KAREN

NEW YORK TIMES BESTSELLING AUTHOR

HARPER

FORBIDDEN GROUND

COLD CREEK NOVEL

New York Times bestselling author

KAREN HARPER

delivers the final gripping chapter in the
***Cold Creek* trilogy.**

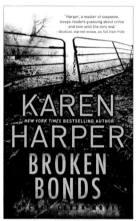

"Harper, a master of suspense,
keeps readers guessing about crime
and love until the very end."
—*Booklist*, starred review, on *Fall from Pride*

Cold Creek is a place with a
dark history. Social worker
Charlene Lockwood is only back in
town to figure out her next move.
She's used to difficult situations,
but soon runs afoul of some locals
who think she's sticking her nose
where it doesn't belong.
Certain something sinister is going
on, when she witnesses Matt Rowan
being run off the road, Charlene
knows she's right…

Available December 30, wherever books are sold!

MIRA®

www.MIRABooks.com

MKH1735IFC

Praise for the novels of New York Times bestselling author Karen Harper

"Harper, a master of suspense, keeps readers guessing about crime and love until the very end, while detailed descriptions of the Amish community and the Ohio countryside add to the enjoyment of this thrilling tale."
—*Booklist* on *Fall from Pride* (starred review)

"Danger and romance find their way into Ohio Amish country in a lively and endearing first installment of the Amish Home Valley series."
—*Publishers Weekly* on *Fall from Pride*

"Harper's description of Lisa and Mitch fighting the river and braving the elements are so realistic the reader can almost feel the icy winds. A tale guaranteed to bring shivers to the spine, *Down River* will delight Harper's current fans and earn her many more."
—*Booklist* (starred review)

"Haunting suspense, tender romance and an evocative look at the complexities of Amish life— *Dark Angel* is simply riveting!"
—Tess Gerritsen, *New York Times* bestselling author

"A compelling story...intricate and fascinating details of Amish life."
—Tami Hoag, *New York Times* bestselling author, on *Dark Road Home*

"Well-researched and rich in detail... With its tantalizing buildup and well-developed characters, this offering is certain to earn Harper high marks."
—*Publishers Weekly* on *Dark Angel*, winner of the 2005 Mary Higgins Clark Award

KAREN HARPER

FORBIDDEN GROUND

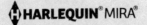

HARLEQUIN® MIRA®

Recycling programs
for this product may
not exist in your area.

ISBN-13: 978-0-7783-1670-1

Forbidden Ground

For questions and comments about the quality of this book, please contact us at CustomerService@Harlequin.com.

Printed in U.S.A.

www.Harlequin.com

DEDICATION

Thanks to my friends and the staff
at the Ohioana Library for their support
and dedication to Ohio authors.
And as ever to Don.

FORBIDDEN GROUND

1

"I think I know what your big wedding surprise is," Kate Lockwood told her younger sister. "You're not the only one in this family who can solve a mystery. It's either you've finally decided to share with your maid of honor, *moi,* where you and Gabe are going on your honeymoon or that you're going to have Detective Vic Reingold give the bride away. After all, he's helped you out twice. I'm betting on the latter. Or is it bridal jitters in general?" Kate asked, leaning closer across their restaurant table. "Tell me."

"I'm going to. I have to," Tess said, suddenly looking as if she was going to cry amid this celebration. "Actually, I wanted a public place to explain it all so you don't go crazy."

"Go crazy? You're not having second thoughts, not after all you and Gabe have been through?"

"Of course not! Never that. I love Gabe, and we've got the perfect life planned out together."

The Lockwood sisters sat in the back booth of the Little Italy Restaurant in their hometown of Cold Creek, Ohio, on a rainy June afternoon, four days before Tess's wedding to Falls County Sheriff Gabe McCord. Kate, who'd lived and worked in the British Isles this year and had flown in only yesterday, had to laugh at the European name and decor of this place, plunked right in the heart of rural southern Ohio on the edge of Appalachia.

Although the Lockwood family's beginnings in this small town had been humble, Kate was used to the international world of academia, where she loved research and fieldwork in her area of anthropology. She was looking forward to writing a book and teaching again at the college level. She knew she'd done well as one of the youngest professors in the country, but it was always onward and upward for her. Her East Coast schooling and Phi Beta Kappa résumé had opened doors in Europe for her studies of the Celtic civilization.

Kate hoped being here for the wedding would give her a chance to pursue her theory that the Celts might be linked to the prehistoric but advanced Adena civilization that had lived in this area and left behind burial mounds. The scattered, man-made hills she'd played on as a child could house skeletons and grave goods to help prove her theory and really make her name. Her stomach always cramped with excitement at that thought, but right now it was more important to calm her sister's nerves.

"It's about the party tonight," Tess went on. "I need to let you know before someone brings it up. Char knows, so you should, too."

Char was their middle sister, who was yet to arrive for the wedding. Kate was thirty, Charlene twenty-six and Tess twenty-four. It unsettled Kate a bit that the youngest of them was so in love when she herself had never really needed a man—except her mentor, Carson Cantrell, at the university, but she'd left the country before permanent plans had come from that. The two older Lockwood sisters were married only to their careers. Char, a social worker in New Mexico among the Navajo, was the family's bleeding heart, but she understood Kate's dedication to her career.

As the oldest, Kate liked to keep control of things. She'd felt that way ever since their father deserted the family years ago. Now Mom had died and wouldn't be here for this happy event—maybe happy, because Tess suddenly looked as if she was going to cry. Kate shoved the bread basket aside, reached across the table and covered Tess's clenched hands with hers.

"I guess I'd better just say it," Tess blurted. "Gabe says that's the best."

"Are you pregnant? Tess, honey, you're not showing, and you wouldn't be the first bride over the ages of civilizations to—"

"No, not that. I know you always take the long view of things—over the ages, the historic, but—Kate, I've asked Dad to come here and give me away for the wedding."

Kate gasped and squeezed Tess's hands. "Our dad?"

It was an utterly ridiculous thing to say, but she was hoping she'd heard wrong or that it was some sort of joke. She felt as if she'd been slapped. She released Tess's hands and sat back hard against the wooden seat. Dr. Kathryn Lockwood always had something to say, but for a moment, she was speechless. Then the words poured out.

"Tess, are you serious? The father who deserted us when we were in desperate need of him after your kidnapping? The man who blamed our mother when you were taken? The man who, for heaven's sake, had an affair with your groom's mother—and she'll be here to-morrow and at the wedding? The man who will then be in the same wedding photos we'll have for decades? At least you didn't just spring him on us when he waltzed in! 'Oh, Kate and Char, look who's here!'"

Several others in the restaurant looked their way. The server, who had been approaching the table with their salads, did a U-turn back toward the kitchen. Kate finally shut her mouth, propped her elbows on the table and leaned her head in her hands.

Tess spoke, her voice shaky. "Like I said, I told Char already. She was surprised, too, but she's okay with it. I've reconciled with him—Dad—over the phone these last months. He's sorry. He knows he did a lot of things wrong. He's rebuilt his life in Oregon with his wife, Gwen. I've talked to her, and she sounds really kind and understanding."

"And I guess I'm not." Kate looked up, now clenching her hands in her lap so she wouldn't pound on the table. "I hope she can trust him not to cheat on her and then abandon her and their kids. He does have children with her, doesn't he? Is he bringing them?"

"Yes, two sons, Josh and Jerod. They're seven and five. He wants them to see where he grew up and to meet all of us. I know how hard you took it—the things he did. You above all, but it's my wedding day, and a father should give his daughter away. Don't you want to patch things up and see him again?"

Kate almost said that she'd much rather have a long-dead Adena warrior resurrected from one of their burial mounds around here, but she managed to keep her mouth shut on that.

"So," Kate said, her voice calmer now. "He'll be at the center of things, not just a guest."

"You mean everyone will talk about the Lockwoods again?"

"I don't care what people around here say. Really. And obviously, Gabe is okay with this."

"Yes, he is. He understands, and we've told his mother. But I really wanted you to understand, just the way my future mother-in-law does. With Mom gone now, I do see you as the head of the family, so it's important to me."

Kate couldn't keep from rolling her eyes. "Head of the family until Jack Lockwood arrives with wife and kids in tow and takes over. Oh, sure, I guess I'm curious about him, but then, I'm curious about everything."

"Like especially what's buried in local Adena mounds, right?"

"Don't try to change the subject. For you, of course, I'll honor your wishes for your guests and who you choose to be in your wedding party. But don't expect your maid of honor to forgive that man. Can't do it, though I'll be civil to him and them. If we've got our crazy cousins coming from that strange religious sect they're in, we might as well have the ghost of child-hood past there, too."

Tess breathed an audible sigh of relief; she seemed to deflate as her stiff stance relaxed a bit and she leaned back. "Once you meet Grant Mason, I don't think you'll be looking at Dad anyway," she said, trying another tactic. "Tall, handsome, deep voice. A Viking revisited, so too bad you're not studying them. Best man, for sure."

"I remember him. But he was older than me, and I didn't really know him. So he's stayed best friends with Gabe all these years?"

Tess nodded and wiped under her eyes. "Right. Even when Gabe was in the service and Grant went to college, then lived out West for a while, working with logging crews so he'd have that background when he took over his family's lumber mill. He's got a gorgeous house with a great view. You'll see that at the party tonight. Wish Char would be here for that, too, but we'll all be together soon."

At least, Kate thought, Jack Lockwood, alias former father, would not be here tonight, so she could enjoy herself. Not only was she curious to see Grant Mason, but she also couldn't wait to examine the Adena burial site she'd found on an old map in the university archives when she was back in the States at Christmas. The so-called Mason Mound was about twenty yards behind Grant's house, and she was much more eager to see it than him.

The caterers Grant had hired from the upscale Lake Azure area had taken over the kitchen, and he didn't want to disturb the setup for the buffet or the bar at the far end of the living room. So he sat in his favorite chair looking out over the back forest view through his massive picture window.

The guests for the party he was throwing for his best friend, Gabe, and his fiancée, Tess, would be here soon—eighteen people, a nice number for mixing and chatting. He'd laid in champagne for toasts to the happy couple.

Gabe and Grant had been best friends since elementary school, when a teacher had seated them in alphabetical order by first names. Grant had been the first to marry. Lacey had been his high-school sweetheart, head of the cheerleaders, prom queen to his king. How unoriginal—and what a disaster.

Four years into the marriage, she had wanted out of what she called "the boondocks," while he intended to make his life here running the lumber mill that had been in his family for three generations. He mingled with the movers and shakers in Columbus and D.C., lobbied politicians to pass green laws and made sure his loggers planted two trees for every one they cut, so it wasn't as if he was always in little Cold Creek. But Lacey's tastes ran to fancy restaurants, import shops and exotic places—probably a life like Tess's oldest, world-traveling sister was used to.

The divorce had been Lacey's call, though he knew he was better off without her. She'd kept insisting she was too young to get tied down with children, too, and he'd love to raise a family here. Yet, when it came to women, he, too, felt caught between two worlds. He might wear work jeans and steel-toed boots and fit in with his good-old-boy loggers and cutters, but he liked tailored clothes and a bit of glitz and class in his playtime—and in a woman.

And he did like this time of year, since the days were getting longer. Not only did they get more done at the mill, but when he came home, he could also look out at this view while he ate or took a run on the path through the thirty acres of hardwood forest he owned. Occasionally, he'd even climb into the great, old tree house Grandpa and Dad had made for him and his brother, Brad, and survey the stunning scene of treetops and, above and beyond that, the blue-green foothills, which fringed the Appalachians.

From that vantage point, he could look almost straight

down on the low, conical prehistoric Indian mound—Mason's Mound, the locals called it. Years ago when he was twelve and Brad was ten, with their friends Todd and Paul, right beneath the huge bird's-eye maple that held the tree house in its limbs and guarded the mound, they had done the forbidden and seen such wonderful and terrible things....

The sound of the doorbell sliced through his thoughts. He glanced at his watch. Someone was early, probably Gabe and Tess so they'd be here when the others arrived. Tess was bringing her oldest sister, Kathryn, with them, the woman who would be his partner for the wedding, the maid of honor to his best-man role. He barely remembered what she looked like, and that was from years ago. As he hurried toward the door, he smelled something delicious in the kitchen, heard the caterers clinking china or glassware.

To his amazement, Brad stood outside, looking as if he'd already been partying but hardly dressed for the occasion. He lived fifty miles away, and he looked like hell. Maybe his high-flying bachelor life was doing him in.

"Brad. You all right? You should have called."

"And get 'nother lecture about not declaring bankruptcy for my paper mill—the Lancaster Paper Mill owned and run by the brilliant, the illustrious Bradley Mason, younger bro of the brilliant, the illustrious, grand Grant Mason of Mason Lumber Mill of Cold Creek? Hell, Grant, I laid off the last workers today and closed the place. America the beautiful's cutting back on paper in this big, bad digital age, and my mill's jus' 'nother victim of that."

Brad's shoulder bumped against the door frame as he

half walked, half stumbled into the house. Grant could smell the liquor on his breath when he got out of the June breeze. Had he driven fifty miles drunk?

"I hope you got your booze just uptown," he told him.

"Yep. My fav'rite ole watering hole in new town."

Looking at Brad, drunk or sober, was always like seeing a slightly younger version of himself, although Brad's blond hair had darkened over the years. Grant was outside enough that his stayed fairly bleached, but they both had their dad's light blue eyes. Grant was slightly taller at six foot two, but their features showed their family ties, and they were both built like the lumbermen from generations of Masons, though since Grant had worked in an office these past years, he'd lost some of his bulk.

"Ah, the old homestead," Brad muttered, looking around. "But looking ever new with the lord of the manor's stamp on it big-time. I'm hoping you'll give me a good job—just tempor'ry—in Dad and Grandpa's old mill, for which you're caretaker now."

"Which I own," Grant said, closing the door behind him. "*Own* because I bought you out and stayed here to keep it going while you skipped town."

"Yeah, well, I still know the ropes. A job there'll do for now, foreman or somethin'."

"You know Todd's the mill foreman. His life is trees, living and dead."

"Yeah, good ole Todd, the modern-day Tarzan, climbing trees when he's not buzzing them into boards for fancy furniture." Brad got only as far as the arm of the leather couch before he sat down, nearly tipping over onto the cushions. He tried to give the Tarzan yell, which came out garbled and made him start to cough.

Grant's heart went out to him, however frustrating he was.

"Hey, you're having a party—with a bar! I see my timing's good. I'll go up to my old room and clean up a bit. Clothes in the car, but I'll jus' borrow somethin' of yours, like in the old days. So, what's the occasion?"

"A pre-wedding party for Gabe McCord, Tess Lock-wood and guests."

"Todd coming, then?"

"And Paul, as a matter of fact."

In addition to Gabe McCord, Todd McCollum and Paul Kettering had been the Mason boys' best friends growing up. Gabe had been away that fateful summer when the rest of them had taken a blood oath, swearing never to tell anyone else about what Grant always thought of as "the death chamber."

"Gabe's deputy, Jace Miller, and his wife are coming, too," Grant went on, trying to keep calm. "And a veteran detective he's close to from the Ohio Bureau of Criminal Investigation. If any of them knew you'd driven in here drunk—even a couple of miles—it wouldn't be pretty. Gabe's mother, who lives in Florida, will be here, too, and one of Tess's sisters…"

"Okay, okay, I get it. Steer clear. Don't embarrass the lord of the manor. Bet you don't even want me to stay here for a while, right, bro?" His voice rose, and he stood unsteadily. "Look, I won't beg, but I'm telling you I need a tide-me-over job or maybe an investment for a new path—and if I don't get some help somewhere…"

"You're welcome to stay here for a while, but I can't free any capital right now, not the kind you'd need to start another business or bail out the paper mill. The digital age would have taken the lumber mill under if I hadn't diversified into things like mulch and log-cabin kits and concentrated on sales to hardwood-furniture stores and some other side projects."

"I don't need that lecture again. I'll go on upstairs," Brad said, holding up both palms as if to fend him off. He suddenly seemed sober, steadier, and his voice turned hard and cold. "Look, Grant. I only have one real big financial asset left, and I'm getting desperate enough to sell it—rare, precious and mysterious as it is. Wonder how much it's worth? Prob'ly priceless."

Grant's head snapped around. "The four of us swore never to do that or even tell others. I wish we could put all that back, erase what we did and saw."

"It's just I need some help right now. So how much you think that big arrowhead would go for on the black market, huh?"

"Keep your voice down. I've got caterers here. Brad, there are laws now that would put you in prison and mean huge fines if you got caught."

"Yeah, and then what if I blabbed about where I got it, right? But I said 'black market.' What did Dad used to say? 'Let the dead stay dead'? Well, my paper mill's dead, but I've gotta find a way to survive and thrive."

"We can discuss it later. I'm sure there will be a place for you at the mill until you get on your feet."

"Cleaning up the back lot? Driving a forklift? Hey, did Gabe catch those timber thieves around here yet? Stealing good hardwood offa people's lots, but for sure, not selling it underhanded to you for the mill, right?"

"That's right, and I don't want you implying anything else, whether you're drunk or sober. I just heard a car door slam outside. I'll be sure you get some food and nonalcoholic refreshment upstairs after you get a shower, and we'll talk in the morning, but I've got to greet my guests. You need help on the stairs?" he asked, taking Brad's upper arm to move him along.

Brad shook loose. "The only help I need's a job from our fam'ly business till I can find a buyer for the industrial rollers, dryers and big, dead building I still own. Go greet your guests, man. Don't look at me that way, like I'm a zombie from the mound out back." He snorted a half laugh. "'Member that old movie with Boris Karloff as a walking, murdering mummy from some old tomb? But listen, I can still think and plan. I'm not an idiot. I may have my life smashed in right now but not my skull!"

Grant's stomach tightened at that final comment and at the nightmare memory that would always haunt him, but he buried it as he hurried to answer the front door.

2

Kate was really impressed with Grant Mason's house and its setting. The contour of the landscaped front lawn, the curved driveway and the surrounding forest embraced the sprawling wood, stone and glass building. Their car had startled a doe and her fawn, which darted away. Like the deer, the house seemed to have emerged from the woods as if it could disappear back into it at will.

She hoped she'd be able to see the Adena mound from inside the house, but dusk was falling. And she'd dressed up even in her one pair of really high heels; though if Grant would show her the site, she'd go barefoot through the woods for a mere glimpse of it. As with other Adena mounds in the area, the foliage probably obscured it, just as the people themselves were so mysteriously hidden by the centuries. She was getting obsessed again, caught up in the mysticism of the Celts and the Adena, but studying them and their amazing cults of death demanded passion as well as reason.

"I said, what do you think of the place, Kate?" Tess's voice pierced her thoughts. Tess twisted around in the front seat as if to see if Kate was still there. Gabe came around to open their doors for them.

"Really handsome."

"Like I said, wait till you see its owner."

"Now, Tess," Gabe scolded. "No matchmaking. Kate, I'm sorry your Ohio State professor friend couldn't be here for all this, because he would have been welcome."

"Carson's had it on his calendar to speak at the Smithsonian for over a year," she explained as she got out of the backseat. "Very prestigious. It's his topic, for sure—Early Indigenous Civilizations of the Americas—but I hope to get him here soon. He knows a lot about the mounds in this area. Maybe we can visit you two once you get back from the secret honeymoon site and get settled."

Gabe had sold his house. Tess's place, their old family home Mom had left to Tess in her will, was next door to his old one on Valley View Road. It was still on the market. The soon-to-be McCord family had bought a place on the old-town edge of Cold Creek and were renovating it as well as adding a three-room addition for the day-care center Tess would open in September. Since the old Lockwood house had not sold yet, Kate was staying there with Tess. Gabe was overseeing the work at their new place, when he wasn't busy trying to bust marijuana growers and, lately, a gang of timber thieves in the area. But he'd said that was like being on vacation after the search for a kidnapper and killer.

Gabe rang the doorbell, and a tall man opened the door. Tess was sure right about Grant Mason, Kate thought. He looked dynamic and just plain solid. He smiled at her in a flash of white teeth against his tanned face as he extended his hand after Gabe's introduction. And for once, it was great to see a clean-shaven man. She'd never liked the scruffy style of half beards so popular these days. Maybe Gabe was shaved close because of his job, but Grant had obviously done so by choice. She should not have been expecting a Paul Bunyan woodsman look just because Grant owned a lumber mill.

His hand was big and warm—just like this house. He lightly touched the small of her back as they stepped in. She felt suddenly nervous but over the moon, as the Brits would say. Trying to get this man to let her explore the Adena mound on his property just went from business to pleasure.

Grant realized he'd been a moron to picture Tess's older professor sister as some frowsy, mousy academic, pale with glasses perched on her nose, plain with no makeup. Kathryn Lockwood was very good-looking. He should have known she'd be pretty since Tess was. But while Tess was quite slender, Kate Lockwood bloomed in all the right places. Her shoulder-length, curly brown hair seemed dusted with auburn like when the sun set through the forest. Her eyes were hazel-hued, alight with amber flecks and fringed with thick lashes. Her mouth was lush, red and pouted right now as she surveyed him. She wore a royal-blue dress that wrapped around her curves. Suddenly, this wedding offered more than just the happiness of his best friend and his bride.

"You have a lovely home," Kate said, her voice warm and mellow. He thanked her but had to pull himself away to welcome others at the front door. He wondered who was keeping an eye on the area since Gabe's only deputy, Jace Miller, and his wife were here. Victor Reingold, from the Ohio Bureau of Criminal Investigation, who had helped solve the town's child-abduction cases, came in and shook his hand.

Todd McCollum and his wife, Amber, soon showed up, too. Grant kidded him about how well he cleaned up. Todd was always overseeing the cutting floor of the mill, and his idea of downtime was uptime—climbing trees. In spite of the fact that Brad had seemed willing to take Todd's job, it was tempting to get him down here to see everyone, but not in the state he was in.

Their other childhood buddy, Paul Kettering, surprised everyone by showing up with one of his fantastically carved tree trunks as a wedding gift. Paul rolled the oak carving into the front tiled foyer area on a dolly, while everyone came to take a look, and Tess clapped her hands in excitement like a young child. Paul's wife, Nadine, beamed as if she'd carved the three-foot-high, in-the-round piece herself.

"Couldn't see hauling it out to the waterfall or lodge for your wedding," Paul told Gabe and Tess. "I'll be sure it gets to your new house when you get back from the honeymoon. I did fairies since I thought it might be nice for your new nursery school, Tess."

Tess was teary-eyed at the array of winged beings that looked like pretty little girls in party dresses, emerging from behind leaves and fronds. "It's wonderful. As you can see," she said, turning to Kate, "Paul is a talented artist. When Grant's group cuts trees, Paul has his choice of trunks and turns them into wonderful creatures like gnomes, leprechauns, fairies or other mythical beings. It's a wonderful, special gift!"

"It really is," Kate agreed. "Do you do assignment carvings, Paul?"

"As long as it fits the Kettering style," he said.

His plump wife, Nadine, spoke up. "These tough financial times around here make living on art a real calling and sometimes a sacrifice, so please tell anyone you know about Paul's work. I have a business card I can give you. Some city folks don't want to drive out into the wilds to find a unique artist, and it's hard to take tree trunks on the road to art shows. A website helps, of course, but I think Paul always underprices his work."

Grant was relieved when everyone arrived and seemed to be mingling well. Despite the high ceiling of the large room, the noise level rose. He had Gabe and Tess go first at the buffet table, and others followed. After they ate, he noticed Kate kept looking out his back window, which, as darkness descended, had turned into a huge, black mirror reflecting all of them.

After much group talk, dessert and a champagne toast, Grant finally managed to talk to Kate alone. She was still glancing out the window. "I'd love to see Mason Mound during daylight," she told him when he approached.

"Gabe mentioned that, huh? It's pretty overgrown. Bushes on top, brush below and surrounded by several huge, prime maples, one with my boyhood tree house in it."

"How wonderful. I love hearing about people's pasts. The mound's never been excavated, right?"

He hesitated, took a swig of his champagne. Either it was starting to get to him or she was. How much to tell this beautiful, interesting and interested woman? "My grandfather and my father both believed in letting the dead stay dead—undisturbed."

"Most mounds in this area are tombs."

"It's only about twenty-four feet high, conical like most of the others, so it's not a big or grand one."

"Which is probably why it's been ignored. I found it on an old map I came across. Actually, the smaller mounds are often more productive and intriguing."

Was it his imagination that the word *intriguing* hung between them for a moment? Of course it was. He just didn't need her questions getting too close for comfort, although that warred with his desire to get closer to her.

"Productive and intriguing?" he repeated as across the room a burst of laughter broke out.

When she raised her voice slightly to be heard, he realized they'd been whispering. "Because," she explained, "if bodies or grave goods are interred there, they would be easier to excavate. In the big, well-known mounds, there may be burials stacked on top of each other in wood-lined tiers but everything's caved in and smashed. Did Tess or Gabe mention I'm fascinated by the Adena and need proof to link them to my major area of study, the Celtic people of northern Europe?"

"Tess told me. Anyway, I look at the mound as a monument—on private land—not to be tampered with or desecrated. But sure, I'd be happy to show it to you. Maybe after all the wedding hoopla. I hear your other sister is coming in tomorrow, so I know you'll be busy. Drop by the mill if you'd like a tour of our facilities there."

She cocked her head, which made her hair brush her bare shoulder. She seemed to study him again. Did she sense he was putting her off about the mound? It actually had been entered in 1939 by his grandfather and then much later—by Grant, Brad, Todd and Paul—but he'd never tell her any of that. Though he had to admit, she was the kind of woman who could probably pry anything out of him if she put her mind to it, which made her damned dangerous as well as a temptation. All he needed was her wanting to take a really close look at the mound, including inside it.

As Kate sat between Gabe's mother and Tess during the bridesmaids' luncheon—at another surprising new-town venue called Miss Marple's Tea Room—Kate could not believe how fast time flew toward the wedding. She knew it would be wonderful, except for having to be nice to Dad and his new family. How many nights had she cried herself to sleep because he'd left them? Before Mom got them an apartment and found a job in Jackson, Michigan, Kate used to be afraid they'd all starve to death, despite the money Dad sent every month. And when she'd later learned Jack Lockwood had cheated on his wife with the sheriff's wife—Gabe's mother, since Gabe's dad was sheriff before Gabe—her pain had turned to stony hate.

Of course, as an adult, she saw there were two sides to every love story, every breakup and divorce. Sheriff Rod McCord had seldom been home, so his wife must have been lonely. Obviously, the affair and divorce had been her fault, too. Mom had always seemed to be raising the three of them alone while Dad traveled for his job. Kate had always blamed him for leaving them at a time when it was crucial for them to bond as a family—right after Tess was abducted and then came back. And now, Kate knew, she'd have to be civil to him as she'd promised Tess. At least she couldn't blame his new wife and their kids for the man he was or, at least, had been.

Char burst out laughing at something Tess had said.

Kate was so glad Char had arrived safely, though her skin was deeply tanned. She'd have to urge her to keep a hat on and her arms covered out there in Navajo land. Char had always been as bubbly as Kate was serious, and she was really enjoying herself now, sitting on Tess's other side, giggling. Well, the two of them had always been close, while Kate had sometimes felt like their second mother.

Char leaned over Tess to speak to Kate. "Isn't it something we have two half brothers? I know it's the sperm that decides the sex of the child, but since we had three girls and now, with another woman, Dad has two boys, you have to wonder if the female doesn't make the difference."

"Char, can we please save this discussion until our real hen party later tonight?" Tess said. "I'd like both a boy and a girl, and I heard, depending on when you have sex, there are ways to hedge your bets on that."

Kate smiled while everyone laughed again. The chatter went on, but it was really hard to wrap her brain around the fact she had two young half brothers. She could only hope and pray they would live better lives than their father had.

Back at the old family house, where the three of them would be staying until the wedding, Sarah McCord, Gabe's mom, was the first topic of conversation while the three of them sat around the kitchen table with glasses of Chardonnay.

"She's still an attractive woman," Char said. "I think she's pretty protective of Gabe, so maybe it's good she lives in Florida. You don't need your mother-in-law over at your house all the time."

"I wouldn't mind a bit if she lived closer to us," Tess insisted. "I'm planning on needing some babysitting help in the future."

"You do have babies on the brain," Kate said. "Don't you want to get your preschool going well before you have munchkins of your own? By the way, I've noticed how Vic Reingold's been paying close attention to Gabe's mother. I overheard he's picking her up at Gabe's for the rehearsal dinner and the wedding, then taking her to the airport after you and Gabe leave for your honeymoon—your mystery spot you still haven't told us about."

"All Gabe told me so far is I need a passport and clothes for some possibly cool weather."

"Ah," Char said with a little laugh as she raised her wineglass. "Antarctica, here we come." Kate clinked glasses with each of her sisters.

"Oh, by the way," Tess, the master of shifting topics, said, "Grant said his brother, Brad, is back in town for a while, so I said he should invite him to the wedding. He's down on his luck lately. Some business deal fell through. What's one more person on top of half the town at the ceremony and reception?"

"Half of *old* town, you mean," Kate said. "I can see that great social divide you mentioned. It's always been the haves and have-nots. We're theorizing now that the lower-class Adenas were cremated and only the upper or shaman class were interred in their elaborate burials—along with a few sacrificed slaves to serve them in the afterlife, much like the Egyptians."

"Kate!" Char threw a wadded-up paper napkin at her. "No talk about funerals past or present right now. Okay?"

"Sorry," Kate said. "I heard you talking about live Navajos, but I only have dead Adenas."

They jolted at a knock on the back door.

"Maybe Gabe," Tess said and bounced up to look out through the screen door. "It's Gracie," she whispered, then called out to the new arrivals. "Great to see you. Oh, and Bright Star. Is Lee here, too?"

"He had a task and couldn't come," Kate heard Grace say.

Kate and Char got up and went to the door, too. They hadn't seen their cousin Lee's wife in a long time. "Grace, hi!" Kate said. "Can't you come in? And your friend is welcome, too." When Grace just shook her head about coming in, Tess stepped outside, so Kate and Char did, too.

Kate was surprised to see the man Grace was with. She'd heard about the strange Hear Ye religious sect and its leader, but to see him in the flesh… She barely remembered Brice Monson, who now went by the name Bright Star. She tried not to stare at the man. She didn't think he was a bit charismatic as Gabe had said. Dressed in white clothes, pale and white-haired, he looked like she imagined a wraith or ghost. Tess had carried on about how he held scores of people, including their cousin Lee, his wife, Grace, and their two children, in thrall.

"I'll just make this quick, but I insisted on telling you in person," Grace said. Kate's first instinct was to hug Grace, but she hung back as if there were an invisible barrier between them now, maybe emanating from this man. Kate tried not to stare at Grace with her braid down her back, her long skirt and *Little House on the Prairie* look.

Tess shot a sharp look at the Reverend Monson, or whatever he called himself, before looking back at Grace. "Did you get permission for Kelsey and Ethan to be flower girl and ring bearer?" Tess asked. "It's not too late to change your mind."

"Oh, no, and I hear you have Sandy Kenton doing that. I'm glad you are so close to her."

"But she'll never replace my own family," Tess told her.

The Kenton girl, Kate knew, was a child Tess had helped to counsel after her terrible ordeal. Tess was tight with the girl's mother, Lindell, too, who would be in charge of the guest book at the reception and was going to work at the day-care center when it opened.

"It's just that…that," Grace stammered and blushed.

"Let me explain," Bright Star said. "Much of the traditional American wedding ceremony, even if held in a church—or outside in nature as yours will be—is based on primitive rituals that our beliefs cannot condone or support. We at Hear Ye have our own ceremony, based on our own tradition and—"

"Gracie," Tess interrupted, her hands shooting to her hips. "You mean you can't even come to our service out by the waterfall at Falls Park or to the reception, either, because you believe something pagan or forbidden is going on?"

"I'm sorry," Grace said, hanging her head like a scolded child. "That's what I came to say. That's what I think is right."

Tess had teared up, and Char was sputtering with surprise, so Kate spoke. "You know, Mr. Monson, I've studied groups with strange beliefs, but this one—to borrow an allusion to a pagan wedding symbol begun by the Romans—takes the cake. Grace, is this man your Caesar, your Napoleon or Hitler, to order you around? You will not be corrupted by coming with your husband and children to your friend and cousin-by-marriage Tess's wedding. Or is it that she's marrying the sheriff?"

"It's obvious," Bright Star said, his voice very quiet compared to Kate's, "that you don't understand our ways, our chosen path. I believe you are the Lockwood sister who studies the pagan beliefs, so I will forgive your outburst and—"

"At this point, I'd rather trust those long-dead pagan ways compared to how you must browbeat and control your people," Kate insisted. "Grace, you and Lee are always welcome to return to your roots, your family."

Grace lifted her teary blue eyes to meet Kate's steady stare. "The Hear Ye people are my family now, Kate. Please try to understand. And, Tess, blessings on your day and your life with Gabriel."

The three Lockwood sisters just stared as Grace followed the man down the driveway and into a black car that was waiting for them.

"That vehicle's a hearse," Char hissed, putting her arm around Tess to draw her back toward the house. "He's not even a charlatan shaman. More like a witch doctor!"

"Like the Beastmaster," Kate muttered. She hurried inside before anyone could ask her what she meant.

3

Friday, the day before the wedding, loomed long for Kate. Though she was dying to see Mason Mound, she dared not trespass on Grant's land, not if she wanted to get closer to him and be permitted at least exterior access to the mound—hopefully, more. Instead, she took her rental car and drove out to the site of two other, long-ago excavated Adena sites.

She was walking around the slant of a mound she'd noted on an old archived map, this one called the Falls Mound. It was not far from the park boundaries where Tess and Gabe would take their vows tomorrow beside the waterfall. That was the spot where, Tess had told her, they had first kissed. Both the rehearsal dinner and the reception would be at the rustic lodge near the falls. When Kate's cell phone rang, she glanced down at it to see Carson Cantrell, her friend and mentor, was calling and it seemed so appropriate to talk to him here.

"Carson, guess where I am?"

"Kate, darling, guess where I am?"

"The Smithsonian? Practicing your talk before some of their indigenous-people tableaus?" she kidded him.

"Sitting out in front of the National Museum of the

American Indian, but it mostly features historic tribes. And—let me guess. You're at an Adena mound, hopefully the Mason one you thought had been untouched by excavation."

"I'm at a mound but one that had some grave goods taken out years ago, according to my research. Some are in the Ohio Historical Museum. Some were stolen and sold on the black market and never recovered. Skeletal remains were too far gone to reveal much."

"How about your smashed-skull theory concerning those sacrificed in the mounds to serve the royals or shamans?"

"No finds like that in the records for this mound. Once again, I think the early pioneer trespassers probably broke things up. As a result, skeletons were useless for examination. I read the pioneers left graffiti on the interior walls, though."

They chatted about his upcoming talk, and she assured him again that nothing but the wedding would have kept her away, not even a Celtic dig in England she was participating in. She did not mention that her father was flying in with his new family today and that his plane had been delayed and he'd barely make the rehearsal dinner this evening. Carson had advice for anything and everything, so she surprised herself in not wanting to share all that. But she was even more surprised by his question. "So what do you think of Grant Mason, the current owner of the Mason Mound property? You think he'll go along with a dig? I looked at his house on Google Maps, but there are so many trees out back, I can't pick out the mound itself from the satellite shot. Even zooming in, all I get is the roof and his curved driveway."

"He seems protective of the mound. His grandfather and father had the theory to let the dead stay dead."

"Which may mean his family knows there's a burial there. But he sounds like a real small-town rube."

"No, he is not! Really," she said, toning down her outburst. "He's a college graduate, business major. Tess says he has ties to the Ohio legislature and even in Washington on environmental issues related to his lumber-cutting and mill projects."

"So you like him. Just remember, I think we're ready to take the two of us to another level. As for Grant Mason, I'd like to visit Cold Creek, meet him, see the mound. Next week I hope, as soon as I get back to Columbus. Stick around there awhile if you can, try to get closer to him—in a highly controlled way. Since he's a business major, keep it all business, okay?"

"Right," she told him. But with her instant attraction to Grant, it seemed somehow wrong.

Kate hated to admit it, but Jack Lockwood, at age fifty-two, looked as handsome as she remembered from her memories as a ten-year-old girl and dreams of "Daddy." As he entered the room reserved at the Falls Lodge for the rehearsal dinner, he let go of his youngest boy's hand and ruffled his older boy's hair. His wife, Gwen, was a pretty blonde, probably fifteen years younger than he was. She looked as nervous as Kate felt, but her father strode across the room toward his three daughters.

Tess met him partway and threw herself into his arms. Char grabbed his shoulder until she, too, was pulled into his embrace. But he looked over both their heads directly at Kate.

"Katie," he said.

She blinked back tears and extended her hand when he stepped free from the group hug. Gabe hovered nearby; she could see Grant watching from the doorway where he was talking to the two young Lockwood boys—her half brothers. She felt frozen in place.

"Welcome back," she managed to say, not stepping closer.

"I know how hard you worked to keep things together, Katie," her father said, lowering his voice. "You and your mother did a great job with everything."

Her brain told her to say thank-you, but the words wouldn't come out. She tried to move away, but he raised her hand and kissed the back of it. The years, the fears, came screaming back as he released her. He had a determined way about him, and maybe she owed her own pluck to that.

Suddenly, everything turned chaotic, meeting his wife, stooping to look into the darling faces of his sons, chatting with them. Dad remembered Vic Reingold, who had helped the sheriff when Tess was abducted, so they shook hands. And then they all held their breath as he came to Gabe's mother, with whom he'd had an affair that helped to end his marriage—though only those closest to him had known.

"Sarah, you're looking great," he said, shaking her hand. "My condolences on the loss of your husband and congratulations that Tess and Gabe have put all the pieces together like I couldn't."

"Yes," she said. "The second generation atones for the mistakes of the former sometimes. That's a blessing."

"It sure is."

Finally, everyone's attention turned back to Tess and Gabe. They all trooped out to the grassy spot where the wedding ceremony would be held. The backdrop was a sky-blue lake with a waterfall crashing into it from granite cliffs. When the wind blew just right—or wrong—mist floated in the air, like nature's attempt at a cleansing, Kate thought, a sort of new-family baptism. If only she could hug her father, forgive him and be glad that he was here, but she just couldn't.

In the wedding rehearsal, Kate walked down the grassy aisle just ahead of Tess's entrance. Gabe and Grant stood waiting next to Pastor Snell and the portable altar. For one fleeting moment, with the whirring rush of the falls in the background, she imagined she was walking down the aisle to Grant.

After Pastor Snell talked them through the ceremony, she walked up the aisle and back to the lodge on Grant's arm. It seemed so natural, actually exciting, to be with him, paired with him, even for someone else's wedding. Strange how her feelings for Carson were so different— admiration, an intellectual bond—while she felt Grant's mere presence in her very bones. He radiated intensity, which shot little shards of heat through her. They sat together at the rehearsal dinner, sometimes talking with others but often only with each other. She wanted to fall into the deep pools of his eyes.

She clung to a bit of rationality, though, telling herself she had just accepted going uptown with him to the English pub for many reasons other than just to be with him. It was still light outside. If only she could talk him into at least showing her Mason Mound before he got busy with his life again—before Carson roared in here next week.

* * *

In Grant's car, Kate was excited as they drove out of the park, when he said, "I know that reunion with your dad was hard for you. But maybe you can forgive if not forget. I know I'd give about anything to have my father back again, and he was no angel."

His cell phone sounded with the old John Denver tune "Country Roads." He pulled over and stared at the phone.

"A call from my home phone number," he told her. "Probably my brother, Brad."

But when he answered it, Kate could hear it was a woman's voice.

"What?" he almost shouted. "Is Brad there?"

"No," she could hear the woman tell him. "Since you and Todd were at the wedding rehearsal, he went to the mill and hasn't come back."

"Phone him, please. I'll be right there. You're right. I didn't order that! Kate," he said, turning to her, "I've got to get home fast. Can't stop to drop you off."

"What is it?"

"That was my cleaning woman at the house," he said as he pulled out onto the main road. "She heard a chain saw out back, but couldn't see anyone. She says the tree canopy has a lot more open sky out the back window. We've had a problem with tree thieves around here, but they surely wouldn't come so close to a house— my house!"

He dropped his phone in her lap. "Call 911 and tell the dispatcher to get Jace Miller. Gabe's been trying to nail that gang, but today and tomorrow—I just can't bother him. Have Deputy Miller meet me out behind the house. These bastards hit fast and disappear, and I've got heirloom, valuable trees back there."

She did as he said while he drove like a man possessed. Well, she thought, this was one way to get near Mason Mound, though her heart went out to him.

Grant could not believe the gall of whoever was tampering with his trees—in daylight, close to the house! He'd helped to spearhead the search for whoever could be sneaking in and stealing from woodlots in the area— valuable oak, maple, walnut and cherry, the very timber he paid big bucks for at the mill. They were robbing people, they were robbing him and desecrating—murdering—trees!

The more desperate people got for money in these tough times, they pirated anything they could, stripping copper pipes from old houses, brass doors and urns off local cemetery crypts—and wood, none of which he'd seen come into his lumber yard. He'd dedicated himself to helping Gabe and Jace stop the crime. He'd put in days trying to convince legislators at both the state and national levels that they needed stricter timber-theft laws, because it wasn't just a problem around here. People from California to Florida were fighting this.

But now it was personal. Had someone known he'd be away most of the day? Were they daring enough to come right into his woodlot to defy him or prove he couldn't stop them? And you might know Brad had left the house, because he surely could have caught on to the fact a chain saw was too close. Mrs. McGirty, who had worked for his family for years, might have a hearing problem, but not Brad.

He roared into his driveway and jerked the car to a

stop. "Sorry to involve you in this, Kate. Make your-self at home. Thanks for the help," he told her, as he grabbed his phone from her, got out and sprinted for his front door.

Kate saw an older lady with a dust rag open the door for Grant. He ran past her. Kate got out and hurried after him, nodding to the woman as she went inside.

Kate could hear Grant run through the house and slam a back door. Thank heavens she was in flats today, since they were wearing them on the grass for the wed-ding. She went downstairs, saw where he'd gone out. She caught a glimpse of him as he ran across the back lawn and disappeared into the fringe of forest. His shouts floated to her. He sounded almost like an enraged or wounded animal. Or had he spotted someone still out there? Even she could see a huge, blank place in the fo-liage that had not been there before.

She found a dirt path and followed it. The shape of the entire mound appeared the moment she started into the trees. Hoping Deputy Miller would be here soon in case Grant was confronting someone, she rushed on. She found him swearing and stamping through a tan-gle of limbs, smashed brush and sawdust that circled a massive tree stump. With nearby bushes crushed and saplings snapped off, she could instantly tell where the massive, missing tree trunk had been felled and dragged away. The trunk Grant kept circling was so close to the edge of the mound that it seemed to be guarding it. And around him lay broken pieces of something built of wood, a deck, a railing, even a broken roof.

She gasped. "The tree with your tree house?"

He stopped and looked up, as if surprised to see her.

He only nodded and turned away, but not before she saw he was in tears.

"Don't come closer," he told her. "I ran a ways on the path where they dragged it away—long gone. This is a crime scene, and I swear, I'm gonna get whoever did this if it's the last thing I do."

Kate stood her ground as Grant called his brother, who insisted he needed to stay at the mill. After Deputy Jace Miller, still in civilian clothes, arrived and looked everything over, Grant allowed Kate to get closer to the scene. He was still furious, spewing out broken threats while Jace followed the trail where the huge, delimbed tree trunk had been dragged, evidently by horses, to avoid making more noise than the chain saw already had.

Jace returned quickly and reported that the huge tree had been hauled away in a truck on the road back of the woodlot. There were obvious tire tracks he was going to make casts from. He also saw prints from another vehicle, which may have held the horse team. He headed back into the forest toward the road, leaving them alone again.

Kate wanted desperately to comfort Grant, but she knew to stand clear while he had smoke coming out his ears. "This is personal. This is someone after me, all I stand for and care for," he said, finally muttering something that made sense to her. "That tree was special, the oldest, and obviously important with that tree house. It's someone who knew me or of me, targeted me, knew I would be away for the wedding rehearsal."

"But you're not usually here during the day on a Friday, are you?"

He looked over at her. "No. True. I'm not thinking straight. You can come closer. I've pretty much checked the ground here, and they didn't leave anything like a glove or tool to help identify them. There may be tire tracks on the road but only horseshoe prints here. The law has got to change to make this kind of tree killing a real criminal case with prison time. Right now it's only a fourth-degree misdemeanor with fines three times the cost of the tree, but that's not enough. This tree was priceless to me."

As she came closer, shuffling through sawdust or stepping over the larger pieces of limbs and leaves, she tried to stop glancing at the Adena mound. She noticed that a huge branch must have fallen near the mound, crushing some scraggly, spiny hawthorn bushes. She joined Grant as he stared down at the newly cut trunk of the tree. The thieves had left about ten vertical inches of the massive, four-foot span.

"I'm guessing from the rings it is—was—about eighty-five years old," he whispered, looking down at it. "It's seen so much of my family's life. It's been like a guard standing watch over the mound. It's beautiful wood.

"Bird's-eye maple, rare and special," he went on, reaching out to take her hand. He held it so tightly it almost hurt, but she was glad to be of help. "No two trees of that are alike. See the oval-shaped eye pattern? It's valued not just for furniture but for crafting guitars and other musical instruments. Bird's-eye can occur in a variety of maples and you can ID it because of the kind of Coke-bottle shapes on the bark, see?" he said, pointing low where the base of the trunk still clung to the ground.

She bent down then stooped as he did. She felt her stocking run up the back of her leg, but she'd probably snagged it on something. And what did that matter next to the loss of this beautiful living being, one that Grant had loved?

"How valuable?" she asked, thinking what treasures might be buried in that mound a mere twenty feet away.

"Going price right now if I had it at the mill—which I never would have, not this one—about $70,000 per thousand-board feet."

He sighed and sank onto the trunk as if it was the perfect seat out here. It seemed quite smooth-cut to Kate, but then, what did she know about it?

"Don't snag your dress," he said and pulled her to half lean, half sit against his knee. "Brad's taking his time at the mill, but Jace should be back soon, unless he found a trail to follow. I—I just can't leave here right now. This was our special tree.... The tree house and so many great memories right in this spot...."

Kate sensed he was going to say something more, maybe something about the mound. His eyes glazed with tears again, but he blinked them back. She figured he did not realize she'd already seen him cry. She wanted so much to hug him, to comfort him, but she put her arm around his shoulders as if to steady herself.

He might not believe it, but she really did feel his agony. She knew the impact on him must hurt the way it would if she could enter that mound and found it completely defaced and emptied. Thank God the brunt of the massive fallen tree had not crushed the top of the mound. She'd known other mounds to cave in, but the top of this one looked rounded and intact.

They stood as Jace came tramping back through the forest yet again.

"A pretty clean, fast job, Grant," he called out as he approached them.

"A personal attack," Grant said, "so I'm taking it that way."

As the two men walked the site together again and darkness fell completely, Kate, despite her good dress, walked around the edge of the mound then sat down on the slant of ground. She tried to be careful but snagged the hem of her skirt on a spiny hawthorn branch of one of the several trees. It was hard to tell, but they looked diseased, dying, and that couldn't have been caused by being crushed a few hours ago.

Grant had suggested she go back to the house and he'd soon drive her home, but, like him, she stayed in the darkness lit only by Deputy Miller's moving flashlight beam. It threw strange shadows, seemed to leap and dance. She, too, was mourning, listening to the men's footsteps shuffling past the wooden tombstone of the tree. But she was thinking of the footfalls of ancient, grieving men and women who perhaps had passed this way to bury their precious dead with sacrificial grave offerings in this dark mound.

4

It was a perfect day for a wedding, Kate thought. Surely nothing else could go wrong. Losing her temper at Bright Star Monson, her father's appearance after all these years and then the theft of Grant's tree had thrown a pall over her mood. Yet today the stunning setting with the waterfall and surrounding forest helped. But did each big, beautiful tree remind Grant of his loss?

The artist, Paul Kettering, and Brad Mason served as ushers, seating everyone before the wedding party walked out from the lodge. Brad, whom Kate had met last night when he finally returned home, resembled Grant but seemed much more edgy, even bitter. Todd McCollum, Gabe and Grant's friend and the lumber-mill foreman, was also in the wedding party, partnering Char.

To a single violin playing "Wedding March," Kate started down the grassy aisle behind the flower girl and Char and ahead of Tess and their father. Standing with the pastor, the men in the wedding party waited before the small altar with its cross and big bouquet of yellow calla lilies. Kate saw Gabe looked nervous; when she got close to the front of the four rows of portable chairs with white covers, Grant winked at her.

It was crazy to feel that wink and look from him down to her toes. He had stopped ranting about the loss of his tree and the insult or threat he felt was meant for him, but she knew he still harbored deep anger. Yet he was determined to help make the day special for Gabe and Tess.

Kate held her own single calla lily and Tess's bouquet while she and Gabe recited the vows they had written and exchanged rings. The old words to honor and cherish were still there. Kate had just learned this morning from Tess that Grant had been married and divorced. What could have happened? Who would not want to stay married to Grant Mason?

Wait! she told herself. She didn't really know the man, though Carson's suggestion that she get close to Grant only in a businesslike, controlled way seemed crazy, maybe impossible. Getting closer to Grant...wouldn't that be an all-or-nothing proposition? She saw him as so much more than just a way to get to that Adena mound on his property.

"I now pronounce you man and wife," Pastor Snell said in a voice loud enough to be heard over the roar of the falls. "Family and friends, I have the honor of introducing to you Mr. and Mrs. Gabriel McCord."

There was a big kiss by the bridal couple. Applause, tears and smiles, a quick procession from the front to the back, where the wedding party formed a reception line before the guests meandered toward the lodge where the wedding lunch would be held. Kate froze when Dad hugged her. She just couldn't hug him back.

* * *

The lunch was lovely, with numerous champagne toasts. Grant gave a short speech in honor of the new couple, hoping they would always support each other through the best and worst in life. Dad gave a toast about loyalty and forgiving each other in hard times. Recalling how their mother had sobbed for days when he left, Kate stepped out for a breath of air on the wide, covered lodge porch, which wrapped around the log building on three sides.

The front section was deserted, but she heard men's voices raised nearby, around the corner away from the waterfall. "I don't care about a bunch of old boyhood oaths at this point!" one man said. "I swear I'm going to do it!"

"Keep your voice down. You'll open up a whole can of worms if you try that. You'll ruin everything. I can only loan you a little, but just shut up about that or else! Now let's get back inside, or we'll have Brad or Grant out here looking for us."

"But Nadine's going to need some long-term medical treatment. We knew we needed insurance, but we were both healthy, and we cut corners. But she's been diagnosed with Parkinson's disease, and that will mean a lot of bills."

Kate knew that voice. It was the sculptor, Paul Kettering. That touch of Southern twang in the other voice sounded like Grant's friend Todd. She didn't want them to know she'd overheard them, so she moved down the front veranda and turned the corner so they wouldn't see her.

And there stood Brad Mason, who was just putting

a small flask back into his inner suit-coat pocket. He looked up at her, obviously surprised.

"You're missing champagne inside," she told him.

"Not my cup of tea," he said, walking closer. A twitch at the corner of his mouth might have been a hint of a grin "Grant's either a beer or wine man, but I go for the hard stuff, maybe because I've been through some hard stuff in life."

"Haven't we all?"

"You mean Daddy Dearest in there?"

"Am I that easy to read?"

"If someone's watching. And I think Grant is."

She turned away from his avid stare. Brad had evidently been studying her, too. The man had liquor on his breath. Though she wanted to know more about Grant, she'd sensed last night when Brad got home from the mill that there had been tension between the brothers. She decided to "pull a Tess" on him and change the subject.

"I understand you own a mill also."

"More or less. Foreclosure. Chapter Thirteen. A paper mill. Now if we could convince people here today to use paper products instead of linen napkins and tablecloths, maybe I'd still be in business," he said with a little snort, not quite a laugh. "I hear even at that wacko Hear Ye compound, they have the words to hymns on a screen, no more hymnals or paper handouts, though I'll bet that dictator doesn't let his flock go online.

"So why isn't Lee Lockwood here at his cousin's shindig?" he asked. "I knew him in school."

"Lee and his family, unfortunately, have been forbidden to attend by their creepy leader."

"That guy's a lunatic, but you're kidding?"

"Wish I were. I met him up close and personal when he made Lee's wife, Grace, come to tell us she couldn't attend a pagan ceremony. At least they aren't protesting this event with placards—paper ones—like some off-the-wall groups do. He got me so upset I invoked the pagan dead. At least I didn't call him the Beastmaster."

"I heard you were an anthropology prof. You study all that stuff? And the Beastmaster? That was a movie and a video game."

"In real life, it was a disguise Celtic shamans used to scare either diseases or unwanted behavior out of people—an antlered head, frightening face."

He frowned, looking upset, but then went on. "In un-real life, I've played that video game. Are you a gamer?" he asked, shifting closer to her and giving her an ob-vious once-over look that meant he fully intended the double entendre.

She leaned her shoulder against a post to give her-self a little more breathing room. Did this guy make a habit of trying to know Grant's women friends—or at-tract them to himself?

"No time for video games," she said. "I have been called Lara Croft, Tomb Raider since I study ancient burial practices, so better not get too close or I might have to go for my pistols."

He actually stepped back. Not only did his breath smell of whiskey, but he also seemed a bit unsteady. "I liked those Lara Croft video games and the movies with Angelina Jolie, especially her sexy, skimpy outfits. But you'll get farther with Grant with a game called 'Kate Lockwood, Tree-Theft Detective' right now."

"He was distraught. Weren't you?"

"Into each life some rain must fall, but we'll get who-ever did that. It was more than an insult. We'll get him."

"Him? Do you have any leads?"

Char opened the door to the lodge and called out, "Kate! Gabe's going to finally announce where they're going on their honeymoon."

"See you later," Kate told Brad.

She hurried after Char but not before she heard him say, "Sure do hope so."

As she hustled back to her seat, Kate saw her cute, little half brothers sitting with the two boys related to the flower girl, Sandy Kenton. Sandy's parents were here, but the child seemed almost like Tess's daugh-ter, since she usually kept so close to her. Dad's wife, Gwen, was keeping an eye on the four boys, but maybe she'd better be keeping an eye on Dad, who was min-gling with people like it was old-home week. Yet he did seem to be steering clear of his old flame, Gabe's mother, who was with Detective Reingold.

Kate got to her seat just before Gabe's announce-ment. "I'm excited to share with all of you that Tess and I are going to be away for two weeks. We're heading to Paris, then going through France on a barge cruise on the Loire River. Sorry, but I probably won't be think-ing much about sheriff's duties, which will be in Dep-uty Jace Miller's capable hands while we're away. I'll be back in plenty of time, Jace, for the next full moon to help keep an eye on the lunatic invasion of outsiders who come in here looking for paranormal sightings and ghosts at the old insane asylum outside town. Mean-while, no cell phones, no 911 calls. We're going to be happily out of touch except with each other."

People laughed and applauded. But Deputy Miller,

Kate noticed, looked pretty nervous. She knew Gabe had assured him that he could handle tracking down the timber thieves. The bigger challenge would be to keep Grant Mason from playing detective or, worse, judge and jury if he figured out who was at fault.

Later, everyone gathered outside to throw rose petals at the departing couple. They were going to their new house to change clothes then head to the Columbus airport to make overnight flight connections to France. One of Grant's mill workers was driving them to the airport. Char was flying back to New Mexico in the morning, so Kate would have the old house to herself.

Kate stood between Grant and Brad, waving goodbye as Gabe's car—with a few crazy signs someone had put in the back window—drove out of sight.

"Nice touch we didn't throw rice, but I guess these are more biodegradable," Brad told Grant and tossed the last few petals from his small sack over him and Kate. "Lacey's Green Tree would be proud."

"I'll see you back at the house," Grant said, taking Kate's arm to steer her away.

"What's Lacey's Green Tree?" she asked.

"Lacey was my first wife—I mean, my wife, but we've been divorced for years. She's really active in Green Tree. It's a Midwest knockoff of Greenpeace. They protest over environmental issues. Ignore Brad. He likes to make waves. Kate, listen. I can drive you back, wait until you change clothes if you want to go see the mill. I need to stop by there for a little bit. Then maybe we can have another private toast to the happy couple, though not at my place. I can't stand looking through that picture window at that spot of naked sky right now."

"Sure, that would be fine. Char's going back to the hotel with my father's family to play with the boys and give their parents a break."

"You're sure you don't want to go with them?"

"I'm sure. I'll go back in to wish them well, say goodbye. It will just take a second. I also want to ask Paul Kettering if I could stop by tomorrow to talk about a special project I'd like to commission, but I see he's leaving."

"I can call him for you, set it up. He lives out a ways, up Sunrise Mountain. I'd be happy to drive you there tomorrow."

"I'd really appreciate that." So easily accomplished, she thought, to spend more time with Grant, though she wished it was at his Adena mound.

The Mason Lumber Mill made a lot of noise and a lot of sawdust, but it seemed like violins and pixie dust to Kate. She loved being with Grant—unfortunately— because after a couple of weeks here, making her own maps of unexcavated Adena burial mounds and hoping to get permission for a team to excavate some, she fully intended to go to Columbus to spend more time with Carson and then back to England to finish her work there.

She also liked seeing an array of Paul Kettering's tree trunks for sale in front of the mill, but was surprised he'd carved Disney characters—though, of course, they were as imaginary as his fairy folk. The seven dwarfs peered from one trunk and *The Little Mermaid*'s Ariel and sea creatures from another.

"I'm surprised to see Paul's carved something so

commercial as Disney characters," she told Grant as they headed inside.

"Money talks. I think Nadine's been on him to expand his horizons. Welcome to my daily world," he added as they went inside through a big double door.

Kate didn't want to let on to Grant that she'd overheard his friends arguing about money earlier today. Paul had threatened to do something she couldn't catch, and Todd had threatened him if he did.

"This mill is huge!" she shouted over the noise of several massive machines devouring tree trunks that came out the other side either stripped of bark or sawed into planks.

"Let's go on up to my office," he shouted back. "It's mostly soundproof, and we can see the cutting line from there, so I can point things out. It's the scaler and debarker making all the noise. We'd need industrial earmuffs like the men are wearing to stay here long. Come on."

They climbed metal stairs to Grant's glassed-in office high above the cutting floor. It helped when he closed the door, shutting them into his lofty observation site.

"I've been making a list," he told her. "Mill owners in a tristate area to call Monday morning to be on the lookout for a big buy in bird's-eye maple."

"Your tree."

"Right. I've been really vocal about stopping the local band of tree thieves and, I'm thinking, they probably decided to show me they can get me back—come in right on private property and do damage. Then they'll leave the area to sell the wood, so I can't trace it to them."

"Could it possibly be someone who has a more personal vendetta in mind—someone who is not that tree thief gang but someone using them as a cover to steal that tree? That way, they figure they won't get blamed."

He sank into his chair opposite where she'd perched across the corner of his huge wooden desk.

"You've been reading too many mysteries or something. I don't take you for a soap-opera fan. No, I don't think that a someone-close-to-me, personal-revenge or vendetta theory's in play here."

"It's just that I've learned to think that way because the world of academia can be cutthroat. In scholarly pursuits, people who have worked together for years might steal research or ideas. It's human nature over the ages. But yes, I guess I do have a suspicious mind."

"You don't mean it could be Brad?"

"I don't mean anyone in particular. But he sure knows the area, and he seems to be upset with you—and he wasn't home when it happened."

"But I know he was at the mill, not that he doesn't know rogue cutters who could have done it for him. Okay, so he is upset with me, mostly because I'm not demoting Todd McCollum to let Brad be mill foreman. Or coughing up big bucks like when I backed him once before." A frown creased his brow. "Then there's Green Tree and my ex."

"You said that group is like Greenpeace, so you meant they're willing to use strong measures if someone's anti-green or polluting the environment? But then, they would never cut down a tree."

"At our logging sites, we plant two trees for every one we harvest, and Lacey knows that, so that's a stretch. I have made some enemies in the Ohio Statehouse and

U.S. Congress, pushing for certain laws. But that's far out, too. Someone had to know how to get in through my back lot, cut that massive tree and get out fast and clean."

"So, no personal enemies?"

"I still think it's that timber gang. But—you know—there was a case out West when I lived in the lumber camps in my twenties. A massive golden spruce of great age and size, venerated by a local Indian tribe, was cut down by an idiot who supposedly loved trees, but wanted to make a statement about others cutting trees. He wanted publicity, to have a voice in a trial if he was caught. Is that crazy or what? The culprit had delusions of grandeur and was on a mission."

Kate shook her head. Being on a mission—she was like that with her theory that the European Celts might have sailed to this continent and became the progenitors of the mysterious, brilliant Adena. If only she could link some of the Adena burial artifacts to Celtic culture. Oh, yeah, she understood someone doing crazy things who was passionate about his or her mission in life.

"I do have a great, happy story about a big tree to tell you," she said, leaning toward him. He looked so downcast she wanted to reach out to him, and she'd better do it with words before she went over to hug him. He looked at her intently.

"Tell me. I could use that."

"Last autumn I visited Sherwood Forest in Nottinghamshire, England. It's much smaller than in the days of Robin Hood, only a little over one acre now instead of the thirty miles by ten miles it was in the old days. But it has a tree called the Major Oak, which is supposedly between 800 and 1000 years old. I think they said it weighs about twenty-three tons and has a trunk circumference of thirty-three feet. I could not believe how much ground its spreading branches covered. And according to legend, the tree was Robin Hood's main hideout while he robbed from the rich to give to the poor. That part about it being his hideout reminded me of the tree house you and Brad used to share in your special tree."

He nodded, his gaze distant, instead of on her. "So maybe someone sees taking that tree of mine as robbing from the rich to give to the poor. You know, growing up, Brad and I, Gabe, Todd and Paul used to play there all the time." He looked at her again. "You've helped me, Kate. You've made me face up to the harsh reality about people's possible motives, but it lifts my spirits just to know that there's a Major Oak out there for every bird's-eye maple or golden spruce some bastard cuts down."

They went back down to the mill floor. Todd had come back after the wedding to work for a couple of hours. Grant asked him to show her around while he talked to some of his workers about keeping their ears to the ground for any word of someone selling bird's-eye maple. As she and Todd went outside amid the mountains of stacked wood waiting to be cut, they turned a corner and ran right into Bright Star Monson.

5

"Oh," Kate blurted out. "I didn't expect to see you here, Bright Star. And Lee!" she cried when she saw her cousin standing behind Bright Star with two other men. "So good to see you since you couldn't come to the wedding."

Lee nodded, but he didn't smile or step forward until Kate went past Monson to extend her hand. She was tempted to give Lee a hug, but who knew what punishment this leader of the pack doled out when someone disobeyed his rules. She could not fathom that Lee and spunky Grace had been taken in by this man. And to have their two kids reared in that repressive atmosphere was tragic.

Lee took her hand, shook it and quickly released it. "We hardly expected to find you here," he said. "We came to buy some wood for an addition at the Hear Ye home."

Home. That word stunned Kate. At least Lee and Grace had a home. And, really, she didn't.

Todd spoke up. "We have salesmen who can show you around, depending on what you need, Mr. Monson.

We deliver and can even put you in touch with architects or builders if you want."

"Oh, we'll do all that ourselves," Monson said. "Brother Lee and others are very skilled at all that. Quite a family we have, talented and diverse for all our needs."

Kate knew she should keep her mouth shut, but this man really riled her. "Lee is from the Lockwood family, also talented and diverse before he changed his life so radically," she said.

"It seems to me," Monson replied in his calm, quiet, infuriating voice, "that your two sisters follow life paths to help the living, whereas you seem to be fixated on the dead. The pagan dead. Don't think we are so primitive that we cannot research people. I know a bit about you and your pursuits."

"You like to seem all-knowing, all-wise, don't you?" she challenged, despite the fact Todd kept clearing his throat and had edged his shoulder between the two of them. "To keep an eye on people, don't you?"

"His eye is on the sparrow, and mine also," Monson intoned. With a nod he moved away down the aisle of wood, with the others following like robots. Lee did not look back.

"Sorry about that, if I lost you a sale," she told Todd. Unlike Grant, whom she had to look up to, Todd was just her height, so she looked at him eye to eye. He seemed very fit, strong but agile, a serious man with bright eyes and a beard to balance his shaved head.

"We're the only lumber mill for miles around," he said with a shrug. "I know he's weird, but, in a way, we all are."

"Yes, we all have our eccentricities. But no one

stands up to him as if it's forbidden, and I can't help disliking him. He's been reading up on my work, which makes me wonder why."

They strolled toward the front of the mill, occasionally avoiding forklifts moving huge pallets of lumber. "I guess you've heard they call me Tarzan around here?" Todd asked with a grin.

"Tarzan? Of the apes? Not because you oversee all these strong men who—"

"Not that. In my spare time I climb trees. I mean way up, sometimes swinging from branch to branch on mountain-climbing ropes. Started that in the days I cut down trees, before Grant took over from his dad and hired me as foreman. There's nothing like a view from a tall tree."

"So you're in mourning for his bird's-eye maple, too."

"And on the lookout for who did it."

"Then consider my feelings toward Guru Monson this way. He's cut down four of my family members. But I'd love to see you climb someday. Did you ever take Grant up with you?"

"Naw, not his thing, though he loved the tree house."

"Did I hear my name?" Grant said, appearing around a pickup truck in the parking lot with his car keys in hand. "I put out the word that everyone's to watch for anyone selling bird's-eye maple. You can't pass that off as something else."

"Someone may just try to hide the tree for a while until things cool down," Kate said.

"Hard to hide something that big uncut," Todd said.

"But another good suggestion," Grant said, taking her elbow to steer her toward his car. "Nothing like a beautiful woman who's also bright. Todd, I'm going to hire her as a consultant," he called back to his friend.

"Better pay her good," Todd said with a grin and a wave as he headed back into the mill.

Grant guided her into his car and closed the door. When he got in the driver's side, he turned to face her. "I'll think of some way to repay you."

She almost said that a real close-up look at Mason Mound in daytime would be a start, but for once, she didn't push that. He'd been reluctant before, so she had to be careful what she said. "Dinner uptown will do," she said. "I'm buying."

"Dinner, yes, you buying, no. This is small-town Ohio, Professor Lockwood, not the ivied halls of higher learning or London, England. And tomorrow afternoon I will drive you to Paul Kettering's art studio so you can talk to him about ordering your special project."

They pulled out of the mill parking lot, just as a huge, loaded lumber truck pulled in. Grant waved to the driver. They immediately passed another car, which honked its horn.

"That's Brad," he said, sounding surprised and craning his neck. "In a Porsche, no less, when his company just went belly-up."

"Do you want to go back to the mill?" she asked. "For the truck or to talk to Brad?"

"No, Todd can handle it. Brad made himself useful on Friday when Todd was away, so I don't think they'll clash. They've been friends for years, though Todd doesn't know that Brad had the gall to ask for his job. But getting back to us…"

He turned down another road toward town. *Getting back to us,* she thought. *There's an "us"?*

"What do you have in mind for Paul to carve?" Grant asked.

She shifted slightly toward him. He seemed far away across the console in the big car. "Since he likes to do mythical beings, it will be perfect," she told him. "There are several Celtic creatures from their artwork I'm trying to link to the Adena culture to prove a splinter group of Celts became the Adena."

"No kidding? So they had the know-how to sail to the New World?"

"They did. The creatures are mostly shaman animal heads, maybe used in burial rites. My favorite is an antlered animal, similar to a deer, but with a very frightening face, and— What?" she cried as Grant swerved the car. "Was an animal on the road? I didn't see anything."

"No. It's okay. I—I didn't, either," he said, but his hands began to tremble before he gripped the wheel tighter. "It's just—when you said 'deer,' I remembered I almost hit one that darted out here not long ago. Muscle memory to swerve, I guess."

She didn't know Grant Mason very well, but she was pretty sure he was lying.

That night, Grant could not get Kate Lockwood out of his head—her or that mythical beast he could picture all too well. The wedding had been great, he'd talked to a lot of folks, but that woman kept clinging to his thoughts. Though there was nothing but yard and thick forest out behind his house, he kept his bedroom curtains drawn as he changed into his jeans and T-shirt with his company slogan—Mason Lumber The Perfect Cut For You. Was Kate the perfectly cut woman for him? No, he told himself. She was damned dangerous. Letting her get closer could bring down everything he'd worked for—and worked to hide—all these years.

He flopped back on his big bed, fingers linked under his head, and waited until it was pitch-black outside before he opened the curtains again. He couldn't stand that bare patch of sky where the tree had been, but you might know a full moon was sitting right above the break in the leafy canopy where the branches used to cradle the tree house. More than anything, that tree had been a monument to his deceased parents and the grandfather he had loved.

Brad had never quite seen it that way, but sometimes Grant thought Brad didn't have a sentimental bone in his body. Not if he could even mention selling his part of their secret bargain on the black market or anywhere else. It had been only a boyhood oath that had bound the four of them, but they'd cut their fingers and mingled blood, so hadn't that meant something? Not to Brad, evidently. At least he wasn't home tonight, probably uptown drinking, or picking up a hottie from the upscale Lake Azure area.

Suddenly, he had to see the artifact he always thought of as simply *the mask* to make sure it was safe. He didn't like to look at it, because it often triggered nightmares of what they'd done, what they'd vowed to hide.

He got up, stuck his feet in his flip-flops and padded out into the dark house, through the big living room, into the kitchen, where he opened the door to the basement.

He'd enjoyed remodeling most of the lower space with oak paneling, thinking he'd have kids someday who could play down here in bad weather. But, of course, he'd planned they'd play in the tree house, too, when it was nice outside. Times changed. Circumstances changed, sometimes for the best, but lately for the worst. Brad's failure had rattled Grant, and he knew Paul Kettering wasn't really making a living lately, either. Paul's wife, Nadine, had been pushing him to sell more art, change his "vision," as Paul always called it, and now that Nadine had medical needs, he was afraid Paul would do something as desperate as Brad might. He'd like to help both of them out, but he was cutting profits close at the mill and had a big staff there to keep employed. And Kate ordering a carving wouldn't solve Paul's financial problems.

He clicked on the basement light and, closing the door behind him at the top of the stairs, in case Brad came back, went down the steps. The basement had a Ping-Pong table, a pool table and a dartboard—all hardly ever used anymore except at the yearly party for employees, which always ended up outside around the fire pit anyway.

His pulse picked up as he went over to the hutch that held his and Brad's high-school sports trophies and his college soccer ones. He slid the piece of furniture out of the way. He carefully lifted the five oak panels that he'd left unattached from the wall behind. Taking the flashlight and old ice hook from the cabinet, he knelt and examined the lowest row of cement blocks the panels usually hid. He stuck the ice hook in the crack around three loose blocks and slowly slid them out.

He put his face to the floor to peer into the niche he'd made there years ago before he went west to the lumber camps. The three-foot square, black metal box was still there, dusty, lonely but for spiders, which skittered away. Grant slid it out and brushed it off.

The key was in a small magnetic box on the bottom of the furnace, so he felt for that, getting his arm dusty to the elbow. He went back into the game room and turned the key in the lock of the box. Holding his breath as if something would spring at him, he lifted the lid and looked down at the crumpled tissue paper inside.

It rustled as he unwrapped the mask. It stared up at him with blank eye sockets through which some ancient man—a shaman, as Kate had said—must have gazed. The fierce face was made from some sort of glazed leather studded with thin mica chips that made it glitter in the light. It still had a few of its terrible teeth—probably from some predator like a wolf. And from its skull base—Grant was pretty sure that was human—were attached with stone pins the antlers of a centuries-old, long-dead stag. Reddish-brown coloring of some kind still clung faintly to the bony points, just like the memories of finding it among the crushed skulls clung to him.

"I appreciate your arranging this," Kate told Grant Sunday afternoon as he drove them in his black pickup truck along the rising, twisting trail to Paul's home and art studio.

"Sure. He'll appreciate the sketch you've made of the two masks."

"I think they were chieftain or shaman masks. Did I use the word *masks* before to describe them?"

"I don't remember. Your drawing just suggested masks, that's all."

"Those two ancient effigies are key to my thesis and what I'd like carved on a tree trunk for my office or home, when I finally settle down in one spot. The antlered one is Celtic, and, of course, the one you've no doubt seen before is the effigy face from the famous Adena pipe found in a mound near Chillicothe. I'd love to link either the Celtic mask to the Adena or vice versa. You've seen the Adena pipe figure before?"

"Right. You know, the only deer-antler information that's made the news lately has to do with banned deer-antler spray some athletes have been using as a performance-enhancing drug. Pro golfers and football players. Like I said, it's forbidden, so they can get fined and suspended for using it."

"No kidding? I'll have to remember that. I read a paper recently that the Celts and Druids probably believed there was some magic power in deer antlers. It makes sense they would think so—power in the pointed weapons of a swift, virile animal."

But Kate thought that Grant was as good as Tess at shifting subjects. He'd seemed really nervous when he saw her sketch of the Beastmaster, and here they were, talking about American sports.

"Wow, this is a long way up here," she observed as they made yet another turn on the narrow, two-lane road with no berms.

"That's why we're in my truck instead of my car. Believe it or not, there's another back way up the other side of the mountain, too. It isn't really a mountain but just one of the largest Appalachian foothills. There's a Boy Scout camp up higher than where the Ketterings live."

"Well, when the snow falls or it's icy, they must just become hermits."

He pulled into a gravel parking area before an A-frame building that reminded Kate of a château. "Built with wood from the mill," Grant said. "Hardwood outside, knotty pine inside. He's here—that's his pickup, but Nadine's four wheel is gone. He said she had to go into Chillicothe for a doctor's appointment, so she spent last night with her sister who lives there."

"Maybe it's just as well she's not here," Kate said as she got out before Grant could come around to open the door for her. "I have a feeling she's really nervous about his art being able to support them. I'm willing to pay his price and even advertise for him, but nervous people make me nervous in turn."

She glanced sideways at Grant's profile. He didn't pause or flinch at that. She must be reading too much into his behavior. He was still just shaken by the loss of his special tree.

Grant led the way up the flagstone path. "He said to come in the side door. Then we'll go down to his work area. He's very protective of his shop," he said.

"How did he start to carve such unique things?"

"You'll have to ask him. I'd say God-given talent inspired by life experiences—a great reader, that guy. Even loved fairy tales, which most boys don't."

Grant rang the bell, then knocked. When he knocked again harder, the door swung open. "He must have left it open for us. Yo! Paul!" he called out. "We're here!"

But once inside, they gasped in unison. The kitchen was a mess, drawers pulled out and dumped, cupboards standing open.

"Something's wrong," Grant whispered. "Stay here."

But she went right behind him into the living room, which had also been tossed. "Thieves?" she whispered, her heart pounding.

"Go back outside, lock yourself in the truck and call 911," he told her. "I don't want you with me if I corner someone. No—wait. Cells don't work up here, so we'll have to use Paul's landline. Where is he?"

Kate saw no phone in the kitchen—unless it was buried under the mess. They shuffled through piles of clothing, books and a sewing basket tipped upside down outside the kitchen. Of course, Grant knew where he was going. She followed him down a hall to peek into a bedroom. It was also a mess.

When Grant found the phone on the floor in the bedroom, its cord had been severed. The mattress was cut up, too, and the pillows slashed.

"The intruder had a knife," Grant whispered.

"What if Paul went crazy? A domestic argument, then..."

"Shh. Stow your imagination for now."

They looked in the bathroom, also chaotic. Grant shoved her behind him as he yanked the shower curtain back and glanced in the tub. Kate picked up a large can of hair spray from the counter and held it up like a weapon.

"Don't leave prints," he warned.

"I don't have my pepper spray."

He just shook his head. She stayed tight behind him as they retraced their steps, back through the living room, then to a hall and out into an area Kate was expecting would be a garage. But the carved door suggested it was Paul's studio.

They went in, and Grant turned on the track lighting. It was, she thought, as she stepped in behind him, like walking into an enchanted forest, maybe one a wicked witch had put under a curse. Tree trunks, some uncarved, some carved, stood along the walls, their fairy or ogre faces peering at them. One writhed with dragons, another with beautifully carved human skulls that looked so real Kate recoiled.

She saw three large, round, rotating platforms like large potter's wheels where he evidently carved his work. One held a tree trunk from which emerged what appeared to be Norwegian trolls with huge noses.

One wheel was empty and tipped and—

"Grant, here! He's here!" she cried and clapped her palms over her mouth to keep from screaming. Feeling sick, she stood frozen, staring wide-eyed at Paul Kettering, obviously dead, with blood on the floor and his skull smashed by his own big tree-trunk carving of the Adena pipe effigy.

6

Grant pulled Kate away from Paul's body. He knew his friend must be dead. His skull was crushed under the top part of the tree trunk he'd been carving. It looked as if it had tipped over on him. At least the heavy piece of wood hid what must be horrible injuries.

The scene in the dark hollow of the Adena mound flashed in his mind—smashed skulls.

Still, Grant felt Paul's cold wrist for a pulse. "He's gone. I want to lift that weight off him, but he's gone," he repeated. "My cell phone has never worked up here. We have to get to a spot where we can call for help. But go ahead—try yours."

He watched Kate fumble for her phone in her purse, try to call out on it.

"Mine won't connect, either. It just says 'searching.'"

"It must have been a freak accident...except for the ransacked house."

"Just in case of foul play, we can't touch more things here. Grant, I can go for help. I'll drive your truck down to where I can get reception, call Jace Miller."

"Yes, good. Can you drive a truck?"

"If I can drive a stick shift on the wrong side of the

road in England, I'll figure it out. I'll go out the back door where we came in."

Grant handed her his keys. His hand was shaking so hard, the keys jingled. "Be careful."

"Keep a good eye out here in case someone's still lurking. We didn't look everywhere in the house or around the grounds."

"I'll follow you out until you're in the truck."

They retraced their steps and rushed outside, just as a vehicle pulled in.

"It's Nadine," Grant said. His heart pounded even harder. "We can't let her see him like that."

"I heard you two were coming," Nadine called to them as she got out. "I've been at my sister's place— stayed there overnight after a doctor's appointment in Chillicothe yesterd— What? What is it?"

Grant put his hands on her shoulders. "When we got here no one answered, so—"

"Did he forget you were coming? His truck's here."

"Nadine, there's been an accident. His carving wheel with a trunk on it fell over."

"Is he all right?" she cried, her voice shrill.

"No, and things are messed up in your house. Kate was just ready to drive down toward town to call Deputy Miller because your phone cord is cut inside and our cells don't work up here. Nadine, he's gone—dead."

"Oh, dear God! He can't be! Let me see him. Here, my cell works, but most don't up here."

She thrust her purse at Kate, then pushed Grant's hands away to lunge toward the house. Grant shot Kate a panicked look and ran after Nadine. He was afraid he'd handled this wrong. But he—and Paul—had handled other things wrong, too.

* * *

An hour later, Kate and Grant sat on the front steps. He had his arm around her waist; she leaned gratefully against him, holding his other hand, which was propped on her knee. Through a front window, they could still hear Nadine sobbing.

Kate saw Grant had tears in his eyes. They were both trembling—he, of course, from losing his good friend in that terrible way, she because the carving that had crushed Paul had an Adena artifact on it, one of the two she'd planned to ask him to carve for her. Pure chance, of course, and yet that shook her to her core. It felt like a curse or a warning to her, and she knew better than to upset Grant more by mentioning it.

Soon after Kate had called 911, people had crowded the house. Nadine was so hysterical that Grant had called Pastor Snell. He and his wife, Jeanie, were with Nadine, and her sister was on the way. The paramedics had been standing around since the county coroner had declared Paul deceased and told them not to touch the body in case there had been foul play. And Jace Miller, who had arrived immediately, still looked shell-shocked. He'd asked the medics to stay in case Nadine needed them. Since she'd insisted she had nothing to do with the ransacking of the place, Deputy Miller had put up yellow police tape around the entire house.

"I suppose," Kate told Grant, "the idea that someone might have robbed the place means it could have been staged to look like an accident when it was really murder. You know, like Paul recognized them, so they had to get rid of him. But since the Ketterings weren't rich, what could someone have been looking for? Drugs? Guns?"

That thought seemed to really upset Grant. Frowning, he shrugged and shook his head. "Around here, folks have guns of their own and can get drugs easily—sad to say. I wish Gabe was here. Maybe Jace should call in the BCI. Vic Reingold was just here, but he's gone."

"Could Paul have owed someone money, and they came looking to collect?"

"Let's leave that up to the professionals, okay?"

"I'm just thinking aloud. Professional jealousy over his art, which turned into an argument?"

"Kate," he said, turning her to face him. "Do you have to dissect everything? Let it go. I said, leave it to the experts."

"I'm trained to ask the what-if questions. And don't you wonder what happened to your friend, what someone was looking for?"

"Yes, of course I do."

She almost mentioned that she'd heard Paul and Todd arguing yesterday, but Grant didn't want to hear any more speculation. Besides, she had no doubt that Todd would have an alibi from being at the mill. Grant was right. This wasn't some Celtic burial excavation where she could theorize which corpses were honored shamans and which were sacrifices.

Jace Miller came around the corner of the house and walked straight toward them. He stopped, put one foot on the bottom step and leaned his crossed arms on his raised knee. Though no one stood nearby, he kept his voice low.

"Two possibilities until we get the forensic specialists here. One, Paul went off the deep end. Nadine admits they're in debt, he's been shook over her medical diagnosis and the house could be foreclosed. So, it's possible he did the damage inside himself. That could make the tipping of that carving pedestal of his an accident or—well, suicide."

Grant shook his head. His grip on Kate's hand and wrist tightened. His voice was shaky. "What about he'd claim a robbery to get insurance money, then the trunk just fell over on him?"

"Nadine says they haven't kept up on insurance payments, not even for good medical coverage, which she needs since she's been diagnosed with Parkinson's disease. Had Paul told you that, Grant?"

"Yeah. He did. Jace, I don't think he'd kill himself."

"I'd go with accident—even murder before that. Nadine insists all three of the carving wheels were stable. From the angle it crushed his skull, either he pulled it down on top of himself or was lying on the floor when someone else pushed it."

"I can't fathom anyone would murder Paul," Grant said.

"Considering any possibility in a situation like this is standard police procedure. I'm going to have to ask you two, since you're the closest ones we have to eye-witnesses, to give me separate statements on what you observed in the house and when you found him. I'd like to talk to you first, Kate, since you spotted him on the floor before Grant did."

Grant nodded. "We understand. Anything to help. I've lost a good friend, and we've lost a talented artist."

Kate surprised herself by clinging to Grant's hand as they stood. Then she let go and followed Deputy Miller around the side of the house where he indicated they could talk in the front seat of his squad car.

* * *

After she'd spent a half hour with Deputy Miller, Kate waited for Grant to be interviewed. Jace Miller seemed understandably nervous to her, but he'd done a thorough job of taking her statement. Remembering Grant's warnings about not theorizing, she'd tried to stick to the facts.

But now, sitting in Grant's truck, waiting for him, Kate began to tremble. If Paul had been murdered, he wasn't the first victim she'd seen, she tried to tell herself. She'd studied deaths, even of murder and sacrificial victims, and their surroundings the way Deputy Miller and the experts would have to here.

But the victims she'd seen were long-dead, dusty skeletons in ancient graves, put to death and buried with their deceased masters to honor and serve them. Discovering Paul that way made her think how horrible it must have been for the Celt and Adena slaves or companions of the dead to have their skulls smashed so they could accompany their betters to the afterlife.

The minute she and Grant drove down the mountain to the level of the town, her phone rang. She glanced at the screen. Carson was calling. She didn't answer the call but saw that he'd phoned her three other times while she'd been out of reach over the past four hours. Well, when she told him what had happened, he'd have to understand.

"Important?" Grant asked.

"Carson Cantrell. You know—my university mentor and colleague. I'll call him back later. Grant, should we talk more about Paul? To debrief or just clear the air? This on top of the loss of your tree..."

"This is worse than the tree."

"Of course it is. I'm sure you want to break it to Todd and Brad."

"Don't want to but have to. Word will get around fast, even if Paul lived out—up—a ways."

"I suppose everyone will say he died doing what he loved. I had a colleague who loved to ski and was killed in an avalanche, but I guess there is a bit of comfort in looking at it that way. Paul's work is amazing—unique and so imaginative. It's a great loss, and I was so excited to have him do a work to link the Celts and Adena. Did you notice the carving that…that hurt him had the well-known Adena pipe figure on it? It's eerie—almost as if he knew that's what I planned to commission from him, with the Beastmaster."

She saw Grant's hands tighten on the steering wheel. Maybe she was wrong to think it would help him to talk about Paul.

He cleared his throat. "Your appreciation of his work pleased him. He was really stubborn about sticking to his art, even when Nadine thought he should take another job—any job—to tide them over or that he should go more commercial. Kate, I was hoping we could have dinner tonight, but I'd better tell our old buddies myself."

He took her home and insisted on walking her to the door and then going in.

"Just to be sure everything's normal in here," he said. He looked around the first floor to convince himself she was safe. "Not much left inside here, is there?" he asked.

"Tess said Grace sold a lot of things after they were done renting it and moved to the Hear Ye community. I guess they pretty much hold things in common there. And Tess took a few things for their new place. I'm only passing through, so I can make do. She did leave me a stocked fridge. Can I get you anything?"

He shook his head but reached for her and pulled her into a tight hug. "I'm grateful you were with me today," he said, his warm breath moving the tendrils of hair along her forehead. "But we can't play detective ourselves, even though I get it that you're used to considering all angles and proving theories. Promise?"

"I know to leave things up to the experts, and this is not my field."

She felt him relax a bit, even though she hadn't really promised what he'd asked. Did he think she'd get hurt by trying to puzzle things through?

"Dinner tomorrow night?" he asked. "To make up for tonight?"

She leaned back a bit to look up into his eyes; that move tilted her hips tighter against his. "Don't worry about me. Yes, I'd love that. But you just take care of yourself."

"I might need some help with that."

"Good. Call me tomorrow. I'll be out and about mapping virgin mound sites, but—"

"Including mine?"

"If you let me."

"Just noting their location and size?"

"For starters, yes."

"Okay. I'll call you about that later, and we can do it together."

Their gazes met and held. His arms around her tightened. He tilted his head and kissed her warmly, but lightly, quickly. She sensed he was holding back for some reason. He was distracted and must figure this wasn't the time or place, darn him.

He hugged her again and was out the door. It wasn't two minutes later her phone sounded—she had it programmed to play "Rule, Britannia!"—and she saw it was Carson again. Strange, but she'd actually hoped it was Grant, which was ridiculous since he'd just left.

"Carson, yes, I'm here."

"Where in hell have you been? I've been worried sick. No weddings today to make you turn off your cell, right?"

"You won't believe what happened. I went with Grant Mason to a local artist's house to commission a carving and we found the man dead—with his skull crushed. And by his own carving—he uses tree trunks—which had the Adena pipe figure on it, like he was psychic that was what I'd order—that and a Beastmaster mask."

"What? Slow down. Unbelievable! A freak accident?"

"His place had been ransacked when his wife was away. She has an alibi—more or less—so it must have been thieves."

"I can't believe you got yourself into that. Are you all right? Is it safe for you to be staying there alone at your sister's place, with lunatics like that loose?"

"I'm not afraid to be out here."

"Anyone you could stay with?"

"Carson, I haven't lived here for years and I was young when I left, but I'll be fine. It might have been a big happy time for my father to be back here seeing old friends, but not me, so I don't have anywhere else to stay."

"So how did that go—with your father?"

"Not that well—for me, anyway. I remember what he was like, though Tess and Char really don't."

"That's my Kate. A mind like a steel trap."

"But I'm sorry I didn't ask about how your talk went. Things got so intense here—"

"Really? Have you convinced Grant Mason to let you excavate Mason Mound yet?"

"I'm working on it, but I can't push. Besides, the murdered man was a good friend of his, and Grant recently had another personal setback."

"That might make him more vulnerable."

"You sound like you're pushing me into his arms."

"My darling, you're the one who is desperate for links, so link away—within reason. I still think you and I could have a brilliant future. And proving the prehistoric Europe-America link could be our big break."

They chatted about his talk at the Smithsonian. She realized it was so unlike him not to speak about himself first. But then, it wasn't every day that a former research assistant and protégée of Dr. Carson Cantrell found a recently deceased corpse instead of an ancient one.

7

For once the floor of the Mason Lumber Mill was quiet. Grant stood on the metal stairs to his office so the staff gathered around could see and hear him. Yesterday, he'd shared details with Brad and Todd about what had happened to Paul and that it wasn't clear if it was an accident, suicide—or even murder. Todd had taken the news badly and was very emotional; Brad was much more stoic. Grant knew people processed grief in their own ways. Their group of five friends was permanently splintered. Gabe, of course, would be back in two weeks, but Grant had decided to let him enjoy his honeymoon. He'd learn the terrible news about Paul soon enough.

"I know you've all heard what happened to Paul Kettering yesterday," Grant told the gathered men and women. "It's hit the news, and Deputy Miller tells me a reporter from the *Chillicothe Gazette* is asking questions around town. Since many of you knew Paul, I just wanted to say a word. He is a great loss to me, to us, to the wider community and, of course, to his wife, Nadine. It's possible the reporter or others may be asking questions, and I'm aware rumors are floating around. Please refer questions to me, since I was one of the ones who discovered his body."

Grant's stomach cramped as he went on to explain that the funeral would be Wednesday or Thursday, as soon as the coroner released the body, and the mill would close so all could attend. As everyone returned to work, Grant realized he didn't see Brad in the crowd. Brad had given him the idea he had been at the mill on Sunday afternoon, helping Todd with inventory since they'd been at the wedding most of Saturday. He'd mentioned that Todd had gone home for a couple of hours. But Grant had noticed this morning that not much of the inventory had been done. He'd inadvertently given Jace Miller alibis for Brad and Todd when he didn't know enough about where they had been.

He tried to avoid heart-to-hearts with Brad since he was so touchy, but he'd better talk to him again about when Todd left and whether Brad was here the whole time. And he wouldn't talk to them together. Grant knew Brad put Todd on edge, so he had to be sure his brother wasn't trying to cleverly, carefully sabotage Todd to get his foreman job.

Lost in thought, he started up the stairs toward his office. Paul was desperate for money. Was he the second one in their once-youthful band of brothers who might have been desperate enough to sell his Adena artifact? It had really shaken Grant that Brad had threatened to do the same.

Gabe had been away that fateful weekend years ago when the other four boys crawled through the old entry to the mound. No way would Gabe approve of years of a cover-up, even if it had started as a youthful mistake. They'd never told him, especially since his dad was the sheriff then. Grant, as head of their pals and the older of the Mason boys, had had first choice of the awesome things they'd seen in the dim depths of the mound, under the timbered roof that held the earth above their heads. He had picked the weird antlered mask Kate had called the Beastmaster, one of the links she was evidently looking for. Brad, choosing next, had taken a large arrowhead, Todd an ax head and Paul the eagle pendant.

Cutting their fingers with the arrowhead and mingling their blood, they had sworn a secret pact to hide the objects and never tell another soul what they'd done. But Grant had been spooked about it ever since, fearing they'd robbed the dead. He'd read a book once about how the people who'd entered King Tut's tomb in Egypt had been cursed for disturbing the dead and had died strange deaths themselves. And he'd never been able to forget that the bodies interred in Mason Mound, the ones evidently guarding the more decked-out corpses, all had their skulls smashed in—just like Paul.

Although Kate wished she was measuring Mason Mound instead of this one down by Cold Creek, it would give her comparison data when she finally did get to the mound on Grant's property. She had a feeling that Mason Mound was special. As far as anyone knew, it had never been excavated as this one had been. Also, Mason Mound was not near a stream, lake or river, which was unusual. This one wasn't far from the falls that had been the backdrop for Tess's wedding.

Kate tried to picture the newlyweds on their honeymoon. The luxury barge on the Loire, drifting through green, glorious France. Gabe had wanted something very different from what either of them had ever done, and he'd found it, all right.

Today Kate was using her notes and the crude map she'd made from an original, amateur Falls County map she'd found filed in the depths of the Ohio Historical Society archives. She'd been recording her measurements of the mound's circumference. When she'd noticed a measuring wheel in the old garage behind Tess's house, she'd asked if she could borrow it instead of just pacing off the ground. The long handle with its small wheel at the end was used for measuring skid marks in accidents, Tess had said. Gabe now had a more modern version, so he'd left it with other goods they were storing until the remodeling of their new house was done.

"This has got to be similar to the size of Grant's mound," she said aloud. "Bodies and artifacts were found here, so maybe there are some in his, too."

She knew this mound had caved in from the top when the upright logs or the roof timbers they supported had rotted. Could it be that Grant's mound, being farther from a water source and underground seepage or even humidity, had not caved in? Could it be intact? She had to get up to the top of Mason Mound, see if there were any signs of a cave-in. But she'd have to be careful or she could start an earth slide or fall right through.

She cautiously climbed this mound and noted where the top of it had settled. She'd read a pioneer-era report written in a fancy, delicate hand that relics and bone fragments had been found in the rubble. Nothing had been brought out intact except a few arrowheads, an ax head, two bone needles and a smashed copper bracelet. Most important, the early settlers had turned up a stone with a carved pattern that showed up on some

Adena art. She and Carson had theorized it was used for ceremonial tattooing. The amateur excavators had also found fragments of skulls too small to piece together. *If Mason Mound is similar to this one, but has not caved in...*

"Oh!" she cried and bent to see what had suddenly glinted in the sun.

Something strange and shiny was standing upright, partly wedged in the grass in the center of the top of this mound, just above the cave-in site.

"Boss, we got us a problem outside." The voice of Keith Simons interrupted Grant's agonizing as he stood on the steps to his office, watching everyone get back to work. Leaning over the railing, Grant looked down at his forklift driver, who stood on the concrete floor below. Until recently, all three Simons brothers had worked here, but Jonas had been charged with ties to a meth lab and Grant had fired him. He thought he'd lose Keith and Ned over that, too. Ned had resigned in anger, but Keith had always been loyal. The guy was a big bruiser, and Grant sometimes thought of him as his bodyguard. "You're not gonna like this," Keith called up to him.

Grant hurried down the stairs. "The reporter's here?"

Keith shook his big, bearded head. "Out on the road, picketers, about six of them with Save a Tree and Don't Destroy Our Forests signs and the letter *S* in the words is a big dollar sign."

Grant swore under his breath. Picketers from out of state had been around before but not for quite a while. He really didn't need this right now.

"I'll go out and talk to them," he told Keith, keeping his voice calm. "That's all we need if the newspaper reporter shows up. It will give him a second story, make us look bad, when I've been working with state lawmakers on green projects."

"I got your six, boss," Keith assured him and joined him as Grant strode toward the big front doors. "One other thing," Keith said. "This time it's Green Tree people, and it looks like your ex-wife's leading the pack."

Kate knew better than to put her weight closer to the caved-in center of the mound's top but she had to see what that shiny object was. Maybe something the early settlers of the area had dropped, for so many of these mounds had been dismantled by pioneers out of curiosity. Whatever was found inside had disappeared into attics and trunks—a few in museums—long ago. Or if stones had been used to shore up the burial sites, early settlers used them for the foundations of their houses and barns. Maybe it was a marker the professional excavators from the 1950s had left. But would the thing be so shiny if it was old?

She hurried back down the mound and came up with the measuring wheel to see if she could use the long handle to reach the object. With it, leaning, stretching, she managed to pry it loose and slide it toward her over grass and weeds, but not close enough to safely pick it up.

She could see it was a star, about two inches across. At first she thought it was a six-pointed Star of David, but it had five points—each one tipped in reddish-brown. As far as she could tell from this distance, nothing was written on it. What was it? Surely not an artifact. A Christmas-tree ornament? She decided she'd come back later with the fishing pole she'd seen in Tess's garage, hook it, examine it. But who had left it here and why?

It was illegal to insert objects into mounds and earthworks. The state of Ohio termed that *vandalizing* or *desecration,* a second-degree misdemeanor. Carson had told her about a couple of idiots who were adding their own fake artifacts to mounds, then trying to sell them as authentic. They had spent ninety days in jail and paid a $5,000 fine—for each mound. Maybe that was what had happened here. She'd have to ask him more about that.

Kate hurried down the mound, vowing she'd be back for that star. But all she could think of now was that she'd tell Grant about it and ask him if she could at least check out the top of his mound to see if there was anything similar. It was an excuse to get a better look at Mason Mound. She was almost tempted to go there first, explain to him later. But she didn't want to get him more upset than he already was over Paul's terrible death. She hoped he'd be in a better mood today than the depths of despair she'd left him in yesterday.

She tossed her equipment into her rental car and headed for the mill.

Grant was trying to keep his temper, but he could see Lacey was reveling in this chance to annoy him.

"All the lumber mills in this state and you choose this one to picket," Grant said as he faced down her little crowd of protesters walking back and forth with the placards just off his property line. "How nice that you wanted to see me again."

"Don't flatter yourself," she said, stopping to face him with one hand on her hip. The clove-flavored gum she liked to chew hit him with its strong scent. "We rotate mills and factories where we protest. It was just your turn, and we had a place to stay with my parents, so it worked out. We'll be back tomorrow."

Lacey had gained weight, her hair was blonder, and she wore a heck of a lot of makeup. She looked a far cry from the natural girl he'd once fallen in love with. Her companions were all pretty young, except for one guy who was keeping a good eye on her.

"Hey, don't just pick on her!" the man said, stepping forward. "We're all in this together."

Lacey nodded and leaned her shoulder against his in a possessive move. Grant just shook his head. The man reminded him of a bouncer or a boxer, when most of the picketers seemed more millennial types. He was good-looking, though, and Lacey had always gone for that. Grant could see Lacey had this guy wrapped around her little finger for anything she wanted or needed.

"This is Darren Ashley," Lacey said when she saw Grant glaring at him. "He's new to Green Tree, and he's all-in."

"I'll bet," Grant said, but he just wanted this confrontation over—nicely, calmly. "Lacey, as you, above all people, know," he said, ignoring the others, "the Masons have always replanted tracts of trees and cut carefully."

"Cut carefully, that's a good one. Oh, I heard about Paul on the car radio, so I'm sorry for that. He was very talented."

"And he used our cut tree trunks for his art, so not even those were wasted, right?"

"Never mind using your smarts and charm on me, Grant Mason. Been there, done that."

Darren Ashley nodded as if he thought Lacey was really handling this. Again, Grant fought to keep calm.

"Well, all of you, enjoy yourself today. Knock yourselves out, but please don't come on my property unless you intend to purchase some of our environmentally harvested products."

"And what about noise pollution, smoke pollution!" Lacey shouted when he started to walk away. That was when he knew she was here for a personal vendetta. Hell, she'd wanted out, and he'd ended up paying her well for leaving him.

"By the way," he added, turning back, "you and your friends should watch out for the big timber trucks that pull in, since you need to stand on the road." Again, he started to walk away.

"You'd like it if we got knocked into the ditch, wouldn't you?" she yelled. He knew he was going to lose his temper, when he thought he'd handled things with reasonable control.

He turned back yet again. Darren Ashley was giving him the finger, and Lacey's little group was all eyes and ears. He fought hard not to leap at the guy and deck him, but that wasn't his way.

"No, I wouldn't like that, Lacey, because we're all busy earning a living here, and I don't have time to call the rescue squad for you. I've got a staff of eighteen men and three women on-site and others in the field who need to feed their families, and we don't even have time to fish you and your signs out of a ditch."

"That's another thing! You should hire at least half women! That's half of the population, you know!" Lacey shouted.

"If I see a qualified or interested woman, one who

likes this beautiful area of the country and the good people who live here and doesn't have pie-in-the-sky dreams of fancy places and exotic people, I hire her!" he yelled just as Kate pulled up, slowly, gawking at the picketers. Luckily, she drove her car between Grant and Lacey's attack dog Darren, who had started toward him.

Grant turned his back on the man and walked toward the mill, knowing Kate would figure out who was behind the Green Tree protest, knowing she'd sense how deeply upset he was. At least the picketers, including Lacey's avenger, had gone back onto the berm of the road.

But as Kate got out of her car, he saw she was upset, too. "Sorry about all that, Grant," she told him, with a narrow-eyed glance at the protesters. She walked into the mill with him. "Is *she* out there—the blonde with the eye makeup?"

He had to grin, the first time in a couple of days, at least. "Yeah," he said, "sadly so. And I'm thinking the reporter the Chillicothe paper is sending out will be here any minute to cover that as well as Paul's death."

"Any more news from Jace Miller about cause of death?"

"Only that he has to consider it suspicious until he can prove otherwise."

"I didn't come about that," she said. "I hate to ask you this when things are so crazy but—"

"Come on up to my office. Noisy in here again, so I hope it drowns out their chanting."

"The protesters were chanting?"

"Yeah, as I started out to talk to them. 'Green Tree says no cut trees! Green Tree says no cut trees!' Are you okay?"

"Two things," she said as they walked into his office. "First, I was measuring the mound out by the falls, the one near Cold Creek. Where it caved in on top years ago, I spotted a shiny gold star—kind of like an old Western sheriff's badge, come to think of it. Gabe or Jace don't wear anything like that, do they?"

"Used to, I think. Didn't Jace have one on yesterday? Did you bring it with you?"

"I was scared to step out where it is, because of the depression, the old cave-in. Grant, can I go up on the top of your mound just to be sure there's nothing like that there? Ohio has had cases where vandals tried to put something into the mounds as well as take something out—and they went to jail for it."

"Whoa! Slow down. I've been up on top of Mason Mound from time to time and looked at it for years from the tree house. I've never seen anything like that."

"But the star looks shiny—new."

"Our whole mound is pretty overgrown. But if I go with you, okay. So what else did you want to say?"

"I should have mentioned it to you earlier—and to Deputy Miller when he interviewed me yesterday," she said. "It was something I overheard, and I think that's hearsay anyway, so—"

"Something about Paul?"

She nodded. He didn't like the fact Ms. Calm finally looked nervous. "What?" he prompted.

"During my father's toast to Tess and Gabe at the reception, I stepped out onto the lodge veranda and overheard Paul and Todd arguing."

"Really arguing or just discussing something? They've been friends for years and neither of them has much of a temper."

"I'm sure they were arguing."

His gut twisted tighter. "Over what?"

"Over Paul being short of money, which we both know about—and, of course, Deputy Miller does now, too."

"And?"

"Paul was threatening to sell something, and Todd was really upset about it."

Grant feared he knew what they'd argued about— maybe the same thing he and Brad had.

"So," he said, quietly. "That's it?" He was suddenly aware of choosing his words carefully. Kate was so bright and perceptive, and gung ho on getting not only on top of but also inside of Mason Mound. He should distance himself from her right now, put her off somehow. His temptation wasn't to sell his Adena artifact, but to keep Kate close yet keep her from realizing what vandals he and his friends had been years ago. Somehow he had to distract her—give her something but get her off on another tack. He'd held back information from Jace Miller, too, that Paul's house could have been ransacked by someone looking for his Adena pendant— if he'd told anyone about it—or if Brad had blabbed. For sure, he'd have to talk to his brother again.

"Grant, should I have told the deputy? Or should I still? I don't want him to think I'm saying he should look at Todd for being the one who came to Paul's house, especially not to continue their quarrel."

"I'm sure Todd has an alibi. He and Brad were doing inventory here, and Todd only briefly went home."

She nodded, but he could see—almost hear—her quick brain clicking through the information—and maybe noting the nerves that showed up in his voice.

But, thanks to Green Tree and Lacey, he had an excuse for that right now.

"Tell you what," he said. "Let's take a look at the top of Mason Mound during my lunch break today. It's almost time. Wait here for a few minutes while I check some things down on the cutting floor, okay?"

"Sure. Great," she said, looking surprised but pleased.

He hoped it would be great, but it sure didn't seem to be his day.

8

Grant fixed them a quick lunch in his kitchen—peanut-butter-and-jelly sandwiches with soft drinks—but Kate was almost too excited to eat. She could see the top of the mound out the window now that the big maple was gone and that, combined with Grant's presence, really made her edgy.

Grant got up to take their dishes to the counter. "We'll just take a quick look on top of the mound," he said. "The grass is high there and things have grown up over the years. We used to roll down it as kids, screaming like savages, until Dad and Grandpa made all of us show more respect."

"For the dead. 'Let the dead stay dead,' your father said."

"Right, even though I'll bet the bodies would be totally gone by now."

"You'd be amazed at what those mounds preserve. Yours, being small with less air inside, hopefully intact with no cave-in, and away from water, could make it a prime excavation site."

"Besides private-property rights, isn't there some

government act that says you can't disturb tribal graves?"

"You've been doing some homework. That's the Native American Graves Protection and Repatriation Act. But that's geared more toward historic Indian tribes, to have bones and artifacts either left buried, or—if the grave has already been tampered with—the things returned to their tribal descendants. But the Adena were prehistoric, and, of course, there are no Adena to give things back to anymore. I hope to prove my theory that they were actually not American Indians but of European stock. They were taller, larger people than more modern Native Americans. My colleague—"

"That Carson Cantrell who phoned you?"

"Yes. He's been moving heaven and earth to get the government to exempt the Adena from the Graves Protection act, although, of course, any relics of them or their culture must be honored, studied and displayed for the common good."

"As for bodies," he said, as they headed toward the back door, "I've read they cremated some of their dead, so maybe there are no corpses in these mounds, though I guess bones and teeth could outlast flames."

"It's been long accepted that the Adena did cremate those of lower castes. But some of us believe that individuals actually chose what would be done with their bodies after death, just like people today can choose cremation or burial. After we check your mound, I'm going back to retrieve the star from Cold Creek Mound."

He seemed to be dragging his feet, but they went out the back door and across the yard toward the mound. Kate's heart rate increased. Bit by bit, she had to convince Grant—maybe Brad, too, though she knew Grant was the one in charge here—to let her excavate this mound.

"You're right," she told him as they stood at the bottom of the mound. "Lots of growth even high up. But I think we can still climb it. No poison ivy, I hope, though those old hawthorn trees will keep us from going up that way. Bet you never rolled down the hill as a kid into those—at least not more than once. They must be diseased. The whole thicket is dying."

"Yeah, I see. I hadn't noticed that," he said, frowning.

She started climbing, bending forward, grabbing at saplings when she could. She hoped Grant was not still staring at the tree-trunk ruin of his bird's-eye maple, but she heard him right behind her.

"Look!" she cried, once the mound leveled out on top. "No signs of cave-ins at all. Even with the bushes and wildflowers up here, it looks pretty solid. I've seen enough mounds here and in Europe to know."

He put his hand around her upper arm. "Maybe we shouldn't add our weight to it, though."

"I'm telling you, I've walked on lots of these. Besides, that star was new and not deep in the ground, kind of sticking up. Shiny, too, so if there's one here, it shouldn't be hard to see. I'm just going to walk around a bit up here, okay?"

For one moment she was afraid she should not have asked him and should have just plunged ahead. Surely, since they were standing here, he wouldn't try to stop her. But his sky-blue gaze was so intense that she felt mesmerized and didn't move. The breeze ruffled his blond hair to remind her that he had once been a little boy who played here, who thought of his grandpa and dad when he was near the mound. Surely that was why he was so protective of this place. And that was only one of many reasons he got to her so deeply, physically but emotionally, too.

Somehow, suddenly, they were in each other's arms. Holding tight, her breasts flattened against his chest, his hands moved to her waist and back. She clamped him to her with her arms hard around his middle. He dipped his head. She tilted hers upward. If he had not been holding her, the kiss surely would have swept her off the mound and far away.

Kate propped her shaking knees against his legs. His right hand moved to caress her hair, tenderly at first, then holding her head as if she would flee, when she wasn't going anywhere.

The kiss went on and on. For once, she couldn't even think, only feel and want. For one insane moment she imagined he was what she had been searching for, not some star or revelation. This was stronger than her passion for discovering things. She wanted to know Grant Mason—she wanted Grant Mason....

When they broke the kiss, she felt devastated, but sanity came flooding back. However desirable this man was, he was dangerous, too. He stood in the way of what she wanted—especially if he became what she wanted more than all she'd worked for. His ex-wife fled being trapped in this little town. Kate could understand that. She couldn't imagine wanting to stay in Cold Creek, but neither could she fathom wanting to leave this man.

Grant held her gently and sighed. He trailed his fingertips down her throat in a light caress to just below her collarbones. His tension had turned tender. Her skin tingled at his touch.

"Can't apologize for that," he whispered.

"You'd better not," she replied. "If that was a diversionary tactic, I'm ready to be diverted again."

"You're not. You're like a dog after a bone—excuse the comparison for a beautiful woman."

They were still breathing hard in unison, making their own breeze up here. Slowly, he set her back, released her. She clung to his upper arms for a moment. This man was as solid as a tree, not thin and wiry like Carson. Finally, she let go.

"I'll wait right here," he said. "Go ahead and look around, but I think all you'll find are a couple of Batman or G.I. Joe figures that Brad and I lost up here years ago."

But Grant was wrong. The grass and underbrush were not a problem because a perfect replica of the other star—clear to the dried brownish paint on the tips of its five points—was stuck in the ground where grass and weeds had been pulled up in a little circle. She used a tissue from the pocket of her jeans to pick it up without putting her fingerprints on it. With Paul's death, Jace Miller probably didn't have time to look into this, but what if it really turned out to be a clue to who had cut down Grant's tree—or something about this mound?

"See?" she said, stepping through the high grass to show him. After they'd examined the face of it, she carefully flipped it over as they both leaned close. Devoid of writing, smooth, it glinted in the sun. "Someone's been here recently and is actually defacing mounds with these stars! That's the legal definition of *defacing*—leaving some object in or on them or tampering with them in any way."

"No writing on it," he said, after she turned it over. "Not even a made-in mark. So why a bright star?"

They looked at each other, wide-eyed. "During my run-in with Bright Star Monson, he insisted Tess's wedding was pagan. I threw back at him something like I'd trust Adena pagan ways compared to how he ran roughshod over his people."

"But if he left these, what's his point? And why wouldn't he leave a cross—a crucifix—if he's trying to Christianize the pagan dead of this mound, or whatever."

"Because he's a cult leader, not really Christian," she insisted, her voice rising. "Maybe he's convinced he can convert the pagan dead to his ways. He's into complete control of his robot congregation and who knows what else. It makes me sick he's got my relatives enthralled and enslaved. In a cult, it always ends up being all about the leader, like that crazy Jim Jones, who got a thousand of his followers to drink Kool-Aid laced with cyanide!"

"Not so far off, maybe, from the ancient Adena leaders. I read their leaders were sometimes buried with others who were killed to accompany them to the afterlife. So don't you go confronting Bright Star yourself. I wonder what the paint on the points means?"

The reality of what she was looking at hit her hard. "I thought it was paint at first, too," she whispered, "but now I think it's old or dried blood."

Back at work at the mill, Grant had another theory about the stars Kate had found. Could she have planted them just so he'd let her get closer to Mason Mound—and closer to him? She'd found the second star pretty fast in that ground cover.

"Grant." A voice cut through his thoughts. Brad stuck

his head in the office door. "Keith said you wanted to see me? A guy that big speaks, ya gotta listen."

"Yeah. Come on in," he said, ignoring the lame joke.

"I mean, it's not like we don't see each other at the house, if this is some big-brother talk," Brad said, closing the door behind him and taking the other chair.

"You're hardly there. I assume the new places uptown are more appealing than my food or conversation."

"Look. I've been trying to help out around here—show you I can be valuable to you. I've talked to everyone on the floor, kept an eye on Todd, and—"

"And that's one thing I wanted to ask you. Todd should be keeping an eye on you, not the other way around. You don't think I'm going to change my mind about demoting him and putting you in as foreman, do you? At most, I can work you in as cutting-line supervisor when Randy Thatcher retires in the fall but—"

"Well, thanks a lot! I come in here, willing to help, and you give me no hope of moving up in our family business. I know, I know, you bought out my share when I wanted to go out on my own. But I'm telling you, if Dad was still alive, he'd welcome me home with open arms like the prodigal son!"

"I'm impressed with the reference. I have no doubt he'd kill the fatted calf for you. And I've welcomed you back, but not at the price of firing or demoting loyal, hardworking men here, and Todd's a longtime friend of ours."

"One we don't want to tick off since he's one of our coconspirators, right?"

"Brad, just listen. I know you understand that Todd's good at what he does and loyal. Dad would not fire or demote him, either, nor would Grandpa or—"

"So, it's family-tree time again. And I don't mean that as another reference to the stolen tree."

"There's something else. On Sunday, when you and Todd were both here, you worked on the inventory, right?"

"Yeah. There any mistakes in it?"

"No. I was just surprised so little of it got done. You weren't arguing with each other instead, were you?"

He gave a little snort, then—after a beat—shook his head. "If you want to know, we both came and went. I went uptown for a few minutes and he went home— or somewhere—for quite a while. I mean, it was the day of rest."

Though they were alone with the door closed, Brad leaned forward and lowered his voice. "I don't want to rat on him, but I actually think Todd went to see Paul about something. I didn't want to say that, thought you'd believe I'd made it up to discredit him."

"You mean, I'd think he could be the one who ransacked Paul's place or worse?" Grant demanded. He was starting to feel sick to his stomach. Kate had said she'd overheard Todd and Paul arguing and now this. "I'll talk to him."

"Better you than Deputy Miller, alias Barney Fife," Brad said. "How many reruns of *The Andy Griffith Show* did we watch when we were growing up, huh?"

"Don't try to change the subject. Jace Miller is doing a good job while Gabe's away. He's been hit with two big investigations—Paul's death and major tree theft, and he's stretched pretty thin."

"Right." He drawled the word as if he didn't believe it. Brad bounced up from his seat, nearly tripped as he headed for the door then bumped his shoulder against the door frame on his way out. "See you later, boss and bro," he threw over his shoulder.

Grant sighed. He hadn't dismissed Brad, but he was glad to see the backside of him. He'd considered bringing up the fact he figured Brad was drinking, even during the day. He hadn't smelled booze on him and his speech hadn't seemed slurred, though his exit was a little shaky. Brad had always held his liquor well. But with so many saws and presses here, the mill had strict rules against drinking or drugs that dulled reaction time. Brad had always joked about this being a cutting-edge business. Grant felt that way now, like he was riding the rails toward a buzz saw—and, despite how much he wanted her, the sharp, clever Dr. Kate Lockwood might just be that blade.

Kate laid out both identical reddish-tipped stars on a cloth on the kitchen table and stared at them. She'd retrieved the second one from Cold Creek Mound with a fishing pole. The design did not suggest Adena symbolism—and they were too new and obviously manufactured—although the idea of them being blood-tipped echoed the way Celtic shamans had probably tipped the antler points of the Beastmaster mask either in blood or ocher pigment. She was picturing the frightening mask she'd seen in a museum in Denmark when a sharp knock on the back door nearly sent her through the ceiling.

Carson Cantrell's clean-cut, almost boyish face popped into view through the storm-door window. With his neatly trimmed brown hair, Carson looked younger than his forty-nine years.

"Wherefore art thou, my Kate? Kiss me, Kate!" he called to her as she opened the door for him.

He hugged her hard and she hugged him back, then moved away from him quickly. After that kiss with Grant today—well, she just couldn't let Carson kiss her.

"You should have told me you were coming, and I'd have baked a cake, but I have something better," she said, walking to the other side of the small kitchen table while he closed the door. "Look what someone left on at least two of the local mounds, including Mason Mound. I think it's blood on the tips, just like on the Beastmaster mask."

The stars instantly captured his attention. He bent closely over them, whipped his glasses out of his suit-coat pocket—didn't he know to dress casually around here? But then, Carson came from old money. His great-great-grandfather had made a fortune in the Akron, Ohio, rubber business, knew Henry Ford, Harvey Firestone, Thomas Edison and all that meant. Carson's beautiful old home in a Columbus suburb was full of various art collections.

Carson had tenure at Ohio State, but Kate figured he could leave his teaching career and his collection of adoring students anytime to become an art collector—his other hobby beyond archaeology. Though he appreciated the finer things in life, he didn't mind getting his hands dirty when he led excavation teams. She watched as he studied the stars close-up.

"Illegal desecration of the mounds," he said. "But I'm glad to hear you've been exploring Mason Mound. That's our target, darling, and we can't just go waltzing in there with trowels, sieves and needle picks. Not until you get the man's permission one way or the other. But, unlike with the old artifacts," he went on, his voice in lecture mode now, "you're right about this being clotted blood, so what's the message here?"

9

As they leaned over the table and Carson studied the metal stars, Kate told him her theory. "Grant and I think there's some symbolic message here, so I'm guessing the blood on the tips ties in to that."

"Grant and I?" he repeated, taking a seat at the table. "I like the sound of that." He produced a penlight from his jacket's inner pocket, slid the cloth with the stars closer to him and shined a thin beam on one of them. "If you two are working together on this, there's more to come—namely getting into that Adena mound on his property. I could try to get a court order, but it would take a while. Eminent domain versus private-property rights is a touchy subject, and we don't need a setback or negative PR."

He smiled at her. "Besides, I'd prefer to set up on his land to explore the interior of the mound, and I'd rather have him on our side. But tell me what you have discovered or analyzed about these stars."

"We're theorizing they were put there by a local religious-cult leader, who calls himself Bright Star. He's got quite a group of followers in the Hear Ye compound not far down the road from here. He doesn't like me. I got upset and more or less told him the Adena were less pagan than he is. His real name is Brice Monson."

"The same charlatan who's entranced the Lockwood cousins you mentioned?" he asked, carefully turning one star over with the tip of his penlight.

"The same. Maybe he thinks by putting these bright stars on the mounds he's symbolizing that his beliefs are above those he calls 'pagan dead.'"

"And the blood? It is the Christian symbol of salvation."

"Carson, like I told Grant, he's not *Christian*. He's a weirdo master controller, not that he couldn't be using blood as some sort of sign or message. Who knows how he keeps his people in line? I swear, my cousin Grace is actually afraid of him."

"Really? I'll have some of my grad student assistants circumspectly check some of the other mounds in the area for more of these. And if we can prove this guy is the one defacing the mounds, we can have him arrested and fined. He could do jail time, though what his flock would consider persecution probably wouldn't free them from his control."

"I swear," she said, sinking into the other chair, "he's cast an evil spell over his followers, like in some gruesome fairy tale. He's an ogre masquerading as a shepherd—the wolf in Grandma's clothes from *Little Red Riding Hood.*"

"Then he's a formidable adversary, so beware. He can't be an idiot to do all this, especially mind control." Carson looked up from studying the second star. He clicked his penlight off and replaced it in his inner pocket. "Maybe he's read up on the Adena, their cult of death, and thinks he can somehow use that to either keep his people in line or scare others off, so he ties the mound to himself—tries to exert control with his namesake symbol above it."

She sighed. Carson was brilliant, though sometimes she thought he was just restating something she'd come up with. Hadn't she just, more or less, said that? "Tess told me he buried a couple of dead infants on his property, but he had permission for that."

He sat up even straighter. "In a mound?"

"Little mounds, I guess, hidden under plastic."

"Stranger things have happened. But all this aside for now, I'm thrilled to see you. No offense, but let's get out of here for a while, as the surroundings in this old place are a bit Spartan. How about heading into the big city of Cold Creek to that pseudo-English pub I passed? I can't wait to tell you about some of the scholars I met in D.C. and how my thesis was received."

"Sounds great. Let me rewrap these stars. You know, I'm wondering if this could be human blood—even Bright Star's. And I do realize it's not a done deal that he's the one who left these."

"Actually, I did spot one tiny hint these stars were originally made to be worn—like a badge."

"Really? I thought of that at first, but dismissed it. Like a sheriff's badge?"

He whipped his penlight out again and trained the beam on the back of one star. "Look here. It's smoothly done, but see those two tiny irregular spots where a pin could have been attached on the back so it could be worn? But I think it's been soldered over. And the metal quality looks quite good—not like it's a kid's cowboy sheriff badge, though I suppose that's another possibility."

"I do see it. I should have used a magnifying glass, but I don't have one here. Under a microscope, maybe something else would show up that's been obscured, like a made-in mark or production number."

"How about I take one and have it checked for that and learn from a lab at the university whether it's human or animal blood? Actually, I'd like to talk to this Bright Star Monson."

"All right, take one of them and let me know what the lab says. But, Carson, don't confront Bright Star, at least not alone. I'm planning to take the acting sheriff if I go to see him. Speaking of blood, Bright Star chills mine!"

As she rose to get a clean dish towel to wrap a star for him, Carson stood and embraced her. "We make a good team, even when apart," he told her, not smiling, so serious. His lips moved against her ear. "My darling Kate, let's continue to work together, however close you get to Grant Mason for the cause, right?"

"Of course," she said, stepping back, then moving away to wrap the stars separately. "But he is a good man, Carson, so I won't lie to him or hurt him."

"And I'm not a good man, struggling to advance knowledge for more than just us? Human, universal knowledge is bigger than just a few small people, Kate. Sometimes the ends do justify the means. Without Howard Carter plundering Tutankhamen's grave or Heinrich Schliemann excavating ancient Troy, mankind would know so much less about the past, even about ourselves. Surely, I convinced you of all that several years ago, at least in the single undergrad course you took from me."

"Yes. Yes, of course," she said. "It's because of that

class and your passion for it that I chose archaeology." It hit her for the first time that, in a way, Carson Cantrell and Bright Star Monson had some things in common. Both were eloquent, charismatic evangelists for their causes, which they fervently believed in. Both were quick with a quote. No way did she want to blindly do Carson's bidding the way someone like Grace toed the line for Bright Star. And it scared her that both men seemed hell-bent on getting what they wanted, whatever the cost or sacrifice.

Grant decided not to question or confront Todd at the mill about whether he'd been arguing with Paul the day he died. Instead, he drove to Todd's house after work. He'd talk to him then call Kate's cell and pick her up about eight. He wanted to get her away from here for a while—clear his own head, too, and avoid Brad—so he planned to drive them to a restaurant he liked in Chillicothe. He didn't mind that he'd be two nights straight at his favorite restaurant. He'd set it up long ago that he'd take Todd and Amber out for Todd's birthday tomorrow.

He pulled into the curved drive at Todd's neatly kept wooden ranch house. Good—his pickup truck was here. He could hear the kids shouting behind the house where there was a jungle gym and swing set. All three of Todd's boys were elementary-school age. Seeing the McCollum family over the years had made Grant long for kids of his own, however rowdy the McCollum kids were.

Amber McCollum had been Todd's high-school sweetheart, as Lacey had been Grant's. Amber saw him arrive and came to the front door. She was a trim natural redhead with light brown eyes and freckles. She'd been a hairstylist in town before the kids, but preferred to stay at home now, more power to her, though Grant knew money was always tight. He tried to give the kids nice gifts, buy gift certificates for restaurants for their family—the family he wished he had.

"Grant, come on in! Aren't you and Todd tired of seeing each other at the mill?" she teased and held the door open.

"I just wanted to run something by him in private without all the noise and interruptions."

"Fat chance with those hooligans out there," she said with a laugh as he went inside. "They'll go bonkers when they see you."

The place looked like a tornado had gone through with toys everywhere and a blanket over a card table as if to make a play fort. It made him think of the mound again. A mounted stag head stared down from the wall. It had colored rings snagged on its antlers as if the kids had used it for a game. It reminded Grant of the argument he and Todd had had over the Adena mask. In their late teen years, Todd had wanted to trade his ax head for the mask with the antlers, but Grant had refused. He just couldn't part with it. There was something so compelling, so hypnotizing—even if terrible—about that mask. Kate's Beastmaster.

They walked to the living-room picture window overlooking the backyard and woods beyond. "Can I get you anything?" Amber asked, turning toward him. "A beer? Can of pop?"

"Thanks, I'm fine. If you can let Todd know…"

"He was upset when he came home. It was more than mourning Paul's death. I don't know why, but maybe you do. He played with the kids a bit, and I haven't had a chance to get it out of him what's bugging him. Pillow talk later will do the trick, I hope."

Playing with the kids…pillow talk. Grant realized he'd like both of those things in his life.

"Grant, are you here about something he did or didn't do? Maybe that's why he's so upset. I mean, I know Paul's death really shook him up, the strange circumstances and all that, but— Okay, I'll tell you where he is," she added when he shook his head and frowned. "Literally up a tree."

"His favorite one?"

"Yep. And I was sorry to hear about the tree-house maple. That hit Todd hard, too. He did mention one thing today—that Lacey brought protesters to the mill and was real mouthy. She's sure changed from our old double-date days, but haven't we all?"

"You're a good friend, Amber, and good for Todd."

"I knew he was Tarzan of our local jungle when I married him. But hey, you just say hi to the boys, then go on out—and tell my man to be home in a couple of hours to help tuck our wild kids in bed."

She walked him to the back door. Jason, the oldest boy, spotted him and started shouting, "Uncle Grant! Uncle Grant's here!"

Three kids barreled at him, and he bent down to give them all high fives and hugs.

You might know, Kate thought, Brad Mason was sitting at the bar in the English pub. When he spotted her with Carson, he sauntered over. All she needed was pressure from Carson not only to get cozy with Grant but Brad, too.

"Yo, Kate of the Adena," Brad greeted her and held

up his free hand, palm forward with his fingers open, two by two, in the *Star Trek* Mr. Spock V. He had what looked like a martini in his other hand. "Just wanted to say hi, but I'll clear out if this is an up-close-and-personal friend."

Kate made the necessary introductions, calling Carson her colleague at Ohio State, where she'd taught low-level archaeology courses before her grant to go to England came through. When Carson heard who Brad was, his eyes lit up just like when he'd seen the blood-tipped metal stars.

"Sit down with us," Carson invited and got up to slide next to Kate on one side of the booth to make room for Brad on the opposite. "Kate and I work together in the study of the Adena. I hear you have a mound on your family's land."

Brad put his drink down and leaned back in the booth. "You're not really BCI undercover here? Some of them dress like that. All you need is sunglasses and one of those earpieces—and to be carrying a gun under that suit coat."

Kate noted that Brad, like Grant, didn't want to discuss the mound. "Brad has just come back to town," Kate started to explain, but Carson cut her off.

"BCI? Bureau of Criminal Investigation? No, though I suppose your brother told you he and Kate found a sort of badge on top of your mound."

"Actually, he asked me if I put it there. I told him he was nuts."

"The thing is," Carson went on, "other than natural growing objects, nothing is to be added to a mound, or it's criminal intent or worse."

"No kidding?" Brad drained his drink. "He didn't say

that, but then, those two seem to be keeping secrets."
He winked at Kate, which ticked her off. "And they're
the ones who found Paul Kettering's body, sad to say,"
he added. "So you're an Ohio State professor, Carson?
Fight the team across the field, Go Bucks, and all that?"

"Can't say I take much advantage of college-life fri-
volities. But I can get good tickets to a football game
this fall if you want to come up and go with me."

Kate rolled her eyes. Carson couldn't care less even
if the Buckeyes lost to their archrival Michigan or never
played another game. But she could see the handwriting
on the wall—the wall of an Adena tomb. If she didn't
get what Carson wanted out of Grant, Brad would be
standing in the wings.

Grant was glad he had his steel-toed boots on as he
hiked up toward the huge pin oak Todd favored for his
climbs. Besides living trees, Grant passed brush with
new saplings peeking through, hardwood sprawl and
downed trees—the generations of a forest. This was
a virgin area, perfect for logging, which Todd would
never do. To him this area was sacred.

Todd had by nature what Grant had worked hard
to gain—brush sense, an instinctive knowledge of the
woods. His lifelong friend was what they called out in
the redwood forests of the West a "brush cat." Although
Grant got along with loggers as well as he did senators,
he'd never have the guts to climb like Todd did. According to the U.S. Department of Labor, logging was the
most dangerous job in America, but Todd would have
reveled in that career if it weren't for his family.

"Hey, you up there?" Grant shouted, cupping his
hands around his mouth.

"You here as boss or friend?" Todd called down, though Grant could not spot him.

"Longtime best buddy!"

"I'll be right down."

From the lofty canopy of oak leaves, Todd descended on a rope, something like mountain climbers used, winching himself down. When he cleared the lower branches, he bounced his boot soles against the trunk, swinging out, then in until he had his feet on the ground.

"Yellow jackets building a nest way up there," Todd told him. "I might have to smoke them out." He started to unstrap his Jumar ascenders and stepped out of his harness. "You gotta come up with me, Grant. The view up there makes things look better."

"Okay. Sometime."

"You got things on your mind we should talk about besides Paul's loss?" Todd asked as he meticulously wound his ropes.

"Are you upset with me?"

"Not you."

"With Brad?"

"For one."

"Has he been trying to edge you out, saying things? You're my foreman on the mill floor, and that's not going to change, at least not for anything I do."

"Thanks."

"I've heard on the wind that you and Paul had a falling-out."

He shook his head and hoisted his gear over his shoulder. "That's a good way to say it, 'a falling-out.' In Oregon, I saw a guy fall from a redwood. He was doing a monkey hang, screwed up somehow. Since the top of the human body's heavier than the lower part, if you're

up over fifty feet, in free fall, you're gonna end up headfirst, skull crushed like that poor dude. Like Paul, right?
I mean, you saw him—that way."

"We're getting off the question about you and Paul
having a falling-out."

"Yeah, okay. He threatened to sell his Adena eagle
piece, and I told him he couldn't."

"Sounds familiar. I told someone else the same."

"Brad again?"

Grant nodded. "So did you go to see Paul the day he
died to continue the conversation?"

"Did you or Brad overhear us arguing at the wedding?"

Grant didn't answer, but took a step ahead of Todd as
they walked through the forest back toward his house.
He turned and put a hand on Todd's shoulder. They
stopped walking.

"The point is, did you see Paul the day he died?"
Grant asked. "If so, you need to talk to Jace Miller.
Maybe you can throw light on how Paul was acting that
day. Jace is even considering Paul committed suicide."

"I didn't see him that day. I was going to but came up
here—way up to the top of my big escape tree. Amber
and the kids were at her folks' place. Her dad is still
giving the kids cowboy guns and outfits, ones he liked
when he was a kid, but they're not into that."

It worried Grant that Todd was not looking at him
eye to eye but gazing slightly over his shoulder. He
seemed to be struggling for words.

"Anyhow," Todd went on, "I didn't go with the family, so they can't back me up on where I was if I really
need an alibi."

"No, that's enough for me, at least. I believe you.

I'd back you up, my friend. It's just that I can't get over Paul's death—can't believe it was either suicide or an accident the more I think about it."

Todd exhaled so hard his shoulders slumped. "Me, neither. Then your old tree being cut… I swear I'd kill someone if they touched my special tree. Well, shouldn't have said it that way. Hey, want to stay for supper? The boys would love it."

"I've got a date, and I guess you know who. I'm going home to clean up, shave, even get out of town. And re-member, tomorrow night you, Amber and me for your early birthday celebration. If things work out with Kate tonight, maybe I'll invite her, too. And I'll handle Brad. You let me know if he steps over the line, but I just can't tell him to keep away from the mill right now, the state he's in. I'd like to find a way to get him back on his feet but I can't see how. And you—you'll have that talk with Deputy Miller and tell him Paul was hurting for money—but not that he was thinking about selling an Adena eagle pendant."

"So, come clean with him, but not clean about what we've been hiding for years, right?"

Grant could only nod and hate himself a little more for telling half-truths to people he respected about their secret, forbidden treasures. Now, for him, that included lying to Kate.

Kate surprised herself by feeling grateful when Carson said he had to get back to Columbus. She was angry with him that he'd mostly ignored her while he'd worked on Brad Mason to get an invitation to visit Mason Mound. Brad had said he—and he'd dared to volunteer Kate, too—would talk to Grant about it, but like his brother, he'd seemed reluctant to agree with Carson's wishes.

After Carson left, Grant phoned and invited her to go to a restaurant in Chillicothe, and that not only suited but excited her, too. She was tired of tragedy, tree or human, tired of looking at her computer screen, and, though she hadn't told Grant, she'd tripped coming down from retrieving the star at Cold Creek Mound. Trying to protect the star, she'd taken some bruises she could mostly hide under her clothes. If any appeared on skin that would show, she'd cover them with makeup.

She took a hot bath and changed clothes, then decided she'd hide both her laptop and the metal star out in the garage amid Tess and Gabe's random things stored there. After all, Paul's house had been ransacked, maybe broken into, and she didn't want that worry while she was away, nor did she want to cart them along on a date.

She couldn't get it out of her head that, since Paul might have been carving that Adena figure when he died, it was like some kind of curse. Some Adena found in tombs had died from crushed skulls, and there lay that carving of the Adena pipe shaman figure right on top of Paul's head.

It was just dusk, not dark yet, so she didn't take a flashlight. As long as she was going out to the garage, she also took the measuring wheel she'd used to measure mound circumference. She didn't bother trying to lift the old, broken garage door. How many times had Dad come out here to work on things or just to sulk when he and Mom were having marital problems? Sensing the tension between them or hearing them argue, her ten-year-old self had watched out her bedroom window until Dad turned off the single swinging bulb in the garage, one that no longer worked. Balancing the dish towel with the metal star on top of her laptop, with the measuring wheel in the other hand, she lifted the unlocked padlock from the hasp and went in the side door of the garage.

It was a jumble in here, but Gabe said he'd clean it out. Mingled smells of dust, paint and junk assailed her as well as the smell of gasoline from the lawn mower Gabe used to keep the grass cut. He'd hired a kid down the road to take care of that when they were away.

Kate sneezed as she carefully put her laptop and the wrapped star on top of some books in a box, then replaced the lid. She leaned the measuring wheel in a corner. The two windows were so dirty that it was a lot darker in here than it was outside. Once she went back out, she'd lock the padlock on the door to be sure everything was safe. She knew the key was in the house, so she'd retrieve everything in the morning and work on her laptop again. She was making a diagram of a virtual mound, laying it out on the screen to estimate the size of upper and lower vaults in proportion to the size she had measured for Mason Mound. She had a theory the mound might have only one room for the burial vault, but she wasn't sure.

She looked at her watch, which was hard to read in the dim light.

Wanting to be ready when Grant came, she hurried to the door. She turned the dusty, loose knob and pushed at the door. It moved slightly, rattled, but didn't open.

She pushed again, harder. Her sore muscles from her fall ached, but she put her shoulder against the door and shoved. She couldn't see how the lock could have slipped closed. She would be a dirty mess if she had to go out a window. Would these old windows even open? She could just see having to break out the glass and get cut crawling out.

She went to the window facing away from the house because it had less junk in front of it. It overlooked the cornfield where Tess had been kidnapped, but the corn wasn't even a foot high now. The window was so dirty she could barely see out.

And then she heard something strange. A growl? A snort? Shuffling? Something sharp scraped along the glass.

She gasped as something brushed close by the window.

She jumped away and hit her head on an old metal lawn chair hanging on the wall. She saw bright colors. She stepped forward and grabbed on to the window-sill so she wouldn't fall, but she still went to her knees.

Had she imagined the thing outside? She was hallucinating from hitting her head, that was it. No, she'd seen the thing, heard those sounds before she'd hit her head.

It came again, the nightmare. A creature was peering in the window—black face, empty eyes—and antlers, sharp, long antlers with red points. She was face-to-face with it through the dirty glass....

Kate's shrill scream hurt her own ears.

10

Grant raised his hand to knock on Kate's door. *Was that a scream?* It sounded as if it came from around the back of the house. It was nearly dark. He didn't see anyone. Her rental car was parked in the driveway and looked empty.

"Kate," he called. "You out here?"

He heard pounding. He sprinted into the backyard. Someone hammering in the garage? "Kate!"

"Here! In here!"

The garage. She must have hurt herself, maybe fell or twisted an ankle. He ran closer. She was pounding on the inside of the door, not the big door but the small side one. He saw an unlocked padlock had somehow slipped into the hasp on the door.

"Kate? Just a sec. The padlock slipped down when you pounded on the door but it's not locked."

The lock looked old but lifted free. To his surprise, she yanked the door inward and threw herself into his arms and held tight. Her hair was a mess, her slacks had dirty knees and she had tears on her face—Kate crying? He couldn't believe it.

He clasped her to him. "What happened? You locked yourself inside?"

"Someone else did it. Come around the back with me."

"Did you see someone? They're still out back?"

"I saw someone—some *thing*. Oh, my head," she said as she dragged him around the back of the garage facing the huge cornfield. "I hit it on a metal chair. Got dizzy, saw colors."

"I'll run you into the Regional Med center."

She turned back to him and gripped his upper arm so hard it hurt. "Grant, it was someone in a mask!"

"What do you mean? If you hit your head—"

"No, I absolutely saw it, heard it. Footsteps, a snort. It was a deer-head mask with antlers like the Beast-master."

Oh, yeah, he thought, she'd hit her head for sure. But the image of his own Adena mask flashed through his brain. "Kate, listen to me," he insisted, reaching out to steady her, trying to sound calm when his heart was pounding. "There *are* deer around here—stags, too. If there was one hanging around this building, the animal could have rubbed against the door, jolted the shackle of the lock into place. I see deer out in back of my house all the time. As for the sounds, it's windy, so who knows what's rattling outside?"

"No, it was a person in a stag mask," she insisted as they stopped in front of the back garage window. "It could not have been an animal, not the way it stared at me—face-to-face with its eyes kind of hidden or sunken in." She bent to look down at the ground. "Oh, no. Just grass here, no footprints."

"Or deer prints."

"But its nose brushed the window—the mask, too."
She bent close to the dirty pane of glass, but he saw
her wobble. He put his hands on her waist and pulled
her back to lean against him. "See!" she insisted, trying to tug him closer to the window. The streak across
the dirty pane was almost impossible to discern in the
dark. Night was sliding down from the hills and creeping across the fields, and her Adena-obsessed imagination had played a trick on her.

"It's getting too dark to see, but that streak could
have been made by anything," he said. "Come on. We're
stopping by the med-center E.R. so they can have a look
at your head."

She turned in his arms to face him. "You have to *believe* me. I hadn't hit my head when I saw it."

"What I do believe is that, if it was a person, you
can't stay here tonight. If someone was spying on you,
tried to trap you or scare you, it's a good thing I showed
up. Who knows what might have happened next with
you locked in there? Come on. Let's get your things,
and you can stay at my place tonight, even longer if
necessary. Brad can easily move out of the guest suite
to his old room. We can tell Deputy Miller about what
you saw tomorrow if you want."

"I'd better get my laptop and the star. I was going
to leave them in the garage, but they're not safe now.
I wasn't scared to be here alone before, but I feel—
threatened. If someone wants to scare me away, maybe
it's Bright Star. Maybe he had someone watching the
mounds and knows I took his stars. Or, if Carson stopped
and talked to him when he left—"

"Carson Cantrell was here?" he demanded, following her into the dark garage. "I have no doubt he's fa-

miliar with this so-called Beastmaster mask, but why would he want to scare you?"

"It can't be him, but yes, he was here this afternoon. I just meant he could have visited Bright Star and got him even more upset at me. Carson took one of the stars to get the blood analyzed in a lab. We ran into Brad uptown at the English pub. Over here, I know right where I left my laptop and the other star," she told him, feeling her way along. "It wasn't dark when I put them here. And let's really padlock the place this time. I'll take the key from the kitchen when I get my things."

Grant took the laptop from her, then kept an arm around her waist as they went out. He put the lock in place and clicked it closed.

The last thing he needed was Kate in his guest suite, but at least she'd be across the living room from where he slept. And he didn't really want Brad next door to him again with his late-night comings and goings. What a temptation Kate would be—and her room would overlook the mound site he knew she was aching to visit again, even to enter. Could she have made up this crazy story so that he would ask her to stay with him? Worse, if she had actually seen a Beastmaster mask on someone, could it have been his? And if he took her home with him, he'd be taking her right into the house where he had it hidden in the basement—if it was still there.

All those possibilities upset him, but it worried him most that she might be telling the truth. But he could not have Kate in danger, so he'd have to endanger himself.

That night, Kate felt really awkward at Grant's house, not only because she still felt so shaken, but also because she was so attracted to him. At least Brad hadn't made a fuss when Grant had called him to explain. Brad had only requested to move his own things, which he had, and Kate had insisted on changing the sheets and towels herself since their cleaning lady wouldn't be here for a few days. Carson would probably be pleased but would order her not to get too involved. And that was much easier said than done.

She was agonizing over her relationship with Grant but also with Carson. She couldn't fathom that the illustrious, fastidious Professor Cantrell would spy on her, then creep around a run-down garage. But he did have a copy of the Beastmaster mask—a mock-up she herself had made. She'd posted a picture of it on her website and left it in his safekeeping when she went to England. She should have asked for the mask back, but with Tess's wedding and all, she just hadn't. Besides, Carson was all brains and business. She could not imagine one reason he'd lock her in and try to scare her. She'd bet on Bright Star first—that he researched her website, saw the image of the mask she'd made, then sneaked around to terrify her, make her want to leave the area. Maybe she was too obsessed, working too hard on this. Maybe she had seen a buck and just panicked. No way was she going to tell Carson about seeing anything weird outside a window.

Then, of course, there was Brad, but where would he get such a mask? Brad had told Grant he'd be "gallivanting till all hours," so at least she didn't have to put up with him, though he would have been a sort of chaperone.

Physically, at least, she was feeling better, except for a headache that wouldn't go away. She did not have a concussion, though the E.R. doctor had suggested she not go to sleep for several hours. She and Grant had managed to have a good laugh when she read him the doctor's only diagnosis, that she'd had "a contusion that made her see stars."

"I've been seeing stars lately, all right," she told Grant as they sat in matching overstuffed leather chairs in his living room, looking out into the darkness of the forest toward the mound. "Stars with blood on the points and antlers with red on them, too. I'm sure of it." With her paper napkin, she wiped sauce off her mouth from the pizza they'd brought back instead of going to the restaurant as Grant had planned.

"I can tell you're exhausted," he said. "You've really been through it lately, but I'm here to keep you awake for a while, then insist you get a good night's sleep. Kate, about that vision of the mask through that cloudy, dirty window into the dusk—"

"Not a vision. I saw it."

"Okay, okay. You saw a Celtic mask you are dying to match to some Adena artifact. You have to admit you're obsessed with things Celtic and Adena. I'll bet you dream of them, and a dream's a step away from a vision."

She frowned but nodded as they both looked out the window. They could see each other's reflections there. A moonless night, it was so dark outside and barely lit in here that the glass once again acted like a huge, black mirror. Still, in the spot where his maple had been murdered—like Grant, she thought of it that way now—she could glimpse pinpoints of silver stars in the heavens.

"Want me to close the drapes?" he asked. "Are you nervous because someone might have been watching you through that garage window, and now we're sitting here? I used to feel this was private, but since the tree theft..."

"You don't have to pull the drapes. I like being close to the mound. I just wish I had X-ray vision like Superman—or woman—to see what's inside it."

He cleared his throat. "So *do* you ever dream Adena?"

"Not lately, but I've dreamed about both the Celts and the Adena. Both were tall, powerful people. Their skeletons attest to that. This may sound crazy, but sometimes my subconscious puts my father's face on a shaman or warrior in my dreams—or nightmares."

"So, in your dreams, they don't wear masks? But the Adena disappeared from this area almost as quickly as your father disappeared from your young life—both tragic mysteries to you, right? So maybe that's the link."

She turned toward him in her big armchair and tucked her legs up under her. He sat so much closer to her than it seemed in the window reflection, so maybe that huge piece of glass distorted things—and maybe that garage glass window had, too. "I never thought of that," she whispered. "Yes—very possible I'd make that subconscious connection. And very astute of you."

"But not like Dr. Carson Cantrell, right?"

"In a different way. People are specialists in their own areas, their own lives. But did I catch a hint of your judging Carson as some sort of intellectual egghead snob when you haven't even met him?"

"Touché."

"My mother always used to pronounce that as *touchy*. We're all products of our past, aren't we? Oh, that reminds me that I wanted to ask you about your grandmother. You seemed so close to your grandfather—that's a photo of them in the room I have, right?

The one in the handsome wooden frame that looks like it was taken in the 1960s or '70s?"

"Yeah, that's Hiram and Ada. I never knew her. She died young, about six years before I was born, so she... she was never talked about much."

"How young was she?"

"Mid-fifties, I think. That used to sound pretty old to me, but not anymore."

"She looks kind of starry-eyed, maybe nervous or distracted."

His head snapped around, and he stared at her. "She did have—a nervous disposition, as they used to say. I guess they didn't like to talk about it, so I didn't know much about her, but lots about Grandpa."

"Well, she was very pretty. She must remind me of someone I once knew, I guess. I didn't mean to pry. Grant, listen, if I'm any kind of problem here, I can stay at Tess and Gabe's new place until they get back."

"I was in there early this morning to see how things were coming with the final details. The place smells like paint. You wouldn't like it—it might make your headache worse, so you're stuck with me."

"You've been so generous and kind." She reached out her hand to him, and he took it. His hand felt so big and strong holding hers. Their fingers entwined. "I appreciate it and want you to know I'm not crazy enough to believe that the Celtic or Adena dead came back to scare me tonight. But that means it was someone wanting me to believe that, someone who hates me or wants me to leave this area. Someone who knows enough about the Adena, he—or she—knew to make and use that mask."

"Then he or she doesn't know you very well. Courageous, curious and calm Kate."

"Not very calm today and tonight. I'm betting it was Bright Star, because I stood up to him. I want to tell Deputy Miller about the stars and the mask. It—it wouldn't be your ex-wife, would it? I mean, I did walk into the mill with you, but then, where would she ever get a mask like that even if she does want to run me off?"

"Lacey? No way. If that was a Beastmaster mask, its appearance was too well planned and sophisticated. The only masks she'd care about were ones for a glitzy costume Halloween party. Besides, she's long done with me and has a guy crazy about her—at least that's how I read it. But as for Bright Star again—yeah, let's talk to Jace first thing tomorrow, and we can also find out how the investigation into Paul's death is going. I told Nadine that, when the coroner releases his body, I want to pay for whatever the staff donations at the mill don't cover for the funeral and burial."

"I'll contribute in another way. I'm going to see if Nadine will sell me that tree trunk with the Adena pipe effigy, and I'll pay her well for it. Surely she doesn't want the piece that smashed his skull. I just wish I could have asked him to put a Celtic shaman or Beastmaster mask on it, linking the two cultures, which I intend to do."

They held hands, their arms stretched between their chairs. She had an almost overwhelming urge to snuggle up to him in his chair, but she wasn't ready for where that might lead.

The next morning, Grant and Kate grabbed breakfast in town, then kept an early appointment at the sheriff's office.

"So, how are you getting along?" Grant asked Jace as they sat in his office.

"You mean, how are the investigations on the timber thieves and Paul's death? Frustrating, to say the least. I'll have a lot to report to the sheriff when he gets back."

There was an edge to Jace's voice. He looked as if he hadn't slept, but Grant himself hadn't slept well, either, with Kate so close. "I'm sure you're doing all you can. You've had a lot piled on you fast."

Jace nodded and sighed. He rocked a bit on his swivel chair, which creaked. He was about six years younger than Grant, so they hadn't really crossed paths in school or on local sports teams. Like Gabe, Jace had gone away to serve in the military.

Frowning, ticking things off on his fingers, Jace told them what was happening. "I've reached out to sheriffs in surrounding counties to find out if any other huge, designer-wood-type trees have been pirated. I know you covered tristate lumber mills. And I gave a heads-up to the highway patrol to keep an eye out for anyone moving a tree—or huge logs—on the interstates. It's a no-go so far on all that."

"But then, with our hills and hollows around here, it could be hidden in our area," Grant said.

"Hills and hollows instead of hills and hollers— sometimes, you all talk like an outsider, Grant."

Kate spoke up. "As someone born here who feels like an outsider, Deputy Miller, I've been impressed to see how Grant seems to get along with those from this area *and* outside."

"Yeah, true," he said, shifting his weight in his chair so hard it groaned this time. "Anyhow, about Paul's death. The coroner is releasing his body to his wife today. I don't know how she's going to pay for his burial."

"I do," Grant said, touched that Kate had seemed protective of him. "My staff at the mill is collecting funds, and I'll take care of the rest."

"That's right good of you," Jace said, looking a bit sheepish. "As for cause of death, the coroner had to rule accidental. Maybe Paul went a little nuts, messed up his own place—who knows, looking for something—then in his rage or frustration, accidentally pulled that turntable and tree trunk over on himself. Or it was just a freak accident. No way we can judge him suicidal since Nadine says no. Until I hear from BCI that there were prints or DNA of someone else—other than himself, his wife and you two—in there, I have no choice but to close the case. And I appreciate you both giving DNA cheek swabs to help with that."

Grant nodded, but he hoped Jace wasn't in over his head with all this, when Gabe had been gone only two days. He still had the gut feeling Paul could have been murdered and that didn't make mourning his loss any easier.

"We also came to tell you that we found evidence that someone—we think Bright Star Monson—has been not exactly defacing but tampering with two local Adena mounds," Kate said. Grant watched as she took the dish towel from her big purse and unwrapped it on Jace's desk.

"Looks like some kind of old sheriff's badge," he said, getting up and leaning across his pile of papers to look at it closely. "But it's not what Gabe or I use these days. What's that stuff on the tips?"

"We think it's blood," Kate said. "But we'd like you to go with us—or with me, since I found them and study the mounds—to the Hear Ye compound and ask Bright

Star point-blank if they are his. It's illegal to tamper with the mounds in any way without permission, but if he admits it, and it has something to do with his warped view of religion, I'd be tempted to let it go—if he swears he'll stay away from the mounds and from me."

"He bothered you up close and personal?"

She looked at Grant. "This is going to sound strange, but someone did," she said. "Let me explain as best I can. I've been thinking that since Brice Monson made a big deal of telling me he had access to the internet and knows I'm an Adena specialist—and I threw that in his face—he might have researched the Adena and be the one who harassed me."

"Explain it to me, then. But I got to warn you about him. The guy is just plain weird, and I wouldn't put much stock in anything he says. He always twists things around—the Bible, too—to suit himself. After all, his initials are B.S., and that's what I think he talks most of the time—but I'm sure not gonna tell him I said so."

11

Kate's goal was to figure out where the original entrance to the burial vault must have been on the slanted, growth-covered circumference of Mason Mound. Some entrances aligned with the sunrise, but she and Carson thought most were positioned facing rivers or streams. As far as she could tell, there was no water nearby. But she had not promised Grant she wouldn't look for streams or ponds on her own.

After they'd explained to Jace Miller what had happened in the garage, Grant had gone to work and Kate back to his house. She tried to throw off the strange feeling that she actually belonged here. She could picture herself sending Grant off to the mill, fixing him lunch, waiting for him to come back while she studied or wrote—or excavated the mound. Surely it was the proximity to it, not to this house or the man himself, that beckoned to her.

"You are crazy, Kathryn Anne Lockwood!" she scolded herself as she headed back into her bedroom to get her purse. "You just get out of here before you make his favorite pie or scrub the kitchen floor!"

She locked up with the key Grant had given her and

drove to Tess's house. After checking that all was normal inside, she went back out. She saw no sign of a scrape or bump on the garage door that could have been made by a deer bumping it so that the lock fell into place on its own. She walked slowly, glancing around, giving the building a wide berth as she went out behind it. The idea of someone watching her, knowing when she left the house to enter the garage, gave her the chills.

Nothing behind the garage. Normal. In the daylight, no footprints or hoof prints.

She sighed and shook her head, scanning the vast, young cornfield with its neat rows of green spears stabbing through the ground. Glancing out about a third of the way into the field, she gasped.

Two does and a buck were grazing on grass or wildflowers. The buck had a good rack of antlers. She pictured the ancient Celtic Beastmaster artifact called the Gundestrup Cauldron she'd seen in Denmark. She shuddered at the memory of the close-up photo she'd bought of the demonic-looking beast with its blank, staring eyes and huge horns. She hadn't shown a picture of its dreadful face to Grant. She wasn't sure she would. Every time she looked at it, even simply printed on paper, she sensed some sort of curse or threat.

Her legs went weak, and she leaned against the garage to steady herself, bumping the sore spot on the back of her head. All three deer looked up and stared at her across the distance. She could feel their eyes on her, could sense their thoughts. *Danger! Intruder!* That was exactly what one of her colleagues in England said he imagined the ghosts of the dead whispered each time he entered an ancient grave site.

Could she have seen that buck's head outside the win-

dow last night and then imagined—hallucinated—the
Beastmaster? Was she letting her obsessions and desires get to her? She'd been so certain, but maybe she
was seeing more than stars. Was being near Mason
Mound—or Grant—scrambling her logic, her brain?

She stared; the deer stared, then bolted away, bound-
ing out of sight, far beyond to the shade of a tall, distant tree.

Still on wobbly legs, Kate hurried to her car, got in,
locked the doors and just sat there, breathing hard. She
supposed she'd have to tell Grant about the deer. At
this distance, safe inside her car, she studied the garage
and the large tree she could see beside it as if it stuck
out from the roof. Tess had told her that Grant's friend
Todd had actually climbed that tree—scaled it, Tess
had said, like someone who challenged tall mountains.
No doubt, from those heights he could look over this
whole area, even hunt from there, like some local men
used to shoot deer from platforms hidden in the foliage
of the nearby hills.

She shuddered at her scrambled thoughts. But the
worst of them was that, not only in her dreams but in
her waking moments, her desires were luring her to
Grant and Mason Mound.

Grant was in a big hurry. He hated to leave the mill
off schedule, but Todd was overseeing everyone, including Brad, so he had to take this time to recheck
that his Adena mask was still untouched when no one
else was in the house. He didn't bother to lock his car
door but did lock himself into the house. It was silent
as—yeah, as a tomb.

He hustled downstairs. This was Tuesday, and Paul's funeral was scheduled for Thursday morning, so he'd put up a notice that the mill would be closed for a half day so staff could attend. He wondered if Nadine would keep her house. Probably not, as isolated as it was. And when she sold it, if she didn't know about Paul's valuable eagle pendant and it was hidden in the house, would the next owner stumble on it?

As boys that day in the death chamber of the tomb, when Todd had dared to joke that Indiana Jones had nothing on them, they hadn't thought about what would happen if one of them died. Maybe they should have told each other where they'd hidden their artifacts, but of course, they thought then they were going to live forever. If he could help Nadine relocate, maybe he could search the house for the pendant—if it was in their house. If he were Paul, he'd have hidden it within one of those tree-trunk carvings, one he'd never sell but keep for his own. He could ask Nadine if one was special to Paul, pay a big price for it as if it were only a keepsake from his friend.

As Grant hurried past the washing machine, he saw a pile of Brad's dirty clothes. Of course, he'd been down here. He'd even played pool by himself the other night after he came back from wherever he spent the late hours uptown. Grant didn't think he'd hooked up with a woman but was much too hooked up with booze. He should check to see if any of his bottles left over from the party for Gabe and Tess had disappeared.

He clicked on the light, got on his back on the floor and felt under the furnace for the metal box with the key. *Not there!* Feeling around some more, he finally found it. He'd been in such a hurry the other day, he'd evidently put it back slightly off position, that was all.

He thought he heard a noise upstairs and froze, listening. If Kate came back—he'd texted her and she'd said she wouldn't be back before noon—what would he tell her? He swore sometimes that woman could read his mind, which was bad news. But no, the house was just creaking in the wind.

He slid the hutch out of the way and lifted the oak panels. He pulled the cement blocks out with the old ice hook then slid the box out. So far everything looked fine. It was just that Kate had been so certain that she'd seen not a stag head but the Beastmaster mask. And with Brad here in the house, though he'd never told him where he'd put his relic, he had to know this hadn't been disturbed.

Disturbed...like he and his friends had done to that elaborate, ritual burial chamber.... Disturbed, like the way Kate got to him when he should keep her away.

He opened the box and exhaled in relief. Yes, it was here, obviously untouched. And yet, had he put the tissue paper back this way, neatly tucked in instead of crumpled? He couldn't recall.

The ancient, eyeless mask stared up at him as if to say, *No answers here. I keep my secrets. But never betray me.*

Grant closed the box fast and slid it back in, then fumbled in his shirt pocket to take out Kate's business card. He leaned it against the box. She'd given it to him because her cell number was on it. He had that memorized, her website and Facebook page, too. But if anything happened to him, and this was ever found—he did have an explanation of it with his will—maybe she'd at least have a chance to see it, study it.

Then, too, if her card was moved, he'd know some-one had found the box.

Still sitting in her car in the driveway of Tess's house, Kate was just getting ready to phone Carson to let him know she was temporarily living right next to the Mason Mound, when a black van pulled in behind her, block-ing her in. She punched off Carson's number after two rings. She'd just put Grant on speed dial this morning and was going to call him if this van meant trouble. Her usual poise and pluck had taken a beating since she'd found those stars and seen that deer head. Bright Star and Grace had come here in a black vehicle the day they'd told her and Tess that the wedding was pagan, so could it be them?

A woman got out of the van. It was Nadine Kettering. Oh, and wasn't that Grant's ex with her, driving the van? Kate put her cell phone in her purse and got out of her car.

"Nadine," she said, walking toward them. They ex-changed light hugs. "I heard the funeral service is Thurs-day. I haven't really had a chance to tell you how sorry I am. Paul was a great talent, and I'm sure a wonder-ful man."

"I appreciate that. I'm glad you got to meet him at Grant's, even if briefly. Yes, he was a wonderful man—temperamental at times. But aren't great artists that way, maybe all men, truth be told? Kate, this is an old friend of mine who's in town for a while, Lacey—Lacey Fencer—ah, she took her maiden name back. I guess you know who she is—was."

Kate and Lacey assessed each other. No handshake.

Two wimpy nods and fake smiles, Kate thought. "I saw Lacey and her friends at the mill the other day."

"Well, yes," Lacey said. "I'm very dedicated to my cause."

"Aren't we all? Would you two like to come in? As you can see by the sign out front, Tess's house is still for sale. I was just getting ready to leave, but you're both welcome."

"If I can sell our place for a hunting lodge, and if the price is right, I would like to look at the house, but too much to do now," Nadine said. "We were just driving past, and I saw your car. I was wondering if you would still like to buy one of Paul's carvings before I give a few to relatives or put them up for sale. Grant said he'd be sure that your sister's wedding gift gets to their new place. Also, Lacey and her group are going to buy one with elves peeking out from behind all kinds of carved leaves for their Green Tree office in Cleveland."

"Honoring the carved trunk as a beautiful work of art, I'm sure," Kate said, "and not using it as an example of tree destruction."

Lacey looked furious. "Well—if we buy it, it's ours!" she insisted.

Nadine turned to Lacey. "You wouldn't do that, would you? I couldn't bear to have his work used in a negative way."

Lacey rounded on Kate, sending a waft of what must be clove cologne at her. "I suppose you think you're clever with comments like that! I hear you and Grant are a real item, and you've moved in with him!"

Kate knew better than to try to explain. "Word always did travel fast around here," she said. "Let me guess. You've been talking to Brad."

"So, do you read minds?" Lacey demanded. "Brad and I are still friends, even if I divorced Grant. You're welcome to him."

Kate turned a shoulder to the woman, wishing she could turn her back. "Nadine, I'm grateful you would still welcome my original offer to buy one of Paul's works. I think they are amazing. And since he won't be able to do a special order for me now, I would very much like to buy the trunk with the Adena figure on it."

"Oh. The one that—that fell on him. Deputy Miller has it now, but yes—I don't want to see it again, and I can understand why you'd want that one."

"I would like to offer you a good price for it, even though I realize he didn't finish it. After the funeral, perhaps we can talk, and I'll see if Deputy Miller is going to hold it for long."

"Well, fine," Nadine agreed with tears in her eyes. "So, will you be studying Mason Mound?"

"I hope so."

Lacey, who had been stewing, piped up. "But you'd rather be studying Grant close-up and personal, I bet. He's moody—just fair warning. And he's real touchy about that mound, like that old hill is some family relic."

"I can certainly understand why he sees it that way. The Mason family legacy means a lot to him. He's probably even more protective of it since someone sneaked in to butcher his beautiful tree. It must have been someone who knew the woods, knew the tree and how much it meant to him, and that makes it even harder."

"Green Tree—and i—detest people who cut down trees for profit, which is why we protest at lumber mills. You—you don't mean I would ever harm that tree just because I know the area or divorced him?" Lacey propped her hands on her hips. The woman was well built and had a pretty face she was hiding under makeup and a bushel of blond hair, but her voice and attitude curled Kate's toes. Grant had said Lacey had changed since their dating days, and that must have been the understatement of the decade.

Kate put her arm around Nadine's shoulders, because the woman had started to cry and was dabbing at her nose with a tissue. "I'm sure no one from Green Tree would harm a tree," Kate said, her voice quiet compared to Lacey's strident tones. "There would be no motive for anyone in your group to want to hurt Grant that much. That is, unless someone held a personal grudge or wanted to get back at him for owning a lumber mill, even though he's very pro-environment. I guess it could be someone who wanted revenge for him wanting to stay in this lovely town instead of taking off for another life, maybe in a great metropolis, like Cleveland."

Lacey gasped. "I get it. You're good with words, like some lady lawyer. But maybe this *lovely* town will do you in like it did me, if you hang around here long enough!" She sashayed away—in stilettos, no less— back to Nadine's van, got in and slammed the door.

"Sorry about that," Nadine said. "She may come off like a bimbo at times, but she's not—really."

"No, it's my fault. I've got a sharp tongue."

"And a sharp brain. I admire that. Look, Kate, I didn't mean to cry over this. I thought I'd gotten hold of myself. I hope Lacey won't blame you if I don't sell her that tree trunk now. I should have thought of that—Green Tree's misusing it as an example of what she sometimes calls 'slash and cut.' I think Grant and Todd have always been good about that, harvesting carefully, replanting and all. I think organizations like Green Tree are good, but they go over the line sometimes, deface property, threaten and scare people. Paul called them 'greeniacs.'"

As they stepped apart, Kate gave the woman's shoulder a squeeze. "Tess will be back in about ten days, but if you want to see the house before that, just call me. Here—my business card, and please don't share it with Lacey. I'd rather not have my office on campus or any of the mounds around here picketed by *greeniacs.*"

A little smile lifted Nadine's lips. "Actually, I believe she and her cohorts were considering putting up a sign on several of the mounds to promote their cause, but they wouldn't dare. Grant could use someone on his side, like you. I'll tell Jace Miller—or we may have to deal with Gabe when he gets back—that the Adena tree trunk is yours."

"For a good price, Nadine."

"I just— I hope you'll be able to get past the fact I think it was a weapon. I can't even stand to say the word *murder,* but I think it was."

They both jumped as Lacey honked the van's horn. Ignoring that, Kate said, "I'll be honored to have it. Paul's imagination was unique, and I'll treasure it. You think someone ransacked the house and killed him?"

"Maybe not in that order. I've got to get going now, and it's obvious the coroner and even Deputy Miller might not agree with me." Nadine turned toward the car, then back again. "Lacey has a meeting with her friends at a restaurant uptown. That's why she honked, I'm sure. See you at the funeral then and later."

Kate headed for her car, too. *If you stay...later.* How long would she stay here to pursue her dream of excavating and studying an untouched Adena grave site, hopefully working with Grant, instead of against him? And if there was a killer loose in the community, she hoped it had to do only with a random theft at Paul's place and didn't tie in to a stolen tree out by Mason Mound.

12

Kate had the strangest feeling she was being watched, even followed. Crazy, of course, yet she kept looking in her rearview mirror as she drove toward Grant's house. She refused to turn into some scared woman who couldn't live life to the fullest and pursue her dreams. She'd watched Tess battle lingering fear after she came back from being kidnapped. Kate knew the signs, and she wasn't going to give in to such destructive feelings.

She drove past Grant's house and turned onto the road that looped around behind his woods. Nadine had mentioned that Lacey and her cohorts had considered putting up signs on some Adena mounds to promote their cause. Nadine thought they wouldn't dare, but would they? Had they somehow picked stars with blood-tipped points to leave there instead of a sign that would identify them? And what was the link between the mounds and their environmental cause? No, Kate scolded herself, she was letting Lacey's hostility get to her, just as she had Bright Star's.

She parked on the curving road that ran behind Grant's property line. Surely, he wouldn't get upset if she just looked around for a possible water source, or remnant of one that could hint at the direction of the entrance to the mound. She wouldn't go near the mound itself, although it drew her like a magnet.

After diagramming the mound on her laptop, she thought its relatively small size might indicate just one burial chamber. Since the mound hadn't caved in, the chamber could be intact. In that case, the entry and covered passageway would go horizontally into the mound, not down or up at a steep angle from a ground-level entry. But she hadn't seen any hint of an entry at ground level just walking around the mound. Finding a water source, even an ancient one, could save a lot of work to locate that shaft.

As she entered the dense, shaded forest, she saw that the narrow walking trail Grant or his family had made was the route the timber thieves had used to drag the big bird's-eye maple tree out four days ago. The path of destruction was obvious with snapped saplings and trails through the thick litter of last autumn's dry, matted leaves. She also saw an occasional hoof print from the horse team that must have pulled the huge tree trunk away to a waiting flatbed truck. The careless destruction here reminded her of Paul and Nadine's ransacked house.

Looking around, she wondered if the ancient Adena had walked this path to bury their dead in the mound. Did the mourners carry them or drag them on a cloth and two-pole travois like historic Indians who didn't have the wheel?

She went off the path in a zigzag pattern, searching for a dip in the ground where a stream might have run. Rills taking waters down to Cold Creek—which was really a small river—from the surrounding hills were

common around here. Folds in the earth, dips and ravines abounded, so the terrain didn't make for easy
going. Maybe a water source once ran where the house
stood today or the street or—

She jerked to a stop. She wasn't the only one rustling
through dead leaves in the rhythmic pattern of human
feet. She heard the slight shuffling sound again, then another step. Maybe she *had* been watched and followed.
It didn't sound like a deer or other animal would walk.

In a slight depression, she hunkered down behind a
thick tree trunk. Her breath seemed incredibly loud. She
had the urge to sneeze. She jammed her finger above
her upper lip and pressed so hard her nose went numb.

Brad strode into view. Although she wasn't sure how
she'd explain herself, better him than Grant or some
stranger. If he saw her, she didn't want to appear to
be hiding.

She started to move, but before she could call out,
he veered away. She watched him from behind the tree.
He headed for a knee-high pile of rocks that reminded
her of some she'd seen in England and Scotland. They
were called cairns, used to mark boundary lines or a
historic spot. This was probably just a place Brad and
his friends had played as kids, maybe the remnants of a
little fort. Stones like that were common around here—
ones, no doubt, the ancients had used to shore up the
big logs that supported more logs for the roofs of tombs
inside their mounds.

Brad bent toward the stones as she stepped out, right
on a dry branch. It snapped loudly. Brad spun around.

"Kate! What're you doing here?"

She was about to ask him the same, but this was his
family's land. Her gut instinct said not to tell him what

she was doing. If she was going to tell anyone, it should be Grant. The last thing she wanted was for him to think she was going behind his back, and he and Brad weren't exactly on the best of terms.

"I've seen the front of this woodlot," she called to him as she walked closer, "but thought I'd take a little hike here in back."

"To see the lay of the land?" he asked with a wink. As she got close, she saw he looked bleary-eyed. She noticed he'd walked a bit unsteadily, not that this was flat ground here. And yes, she smelled liquor on him again, and it wasn't even noon.

"So, you had the same idea?" she asked.

"Thought I'd clear my head. And relive the days of buried boyhood treasure. Actually, ah—this is where I buried a favorite dog years ago, Max. Silly, I know, but I still miss him—a collie."

"I understand. It's a beautiful burial place."

"For your pet Adenas as well as Max, right?" He shook his head as if to clear it. "It was my dog, not Grant's, maybe the first thing we didn't share."

"So you marked his grave with a pile of rocks instead of a single stone?"

"Kate the curious," he said, sounding annoyed. "Look, if you're meeting Grant for lunch, just tell him the *babysitter* he had drive me home from the mill dropped me off on the back road and someone's picking me up, not to worry. He told me to head home to sleep off a slight hangover. Big Brother is watching me and didn't want little Bradley to get hurt by a big bad saw or fall off a catwalk at the mill."

"It's nice he does worry about you," she said. "That means he cares."

"He worries about you, too, you know. That means he cares—for you and that you keep your hands off the mound. Family tradition to let the dead stay dead. Poor Paul, huh?"

"And Nadine. She stopped by Tess's house this morning, might even consider buying the place. Lacey was with her, and I got the impression she's been talking to you—about my staying at Grant's for a while."

"Lacey swore off Grant long ago, but I was glad to see her again, that's all. So, enjoy your walk—your exploration," he said and, with a glance at his watch, started away without further comment.

Kate gave him a good start then followed him out toward the road. She watched him from behind a bush. Here she'd felt she was being followed and now she was doing the same. Brad paced, looking a bit tipsy at times. Kate gasped when she saw Lacey drive up in her van and pick him up. They headed not toward town but out toward the hills. And they'd exchanged a quick kiss, not on the cheek, but mouth to mouth. Then a second one that was much longer.

When Kate finally emerged from the forest, she was tired and hungry. Feeling she owed Grant for his hospitality and wanting to get him on her side about the mound, she drove into town, hit the small supermarket near the Lake Azure area then hurried back to fix him something for a late lunch—he'd said he'd be home around two.

She'd come to some conclusions in her trek around the back forest area after Brad left with Lacey. Though she was certain Brad was up to no good, she herself had made a good discovery—there was a definite shape of a now dry streambed on the back side of the mound, away from the house. Despite overgrowth, she'd followed it for nearly half a mile up toward the hills. She theorized that in the spring and summer, when it rained hard, it used to be full of water. But growth, stones and other debris higher up had diverted the water elsewhere over the centuries.

What had excited her almost as much as that discovery was that she'd seen a bald eagle's nest high in an oak tree, with what must be a mating pair in it, swooping out now and then to guard it or to find food. She was proud of that discovery, not because the eagle was the national bird, but because the Adena had venerated it as a symbol of spiritual power. She knew it was possible that eagles had nested in that same spot, between the dried-up stream and the mound, for centuries. She couldn't wait to tell Grant. And she figured she'd have to tell him about Brad and Lacey, too.

Grant walked in exactly at two, when she had the chicken quesadillas and iced tea ready.

"Looks great," he told her. He washed his hands at the sink and sat across from her. They had an awkward moment—she a stranger taking over his kitchen, he not sure whether to help or just sit down to be served.

"Fresh strawberries in clotted cream for dessert. Terribly British," she said with a touch of accent. "Oh, Grant, I took a walk on the far side of the woods today and saw an eagle's nest and both birds!"

"You'll have to show me where. I've seen them in the air. I think that pair comes back each year. They mate for life, you know."

"I took them as a good omen since they were key

symbols of spiritual power to the Adena. There's a site in Georgia, where the Adena built a gigantic effigy of an eagle with white sandstone slabs. In a different burial site, two amateur anthropologists found a stone eagle with the skeleton of a man laid out on the left wing and a female skeleton on the right wing. Both were stretched out on raised biers with rich burial offerings around them of copper, flint and bone. And two smashed human skulls lay at the feet of the man and one at the woman's feet…" She paused for a moment. "Not such a good lunch-table topic," she admitted.

During that gush of information, Grant's eyes went wide, and his lower lip dropped. "Crushed skulls? But—those grave sites—sound amazing," he stammered, then took a big swallow of his iced tea.

"That last one I mentioned is near the little town of New Benton, between Youngstown and Akron. That Ohio mound was owned by a private family, but thank heavens, they let it be studied."

He put his glass down on the table with a thud. "I hear you, Dr. Lockwood."

"I didn't go near your mound. I'd like you to be with me when I do—with your permission."

"Was that Ohio site a small mound you just described?"

"No, it was quite large, but it had a single entrance, and I think Mason Mound does, too."

"You surely don't think you'd find something spectacular like that here? Eagles, skeletons, skulls?"

"I'd like you to talk to Carson Cantrell about the importance of the possibilities. But, not to ruin your lunch, there's something else while you're sitting down. Maybe you know this already. Brad's evidently been telling people, including Lacey, that I moved in with you. I might as well tell you—I saw Brad when I was in the woods. Lacey picked him up on the back road and they drove off toward the hills. He was with her last night, I think, and when he got in the van with her, they looked…cozy."

A frown creased his forehead, but he surprised her by keeping calm. "Putting on a show for you maybe, so you'd tell me."

"I was hidden. He'd just been in the forest, and we'd talked briefly. He was visiting that pile of stones where he buried his boyhood pet collie, Max."

Grant's eyes widened. She could almost hear his mind working but didn't know what he was thinking. He cleared his throat and took a sip of his iced tea. "He was drunk at work midmorning," he told her, glaring down into his glass as if there were tea leaves to read. "We had words, especially when I took his car keys and had someone drive him home."

"I'm sorry. Yes, he did seem…unsteady." But, she thought, that was definitely not the first time he'd been with Lacey lately; it wasn't some retaliation for a scolding at work.

"Him and Lacey, huh? Can't say I like the sounds of that and not for the reason you're thinking."

"You think she's out to turn him against you?"

"It wouldn't take much. So—big news day, and on top of your fixing this great lunch for me. I'd better eat fast and get back to work in case the two of them are planning something there. As for Carson Cantrell, I'd rather deal with you, because I'm hoping you'll understand. And I wish I could go with you and Jace to talk to Bright Star this afternoon, so you don't get all the blame. Maybe we should just let Jace go question him alone."

"I want to be there, see if I can read him. I'm the one who found those stars."

"And you want to find much more than that or eagles or where Brad put his dead dog. So, that pile of stones must have been off the beaten path, right? Just like him to hide it from me."

"Yeah, it was," she said, surprised to realize he didn't know where that old dog was buried. Had the two brothers not gotten along as kids, either? "The pile of stones was kind of west of the main path about a quarter mile in from the back curved road, behind some kind of bramble thicket."

He nodded. "Kate, I just don't know about a dig in the mound, and I'm hoping you won't try to go around me on this. I need you—I want you—on my side."

She nodded, too, before she realized he might think she was giving in to him. Nadine had said much the same about Grant needing her. She loved the sound of that, but hated it, too. If anyone could seduce her out of what she wanted most in life right now, unfortunately, it was Grant Mason.

Kate was much more nervous than she'd thought she would be when she and Deputy Miller were finally escorted in to speak with Bright Star Monson in a room their guide had called "the retreat." To her amazement, both her cousin Lee Lockwood and his wife, Grace, were in the room. Monson himself sat behind a large glass table that must serve as his desk, although it didn't have a book or paper on it. The entire room was white with only glass objects, maybe to give the appearance of light, even of weightlessness. Some sort of lighting system through the thick glass walls made the room seem to glow. Well, she thought, this phony hadn't chosen the name Bright Star for nothing.

Even Lee and Grace were dressed in white instead of the down-home, prairie look. Lee stood like a sentinel in one corner, and Grace, a marble statue, in the corner near the door. Kate, not caring if she was defying some rule, went over to hug Grace, who hugged her lightly. "How are the children?" she asked.

"Oh, fine. Thriving. Thanks."

"I'd love to see them, and I know Tess would, too. Perhaps when Tess returns from her honeymoon."

Grace looked immediately at Bright Star, as if for permission to answer. "Please sit down and explain this visit" was all their leader said.

Kate could see Jace was nervous, too. She could feel the hostile vibes in here. Maybe insisting on direct confrontation wasn't the way to go, but it was the way she'd lived her life. She hated secrets, things half said or hidden.

She unwrapped the star she still had, wondering when Carson would get back to her about the blood on the other one. "These have been found atop two of the Adena mounds in the area, and since they are bright stars, which almost sparkle in the sun—to glow, almost like this room—we were wondering if this is your calling card, perhaps? Especially since you made it obvious earlier you would like to ignore, perhaps to erase, such *pagan* practices as Christian weddings or the ancient Adena culture."

She realized she'd come on too strong again, but he didn't take the bait. "That is not mine or ours," he said after glancing briefly at the star. "What are the Adena that I would be mindful of them or visit them? I declare such things under my feet, but I have not visited those savage places. My place is here with my people."

Kate thought he was scrambling scripture again, but she wasn't quite sure. She was aware that Grace was fidgeting, but Lee looked stoic. She knew Jace wasn't going to be much help.

"Asked and answered, I guess, Kate," Jace said. "You see, Mr. Monson, there's dried blood on the tips of the star, which means we need to find out whose and why."

"Is that so? Then it suggests some sort of sacrifice, you mean. I regret I can't help you further. Thank you for visiting us, and I'm sure Grace and Lee will be happy to receive you in the future—and, of course, your sister and Sheriff McCord when they return."

Bright Star stood. Kate felt frustrated and furious, but Jace rose, so she had little choice but to leave, too. She hated being manipulated by this man who, she was certain, had some sort of evil hold over her cousins.

Kate turned her back on Bright Star and, with Jace right behind her, started from the room. She could feel Bright Star's eyes boring into her back. It was the same feeling she'd had when she thought she was being watched earlier today, but that was nonsense.

Kate glanced at Grace as she opened the door. Bright Star was talking to Jace about providing protection for the group when they sold things at the weekend market uptown. And in that moment, when no one could see Grace but Kate, the woman drew a five-pointed star just above her left breast, once, then quickly again.

Kate stared, almost stumbled. When she hesitated,

Grace tipped her head toward the door, as if telling her to move on, so she did.

As they left the compound through the guarded gate, Kate's mind raced. Was Grace trying to silently send her love or to indicate that their holy man was lying? Or had Grace tried to tell her that she had worn such a star?

The motion had also brought back memories of how she and Grace—who had been a playmate and neighbor years ago—along with Tess and Char, had often used that sign when they'd sworn to keep a secret. *Cross my heart and hope to die.*

13

Late that evening, Grant was glad he finally got Kate to one of his favorite restaurants in Chillicothe. The thing was, they had Todd and Amber with them. Grant took them out for Todd's birthday—an excuse to get them out of their house. Amber's parents always did babysitting duty with the boys. Grant and Todd had liked this place for years because it had wood from the mill everywhere, including tables, booths and wall paneling. Some diners were out on the patio, but Grant liked it inside, with all the wood around.

They'd started out sharing reminiscences of Paul and talking about the funeral plans. Grant and Todd—Brad, too—were going to be pallbearers. Losing Paul and the worry about where his Adena eagle pendant could be depressed Grant so deeply he was afraid he wouldn't be a good host this evening. But despite Kate being a newcomer, she fit right in with the three of them.

"Great food," she said, tucking into her garlic mashed potatoes. When Grant had heard her order them, he'd asked for the same in self-defense, since he was planning on some kissing later. He hoped she didn't think his attentions were a prerequisite for his letting her study the mound up close, though he wanted to study her that way.

Todd took a sip of beer and turned toward Kate. "So, Grant told me about the metal stars stuck in the mounds. And that you confronted Bright Star over it."

"Right, but I had Jace Miller riding shotgun, so to speak. The great guru denied knowing anything about the stars, but I'm thinking they might have been pins of some kind."

"You know, my dad gave the kids some sheriff and deputy cowboy stars to wear with their outfits," Amber said. "I wonder if the mound stars are anything like that. Todd, do you know where those went?"

"Nope. With all the stuff the boys have around, who knows? Probably on their *Star Wars* outfits instead. So, how do you read that weirdo Bright Star, Kate?"

"As *very* weird and probably dangerous. I think the stars were his, maybe put there to place his blessing—or curse—on the long-dead pagans in the mound. Maybe he's like the Mormons, thinking they can get dead people into heaven. Todd, what? Why are you looking at Grant that way?"

"Just that—that you seem to be sure there are corpses in the local mounds."

"Mason Mound, especially. I've been telling Grant the odds are good. No sign of a cave-in, and the smaller mounds are usually more sturdy, which means well-preserved burial chambers. Mason Mound is evidently intact, never entered, probably with one horizontal entry shaft that shouldn't be too hard to find and dig through. As for Bright Star, I was telling Grant what upsets me more than his lies about the stars—I get that, because any tampering with such a mound can mean big fines or prison time—is the hold the man has over his people. Namely my cousin Lee and his wife, Grace. She was a friend of mine and my sisters' from way back. I swear, she's like a zombie now, but she tried to give me some sort of sign—I think—about wearing a star. Bright Star does brainwashing at best, terrorizing at worst. Everything's so guarded and secret I can't get near the Hear Ye compound to find out what's really going on in there."

"Of course," Todd said, "we could peer down into it."

"No way," Grant cut in. "Because I know you're not talking about renting a helicopter."

Todd thumped the table with his knuckles. "Grant, there are three really tall trees close together on the hill above Cold Creek that look down into the compound. And not on Monson's land—on public land. I've only climbed them once years ago, but—"

"Amber, can you talk to this maniac, please?" Grant said. "I wouldn't trust Monson not to take potshots at him and claim a hunting rifle just misfired."

Kate placed her hand over Grant's. "But it is an idea. We have to get something on him to get some leverage. I can tell Grace and Lee are too scared or doped up or whatever to talk, and their kids are prisoners. Who knows what people will do if their children's well-being or safety's at stake?"

"The sad thing is, they went there of their own free will," Amber put in. "This is the U.S. of A., and people are allowed to make fools of themselves, targets, whatever. People seem to be content there. I've talked to some at the Saturday market, and everyone seems loyal."

"Back to tree time," Grant said. "Kate, you'd better

take a look at how this guy climbs and swings around in tall trees before you go so gung ho over this idea."

"That's my Todd," Amber said. "Kate, let me tell you. Grant, Brad, Gabe and Paul used to play or hide out in the tree house behind the Mason house, and Todd would be above it, way up in the tree."

"All right, I'll take things one step at a time," Kate promised. "I'd like to see how he climbs, if the offer's still open. I've done stranger things to get answers. How about a demonstration soon? Then maybe I'll go up with you, Todd."

Grant had no choice but to keep his mouth shut at that point, but this was ruining his dinner. He wasn't her boss, wasn't her husband, wasn't even her significant other, despite how natural and cozy this dinner had been. She'd ruined his mood to romance her tonight. Besides, what worried him more than Kate's climbing trees was her declaration she'd done stranger things to get answers. He hoped that didn't include trying to get into his heart just so she could get into his Adena tomb.

Carson called Kate just after ten the next morning to tell her he was at the coffee shop in the new part of town. "I'm assuming Grant's at the mill. I can be there in ten minutes, and we can take a good look at the mound, see if we can locate the entrance. I'll meet you in front of his house," he said.

"No! Carson—no. I promised Grant I wouldn't go near it alone."

"Great. You'd be with me."

"He meant without him. And his cleaning lady's here, the one who tipped him off too late about his beautiful tree being stolen. I'll meet you in the coffee shop. Don't you teach a doctoral class today?"

"At three. I came with information about the star, but you've got to get us into that mound."

"I have to do things his way."

"Really? That doesn't sound like my Kate."

"Never mind. I'll be right there."

She realized she hadn't mentioned that Grant was upset at her for saying she might climb a tree with Todd. Or that she was certain he was stalling her about taking a closer look at the mound.

She told the cleaning lady, Mrs. McGirty, that she was going out then drove to meet Carson. Of course he'd gravitated to the tony end of town, even though it was a farther drive for him. She admitted she'd become a bit of a snob, too, in her years away from here, but now she enjoyed the people and the place. No way could she sympathize with Lacey, looking down on this area, especially since she'd been married to Grant Mason. Damn, there she went again with wayward thoughts and just when she was going to meet Carson, whom she'd dreamed about for years.

He had coffee just the way she liked it delivered to their table the moment she appeared. "How thoughtful," she said. "Thanks." She gave him a peck on the cheek and sat across from him. She hadn't been in here before. The place was decorated 1950s retro, and she liked it.

Carson still looked ticked off at her refusal to play things his way. "So how did the meeting with the cult guru go?" he asked without producing the star he'd promised to give back.

"He not only denied everything, but used part of a biblical quote he probably thinks I didn't pick up on. I finally found it from Psalm 8. In answering as he did, he seems to be putting himself in the place of God. The Psalm starts out, *O Lord, our Lord, how excellent is Your name in all the earth,* and it goes on to mention the stars the Lord has made. I was thinking, since in The Book of Revelation, Jesus describes himself as 'the bright and morning star,' Monson probably sees himself as a modern-day Messiah."

"Which is what most whacked-out cult leaders claim. That's a far-fetched jumble of clues, but with a madman, anything is possible."

"I swear, years ago that man would have been admitted to what was then called the lunatic asylum right outside of town."

"Really?" he asked, momentarily distracted. "So it's defunct now?"

"They did terrible things like lobotomies and electrotherapy. I hear the grounds are derelict now except for a children's playground."

"An interesting relic of Americana, just as are the mounds of Adeniana," he told her, making up that word, but he was right on with the societal observation as usual. However clever she was, Carson was always a step ahead and that had absolutely snowed her for years.

He took a small, flat box from inside his suit-coat pocket. For one moment, her heart skipped a beat. It was a jewelry-size box, and he'd hinted at giving her an engagement ring, but surely not now.

He put the box on the table between them, on his ironed pocket handkerchief as if the table were contaminated. Even here among the country-club golf and tennis crowd, Carson stood out as retro as the decor.

She'd found that so alluring about him when she was younger, but now it seemed elitist and even snobbish.

"Oh," she said as he opened the box. "The star."

"The blood on the tips is human. Type A positive, as a matter of fact."

"Great work." She sighed. "Now I just have to talk Bright Star and his followers into telling me their blood types or letting me give them a blood test. O positive is the most common blood type anyway."

"If I were writing a horror story, I'd make up the fact that the Adena were mostly A-positive blood types, and their ghosts placed the stars as an invitation for one Kathryn Anne Lockwood to come visit their resting place to pay her respects. And, of course, I'd include the fictional factoid—excuse the paradox—that they themselves are the walking dead, out to haunt beautiful women who sleep close by and don't come quickly enough to visit—and who are distracted by men who hold the keys to their mound."

He grinned at her without showing his teeth. "The Adena did some metal work, of course, only this die-cut star is a bit advanced even for them, and—"

"Carson, stop it! Enough!" she protested, but his mentioning the walking dead made her think of poor Grace again, trying to give her some sign, looking like the walking dead herself. Had this star indeed been a pin as Carson had surmised earlier? Had Grace worn one? But to signify what?

When Carson looked surprised at her outburst, she explained. "I know you're upset with me, but as I said, I have to play things Grant's way."

"What happened to Carson's way—our way?"

"We have to be patient. Worthwhile things are worth waiting for."

"Really?" he said, again using his favorite subtle—even snide—challenging comment. "I think you're starting to really enjoy doing things *his* way."

"*No.* He's angry with me right now because I said I'd like to see how his friend Todd scales trees. Actually, I'm hoping to go with Todd into a tree above the Hear Ye compound and look down into it—spy on Bright Star and his poor robots. I'd also like to pay Todd for his time, since Grant says his family—they have three sons—can always use extra money."

Carson rolled his eyes and shook his head. "You'd better concentrate on our task at hand. But if you must go off on a wild-goose chase after this Bright Star, be careful in the air let alone on the ground, darling. I want you with me, intact—and willing—when this is all over. Kate," he said, leaning forward and capturing her hands in his, "I swear, you are on the cusp of linking two great prehistoric cultures. One unique artifact in common, and you're partway there, next your articles in the professional journals—even the likes of *Time* or *USA TODAY.* I'm sure of it! So let me guide you through all this."

Again, she scolded herself for not telling Carson about thinking she'd seen the Beastmaster at the garage window. She'd meant to, but she didn't want him to think that she was losing her grip on reality—or that she might suspect him since he still had the mock-up of the mask she'd made.

"Carson, next time you come, would you bring the facsimile of the Beastmaster mask I left with you?"

"I use it in class, you know. And would like to soon again. Do you need it now?"

"I can show Grant my photo of the Beastmaster artifact, but I thought my mask might show him the kind of thing I'm after in an Adena mound."

"Of course, darling. Mind if I have one of my grad students copy it first so I still have one? I'll get back to you on that, and you keep in touch—with me."

"I hear you. I do have to move carefully, unless you want Grant to dig in his heels. As for Brad—"

Carson shook his head. "I've carefully asked around. Grant would have to be as dead as the Adena before Brad would inherit one penny or one breath of say-so over the mound."

With Paul's death, and possibly under mysterious circumstances, Kate didn't like the way Carson had phrased that. She made a move to slide out of the booth, but he held her hands. "Remember that W. H. Auden quote about asking questions, the one from Anthropology 201 that I made everyone memorize when you were just a neophyte—but a neophyte of mine?"

She nodded. "'History is, strictly speaking, the study of questions; the study of answers belongs to anthropology and sociology.'"

"Right. Top marks for my girl. So be sure you ask the right questions from the right people. Then use your knowledge of anthropology and sociology, not sexology, to get what you want from Grant Mason. Save the latter for me, understand?"

"I understand a lot more than I used to."

"Then put it to good use, and I'll be in touch. Really in touch, next time."

Kate made a show of looking around as if she didn't

want strangers to see them together, see them kissing.
She pulled her hands free and walked out.

Kate knew she was taking a big chance by sharing her photograph of the Beastmaster with Grant, but
until Carson gave her mask back, it would have to do.
Even the mere photo was so stunning, so compelling,
that surely he would realize the possibility of the valuable artifacts within Mason Mound. She waited until
they'd been home awhile and had enjoyed a glass of
wine after dinner. Grant had even told her a bit about
his and Brad's boyhoods. She could tell he was worried
about where Brad was tonight, not that he kept tabs on
an adult brother, but the Lacey connection was obviously bothering him. Maybe this would take his mind
off his worries.

"I'd like to show you a copy I have of a famous Celtic
artifact that's housed in a museum in Denmark," she
told him as they sat side by side on the couch before the
fireplace. The June night was amazingly cool with rain
streaking the huge picture window, so he'd built a fire.

"Not of something you found?" he asked, turning
toward her with one bent leg propped on his knee. "I
thought you were working in England."

"I was, but I made a special trip, a sort of pilgrim-
age, just to see this in a museum. The Celts were all
over northern Europe, too. Let me go get it."

She rose from the soft leather cushions—his weight
close to hers tipped her toward him, and she was so
tempted not to move. She went to her room to get the
picture. It always fascinated and chilled her to look at it.

"See," she said, sinking down beside him with their
shoulders touching again. "This silver bowl, called a

cauldron, depicts the so-called Beastmaster. He got his name because he's surrounded by various beasts or animals and appears to be in command of them. Scholars believe he's the Celtic horned deity of fertility and nature named Cernunnos. Humans are always depicted as very small compared to him."

Grant drew in a sharp breath, so she knew the impact got to him, too. He looked transfixed, his eyes wide, his lips parted. "Beautiful but in a bizarre way," he whispered. "With his horns and holding a snake, it reminds me of some paintings of Satan."

"I've thought of that. His cult and significance in the Celtic religion is unknown, but if I could just find anything shown on this cauldron in Adena art—especially depictions of the Beastmaster—it would really help me to prove my theory that their cultures are linked. What? You have the strangest look on your face."

"Doesn't it—he—have a terrible effect on you?" he asked. "So strange with those wide, staring eyes. I'll bet you could have imagined this face when you saw a deer through a dirty garage window."

She sighed in frustration. Did he always have to fight her about this? "Both the Celts and the Adena were larger than average people," she told him, ignoring his attempt to sidetrack her. "Celtic skeletons have been found that show them almost as giants, some six feet seven, another six feet ten tall. And the Adena were tall, too. Even their skulls—the ones that aren't smashed—are large. Smashed skulls were used in their burial rites somehow."

"Smashed human skulls?" he whispered. "Like human sacrifices with other dead people, maybe the upper class?"

"Yes, possibly chieftains or shamans. I just want you to know how important more knowledge about these two cultures would be."

He tossed the photo on the coffee table, then put his arm around her. "The truth is, Dr. Lockwood, this all kind of creeps me out, maybe partly because of Paul's crushed skull. So, what's that around the Beastmaster's neck that looks like a rope, like he could be strangled?"

"That's called a torque. See," she said, leaning over to retrieve the photograph and pointing at it. "He's also holding one in his other hand. It's a rigid neck ring, kind of like a necklace. A sign, I think, of honor, as some have been found around neck bones both on the Celts and the Adena."

"So there's your link. You don't need to be searching for other horrible Beastmaster images or masks."

"But more proof than a style of jewelry is needed. Masks are too common to be another link, unless it's a particular mask."

"You're really passionate about this," he said, pulling her closer, turning her head toward him with one big, warm hand. "And," he said, as his hand drifted lower to cradle her throat, "if a torque was solid metal, it stayed on for life, right?"

"Right," she agreed, but with that short response, she knew her voice had gotten softer, breathier. Like a wedding ring for life, she thought. Like one she did not want from Carson, though for several years, she'd thought she did. But this close to Grant, almost in his arms...

They moved together in a mutual caress and kiss. *You are really passionate about this,* he'd said. But this sweeping, spinning feeling was a different sort of passion, not of the head but of the heart. She clung for one moment, not only to him, but to sanity, as well, to whatever she had been telling him, trying to get him on her side. But this—was this the way? Then why did she feel she was the one being convinced, converted to something he wanted?

She half sat, half lay across his lap as their kisses deepened, lengthened, as his hands moved over her. They sank into the couch as if they floated on a bed, pressed together, lying full length now, with his leg atop hers as if to hold her down when she had no intention of going anywhere. She couldn't breathe—she, her family's bright student, big achiever, going places—didn't want to go anywhere but here. But something crazy that Carson had said crept in when they lay, holding tight, pressed together, gasping for breath. *You don't have to do things Grant Mason's way.* She began to tremble.

"You okay?" Grant whispered. "Didn't mean to push things—us. I don't mean to take advantage of your being a guest here."

"Or of trying to distract me?" she managed to answer. "But you do."

"If we get together—I mean, not only like this—I don't want it to be because you want to convince me you should explore the mound."

That was the splash of cold water she needed. She struggled to sit up, and he helped her. They sat, still facing each other. "Nor do I want you to think my response is any sort of bribery," she told him.

They were so close she could see her reflection in the dark depths of his eyes, flickering firelight, too, as if flames danced within. Could it be she'd known this man for less than a week? In a way he was her enemy, but she felt so close to him. She was suddenly afraid of him and herself. He'd come closer to convincing her to want him, even to love him, and wouldn't that mean putting what he wanted above her own needs?

That night, Kate couldn't sleep. Her mind raced over things Grant had said and done—Carson's words, too. For a while she studied the photo of his grandmother Ada. She looked so unique, as if she knew things she couldn't quite say or was a deep thinker. For some reason, Kate related to her, instinctively liked her. She turned out her lights, then stood at her bedroom window, staring out toward the mound. The slash of moon seemed like a tilted grin, like the one the Beastmaster wore. And she kept thinking of Carson's silly story about the walking dead coming to get her to make her visit their graves in the mound.

Paul Kettering's funeral was tomorrow. He'd be laid to rest not far from here, according to current customs, embalmed, put in a coffin, then a concrete burial vault six feet under, his grave marked with a stone. The Adena had buried their beloved, too, but according to their ways, under a mound. It was still a mystery how Paul's skull had been smashed. It was a mystery how the Adena of Mason's Mound had died, and she yearned to—

She heard a fierce, single, distant shout. Surely, that hadn't come from outside—from the mound! No, it was muffled, but definitely Grant, unless Brad had come back, but she hadn't heard him.

Could Grant be sick? Calling for her? If Brad was back, was it an argument? An intruder like at Paul and Nadine's?

Not waiting to grab her robe or stuff her feet in her

slippers, she grabbed a brass bookend from the dresser for a weapon and ran from the guest bedroom into the dark house.

14

Kate rushed headlong across the living room with fire embers still glowing in the grate. She had not even been down the hall to Grant's bedroom. Several doors stood open like dark, yawning mouths, but two of them were closed.

"Grant? Grant, are you all right?" she called out.

Wearing only black boxer shorts, he opened his door and leaned against the frame. He looked frazzled and disheveled. She wanted to comfort him. Though his bedroom was dark and the hall was dim, she could feel his eyes on her body. She crossed her arms over her breasts, surprised she still held the heavy bookend in one hand.

"Sorry," he said, shaking his head as if to clear it. "Nightmare. So real. I must have yelled. You got me thinking too much about what could be inside the mound—ghosts or something."

"You don't have to apologize for that. Welcome to my world," she said to try to lighten the mood, but she could tell he was embarrassed.

"Ever see one of those old mummy movies—Boris Karloff, I think?" he asked. "It's your fault, sweetheart, for hauling out that picture."

Sweetheart?

"Grant, I'm sorry. How about we form a team with Carson Cantrell and his staff and excavate the mound, even if it's just to prove there's nothing of interest or value there? You know—debunk any strange thoughts we might have about it. Since many of the mounds were entered and pillaged by pioneers years ago, maybe there is nothing left, but don't you feel curious?"

"Isn't curiosity what killed the cat? But yeah, I'm curious about you, at least."

Despite priding herself on being rational and careful, she walked closer. Talk about that mound being a magnet—this man enticed her as much...more.

A voice cut in so close she jumped. "Din't mean to ter'rupt your foreplay or afterglow," Brad said. "Or," he said, staring at the brass bookend she held, "a lover's quarrel. I'm goin' to the room you two 'signed to me. 'Scuse me, please."

Now Kate felt really undressed. "Grant had a bad dream and called out," she said as Brad propped himself against the wall, not moving despite what he'd said.

"No need to 'xplain. I swear you two are fated to be mated, so full steam ahead."

"You weren't driving in that condition, I hope," Grant said, putting Kate gently behind him. "I thought we were agreed on that."

"Nope. Had a lady friend. Don't we all? She dropped me off—not dropped me." He snickered at his own stupid joke.

"Lacey?" Grant demanded.

Behind him, Kate grimaced and shook her head. Brad might guess she'd spied on him now.

"Word sure travels fast in these parts," Brad said.

"Yeah, Lacey, just for old times' sake, man. Sometimes I think 'Bad Brad' was better for her'n you were."

"Kate," Grant said, his voice hard. "Head to your room, please. Brad and I need a discussion that's been coming for a while, and not just about Lacey."

Kate was only too glad to scurry away. She went into her room and closed her door but could hear an occasional shouted word—mostly Brad's slurred ones, because Grant pretty much kept his voice down. She heard Lacey's name, but they were also arguing about Todd remaining foreman at the mill. She tiptoed to her door and opened it a crack.

"Didn't blood used to be thicker'n water?" Brad demanded.

Grant finally started shouting, too. Somehow they'd gotten on the fact that "Tarzan Todd" had invited Kate to climb trees to spy on Bright Star.

"Yeah, well, I'll go 'long, too!" Brad insisted. "And I'll lay off the booze before I do, so hope that suits you. Course, you'd prob'ly rather have me just fall out of a tree and out of your hair for good! And don't start in with me 'gain about whether I'm bugging you by planting metal stars on the Adena mounds round here! If Mason Mound was mine, I'd let Kate and her college cronies dig stuff up in a second if it meant I could get some funding from what's there to restart my mill and get the hell out of here!"

"Would you keep your voice down? It's not your call! And you'd damn well better sober up before you drop Paul's coffin at the funeral in the morning. It's only a few hours away, so go sleep it off!"

That was the last thing she heard before two doors slammed.

* * *

The day of Paul's funeral had beautiful weather, although Grant felt a storm would have been more appropriate. In the church, he sat between Brad and Todd
in the second row behind Nadine, her sister and Paul's
relatives, a couple of whom were also pallbearers. Of
course, it was a closed casket. No way could the funeral director have made Paul's head presentable. He
still couldn't understand what had happened. Grant had
learned from Jace that Paul's wallet was on his dresser,
untouched with money and credit cards in it. Paul's
guns weren't taken, and there had never been any hint
of drugs in the house.

The funeral service, led by Pastor Snell, was emotional but blessedly brief. Still, Grant's eyes burned with
unshed tears, especially when he saw the tree trunk Paul
had been working on for the church. It depicted angels
with swirling robes flying toward heaven. It must be
incomplete since the angels' faces were blank, and Paul
always did great, detailed faces. Or could he have meant
to leave them that way? But what really bothered Grant
was that he kept imagining the terrible Beastmaster face
on the angel that had arms stretched upward, because
that reminded him of antlers.

What else had Paul been working on besides this angel
carving and the one of the Adena shaman? Where had
he secreted his eagle pendant—the symbol of Adena
spiritual power, as Kate had put it? Maybe Paul saw
that beautifully carved artifact as inspiration for his ar-
tistic talents. That would make it logical that he'd hide
the pendant inside one of his carved tree trunks—inside
that one with the angels or even the Adena carving Kate
wanted. Maybe during the lunch here later, he'd slip away

to come back into the sanctuary and take a close look at this carving, at least.

At the end of the service, the six pallbearers rose and carried the coffin out. Grant saw Kate sitting partway back in a pew with Amber, her sons and Amber's parents. Kate had said at breakfast she was going to watch Todd climb his favorite tree tomorrow after he got off from the mill and maybe go up with him in a tree overlooking the Hear Ye compound. Brad still said he'd go, too, so Grant would reluctantly join them, just to observe, at least.

Lacey was here, with her elderly parents. He'd seen her talking to Brad outside the church. Both Lacey and Kate got under his skin, but in very different ways.

Above all, Grant scanned the rows of faces for a stranger. He and Jace had talked about the fact that some murderers were drawn to attend their victim's funeral, even to visit the grave. Could such a person have dared to come here? Worse, was it not some stranger, but someone Paul—and Grant—knew?

The coffin was heavy, his thoughts, too, as they approached the waiting hearse, which would lead the funeral procession the short distance to the cemetery. After they slid the coffin into the hearse, Grant went to his car and got in line with others, all sporting magnetic blue and white funeral flags. He drove with Kate beside him and Brad in the backseat.

The cemetery staff had erected a green canvas tent to shade the grave, though the sun felt warm and the breeze gentle. He pictured the dusty, log-lined and covered roof over the interior of the Adena tomb, dank with earth smells and dark but for his and his friends' darting flashlight beams.

It had been this kind of weather the day the four of them had dug their way into the mound. Gabe—who always did things on the up-and-up—was away that week, and Grant and Brad's dad and grandfather had gone to a lumberman's association meeting in Cincinnati. The boys would probably not have dared to check out the mound otherwise.

The horizontal entry shaft had been mostly cleared decades before when Grandpa had gone in for a look. According to what Grant had overheard, he'd really had to dig his way in. He hadn't refilled the narrow passageway when he'd backed out and resealed the tomb. A pile of dirt and stones had been outside the mound for years, until it had been carried away for various uses. In front of the entrance, he'd planted prickly hawthorn trees. The four of them had belly-crawled under the reach of the lower limbs.

Grant realized now that the old pile of rubble was probably where Brad got the stones he'd put back in the woods. He'd told Grant once he was just marking his favorite spot—the place he'd told Kate he'd buried his nonexistent pet. He'd even made up a name for the dog. That well might be where Brad had hidden his Adena arrowhead, so he hadn't told Kate that Brad was lying about burying a dog there. But now—unbelievable—they were burying his dear friend Paul.

They slid the coffin atop the frame that would lower it into the ground. The funeral director placed an arrangement of foliage and roses on it that read *Husband, Friend.* Grant scanned the cluster of people again, then gazed at the coffin. He'd have to make up with Brad somehow. Life was too short—too unpredictable—to be arguing with someone close. Even if people couldn't forget, maybe they could forgive. If he got a chance, he'd try to get Kate to reconcile with her father, too.

At the reception following the burial, Kate looked around the crowded Fellowship Hall for Grant. He'd been greeting people, helping Nadine. She wasn't sure he'd gotten any food from the long buffet table. She hadn't seen him for a while, surely longer than a men's-room stop would take. She knew he was depressed. However, he'd put on a good show today, and she was worried about him.

She kept busy helping Amber with her three boys, as Todd, too, was mingling, and Amber's parents had gone home because her mother had a bad summer cold. Like Grant and Todd, Brad had mixed with others— briefly—but now sat at a table in the corner, talking to several people she didn't know. At least he was drinking only coffee. Lacey was here, not sitting with Brad but close to him.

"Nadine seems to be holding up okay," Amber told Kate. "I'd be a basket case if I ever lost Todd." Amber had brought crayons and paper for her boys. They were eating chocolate-chip cookies and scribbling away at pictures, sometimes proudly showing them to their mother and Kate. The younger boys, Aaron and Andy, were drawing trees with a man way up in them, but the oldest, Jason, had drawn a cowboy with a brimmed hat, two guns—and a big, yellow star on his chest.

"Oh, what's that star for?" Kate asked him.

"He's the sheriff. I named him Gabe. It's a badge like Grandpa gave us, but I can't find it, none of them."

"So Grandpa gave you more than one star?"

"Three, 'cause there's three of us."

"Oh, Mary Ann, how are you?" Amber said and bounced up from her folding chair to greet a woman who'd approached with a very elderly man. Kate had noticed them at the funeral. "And it's so nice to see your dad again," Amber said, in a loud voice, shaking his hand. "Hello, Mr. Custer!"

"A nice turnout," he said, nodding so hard that his white, shaggy mane bounced. "Sad occasion. I've seen many a passing, but that's what you get when you're old as the hills. I wanted to see this young lady here," he said, indicating Kate. "I knew her daddy years ago."

Kate stood and shook his hand. She still felt guilty over giving her father the cold shoulder when Tess and Char had been so glad to see him.

Amber introduced them all around. "Mr. Custer was a friend of Grant and Brad's dad, too," Amber told Kate in the awkward lull when Kate didn't pursue the comment about her father.

"And, goin' way back, knew their granddaddy," the old man said in a loud voice. "We was hunting buddies when the Mason men weren't working at their sawmill. Got us venison in the woods out back of their house, more'n once."

"Kate's a professor and explorer of Adena mounds like we have around here," Amber told him, also speaking loudly, so Kate took the hint the old man was hard of hearing.

And when he repeated the information about being a hunting buddy of Grant's grandfather, Kate realized he was forgetful at best, had dementia at worst.

"I'm hoping to get permission to excavate the Mason Mound behind their house," she told him, raising her voice. "And maybe some others in the area."

"Mason Mound? Why, the boys' granddaddy looked into it. Let's see—must have been in '39, coupla years before a bunch of us got drafted and sent to the Pacific. I knew men who'd survived Pearl Harbor but was sent on a battleship to Iwo Jima, myself. Lived through that hell, you can live through anything, so I'm almost ninety-two now."

The elderly man went on, while his daughter tried to shush him. The McCollum boys started to squabble, and Amber had to settle them down. But Kate's mind had snagged on the fact the old man had said Grant's grandfather had *looked into* Mason Mound. Did he mean he'd entered it or just studied about it? It surely must be the latter.

Kate wanted to ask about that. He did seem clear on things the further back he went, and 1939 was pretty far back. But Mary Ann was tugging her dad away. It touched Kate to see how devoted she was to him. It made her feel guilty again about how she had treated her own father. She should have asked Mr. Custer about his memories of her dad. His memories could be jumbled, warped information from an elderly, forgetful man, so she'd just ask Grant—if she could find him.

In the deserted sanctuary, Grant knelt next to Paul's angel carving on the tree trunk. He'd tipped it over and looked at it from all sides, especially the bottom, wondering if there was a place Paul could have secreted a package with his Adena eagle pendant inside. If it was not in this carving, he'd try to check out others. Each crack intrigued him but nothing seemed to outline a hiding place.

"Grant. Are you okay?"

He jerked his head around. Kate, alone, walked down the center aisle.

"Yeah. Just wondering how Paul did this. I never really watched him work," he told her, quickly tilting the heavy block of wood back on its base.

She came closer, her dress swishing against her bare legs. She leaned down and put her hand on his shoulder. "It's strange how once someone's gone you think of all kinds of things you wanted to say or ask."

He nodded and stood, brushing bark off his hands. They sat in the front pew, silent at first.

"Grant, I met old Mr. Custer and his daughter."

"Now, there's one who goes way back. Sam's ancestors probably knew the original Falls family that pioneered this area."

"He said he knew your dad and grandfather. And he said a funny thing…that your grandpa once *looked into* Mason Mound. He even knew the year."

Grant fought not to react, but he was upset to hear that Sam Custer knew Grandpa had entered the mound. Dad had learned about it, since he was in the discussion Grant had overheard years ago. Grandpa had been so awed and scared by what he'd seen inside the mound that he hadn't touched anything—unlike his grandsons years later.

He cleared his throat. "I wish my folks had lived into their nineties like Sam Custer. But Sam gets pretty mixed up on things."

"He said it was 1939. He seems pretty clear when he gets that far back. His exact words were he *looked into it*."

"He must mean Grandpa got information on it somehow—checked out what the mound was—might be.

When he learned it could be a burial spot, he obviously decided to honor the dead and passed that idea on to Dad and me. After all, we wouldn't go digging up graves where we buried Paul today, so the ancients deserve the same respect."

"Sorry to bring it up today. *Looked into* could mean they studied it, of course. Did you ever come across any notes on it, something like that?"

"No. Kate, you've got to let up on this. If I were you, I'd spend my time trying to nail Bright Star for leaving his own relics on the mounds, see if you can rattle his cage and maybe pry your cousin's family out of that cult, one that's hurting modern people."

"I intend to do that, too. I know you're grieving and have a lot on your mind. I shouldn't have brought this up now."

"Thanks for understanding. Your support means a lot and—"

He saw a big shadow on the wall, turned and stood. It was his forklift operator from the mill, Keith Simons.

"Keith. What is it?"

"Sorry, boss. Just noticed you were gone awhile and wanted to check that you're okay. But I see you're well taken care of. Again, my regrets for the loss of your friend. See you at work tomorrow."

And he was gone.

"He moves fast for such a big guy," Kate observed. "And I'm glad you have someone watching out for you there, even if you are the big man on your own campus."

"We'd better get back downstairs before everyone else looks for me or leaves, okay?" he said, trying to keep his voice light.

They stood. At least, she'd taken it well about his

grandfather *looking into* the mound, but he felt rotten about deceiving her again. What was that old saying about what tangled webs we weave when we deceive?

She put her arm through his as he escorted her toward the back of the church. They'd probably never walk a church aisle together as man and wife—too many differences and contrasting goals. He had to be careful he didn't make another mistake like he had with Lacey.

That thought disturbed him, and he stepped away from Kate at the top of the stairs. He could hear the buzz of voices below. He wanted to say goodbye to Nadine, tell her he'd like to stop by to look at Paul's carvings, choose one or two to buy—and, in the process, check them for the eagle pendant. If only they'd left the relics untouched that day!

"It's a lovely old church," Kate said, turning to glance back at the sanctuary. "But I like the way they've updated it, too—a good blend of honoring the past but with the modern."

Was she subtly trying to work on him again to let her modern techniques study ancient Mason Mound? He turned back to look at the altar, the cross. And he felt doubly ashamed that not only had he lied to her again, but he'd done it in the heart of the church, too. What shook him more than that was, for a blurred moment, again in his mind's eye, he saw the dark sanctuary of death in the mound, the ornaments of Adena worship laid out around the two main skeletons, circled by human sacrifices with their skulls smashed.

15

Kate was appalled she'd slept late the next morning, but she and Grant—Brad, too, sober—had stayed up late talking about everything except Mason Mound. She'd promised to get their breakfast, but they'd obviously been quiet and just let her sleep. The house was silent.

She got up, threw on her robe and padded into the kitchen. They'd left some coffee, so she poured a cup and stared out the window. The mound beckoned to her, just as it must have to generations of inhabitants here. Especially, it seemed, Grant's grandfather.

She looked around for a local phone book and found a skinny, old one that covered the whole county. Amber had said Sam Custer's daughter Mary Ann was unmarried. Kate was guessing the old man might live with her. Despite Grant's smooth shift of topics and his comments that Sam was senile, which she'd seen for herself, she wanted another interview with the man.

She called the Custer number. *Yes!* Mary Ann lived in her parents' home not far from here, and Kate was welcome to come over. "I meant to ask *your* father more about *my* father yesterday and didn't get a chance," she told Mary Ann. Kate had to admit to herself that if Grant was bending the truth, he wasn't the only one. Yet she would be sure to make what she'd said true—she would ask Sam about her own father, too. Maybe it would be a first step to understanding not only Sam, but also her dad, at last.

Grant had spoken to Nadine about Paul's carvings after the funeral. She'd told him to come by, and she'd give him first choice on the ones she was selling. She also told him Jace Miller said she could collect the one that had killed Paul.

"How about I stop by the police station and bring that back to you?" he'd asked her, so here he was, rolling the Adena carving up Nadine's driveway in a wheelbarrow. When he'd loaded it on his truck, he'd carefully looked it over for a hiding place.

"Thanks so much, Grant," Nadine said as she opened the garage door for him to roll the trunk into Paul's workshop. Grant noticed the chaos had been straightened; order restored; things rearranged. Of all the places over the years Grant would picture his longtime friend, it would be here or up in the lost tree house, cut down just as prematurely as Paul had been.

"You know Kate wants to buy this," he reminded her as he carefully tipped the wheelbarrow and slid the tree trunk to the floor where she indicated, among the others.

"She said she'd stop by soon, but I suppose she'll need you to haul it. I'll be glad to get it out of here," she admitted, throwing a canvas work apron over it. He saw her shudder. "That squat, strange Adena shaman he carved always gave me the creeps anyway, like he was guarding something with a curse on it. It's almost like it came to life and struck Paul down."

Grant felt a chill slither up his spine, too. That was all he needed—Nadine as well as Kate obsessing that the ancient Adena could come to life and haunt humans who disturbed their resting places. In a way, that was what had killed his grandma Ada.

"Grant," Nadine rushed on, turning toward him before he could find something comforting to say. "Paul's death had to be either an accident or—or worse. As soon as Gabe gets back from his honeymoon, I'm going to talk to him about making a full investigation. I can't stand being here alone at night anymore, so my sister's coming to stay for a while—to help me get over...over Paul's loss."

"That's a good idea, Nadine. I'm sure she'll be a big help."

Grant recalled Jace had told him Nadine refused to use the word *murder,* but that she thought that was what it was. And she'd been doubly upset, he'd said, when Jace checked with her sister and the gas-station attendant in town to be sure the time frame she'd given him for her whereabouts the day of the murder matched what she'd said, so that she could be ruled out of being a person of interest.

A person of interest. Nadine was that to him partly because she was battling an illness and needed support and money, partly because she might have an idea about where Paul would hide something priceless. Grant figured Paul hadn't told Nadine about the eagle pendant or she wouldn't be hurting for money—unless she'd promised to keep her husband's secret, keep his precious boyhood find hidden.

"Everything all right with Paul's will?" Grant asked. "Do you need any help with moving stuff out or cleaning the house before you sell it?"

"You Mason men are so supportive," she said. "I'll let you both know when I'm ready to take you up on it, because Brad's insisted he'll help me go through Paul's things."

"Your daddy was sure a handsome man, good salesman, too," Sam Custer told Kate as she sat with him in the old farmhouse his family had lived in for years. Mary Ann still referred to this front room as the parlor. "Like all of us, he done some wrong in his days, but at heart he was a good man—a man's man."

Kate nodded, though she disagreed with most of that. Her father had not acted like a good man. He was a woman's man, and not just one woman. She listened attentively to Sam's renditions of times Dad stopped by to see him.

"Course, I understand what a tragedy it was when he left you girls. He hated hisself for that part of it, but it always takes two to tango—two to break up a marriage, too."

She bit down the instinct to come to her mother's defense; maybe there were things she didn't know. Besides, she wanted to get on the subject that had really brought her here, before Sam went off on another World War II tangent.

"I found it interesting that you recalled Grant's grandfather looking into the mound behind their house—your old hunting grounds," she said when she finally got a word in, remembering to talk loudly. "But did you mean he just looked into information on the Adena or did he manage to actually look inside the mound?"

"Oh, sure, that's it. Don't think many knew. Cleared hisself out a real narrow passage in, so he said. Had to move stones, dirt, coupla fallen beams—solid, old wood, oak, he thought. Took him years to clear away the debris from that, saw the pile of it more'n once when we was after deer over there. Whatever he seen in that mound scairt him bad. You know, I swear deer was thick as mayflies round their woodlot sometimes. Shot me a big buck there right after the war, twelve pointer. Venison's a far cry from what we ate in C-rations during the war, you know...."

Kate nodded but she was hardly listening. Grant's grandfather had entered the mound. That meant Grant was either ignorant of that or lying to her. Talk about going to war... If the latter were true, that made Grant her enemy. And that changed all the rules.

"Hi, Carson," Kate said into her phone the minute she got his voice mail. She didn't bother to identify herself. She was sitting in Grant's driveway, hadn't even gone into the house, as if it might have ears.

"I need a favor—for our cause," she said, talking fast. "I know you're teaching a class, but when you get a chance, can you send a grad student to research something for me in the university library archives? In the stacks on Kenny Road last year, when I was home from England for Christmas, I found some mid-twentieth-century reports from this area about mound entries and finds, which were recorded by hand, of course, and filed under Falls County reports about crops, no less. I copied some stuff about the Cold Creek Mound, but maybe

I missed something in there about Mason Mound. I've heard a rumor—even have a fairly reliable secondary witness—who says the mound might have been entered in the late thirties. So if you can—"

His recording beeped. Out of time, but she'd said what she'd needed to. She knew how much Grant had loved his grandfather, that the lost tree house had revived many memories and how much he'd love to have him back. Now Kate wished his grandfather was back, too, because she had a lot of questions.

Late that afternoon, not having heard from Carson, Kate drove to Todd and Amber's place to see Todd demonstrate his climbing techniques.

"Brad and Grant are coming, too," Amber told her as she let her in. "The boys and I will go along with you all. It's good for them to hear their father's lectures about safety now and then, but they're much too young to go up with him. I don't even want them standing under the tree just looking up. If something gets dropped from that height, it's going fast and hard when it hits the ground."

"I see they like to draw pictures of Todd up in a tree."

"Sure do. I suppose it's inevitable, but I'd like to think they won't follow in his footsteps that way. I still worry about him."

While the boys played out back, the two of them sat over coffee and peanut-butter cookies until the men arrived. Grant and Brad came together in Grant's truck, as if he still wasn't letting Brad drive. Amber evidently loved to have company and served everyone with a smile on her face. It made Kate wish she was better at hospitality, a real gift, but her mother had seldom entertained because money was so tight, once again, thanks to her *good man* father.

In the living room, Todd produced a sample harness and proceeded to show the safety features and explain how he climbed. He was so knowledgeable and interesting he reminded Kate of some of the better lecturers she'd heard over the years of entirely too much schooling.

"If you've got an extra rig for me, I'd like to go up with you today," Brad said. "I know Grant prefers to be earthbound, and he'll never let Kate climb without any practice, but I'm ready. You got an extra harness and gear around here?"

"You bet. I was showing Keith Simons how to climb the other day. He's a big guy, probably too big to try it again, but if this harness can hold him, it can sure hold you."

Kate could tell Grant didn't like Brad showing off today. She could almost hear his thoughts. *Brad's sober right now. I can't keep trying to control him even if I am his big brother. He's had a hard time, losing his company. I may be mad at him about hanging out with Lacey, but I've got to keep my mouth shut, especially since we had that big argument night before last.*

They all trooped outside and through the woods toward what Todd called his favorite tree. Amber got a call on her cell and dropped back a bit to talk, so Kate took the hand of Aaron, the middle boy, while Grant carried the toddler, Andy. Their oldest, Jason, kept right up with his dad.

As they got deeper in, Kate saw deadwood had fallen and sprawled over living growth. As if he'd read her mind, Grant explained. "A lot of downed trees from a straight-line wind here two years ago. When nature does it, I don't mind, but I'm still going to find out who cut down my maple. It's just that losing Paul took precedence."

"I understand," she said, but she couldn't really understand why he fought her so hard on further examining Mason Mound. Or did she actually have his long-gone grandfather to blame? Had he made his son and grandson vow never to let someone tamper with their mound? What could have *scairt him bad,* as Sam had said, inside it? She doubted he'd been scared by a cave-in since the exterior seemed intact. Could he have seen decayed corpses inside—even a horrible mask?

"Todd can ID types of trees by the texture of their bark and the smell of their leaves." Grant's voice interrupted her thoughts. "If it wasn't for him, Mason Mill probably wouldn't have branched out—excuse the pun."

"Oh, yeah," Brad said, turning back to get into the conversation. "Here we go with the environment, diversity talk. Okay, you told me to do it, too, with the paper mill and I didn't listen. Save this green goal stuff to get Lacey to back off."

"She's backed off me. How about you?" Grant shot back.

Before this escalated again, Kate interrupted them. "What side products does the mill sell wood for besides furniture?"

"Things made from wood flour," Grant said, still glaring at Brad, who turned his back on them and continued to cart his climbing gear along behind Todd. "That product is basically wood pulverized to dust, bleached and rinsed, which we don't do on-site. Bet you didn't know wood flour's in such things as nondairy milk shakes—water, sugar, flavoring and wood flour. Yum," he said with a chuckle.

"You've got to be kidding."

"It gets weirder than that. Other items we contribute wood pulp, not flour, to are the cups you get your coffee in at places like Starbucks."

"He probably won't mention tampons," Amber said, catching up with them. "And I won't repeat a couple of jokes Todd told me about that. Grant, that phone call—it may be nothing, but a friend of mine says up by where her brother lives on Shadow Mountain, a man keeps a team of big Amish-type horses that come and go in a truck sometimes. Didn't Todd say that you think a draft team might have hauled off your tree?"

"Yeah. Can you give me directions?" he asked. "I'm looking for any lead. No Amish live around here, far as I know, so it's worth looking into."

"Sure, can do" was all she got out before Todd stopped under a huge oak and everyone looked up at its lofty height.

"This is the site of your field trip, boys and girls," he said with a grin as he clapped Brad on the back.

"But, Dad," Jason said, "we only have us boys here, not girls. Mom and Miss Kate are ladies."

Todd grinned as he put his gear down then went to Brad and started to hitch him up. "I've already got climb lines all over this tree, or else we'd have to throw and secure them," he said, as he pulled gear from his backpack.

Again, he demonstrated the Jumar ascenders he'd shown them before, devices with handles a climber could hold and teeth that gripped a rope. Jumars attached to a harness that held the climber around his hips and thighs and kept him from being detached from the rope. Todd then climbed into his harness.

"Do a monkey hang up there today, Dad!" Jason called to him as the two men walked over to the ropes hanging from the tree.

"Not today," Amber chimed in. "Todd, please, no branch-walking, either, even if you have an audience."

"Yes, boss," Todd said and blew her a kiss. "Don't worry. I'm just going to take Brad up a ways and let him look around. Then if Kate is still game, I'll give her a couple of lessons before we climb near the Hear Ye compound. Brad, up we go. Let's convince these groundlings that this is a walk in the park."

"I don't usually watch him climb," Amber whispered to Kate as the men started winching themselves up separate ropes with the help of ascenders. "At least he's been doing this for years without a hitch. He says it's a whole new world up there, but I've just never—never needed that. And now with the kids, no way, however sure-footed he is up there. Grant, I didn't know Brad was such a risk-taker."

"You'd be surprised, especially lately," he said, keeping his voice down and his eyes up.

"Besides drinking? You mean Lacey?" Amber asked.

"Yeah, she's a risk, but he's welcome to her. You know about that?"

"Saw them uptown together. Todd told me that he was afraid Brad was after his job, but Brad assured him he isn't, that the two of them kind of made up for bad feelings."

Kate thought Grant looked relieved.

Amber cried out in a loud voice. "Okay, boys, look at Daddy go!" The two youngest clapped and cheered.

"Just like I drawed you in the tree, Daddy!" Aaron shouted and ran to the tree.

Grant shifted Andy into Amber's arms and retrieved Aaron. "Let's just watch Daddy from over here," he said and tugged the boy away.

"But I can't see him."

Todd, then Brad, had disappeared into the foliage of the tree. Between branches, they appeared again, sometimes standing on them, sometimes—with Brad following Todd's lead—slightly swinging out from the main trunk with their feet on it, then back in again. "Woo-hoo!" Brad's triumphant cry came down to them.

At least this was something Brad could feel good about, Kate thought. He'd finally got something over his big bro, too—literally—high above them all.

Looking up, she felt almost dizzy. She held her breath. Maybe she'd just let Todd climb a tree above Bright Star's commune. It didn't scare her to go underground in small, tight places, but this... She found a new admiration for Brad, despite how she knew Grant was more logical, more like her. After all, there was nothing wrong with caution—up to a point. But when you wanted something so bad, onward you went.

Her neck started to hurt from looking up. Like Amber and Grant, she shifted her position to watch the climbers. They were very high. In that moment she made two decisions. It might be exhilarating, but she was not going to climb a tree, even to spy on Bright Star. She was going to get even closer to Grant. She'd convince him to let her help search for his own big tree, starting with checking on some draft horses up on Shadow

Mountain. But meanwhile, she had to find out why he kept putting her off about Mason Mound—and somehow get inside it.

In a way, watching like this, hearing Brad cheer in exultation, Grant wished he'd climbed with them, but that was Todd's realm, like art had been Paul's. He'd encouraged Brad to do this only because he was hoping he'd find some new strength, a sort of victory, to pull him back from too much booze. And yeah, maybe give him something to do besides lust after Todd's job and Lacey, no matter what Amber had said about him and Todd mending fences. Brad was welcome to Lacey, except Grant didn't want her around if they got serious. All he needed was Brad being converted to a tree hugger, turning against the family business generations before them had built.

"Changed my mind about trying that," Kate told him. The wind blew her hair; her cheeks looked flushed. At this moment—most moments—she was so beautiful, so desirable.

"Good," he told her. "We agree on that, so what's next?"

She smiled, but it looked forced to him. She'd seemed a bit wary of him today, almost cool.

A shout came from above.

He heard Todd's voice. "What in the…? Hang on, hang on! No, not to me! Your rope—the branch…"

Branches snapped, cracked. Very high in the tree, limbs and leaves shuddered and shook. Amber screamed. Grant rushed toward the tree as a body bounced off high branches, hurtling downward.

16

Amber screamed again. Kate threw her arms around her as they both stood transfixed. Grant lunged toward the tree as limbs snapped. Another shout came from above. Brad? He must have fallen.

It seemed an eternity before they saw him—not Brad but Todd—crashing into the branches, clutching at them, bending them. But the last twenty feet were a free fall. Grant ran forward as Todd hit the ground. The two youngest boys started to wail. Kate grabbed them, turned them away while Jason shouted, "Dad! Dad!"

Grant reached Todd first, Amber right behind. He had not fallen headfirst, but sideways.

From above, Brad's panicked voice called out. "Is he all right?"

No one answered him. "He's breathing," Grant said to Amber.

"Oh, dear God, don't let him die. How could he fall? Not Todd!"

"We don't dare move him. Kate! Take Amber's phone and the boys. Go back to the house and call 911 as soon as you get a signal. Tell them we need a chopper. They should land in the grassy field southwest of Pleasant

Drive, and I'll meet them there. Amber. Amber! Give Kate your phone."

Jason ran forward and wrapped his arms around his mother's neck where she crouched beside Todd.

"Jason, listen to me," Grant told the boy. "You have to go with Kate and your brothers to get help for your dad. We'll stay with him. I'm depending on you."

Her face streaming tears, looking stunned, Amber thrust her phone at Kate. "Come on, Jason," Kate cried. "I need your help. Come on, right now."

Sobbing, the boy let go of his mother and turned toward Kate. "Take Aaron's hand and try to keep up," she told him, fighting her own tears. "I'll carry Andy. We have to get your daddy an airplane to take him to the hospital so they can fix him."

"Is his legs broke?" Aaron asked.

She scooped up Andy. "The doctors will take care of him."

Kate stretched her strides, juggling the child and the phone until it stopped searching and took her 911 call. She put Andy down and spoke over his crying. She told the dispatcher what Grant had said, gave Todd's name and address, explained what had happened, gave them her name and Grant's. "In the field southwest of their house," she repeated. "And maybe for a flight to Columbus, not just Chillicothe."

She collapsed on the grass with the three boys huddled to her, all crying, while she tried to cuddle them and tell them everything would be all right. But would it? She could not believe it was Todd who'd fallen and not Brad. How could it have happened? And now would Brad get what he wanted at the mill if Todd was too badly hurt to return to work—or never did?

* * *

"If you can't come down safely," Grant bellowed up at Brad, "just hang on until the volunteer fire department gets here. 911 always sends them, too."

"But is he going to be okay?"

"He's unconscious, looks bad, so just hang on."

"I swear, I don't know what happened! I don't like it up here alone."

Amber hovered over Todd, but Grant kept her from moving him. Who knew what bones could be broken? Grant's eyes stung with unshed tears. His friend looked crumpled. His legs for sure must be broken, maybe his back, however skillfully he'd managed to turn himself so he didn't fall headfirst. But he was unconscious and had a huge bruise rising on his forehead. If it wasn't his imagination, Grant saw Todd move his left foot about an inch from the grotesque position it was in.

Time stretched into eternity. Jace Miller arrived, jogging, his equipment bouncing on his duty belt.

"Got the 911. Saw Kate and the kids on the way in. Can't believe it," he said, bending over them, out of breath. "Not Todd from a tree. I'll have to look at the ropes, his gear. See what happened."

"Brad was with him," Grant said. "He's still up there, so we'll need help to get him down."

"At least he can tell us what happened."

"He says he doesn't know."

What he'd been trying to ignore hit Grant hard. Had someone—surely not Brad—tampered with Todd's gear? He was always so careful. It would take a while to get that harness off him to examine. It would probably go with him to the hospital, where they'd have to cut it off anyway.

While Jace shouted up to Brad, Grant kept his hand on Amber's shoulder where they knelt next to Todd. She was shaking; tears dropped off her chin onto her clasped hands as she kept murmuring prayers.

The minute they heard the chopper, Grant took off running to bring them in from the field. He saw Kate and the boys huddled halfway to the house. In the midst of his panic and fear, an errant thought hit him—she looked like a mother comforting her kids.

He raced into the field, waving his arms. A huge wash of wind rippled the grass and ripped at his hair and clothes. The helicopter set down. Two medics jumped out with a portable stretcher and a med bag. Before the rotors stopped, they ran with Grant toward Todd's favorite tree.

Hours later, still shaken, Kate and Grant slumped at Todd and Amber's kitchen table. It was dark outside, after nine. Amber's parents had arrived, put the boys to bed and would stay the night. Kate and Grant had promised to take the three kids for a while tomorrow to allow the grandparents to drive into Columbus, where Todd had been taken to the Ohio State University Hospital. He was alive—for now. That was all they knew until Amber phoned.

Kate clenched her hands in her lap while Grant got up and paced around the kitchen table. Amber was talking so loud, sounded so frenzied, that Kate could hear her. She recalled how Amber had told her she'd be a basket case if anything ever happened to Todd as it had to Paul. Grant's second close friend to experience tragedy. She prayed Gabe was safe with Tess on their honeymoon.

"Broken ribs...both shoulders...both femurs..." Kate could hear Amber telling Grant. "Spinal cord...not sure but they're doing MRIs and CT scans before surgery... internal injuries. Grant, I just can't believe he fell, not Tarzan Todd. Did Brad get down okay?"

"The volunteer fire guys went up partway and talked him down. Can I help you there? Do you want some company to get through the night?"

"It won't do any good here now. Maybe later. Oh, if you could help my parents with the boys tomorrow, because Mom hasn't been well, and it takes both of them. They're going to come here, bring me some things."

"Listen, you have to take care of yourself so you can take care of Todd while he recovers. And yes, Kate and I already planned to take the boys for a while, no problem."

"I don't know how we'll make it without his salary."

"That's the least of your worries. He has company insurance, not only for injuries on the job but off. He'll get his salary—sick leave, too. Don't worry."

"So I guess—I guess Brad can cover for him," Amber said.

Kate saw Grant's head jerk, as if he'd been so focused on Todd's injuries that he hadn't thought of how Brad would benefit. But Amber was still talking.

"Thank Kate for me. Oh, meant to say, the E.R. doctor said it's a miracle Todd managed to turn himself in the air. You know, falling that far, it's almost always headfirst. Thank God his skull didn't get smashed, too."

Like Paul's, Kate thought. Surely, the two tragedies couldn't be related.

Grant leaned back against the kitchen counter as his gaze met her wide stare. He must know she could hear because she gasped and covered her mouth with both hands.

But it was Grant, who had been so strong through all this, who collapsed in a chair and looked agonized. He didn't even say goodbye, and Amber hung up before Kate could take the phone from his trembling hands.

"Like their ghosts are after us," he whispered to himself, before he jumped up and went into the bathroom down the hall. He closed the door but she could still hear a single, sharp sob.

It was time, Grant thought, to come clean with Kate, at least about some things. Maybe leveling with her about his grandmother would make her realize she had to back off about the mound. After all, Kate had already been "haunted" by thinking she saw the Beastmaster stalking her. At the least, he could explain what he'd said about ghosts, which he'd put her off about last night. She'd let up, probably because they were both so devastated and exhausted.

He didn't want her to think he'd meant there was a curse on Paul and Todd, because she'd try to find out why, keep digging at him since he wouldn't let her dig in the mound. He didn't believe in ghosts or a curse. A fatal crushed skull and a freak accident that could have meant another crushed skull were catastrophes for sure. But even if some of the corpses they'd taken things from in the tomb had their skulls crushed, it was just a scary coincidence. Besides, wouldn't such a crazy theory of ghostly revenge mean Brad or he was next? For sure he had to explain some things to Kate—and to himself.

The two of them took the McCollum kids to McDonald's for Happy Meals, and then he drove them all to the playground on the grounds of the long-deserted Falls County Mental Hospital, which had started life in the 1880s as the Cold Creek Lunatic Asylum. A wealthy businessman who'd been born in Cold Creek had left money in his will for an amazing array of swings, slides and jungle gyms for the disadvantaged children in the area. No way were they going anywhere near the woods today. They all needed open spaces.

"The derelict buildings here give Gabe fits," he told Kate as they pulled into the playground area. "They have Do Not Enter signs, but some people think the old places are haunted and go ghost hunting. Vandals hang out here. Graffiti's everywhere. We need another benefactor to restore some of the old buildings for youth retreats or artists' studios, something. An artists' retreat was Paul's idea. And, I hate to bring this up, but Bright Star's put up a lot of money to buy some of the acreage to expand and further segregate his Hear Ye flock, move them all here."

"An old mental institution sounds like a great place for him and anyone who trusts him, including my cousin Lee and his wife. I'll have to find another way to spy on that cult or pry Grace loose to talk to her."

"Bright Star was turned down at first but made a case, claiming prejudice against religion, so a state-senator friend of mine told me."

Kate just shook her head, and for once, Grant marveled, she didn't have anything to say.

They pushed the kids on the swings and watched them come down twisting slides and crawl through wooden tunnels. "Our best hardwoods," Grant told her. After that the boys wanted to roll down a small hill that was close to the old asylum cemetery. A mound and a cemetery seemed the perfect setup for what he wanted to tell Kate.

Waiting for the right moment, he sat on a bench next to her while little Andy slept with his head in her lap, and his two older brothers ran endlessly up the hill, then rolled down. Again, Grant was struck by how good she was with these kids, how natural. Kate the clever, ever the professional Professor Lockwood, looking like a young wife and mother. Kate, who had assured him just by looking at the hill that it wasn't an Adena mound.

"You asked about my grandmother the other day," he said, his eyes on Jason and Aaron. Shades of him with his friends in their very young days, he thought.

"Yes," she said. They didn't bother to keep their voices down, since the oldest two were whooping up a storm, and Andy hadn't budged. "I can see why you don't know much about her since she died so young."

Where to start? "She died here," he said in a rush.

"Here? What do you mean?"

"Here at the asylum—the mental hospital. Kate, the look you saw in her eyes in that photo in the guest room—she was what we'd call schizophrenic today. She heard and saw things that weren't there."

"Poor woman. Like what?"

"Like what she called Indians coming out of the mound to kill her."

Kate gasped and jerked so hard that Andy stirred. She soothed him. "Delusional about your mound—so close behind her house?"

"Right. The thing was, she had a great-grandmother who was massacred with her family by Indians, the historic ones in these parts. I think that played on her fears."

"So, Grant, did your grandfather ever enter the mound to assure her there was nothing to be afraid of? And was there?"

That sure as hell wasn't the path he wanted this revelation to take. "Look, Kate, all I know about this is what I overheard as a kid. Her so-called insanity wasn't exactly a big topic of family conversation at the dinner table, let alone with friends, but you asked about her earlier, and I wanted you to know."

"Can you tell me more of what you do know?"

"She was admitted to the asylum in the early 1970s, but the care here didn't seem to help her. She had electroshock treatment, and it might have made her worse. In 1974, she broke away from a nurse, ran down a third-floor hall and threw herself over the banister, down the staircase to her death. Broken neck..." His voice caught. "Broken skull, too. I guess my grandfather and dad finally got the caretaker to admit that she was screaming that the savages were after her again. That's about all I know. She just couldn't shut the mound out of her mind—and that really did her in. She obsessed about it, and that wasn't healthy for her."

Kate narrowed her eyes at him. "Why didn't your grandfather move away with her, away from the mound?"

"He did once, moved in with the Custer family, but it didn't help, and he didn't have the ability or money to move her farther away. He needed to stay close to the mill or it would have gone under."

"So *she* went under. You know, it's tragic what people used to call insane. Female patients were often committed in the old days for things like postpartum depression or menopause problems—even epilepsy. She isn't buried here in the cemetery, is she?"

"No. She's in the Mason family plot with Grandpa and my parents not far from where we buried Paul. But I just want you to know the fact that she was haunted by the mound is another reason I want it left intact, untouched—kind of like, in her memory."

"I can't help but wonder if she would have been better off if it was opened and relics or Adena skeletons—if they are there—were taken away."

"Let's take these three home to their grandparents and get a report on how Todd's doing today. I also want to find out if Jace has learned anything after getting the climbing harness back from the hospital. It could have been faulty somehow. The man climbs enough that it could have frayed."

Damn, he hoped that was the case, Grant admitted to himself. Because despite Brad's novice climbing abilities and the fact he was shaken to be left hanging in the tree alone, he had a big motive for hurting Todd. And Todd's shout from the tree ordered Brad not to grab at him....

"Grant, I'm glad you told me about Ada. Of course, her fears could have been linked to the tragedy that befell her own ancestor. I'm so sorry she felt haunted and paid a big price for that. In a way—a more sane way—they haunt me, too," she admitted.

Kate carried Andy while Grant corralled the other two boys, and they headed back to his car. He wasn't sure Kate had gotten the message not to get too involved with Mason Mound, but Kate was Kate and always managed to turn things back on him. He didn't believe in ghosts, but damned if he'd tell her how the mound obsessed him, too, but in a different way. He couldn't let her in there, however much she was working her way into his life and heart.

Even more sobering than that, if an outsider knew the four of them had stolen priceless artifacts from the ancient dead, Grant feared he might be next on someone's hit list.

17

"Hi, darling," Carson said the moment Kate answered her phone. "I got your message and sent a grad assistant over to the library archives to comb old records for any mention of Mason Mound, but no go."

Disappointed, she exhaled hard. It seemed so long ago she'd been his grad assistant, doing his bidding. At least now, he was doing hers—or was it still the other way around?

It was Sunday afternoon, and she'd been changing clothes after church when Carson called. Wearing only her bra and panties, she paced in the bedroom as Carson went on and on about his ideas for a speech he'd been asked to give in California. Now and then, she interjected with pleasantries but her thoughts were elsewhere.

Only she and Grant were in the house, and he'd said he was going to fix them a quick lunch. Brad had attended church, sitting in the back with Lacey and her parents, then had driven off somewhere with her. She'd even picked him up at the house and honked for him to come out like some teenager.

When Carson called, Kate had been staring at the

photo of Grant's grandparents, Hiram and Ada Mason, wishing she could crawl into that picture and go back in time to talk to them. Poor Ada. Kate really empathized with her seeing visions. Her memory of the Beastmaster she thought she'd seen out that smeared garage window was still vivid. Sometimes in the middle of the night, it came at her like flashbacks lit by a flickering strobe. Like Ada, Kate felt haunted.

She cleared her throat and told Carson her search-the-archives idea was just another stab in the dark. "It's how I feel I'm operating around here. I'd love to have a crew tackling the Mason Mound entrance right now."

"Kate, for heaven's sake, you're living with the man who owns and controls it. When he's not around, walk out there, check it out. Especially if it was entered in the last century, and you found the side facing an old water source, you can figure out where the entrance is. Even a little excavation could tell you if it's a horizontal entry shaft, which will make things much easier for us. Meanwhile, if someone made a solo entrance years ago and covered it up, you could, too. If it was dug out once, another entry should be a piece of cake."

"Carson, no way! Grant trusts me. He's helped me, taken me in."

"Evidently, taken you in in more ways than one. We're talking the universal knowledge and preservation of human experience here."

He began to talk about his work again, saying he'd send her a copy of an article he'd published about Etruscan tombs in Italy, that she should read it and "take it to heart."

She sighed as her thoughts drifted again. Carson... Italy...everything but Grant and Cold Creek seemed so far away. She was pretty sure the Mason Mound entry lay behind those hawthorn bushes, which looked either old or ill. They seemed to be dying, so she wouldn't feel too bad about cutting them back some. Since she hadn't noted any others of those spiny trees in the area, could Hiram Mason have planted them there, either to assure poor Ada the mound was sealed—or to make sure no one else entered it after he did? But if she cut her way through them, or asked to dig them out, Grant could tell her to keep away for sure.

Either he was just plain ignorant of the fact his grandfather had entered the mound—and he was not an ignorant man—or he was lying to her, trying anything to keep her from getting into what must be a burial chamber. But she'd been so certain he cared for her. Was that just an act to sway and control her? And was it only because he'd promised his father or grandfather that the dead should stay dead, or was he hiding something else?

"So what are your plans today?" Carson finally asked something that brought her back to reality.

"We just got back from church. With Paul Kettering's funeral this week, I feel like I've been living there."

"Church again. Really? Am I talking to the cosmopolitan, world-traveler, hard-driving, work-on-Sunday Professor Kathryn Lockwood?"

That annoyed her. In the church service, Pastor Snell had led a lovely prayer for Todd's full recovery, which they now knew would take months, maybe longer with casts, a wheelchair, pain and rehab, but at least he was alive and his brain hadn't been damaged. And Kate felt good that she'd helped Amber by calling a friend who lived near campus in Columbus and would let Amber stay with her while Todd was hospitalized nearby so she didn't have to drive back and forth or pay for a place to live there. More of Todd and Amber's relatives had come in to help with the boys, though Kate was surprised to find herself missing Jason, Aaron and Andy. But if she tried to explain that to Carson—or even to herself...

Carson's words cut through her agonizing. "Look, back to business. I'd love to have you excavating that mound, too, but it will happen one way or the other."

"What do you mean by that?"

"I'll find the right senator to get a bill passed to allow the betterment of human knowledge over private-property rights—something to bring pressure to bear on Grant Mason. The Adenas have slept there for centuries, so they can wait for us a little while longer, but I'm relying on you to get us in ASAP. Get Grant to let you at least do a solo entry, if not with all the crew and equipment. Toward that goal, how's it going?"

"Complicated."

"By feelings? His, I hope, and not yours."

She couldn't figure out what to say. What *did* she feel for Grant, for this town, for her new friends here, for those darling McCollum boys? Carson plunged on. "Oh, by the way, I have your faux Beastmaster mask to return to you, now that my best grad assistant's made a copy, so I'll drive down this evening. Dinner? Maybe with you and Grant to chat about the mound?"

She hesitated. "I want the mask back, but—"

"Don't want me back?"

"I didn't say that. Grant and I are helping out with the kids of a friend of his who took a bad fall from a high tree."

"When the mill's loggers were cutting it down? Or

something like that old tree of Grant's you mentioned that was taken?"

"Oh, did I tell you about that? No, this guy climbs for a hobby and was up high giving Brad Mason a climbing lesson. He fell—Todd, not Brad—was gravely injured and is now in OSU Hospital, as a matter of fact."

"That's terrible. So you're babysitting kids? Ha, that's a good one."

"It isn't, not the way you mean. I helped raise my younger sisters, you know. But yes, it is a good thing to do."

"All right, if I'm persona non grata there for now, I'll send my grad student Kaitlyn Blake down with it late tomorrow—and with a copy of my latest article. But I hope you can find a space soon on your backwoods calendar for your mentor—who wants to be much more to you. But, Kate, I'm trusting you to get us into that mound, get *yourself* into that mound at the very least. If it's complicated, you're good at finding your way through the maze. Call me for an update when you can see the—sorry for putting it this way—the forest for the trees."

"I hear you, Professor."

But the truth was, for the first time in the twelve years she'd known Carson Cantrell, she was going to do things—though things he wanted—her way.

The minute Kate joined Grant in the kitchen for lunch, he had news for her. "I think I've got a lead on how you can check on Grace Lockwood and what she might have meant by drawing a star on her chest when you saw her in Bright Star's inner sanctum."

Despite the fact the weather was gloomy and threatened rain, they were planning a ride up Shadow Mountain to search for the team of draft horses there—and who owned them and why in such a rocky, gravelly area. But her stomach flip-flopped to hear he had a lead on how to get to Grace.

"Tell me. Can we go today?"

"Not so fast. On the Sabbath, you just try to talk to a Hear Ye convert about anything but what Bright Star's preaching. No, Keith Simons, who works for me at the mill, may be our missing link."

"The big guy who also doubles as your bodyguard when needed?"

"The same. He's become a friend." He put the plate of bread, cold cuts and cheese on the table where the two of them sat across from each other. "I remembered he told me last week he's having a fence repaired on his property, and your cousin Lee's doing the work. So if you dropped in around lunchtime tomorrow—with me—at the Simons place, maybe you could talk to Lee at least, find out about what Grace was trying to say."

"Great, though I'd rather talk to Grace. Lee seems to be really closed up, whereas she— I don't know. Is he working there without another Hear Ye member? I'd want to talk to him alone. Can you set it up for tomorrow?"

"Whoa! We'll have to play it partly by ear, but I'll call Keith, and we'll see."

"And please tell his wife I'll bring lunch from somewhere uptown. She shouldn't have to feed us over this. Isn't Keith the brother of the police dispatcher Gabe used to date? Tess told me Gabe arrested one of their brothers, a guy who worked for you."

"True, but despite his siblings' hating Gabe's guts

and evidently blaming me, too, Keith's been my right-hand man after Todd. Keith stuck with me loyally when Jonas was sent to prison and Ned, another brother, quit the mill. Keith may seem like a man of few words, but the guy's ambitious and sees everything. If I have Brad fill in for Todd—and it looks like I'll have to do that—Keith will be a big help to him. As for his wife, Velma, in true Appalachian style, I'm sure she won't take to guests bringing their own vittles, so you'd better just take her a present afterward—not right then if we go there for lunch. Speaking of which, eat up right now. So much has happened I haven't been able to track my tree any more than you've been able to get to Grace alone, so let's hustle here."

He winked at her, which made her spirits soar. Despite all he and they had been through, Grant had a solid core of strength that emanated from him. Like a tall tree with deep roots, one, hopefully, that could not be cut down as two of his best friends had been.

On the half-hour drive up Shadow Mountain, Grant and Kate discussed Todd's accident again. As upsetting as that was, Grant thought, it was better than the topic of his wanting to keep Mason Mound untouched.

Jace Miller had retrieved Todd's harness from the hospital and checked it over. He'd said a thorough examination didn't reveal if the snags, two large tears and several cuts had occurred before or during his fall. To complicate things, the emergency-room team didn't recall how many of those they had made when they'd cut it off Todd. According to Brad, Todd had seen some problem and had tried to shift himself onto another rope, but *something just gave way*. That something had been Todd's harness, not the rope, as Jace had first suspected. Though Todd had regained consciousness in the hospital after his surgery, he couldn't recall any details about the climb or his fall. His last memory was walking up to the tree with everyone.

Considering how skilled Todd was at climbing, Grant was afraid someone could have tampered with his harness. Jace had interrogated Brad, but Brad had no access to Todd's gear and basically didn't know what he was doing. Despite having a motive to get rid of Todd, Jace had ruled the accident just that, and Grant agreed. However much Brad wanted the foreman job at the mill, he would not have hurt their old friend to get it, nor would he have chanced leaving himself dangling high in a tree.

Since Jace was busy with an investigation into Paul's death and Todd's accident, Grant hadn't even mentioned that he was going to follow a possible lead about draft horses in a field up on this mountain.

"You might know," Kate said, "this place is called Shadow Mountain, like someone's hiding in the shadows who could have taken your tree. Even though the rain's letting up, this place reminds me of something from the Brothers Grimm, where there's a witch in the forest and an ogre under the bridge."

Grant shook his head. "That sure cheers me up, Kate. Gabe said arresting the local timber thieves would be his top priority when he's back. But it won't be now since so much has happened. I can't believe it's been nine days since my maple was butchered, so the trail may have gone cold. Still, the idea of a team of draft horses up here, where the ground can't be tilled, is worth a look."

"Have you been driving around anywhere else, looking for traces or clues of other tree thefts, or leaving it up to Gabe?"

"All of the above, but we've found nothing. So far, that is, but I'm not giving up, especially now with what I see as a direct challenge to me—revenge, even. I don't know. But there are so many old barns, wild woodlots and deserted places in these foothills and the Appalachians beyond that it's needle-in-a-haystack time."

As Grant drove them upward in his truck, the wet, twisting road became a single lane with sporadic pull-offs so vehicles could pass. He could tell Kate tried not to look over the steep sides when the view was straight down. "Plateau coming up here," he told her. "I'd give you a hug, but need both hands on the wheel."

"I'm fine."

"That you are."

The lay of the land slanted less steeply with a log-fenced, grassy field near the area Amber had mentioned. As they drove past a small farm with chickens and goats in ramshackle pens, Grant recalled who lived around the next bend in the road.

Lacey's parents had a summer home—actually, a fairly crude log cabin—up here. Could that mean anything? But Lacey was into protecting trees.

"It didn't hit me at first," he said. "A little farther on, Lacey's folks have a small retreat—not much of one, probably, by your standards. Kind of a hunting cabin. It's just through that stretch of trees."

She sat up straighter, turned toward him. "Can there be some link to them and the horses? I saw her folks in church. They're not that old-looking, like they could handle large horses and chain saws. Do they hold a grudge against you for divorcing her?"

"*She* divorced *me,* and that was for the best for me, too. Her mother kept her mouth shut, but I heard she took my side and said Lacey was flighty and the two of them quarreled. Her father—she was a Daddy's girl— reacted just the opposite, so he blamed me. I used to think he might come down and take potshots at my picture window."

"What occupation was her dad in? Not a competitor to the mill?"

"Worked in a sporting-goods store halfway to Chillicothe. He was known for getting the biggest bucks during hunting season—always proud of having his picture in the *Chillicothe Gazette.* Look, it's obvious this field is empty, and that tiny shed won't hold more than those goats and chickens, but I want to stop and check the field anyway."

"You're looking for, let's say, relics or artifacts that big horses would have left behind even if they've been moved on?"

"You got it."

He pulled over and got out at the edge of the log- fenced field where it was shaded by a woodlot. In the light swirl of mist, Kate got out and followed him to the fence. Shorter than he was, she climbed on the lower rail and looked over.

"I smell it," he said. "Horses—and a rat."

"Me, too. And look, I see the horses' calling cards in the grass. Someone might have moved the horses, but they could hardly clean this big field."

"The hill folk call those 'horse apples.' So the draft horses were here and they've been moved—maybe for their next job hauling off a big tree. Let's look around behind the outbuildings. My tree would be too big to hide intact, but maybe the thieves are cutting the trunk and limbs up here then moving them. Watch where you step."

"No kidding."

They ducked through the fence logs and stuck close to it where the grass seemed to be just grass. "Where's the farmhouse?" she asked, keeping her voice down, though she wasn't sure why. "It's just a few run-down outbuildings?"

"I think it burned years ago, so the goats and chickens we saw may be a cover."

The minute they walked behind the cluster of ramshackle buildings, they saw Grant was right. The ground was littered with so many wood chips, trails of sawdust and abandoned sawhorses that Grant swore and Kate gasped.

He bent to pick up some of the bigger chips. "Bird's-eye maple," he said, giving her one of the pieces with the distinctive pattern. "*My* bird's-eye maple, damn them."

"But who is *them?* At least next time someone reports trees taken, you, Gabe and Jace will know where to look for them to be cut up."

"But I want the bastards now."

"Believe me, I understand. It's hard to have patience when you want something so close—want it now and—"

Something pinged past them into the shed. Wood splinters peppered them. A loud crack seemed to echo from afar. Kate squealed as Grant yanked her down and threw himself on the ground beside her. The air slammed out of him; he tasted sawdust. Though it happened so fast, everything seemed to go into slow motion.

"Bullets!" he said, throwing an arm over her and

shoving her head down when she lifted it. "Maybe from the woodlot. And it's not somebody after deer!"

Kate was as angry as she was scared. Two more bullets whizzed past them, and then one struck so close, wood chips hit them and she got sawdust in her eyes.

"Mist or not, he's getting the range," Grant muttered. "We're going to roll into that shed. Keep your head down. Go!"

She did as she was told with him so close behind that his elbow hit hard into her ribs. The boards were worn with spaces between them, and she feared this ramshackle shed would be no protection.

Grant half shoved, half dragged her behind what must have been an old feed trough. She blinked back tears to get rid of the sawdust burning her eyes.

He hunched down beside her. "I thought there might be a door out the back so we can get into the woodlot and run for the truck. Stay down. This wood's so old I'm going to make us a way out."

"The shots have stopped. Maybe he's gone away."

"Or is changing positions to get at us better." He sat on the floor and kicked at some low boards that looked half rotted. He made a hole, then kicked at it to make it larger. "We can't stay trapped in here. I'll go out first in case he's moved around this side, but I think the shots were distant. Hope he doesn't have a scope. If it's clear, you come right behind me. Belly-crawl."

"But if he's in the woodlot…"

"Trees may be his friends, but they're ours, too. We can't run clear to the truck in the open."

With a grunt, he crawled out on his elbows and stomach. She could see only his feet as he stood, obviously making himself a target. First Paul, she thought, then Todd and now...

She held her breath, every muscle tensed, fearing another shot. Nothing.

"Now!" His voice came to her, and she crawled out, somehow snagging the back of her belt on one of the broken boards. Grant reached down and hauled her out, then to her feet. "Go!" he told her. "I'm right behind you. Run zigzag."

They ducked through the old log fence and sprinted into the woodlot. Grant pressed her against the trunk of a big tree away from the direction of the shots. Her cheek and breasts pressed against the rough bark with his big body as strong as the tree tight against her back and butt.

The woods seemed quiet now but for the breeze rustling the branches, bird calls and their hard, rhythmic breathing. Damp foliage sputtered drops on them, but it wasn't misting in here. Strange, but held so close by Grant like this, she almost forgot to be afraid.

"What's your best guess?" she whispered.

"For the shooter or his position?"

"Both."

"I think he was far enough to the north that he can't have worked his way behind us yet. Remember those old cowboy movies where they darted from tree to tree?"

"Cowboy movies? I was hooked on *Indiana Jones and the Temple of Doom*."

"I don't want to hear the word *doom*. I'm going first. You follow—if you don't hear another shot. If so, get flat on the ground again."

Still in a zigzag pattern, he went tree to tree with her right behind him. No noise but crows cawing. They worked their way toward the road and made a dash for his truck. He gunned the engine to pull away up the hill.

"Can we turn around somewhere and go back down?" she asked. They hadn't even taken time to fasten their seat belts, and the warning buzzer kept sounding.

"Hate to say it, but I'm going to stop at Lacey's folks' place so we can call Jace. Pretty soon he'll stop taking our calls at all."

"I think we should turn around at their place, go back down, get out of here then call Jace."

"You're not in charge right now, sweetheart!"

"You mean our cell phones won't work up here? But we're so high."

"Lacey's folks have one of the few landlines up here, which will surprise you when you see their small place."

"But if they're not there, you aren't going to break in, are you?"

"Nope. Then we'll go to plan B. As you know, I don't approve of people breaking in—and that's not a reference to Paul's place."

She knew he meant the mound, and it upset her even more that he thought a careful archaeological excavation was like breaking in.

Still wiping sawdust from the corners of her eyes, she saw where they were going, maybe a half mile ahead. The light rain had almost stopped, but the pavement was still wet. A small log cabin stood on a rise with trees behind but not in front. It must have a stunning view of the valley far below, maybe clear to Cold Creek from the steep drop-off across the narrow road. As they got closer, she saw an old pickup parked there and, next to it, the car Lacey had driven earlier today. So both Lacey's father and Brad had been within shooting range. At least, she thought, if Lacey's parents were here, too, they weren't going to barge in on Brad and Lacey in bed together.

Grant muttered something she couldn't decipher, so maybe he was thinking the same thing. She was going to suggest he turn back again, but the back window shattered. Kate screamed. A second shot evidently struck a tire, because as Grant hit the brakes, the truck started to spin wildly toward where the road met nothing but gray sky.

18

The last person on earth Kate wanted to see when she opened her eyes was bent over her, dabbing at her forehead with a damp cloth. Lacey Fencer. A cloud of clove scent hit her. Oh, the woman was chewing reddish gum.

Suddenly, she remembered. Grant's truck had spun out on the road. Had they gone over the cliff? No, she was obviously in the Fencer cabin and wasn't in pain except for her head. But as she gazed above Lacey, a horrible animal face with horns glared down at her. Was she hallucinating again, like when she'd seen—or thought she'd seen—the Beastmaster?

No, it was a stag head mounted on the wall over the narrow couch where she lay, one like in Todd's living room. Did everyone decorate this way around here?

"Where's Grant?" she managed to ask.

"He's here," Lacey said. "Both of your air bags deployed. He's washing up in the bathroom. You lost consciousness, but he didn't."

"But is he okay?"

"He is. The truck isn't. He chose to put it against a tree instead of taking flight. He says you weren't tailing Brad and me."

Kate put a hand to her head. Yeah, it hurt. She was a little dizzy. "We were looking for his stolen maple tree and found where it was cut up. Got shot at," she said.

"So's we hear," came a male voice as a grizzled face appeared behind and above Lacey's to block out the stag head. Lacey's father, Kate thought. She might not think much of the woman, but at least she must have a good relationship with her father. Kate recalled he had blamed Grant for his daughter's divorce and, Grant said, was likely to shoot out his picture window. At least her head was clear, even if every muscle in her body ached, and the skin on her face felt sunburned, evidently from the air bag.

Kate heard Brad's voice. "Grant, I can't believe you found where the tree-house maple was cut up or that it was up here. Clemmet, you have an idea on who could have done that over there?"

"Or who could have fired at us?" Grant asked. "Someone who's either not that good a shot or just wanted to scare us off—except for that bullet in the tire."

"Don't you go lookin' at me, boy," Clemmet Fencer said. "If'n I was the one shooting, I'd of hit you. Folks here 'bouts can tell you I been on these grounds, not a runnin' through some woodlot. And know nothing about someone takin' or cuttin' up some tree neither— though some skunk cut our phone wires."

"Yeah, the phone's dead, all right," Brad said. "At least Grant and Kate aren't, but you two have got to quit getting into trouble."

"Yeah, and you should talk," she heard Grant mutter.

For a man of few words, as Grant had described Lacey's father, he'd given quite a speech, Kate thought. She leaned on her elbows and sat up. A wave of dizziness hit her as the cabin seemed to tilt, then righted itself.

This small living room had no ceiling; she could see clear to the rafters. There appeared to be a sleeping area partitioned off as well as a small bathroom and, across the way, a small galley kitchen by the back door. It was bright—lots of windows to take advantage of the view.

Grant came over and leaned down close to her. Lacey almost jumped off the edge of the couch and moved over by Brad at the small table where her parents now sat. Kate saw Grant's clothes were dirty and torn; hers must be, too. No wonder Lacey was washing her face. She was probably a mess.

"Like they said, someone cut their phone line here, so we can't call Jace yet," Grant told her. "I'll drive you to the doctor's in Cold Creek for a checkup. I don't like it that it's the second time you've hit your head. I'll have to call the doc to come into his office since it's late."

"I'm all right," she insisted. "But is your truck okay?"

"Except for a shot-out tire, a blasted window and a scraped, dented driver's side. We'll call Jace when we get down the mountain. Brad's going to help me change the flat tire so I can drive. You just rest here, and I'll be back soon."

"I told you Lacey and I can drive you down, Grant," Brad said.

Grant ignored that. He squeezed her shoulder and stroked the backs of his fingers gently against her cheek before standing. She felt he was leaving her in the lion's den. She'd rather help change the tire, but maybe she could get something out of the Fencers about who might have shot at them—and taken Grant's tree.

* * *

"Just sit down and rest if you're woozy," Brad told Grant as he dug the jack and other tools out of the box from the bed of Grant's truck. "I can handle this."

"I'm just shook up. I'll help."

"My sentiments exactly—I'll help. Here and at the mill. Look, Grant, I swear I'll just try to support you and hold Todd's position for him until—if—he gets better."

They squatted by the back driver's-side tire, jacked up the truck, and then Brad pried the dented hubcap off. "Don't talk about *if,*" Grant insisted. "Can you imagine Todd in a wheelchair or partially paralyzed? Operations and rehab have to bring him back, even if he never climbs again. But yeah, I can use your help at the mill. Here, I'll help you unscrew the lug nuts. And Keith can help you oversee the mill floor when I'm not available."

"You going somewhere?"

"Hope not. But doesn't the fact that Paul, then Todd had tragedies, then I almost did, make you nervous?"

"You mean like we're targets? Like there's some curse on us for taking stuff from the tomb?"

"So you thought of that, too? Nadine told me you asked her if you could help her go through Paul's stuff. You're wondering where his eagle pendant's hidden, aren't you?"

"Yeah, aren't you? The guy was having financial problems and then with Nadine's medical treatment on the horizon... What if he sold it to a middleman, a fence, or whoever he consulted, and that guy came back to see if he had more?"

"Yeah. I know." Grant knew that Paul wasn't the only one having financial problems. Brad was desperate to bail out his business, but the conversation just couldn't

go there. He couldn't get his mind around the idea that
Brad would hurt Paul or Todd to get his hands on their
artifacts to sell. Brad was his little brother. Surely, he
would never deceive him like that? Grant decided he
had to make sure Brad's big arrowhead was where he
must have hidden it, under that pile of stones Kate had
spotted. The grave of his nonexistent pet dog.

"Okay, let's lift the wheel off together," Brad said as
they pulled the flat tire away from the axle. "Speaking
of together, you and the professor have a thing going?"

"No, don't roll that tire over the side!" Grant told him,
grabbing his arm. "I want Jace to check it for bullets."

"Even if it matches a shotgun or hunting rifle—even
if it matches the one Lacey's dad has—he might hate
your guts, but he wasn't out of the cabin shooting at anything, including you. Or cutting his own phone lines. I
can vouch for that."

"And he and Lacey can vouch for you. Speaking of
together…" Grant said as he reached for the spare tire.
"You and Lacey?"

"You think she'd stay in Cold Creek for anyone?
Though ultimately my goal is to get out of here, too.
And I suppose Professor Kate Lockwood wouldn't be
happy living here, either, right?"

"Right," Grant admitted, but he wished he could say
wrong.

That evening Kate had dinner for Grant pretty well
under control, which was a good thing because she felt
exhausted, as if she'd run for miles. They'd made it back
down the mountain—slowly—in Grant's beat-up truck.

The local doctor had come into his office and checked
her over. No concussion this time, he said. She'd just

blacked out. Then they'd driven directly to see Jace, even though they'd looked as if they'd rolled down the mountain.

Jace, spending Sunday afternoon at his office, had said he'd send the two bullets from the tire to BCI for ballistics analysis, but that could take a while. He promised he'd also try to retrieve other bullets on-site. But it was a tense exchange between Grant and Jace that had really bothered Kate:

Grant had told Jace not to waste time interviewing Clemmet Fencer or Brad. They'd just alibi each other—as would the women. "Besides, I believe Brad."

"Maybe that's a bad move," Jace had said, sounding more uptight than Kate had felt. "Your little brother keeps turning up at the site of crimes, Grant, or at least could have been there. If I hear his name tied to one more thing, I— Listen, I don't mean to jump the gun here, but are you sure he's on your side?"

And he'd said something else that had really shaken her up: "You don't see a trend here, do you, Grant? I mean, could the shooter have been aiming for your head? After Paul's skull was crushed, then the E.R. doc kept saying that Todd was the first patient he'd seen who had fallen more than twenty feet who didn't go head-first and crush his skull, I mean…"

"No," Grant had said and reached out to hold her upper arm as if to steady her. "Kate's the one who's hit her head, but she's all right."

Now Kate raked her fingers through her hair, which she'd finally gotten clear of sawdust, leaf litter and dirt. She'd taken a long, hot shower and washed her hair after they'd left Grant's truck at the local body shop and Jace had driven them home. She jumped when the doorbell rang. Brad wouldn't ring it, and Grant was taking a shower. Jace back again with something new?

In her cutoffs and T-shirt, she went to the door and looked out through the peephole. She was surprised to see almost a mirror image of herself—her younger self, anyway—standing on the front porch with a big box in her arms. The woman looked more like she could be her sister than either Tess or Char. She wore skinny jeans and an Ohio State scarlet-and-gray sweatshirt. Oh, must be Carson's graduate assistant returning her Beastmaster mask, but hadn't he said she'd come late tomorrow?

Kate opened the door, and before she could ask, the girl blurted out a greeting. "Hi, I'm Kaitlyn Blake, Professor Cantrell's GA. I have your Celtic mask and I tried to copy it exactly for him to use in his Indigenous Native Americans class, but I think you did a great job with it and I've read all your Adena-Celtic articles. Very convincing!"

"Kaitlyn, won't you step in? I got confused, thought you were coming tomorrow."

"I was, but I have to help grade exams then, and I was eager to meet you. Actually, I mean—I hope helping the professor will get me started on my own great career, just like you. I've been researching Etruscan tombs but I'd love to get inside an Adena one."

Kate's mind raced. Kaitlyn even had a similar first name and echoed Kate's primary goal. She took the box from her, put it on the entry-hall table and opened the lid carefully. The Beastmaster mask she'd made so long ago glared up at her despite its empty eye sockets. Its stag antlers she'd worked so hard to find were intact. The mica-chip skin glittered despite the dimness of the hall. As glad as she was to have it back, the thing unsettled her, and she put the lid back on quickly.

"I know you're busy," Kaitlyn said, "but I was just wondering if I could see the Adena mound that Professor Cantrell said is on this property, maybe just the entrance to it, even."

Right, Kate thought. Carson must have told her to say that. Or did he? When she was Kaitlyn's age, she was so eager to make discoveries, to prove things, to take steps to make a name for herself in the well-trodden field of archaeology—just like now.

"You can see it really well from this picture window back here, but I can't take you out closer. When I get the chance to excavate it, I'll remember to ask for you on the dig crew, if you're available," Kate said as they stared in silence, almost a mutual reverence, at the mound.

Kaitlyn sighed and gazed through the glass. Even if this woman had been sent here as Carson's spy—or if she was a new-tread replacement for the eager ingenue Kate had once been—she understood this girl's aspirations and ambitions.

They spoke awhile longer. Kate offered her a glass of iced tea, which she turned down, and then she showed her out. And when Kate returned to the living room with the box in her arms, she gasped to see Grant, leaning in the hallway, arms crossed over his chest, frowning at her. Somehow, instantly, she knew he'd been there for a long time, had seen and heard her with Kaitlyn.

"She looks like—acts like—your clone, doesn't she?" he asked, his voice hard.

"You should have said something. I would have introduced you." She felt like a kid who had been caught with someone else's property in her hands.

"I'll leave her to Professor Carson Cantrell, who obviously likes auburn-haired, green-eyed beauties as his assistants. Since you told her you'll have her back on a dig crew and that's not likely to happen, I'll probably never get to meet her. But it's interesting to hear you have plans for a dig here."

"I didn't mean it that way. I wanted to encourage her. She just brought back the Beastmaster mask I made. Carson had her copy mine so he'd have hers to show his classes."

If it was possible, Grant looked even angrier. His square jaw set hard. The furrow between his brows deepened.

"Would you like to see the mask?" she asked.

"The drawing you had was bad enough. That nightmare I had, remember? If you have to keep it around here, hide it from me—I mean, just keep it in your room. I don't see why you needed it here."

He strode past her and went into the kitchen, where she heard him slam a cupboard, then pull back his chair and sit down hard. She went into her bedroom and put the box under her bed, then went into the kitchen and started to ladle out the three-cheese macaroni she'd made from scratch because he'd mentioned that he'd loved it as a kid. She put his plate down next to the tossed salad and the zucchini bread, put her own plate down a bit too hard.

"I'm sorry if I upset you," she said, grabbing her fork in her right hand, ready to stab it into the salad.

How many meals had she seen in her childhood that had started like this between her parents before Dad left them? Hostile silence at the meal, unspoken bad feelings, banging tableware, stomping out. But her father hadn't loved her mother then, she was sure of that, or he would have broken the dreadful silence, reached out to her.

Tears sprang to her eyes as Grant reached across the table, loosened her fingers from her fork. He held her hand, silent for a while. Even if their meal was getting cold, she knew something important was coming. He was probably going to ask her to leave. To go back to Tess's house, get far away from his mound and stay away. He was going to desert her.

"Sorry, sweetheart," he said, his deep voice catching. "It's just so much has happened lately that I'm a mess, and I don't mean to take it out on you. The meal looks great. Comfort food—and your company—is exactly what I need to keep myself sane going through all this."

Passion and trust and messed-up parents and danger aside, that was, Kate knew, the exact moment when she realized that Grant really did care for her. And that she loved him.

19

After dinner, Kate and Grant drove to Columbus to visit Todd and Amber at the hospital. They'd thought about taking Jason, but Amber said Todd looked pretty bad, and they'd better wait on that.

They drove along the Olentangy River, which ran through the sprawling Ohio State campus near the cluster of large hospital buildings. "This area must be really familiar to you after the years you spent here," Grant said. "I thought about going to OSU, but opted for the smaller Ohio U."

"A lot of good times here, a lot of hard work, dreams and hopes," she said as her gaze drifted from the distant, huge football stadium to the tall main library building.

"Was Carson Cantrell your favorite prof?"

"I must admit he was. Still is, I guess."

"You guess?"

"He's been my mentor, my sounding board and champion for years. I owe him a lot. He believed in me from the first and opened doors for me."

"And now that must be the case with him and—what's her name?—Kate Blake?"

"Kaitlyn, but I get your point. I'm not an idiot, Grant."

"Far from it. The fact she resembles you—and seems so, well, bright and ambitious—could just be a coincidence."

"The thing is, I understand her, can't dislike her. She's more like me than Tess or Char in looks, head and heart."

He drove toward the hospital. "So you don't think she's a setup. A participating or even an innocent go-between for you and Carson, reporting in to him, someone on his side."

She turned in her seat belt to face him full on. "Grant, *I'm* on Carson's side. We both agree that archaeological discovery is an important endeavor for all mankind. You've heard if we don't learn from the past, we're condemned to repeat it. I believe that."

He frowned. The car interior dimmed as he turned into the parking garage, where he stopped and punched the button to take a timed ticket and make the gate lift. She thought he'd say she should forget plans for the mound again, but he didn't. "If it's okay with you, I'd like to talk to Todd alone for a little while tonight."

"Of course. I'll show the pictures the boys drew for him to Amber, and she can show them to Todd if she thinks it's a good thing to do. Jason's was pretty awful. He may need some counseling to get over seeing his father fall. He's imagined it in a different way. He drew the injured figure on the ground with his arm cut from some sort of handleless ax head with blood all over. I didn't even see any blood on Todd. I hope Jason hasn't been allowed to watch one of those ax-murder or slasher movies."

As they drove upward through the spiraling levels of the garage, Grant looked stunned. She could almost hear the cogs of his mind clicking, and it surely wasn't just over finding a parking spot in this crowded place.

"Grant?"

"Yeah, I'll talk to Jason tomorrow. I didn't see that drawing, only the scribbles from the younger two. Show it to me in the lobby before we go up to his room, okay?"

Once they were inside the hospital, Kate pulled the drawing out of her big purse and extended it to him. "Strange, huh?" she prompted when he just stared at it, silent and frowning. She couldn't believe it, but this big, solid man's hands were shaking. He almost rattled the paper before he thrust it back at her.

"Yeah, weird, but pretty good art," he said.

"Especially the detail on that oversize ax head. Definitely looks like an Indian one, but he's drawn it so large. Wherever he got this idea, it made an impression on him."

"Maybe we have a fledgling artist who will pick up where Paul left off someday."

"The ax is probably something his grandfather showed him, along with those sheriff's badges that went missing. Maybe he thought it was an arrowhead. Back to cowboys and Indians. That sort of artifact's been found in our area at home, only much smaller."

She could tell his smile was forced as he took her elbow, and they started toward the bank of elevators. "A Shawnee Indian relic probably," he said and punched the elevator button hard. "And I like the way you said *in our area at home.*"

"I did, didn't I? But I'm glad you're going to talk to Jason because there's a lot of fear in that drawing. Out

West, Char has the Navajo kids draw to get them over violent domestic situations where their parents drink and fight. And Tess said she drew some pretty strange stuff after her captivity when she was getting some counseling."

She stopped talking as others got in the elevator with them. Funny, she thought, how modern life put strangers so close together in small spaces, as if they were intimate. Everyone stopped talking and didn't really look at each other as the elevator went up. Kate said a little prayer that, since she and Grant were getting closer every day, he would continue to open up more, but it always seemed he was holding something back.

They both hugged Amber, and she gave them a progress report on Todd. "He's awake and alert, but still, like he told me, not out of the woods," she explained, "and I think he meant saying it that way as a joke. But he's angry, mostly at himself."

Amber and Kate went down the hall to the waiting room. Amber had said Grant should go on in to Todd's room. Grant shuffled over to the elevated bed framed by monitors and racks with dangling IV tubes.

Todd was staring at the ceiling as if he could see something there. His narrow-eyed gaze darted to Grant. "Yo, best bud and boss."

"You bet I'm still your boss, and I need you back as soon as you can get around at all."

There was a chair next to the bed, but Grant stood, leaning over so he could see his friend, who lay flat on his back. Both legs were in casts. One arm was in traction, the other in a cast, elbow to wrist with his black-and-blue fingers sticking out. He was bare-chested, his ribs wrapped with tape. His bruises were every hue from black to pale green, and scratches crisscrossed his bare skin, including his face. Grant tried not to let his dismay register on his own face.

Todd looked up at him through swollen, purplish eyelids. "I can't believe I fell. I never fall."

"A freak accident? I'd give you a hug or a high five but later, when you're better."

"Don't try to cheer me up. I'm not a patient man, Grant. Not a good patient in general. For the family's sake, I'm grateful to still be here." He spoke slowly, taking shallow breaths and almost whispering. Grant leaned closer to hear. It obviously hurt even to talk.

"Listen, we'll help with the boys," Grant tried to reassure him. "Kate's amazingly good with them. They sent you some drawings that Kate's showing Amber. Jason drew your fall—but with an ax head cutting your arm with lots of blood, so he's mixed that up somehow. He drew it big, Todd, too big to be a normal ax head or a pioneer or historic Indian one a kid would find."

Todd screwed his eyes shut, then opened them. "So, you recognized it after all this time? He found it last winter where I had it squirreled away in the attic. Somehow, he managed to cut himself on it. There was a lot of blood, and I had to assure him he wouldn't die before we got him stitched up. I told Amber I'd found it in the woods, that it was Cherokee or Shawnee, and she never questioned it. Did Kate recognize it in the drawing as Adena?"

"No, thank God."

"She still has no idea you—we've—been in the mound?"

"Look, I didn't mean to get into all this. You need your rest and—"

"I need to talk, Grant! To figure out how I could have fallen. It's all I've been able to think about—that and worrying about the family without me. I swear my harness must have been cut and not by me!"

"Calm down. You heard that Jace cleared Brad—"

"Yeah, I know. Gotta admit he didn't know what the heck he was doing, and I mostly took him up thinking that would get you to climb with me sometime. I was keeping an eye on him before we went up—then can't recall the climb itself at all. But just in case something goes wrong with another operation to set my bones or something—Grant, pretend I'm grabbing your hand right now, and we're making a life-or-death promise. I'm going to tell you where the Adena ax head is, just in case someone wants to kill me."

"That might be true of Paul's case, but you had an accid—"

"Just listen. With my broken ribs, it hurts like hell when I breathe, let alone talk. I wedged and nailed the ax head in a wooden case way up in a crotch of my tree where no one can get to it but me—and now maybe never again. But if something happens to me, promise you'll get a climber to retrieve it and see Amber gets it. I swear, if she'd sell it, she could put all three kids through college. She can just say she found it. Promise me!"

"You're going to make it, Todd. You're going to be in a wheelchair for a while and rehab, but you'll be tooling around the mill floor in no time. But as for climbing again…"

"I will. I swear I will. And please promise me—only

if I don't make it—Amber gets the ax head, and you'll help her sell it on the sly."

He gasped—either for air or in pain—and started to cough, moaning. Grant pushed the red button by the side of his bed, and a nurse came running in.

"He's been talking too long," she said, assessing the situation. "He's not to become overly animated. Now, Todd, I've told you to keep calm, or we'll have to increase the dose of morphine. Then it will be off to dreamland."

"Bad dreams. Don't want that," Todd muttered as Grant moved back and put his arms around Kate and Amber, who had heard the alarm and come rushing in. He and Kate stepped out into the hall and could hear Amber speaking soothingly to Todd.

"So much for visiting and comforting him," Grant whispered.

"What got him so riled? Worried about his job again?"

"He's upset he fell, can't believe he fell."

Kate, still clutching the sheaf of crayoned drawings, leaned against him and stayed silent for once, not one word. Now, he thought, at least he knew where Todd's relic from the death chamber was, high in the air, higher than the attic where Jason had cut himself on it. And all this had made Grant decide to keep looking for Paul's eagle pendant, and Brad's arrowhead, starting under that pile of stones in the woods. Because, despite the fact Kate had missed the clue in Jason's drawing, all he needed was for her to get on the scent of anything coming out of that mound, most of all the Beastmaster mask in the basement right under the room where she slept.

* * *

Grant and Kate were exhausted. They fell asleep on the couch where he'd been holding her, legs and arms entangled as they talked about everything but the mound, which lay dark and silent, outside the window.

After she'd gone to bed, Grant sat back down, looking out, waiting for her light to go off. A wan shaft of gold threw itself onto the lawn until she finally turned it off. Fighting sleep himself, he sat there for another half hour, then tiptoed to the basement door.

He quietly closed it behind himself, turned on the light and tiptoed down in his bare feet. How crazy that she'd brought a Beastmaster mask into the house, even one she'd made herself. He hadn't even wanted to look at it, but he had to grimace at the thought that the two masks could escape their boxes and meet at night in the house—to mate.

Man, he was losing it. Exhausted. Conflicted. Scared.

He went through the ritual of getting the box out of the wall, setting aside Kate's business card. He opened the box, pulled away the tissue paper. The mica chips on the skin gleamed in his flashlight glow; the dried blood on the spiked points of the ancient stag antlers seemed to move in shifting shadows. Maybe after all these years, he should put it back in the death chamber. Put Todd's back, too, and Brad's, if it was under that pile of stones. If he could find Paul's eagle pendant, return that, too. Then he could let Kate excavate the mound, remove the bodies, the precious relics—the burden and curse of the place. But to enter the mound, he'd have to see and be haunted again by the smashed skulls and skeletons all laid out in dreadful death.

On the other hand, his gut instinct was to get Kate

away from here, however much he wanted to keep her. Even if he returned things and let her in the mound, she'd surely ferret out that he'd lied to her, led her on—been in there before.

He gazed into the eyeless stare of the beast, trying to decide what to do with this, with Kate. He returned the mask to its tomb and hurried back upstairs to bed.

Kate sat up in bed with a start. Peering into the darkness, she strained to listen. Nothing. She heard only the wind outside, the air conditioner as it hummed low.

She looked at the bright red readout on her bedside digital clock. 2:13 a.m. She'd been asleep over an hour. She and Grant had been just like an old married couple tonight, talking, cuddling, kissing, dozing. So natural, no talk of the things that could divide them. Yet tension always twisted between them, desire on a leash, waiting to be loosed. Was that what had wakened her now?

Other thoughts crowded in, things she'd passed over during the day. Carson had said he'd send a copy of his article on Etruscan tombs, hadn't he? And that she should read it and take it to heart. Now, what had he meant by that? Was it in the box with the mask, and she'd ignored it?

And then her young double, Kaitlyn, had mentioned that she'd been researching Etruscan tombs. So wouldn't it be just like Carson to take his GA's research to write his own article, citing Kaitlyn's sources as his own? How often had he done that with Kate's own work on the Adena when she was with him? But he'd done so much for her—she cared so deeply for him—that she had not protested. If she hadn't spent so much time pursuing the Celtic-Adena link, would she have had her own career at all?

She'd been wrong to idolize Carson, and she didn't want Kaitlyn to do that now. Funny, but she'd felt an instant sisterhood or camaraderie with the girl, but maybe she was just missing Tess and Char. She never used to miss them as much as she did now here in Cold Creek. At least Tess would be back in a few days, and maybe Kate could visit Char out West before she went back to England, if the mound excavation was impossible here. Though Char worked with Navajo children, Kate had always wanted to see the Anasazi Indian burial places out there. She'd heard some pretty strange things about their death rituals.

She clicked on her bedside light, got up and pulled the box with the mask out from under her bed. She lifted it onto the mattress, pulled off the lid. There was an envelope stuck along the inside of the box. As she reached for it, her fingernails snagged some of the mica chips on the side of the mask. She'd have to glue the chips she'd loosened.

She closed the box, shoved it back under the bed, wishing she had a better place to keep it. Sitting there, she knew she was putting off reading Carson's article, and she wasn't sure why. If there was something in it to take to heart or help with the mound here, she should study it now. Or was it just Carson she was trying to put off? She still wanted to get into Mason Mound and with him at her side.

She took out the article and opened it. She read Carson's neat, tight script across the top. *Had we world enough and time, this coyness, lady, were no crime...*

She recognized the quotation from a 17th-century

poem called "To His Coy Mistress." And she got the hint. He was upset. He thought she was stalling, that her putting him and the mound off was a crime against knowledge, archaeology, mankind—and him.

She skimmed the article. It was about two-thousand-year-old Etruscan tombs in Italy being broken into and looted by thieves called *tombaroli*.

A couple of blows from a pickax breaks the ceiling into the burial chamber, the roof caves in, and the tomb, crammed with antiquities and even bodies, is ransacked and the precious artifacts sold to illegal dealers and museum curators.

She'd heard of that, of course, but was Carson suggesting that someone—maybe someone who had marked several local mounds with metal stars—would break into them if they weren't properly, quickly excavated first? The poem reference and this article implied she was running out of time.

She gasped as she read that the Italian police often looked the other way as did European and international law enforcement. Places with excellent reputations such as Sotheby's auction house in London, the Metropolitan Museum of Art in New York and the J. Paul Getty Museum in California had been accused of buying antiquities that were looted. And her eyes were drawn to the line with the word *mask*. A stolen 2,500-year-old theater mask had been found in an art dealer's briefcase, one maybe close to the age of the Beastmaster cauldron and mask.

She put Carson's article in the bedside-table drawer and turned out the light. She lay back down in bed, staring at the dark ceiling, agonizing about what to do, whether to beg Grant, buck Grant, sneak around him to check the entry, whether—

Something scraped or scratched against her bedroom window. A branch? It was almost like fingernails on a blackboard. Chills shot through her. Had the wind picked up? Squirrels sometimes got on the roof. That could be what she'd heard, but they usually stayed away after dark. The bushes outside were cut low, which pleased her, since it made it easier to see the mound.

The sound came again, more like a growl or snort this time—just like before in Tess's garage. Her heart pounding, she got up, went to the window, parted the drapes a few inches and peered out.

Nothing. Nothing but the night, the lawn, the woodlot beyond and the mound, which always beckoned to her. Again she recalled the stag outside the garage window, the sounds it had made, but maybe she'd been half-asleep and had hallucinated this. There was absolutely nothing out there to make sounds on the window, no animal in the yard.

Yet the face of the Beastmaster mask under the bed flashed through her mind. Suddenly, she didn't want it under her bed. Grant didn't want it in the house, as if it were evil. She had to get it out of this room or she'd never sleep tonight.

She dragged the box out again, took it down the hall, into the kitchen and clicked on the basement light so she could take it downstairs. Hurrying now, feeling cold to the core, she put it on the Ping-Pong table and scurried back upstairs. In the morning she'd suggest to Grant that he get safety lights that clicked on where there was movement outside, like Mom had put in years ago at their old house after Tess had been taken.

Trembling, Kate got back into bed and pulled the covers up as if she were a kid afraid of the dark. She left her bedside light on, turned her back to the window and curled up in a fetal position. Yet, despite the fact the curtains were closed, she felt exposed as if the eyeless mask was outside, staring in at her, able to see right through walls, right through the centuries.

She got up, dragged her bedding to the floor and, with the bed as a buffer between her and the window, made a messy little nest on the carpet to comfort herself. As she lay down again, she pictured the darkness outside.

As she tried to doze, her thoughts flitted past like bats in the night, sharp ideas like deer antlers, faces wearing masks—Brad and Lacey, Kaitlyn, Carson. Could she really trust anyone?

Then a vision that shot her straight up, wide awake, in her ravaged covers. Could she trust Grant, smiling and seductive, staring at her from behind his mask?

20

As soon as daylight seeped into her room, Kate got off the floor, stretched her sore back and whipped open her curtains. The forest and mound were still in shadow, but looked so normal. Just another June day—Monday. Gabe and Tess would be home in five days. She pictured them sipping wine, sitting on the deck of the riverboat, gazing out at old châteaus and castles along the Loire… man and wife.

She yanked the curtains closed and hurried to take a shower and get dressed. The house was quiet, so she'd fix breakfast for Grant. And Brad, if he'd come in last night. Today she and Grant were going to Keith Simons's house for lunch so she could talk to Lee. But before any of that, she was going outside.

She went out the kitchen door and checked outside her bedroom window where she thought—no, she was sure—she'd heard sounds, scratches, even snorts or grunts last night. Could Brad have come home drunk with Lacey and they were goofing around in the back-yard? She doubted it, but that thought made more sense than what was really tormenting her, that the stag she'd seen outside Tess's garage window had been here, too.

Just a deer, she told herself, not someone in a Beastmaster mask—or worse. No, the only ghosts she believed in were ones from a person's past, like her dad, not the dead-come-to-haunt-you kind.

Under her bedroom window, she was certain the hosta plants had been trampled like someone had stood close to the house and her window. There was definitely disturbed foliage, and, since it had rained yesterday, she wondered if she'd find footprints in the soil under the bent leaves.

She pushed the green-and-white-striped leaves of the plants to the side so she could see the ground. Damp soil, vague shapes, but nothing distinct, as if a person's standing on the large leaves had blurred any prints. But something on the ground glittered. She saw small flakes that looked like pieces of the broken record her mother had kept because it was from Dad's old Johnny Cash collection, and she was sorry she'd smashed it against the wall when he'd walked out.

Kate reached down for a handful of soil and looked closer. Mica chips! Thin mica chips just like the ones from the Beastmaster masks! She'd go around to her rental car and get some of her smallest handpick tools and a sieve.

"Kate!"

She gasped and jumped to her feet. "Oh, Grant. I just... I heard noises out here last night and wanted to look for prints. But look, look!" she cried as she showed him three small chips of the black mica on her dirty palm. "Proof someone was out here with a Beastmaster mask, since it has a mica covering! I heard scratching and snorting and—"

He held up his hands as if trying to stop traffic.

"Kate, sweetheart, this whole area has mica chips in the soil, and there's a vein of it a little ways back in the woods. Besides, they put mica in potting soil and a bunch of other things. A garden store from Chillicothe once asked if they could dig out the mica back there, and I said no."

"Of course you said no digging," she retorted, instantly angry with him again—and at herself for being so foolish.

He looked almost smug, but she'd fix that. Her old competitive drive took over. "Mica in this area and in the woodlot near the mound? That's great! So the Adena in this area could easily have used that mica to adorn their clothing or masks. I can't wait to see that vein, if you'll show me. You might know about potting soil, but I'm telling you the ancient Egyptians, Greeks, Aztecs— and Adena—valued mica. So, you've given me another great piece of evidence that something important is in that mound. But can you explain how beat down these hosta plants are?"

He frowned at her, at the foliage. "Beat down by yesterday's rain, maybe, or the guy who washed the outside windows a week or so ago. Kate, I know this sounds like the same old song, but wildlife, especially deer, eat a lot of the plants here. They could have stood there grazing."

"Well, they haven't eaten these recently. They looked stepped on not chewed up."

"Look, I've got to get into work early since Brad's going to start covering for Todd, and I need to explain that to the staff. I had coffee, so I'll just grab toast and juice, but I'll be back about eleven to pick you up to go to Keith's so you can talk to Lee."

Still clutching the mica chips in her hand, she tried

to keep up with his long strides. "Grant, I'm sorry I seem so paranoid. And I appreciate your taking the time for this lunch when I know you're extra busy at work. I'll go in to help with breakfast. Does Brad need something, too?"

"He never came home last night. I thought he'd be trying to toe the line since he's going to manage the mill. I just—with two of my friends hurt—I just hope he's all right. If he's not stone-cold sober, I'll put Keith in as foreman, despite what I promised Brad. And, Kate," he said, turning back to her. "Please don't go looking for the seam of mica yourself. It's hidden by overgrowth. And don't get too excited about the mica connection. You're clutching at straws."

"Sometimes, I think that's all I have, and here this fantastic mound is, sitting within view...and reach."

"I want to be out of here in ten minutes," he said, opening the back door for her then following her in.

She muttered under her breath as she washed the mica chips and her hands, then got the juice out of the fridge. The mound might be in physical reach, but it seemed so far away—sometimes as far away as Grant.

On the way to Keith Simons's house, Kate hit Grant with another surprise. "Oh, by the way," she told him, "I put the box with my mask in the basement. It's better down there than under my bed—humidity, dust and all."

He turned to her as they drove up the road on Black Mountain. "Where in the basement?" he snapped much louder and harsher than he'd intended.

"Just on the Ping-Pong table. I can move it, if that's a problem."

You are a problem was his first thought, but he managed to keep his mouth shut. She frustrated and infuriated him, even as he was trying to be her host and protector. She was a woman who could cause him all sorts of trouble—hurt Todd and Brad, too. Man, she ticked him off yet he was tempted to just grab her, kiss her, put his hands all over her and…

"No problem," he muttered. "I was just surprised. I'm on edge after having to tell everyone about Todd and explain Brad taking over today…."

"So he did show up?"

He was grateful that she went for his change of subject. Again, he could picture those Beastmaster masks— her phony one and his authentic one—getting together down in the dark…breeding more masks, more trouble. Damn, he was getting as off base as she sounded sometimes with her fears about Adena demons peering in windows. But considering what had happened to Paul, when there were no prints to suggest a home invasion, and then Todd, of all people, falling from a tree…

"Was Brad sober?" Kate asked, yanking him back to reality.

"Ah—yeah. And ready to go, there before I was. It went unspoken that he'd obviously spent the night with Lacey somewhere, but he's welcome to her. And he volunteered to stay at the mill during the lunch break, go around and talk to the guys, so that Keith and I could both be away. I explained to Brad why we'd set this up for you, so he didn't think Keith and I were plotting something behind his back. I hope this new responsibility will settle Brad down, bond the two of us again."

"Sometimes I wish something would make me feel that way about my father. I was awful to him when he was here, but I just couldn't help it." She sighed. "So

Keith's wife's name is Velma. Do they have kids at home?"

"Two in high school, but they sent them to camp for the first time this year. Keith came into some money from an old Desert Storm buddy who died and didn't have a family. It sounds like he and Velma have been spending money like it was water—a new truck, furniture, not sure what all. And, of course, having Lee, so Keith tells me, not repair but *replace* their fence."

"Maybe Keith will try to help out his sister and brothers, though not much he can do for the one in prison. It's a real blessing one of them seems on the right path, to stick with you, not blame you and Gabe for the troubles of the others."

"Yeah, I never did understand that guilt-by-association stuff when Gabe's the one who arrested Keith's brother, not me. I need all the help I can get right now. And I appreciate your helping out Nadine financially and Amber with her kids. And reaching out to me," he said, putting his hand on her knee.

As usual, merely touching her sent a jolt of energy through him. If he made love to her, possessed her body, would that stem the ache she'd created in his life?

Kate thought Keith and Velma Simons made a strange team. She was as short and wiry as he was tall and brawny. She had hair bleached so blond it looked almost white, while his was dark. She talked a lot; he was a man of few words. Velma was proud of their new things and showed them off, while Keith seemed a bit embarrassed by them.

"Your cousin just took a break and is eating his lunch

over on the hillside," Keith told Kate, pointing. "You can see the hill but not him from here."

"I fed him up good yesterday," Velma said. "Today I wanted to keep him off by hisself for you to talk to. So nice to meet someone's been all over Europe, like you, Kate. I got Keith here to promise me we might go to Paris someday, so's if you can fill me in on that, much obliged."

"I'd be happy to," Kate told her, looking out the window in the direction of the hillside. "My sister and Gabe will be back this weekend from France and—"

The moment that was out of her mouth, Kate realized these people wouldn't want anything to do with Tess and Gabe, since it was their evidence that had sent Keith's brother Jonas to prison for working with the meth gang. And Gabe had fired Keith's sister, Ann, whom he used to date, though she'd pled to a lesser misdemeanor and was only on probation.

"But sure," she said quickly. "Never mind them. Let's talk about Paris at lunch."

"Better go out to see to your cousin now," Keith said. "You know, while he's on break, not working. See— we understand how blood's thicker'n water, if'n you get what I mean, that you're worried about your kin."

"And you're worried about yours," she said. "Of course, I understand that and thank both of you for helping Grant set this up for me. I do worry about Lee, Grace and their kids at that commune."

"Oh, yeah," Velma said, hands on her skinny hips. "For sure that squirrel—Bright Star—got more than one screw loose. We'll hold lunch for you now."

Kate was grateful they'd given her a pass on her misstep. One thing she recalled about this area fringing the Appalachians was that kin counted. Grudges and insults could go on for decades, kind of like the Hatfields and the McCoys. And here she was, sister-in-law to the sheriff. At least Keith didn't hold it against Grant.

As she left the three of them talking, she saw Grant position himself so he could watch her out the window. Kate crossed the front porch with its new lawn furniture—Grant had said there used to be a beat-up, old couch there—and toward the hill. She could see the white picket fence Lee was erecting and painting. She supposed they got the wood from Mason Mill.

She passed Lee's tools neatly laid out on the ground, his closed can of paint, the few slats and boards he had yet to assemble. A longing for her own excavation tools laid out on the ground near a dig swept through her. She spotted the top of Lee's head first, then saw he was sitting down the hill and had finished his lunch. He was dressed in the muted, nondescript clothes the Hear Ye male converts tended to wear.

"Lee," she called so she wouldn't startle him by coming up behind him. "Grant Mason and I are having lunch here today, and they mentioned you were working on a fence out back. I thought I'd just take a minute and say hi."

He sprang to his feet and turned to face her so fast that she thought he might tumble down the hill. He looked dismayed, as if she'd caught him at something.

"Kate. What a coincidence."

"I guess so—a good one. After all, the last time we were together, Bright Star ran the show."

"He always does—more than a show. Reality. Eternity."

She wasn't sure what he meant by that, but she didn't

want to get confrontational or stuck on some philosophical topic. "Well, it was good to see you and Grace anyway. How's everyone doing lately? I will make an appointment to visit both of you and the kids. Tess will be back this weekend, so you'll see her soon, too."

So she didn't seem to tower over him, she walked down the hill a ways. She was tempted to sit, but she didn't want to invade his space. She was an outsider to him, maybe a dangerous one if Bright Star found out about this private chat. Would Lee have to confess it as if it were a sin?

"I thought Grace looked good," she rushed on. "Maybe a little tired."

"She works hard. The angels do."

"The angels?"

"Like, ah—those who are specially chosen."

"Leaders in some way?"

"For sure," he said, but she couldn't decide if he sounded proud or angry.

Kate had meant to question Lee about what the star Grace had drawn on her chest could mean, but suddenly, she hesitated. If Grace had been trying to give something away or even call for help, could she be punished by Lee or Bright Star? It had been obvious that she'd meant to show the sign only to Kate.

"So," Lee said when she hesitated. "Are you going to be allowed to dig in the ancient mound? The Adena were infidels, you know, pagan people. Pieces of their past, things they left behind, should be buried for good, not brought into the light of day, where they would be studied, cherished and idolized."

She wondered if those were Bright Star's words, not Lee's. And it annoyed her that he seemed to be on

Grant's side. "But we can learn from them," she said. "What they did, what not to do, since they disappeared almost as quickly as they arrived in this area."

"A warning then that modern men and women can disappear in death as quickly—or so Bright Star says."

"What does he mean by that?"

"Just that life is short. Living people matter, not dead ones, not places."

"But I heard somewhere that he's buying the old insane-asylum grounds outside of town. I can see why he's attracted to it. That place must matter to him."

"Are you implying something is off with Bright Star? It will be Eden on earth for us there. We pray it will come to pass soon. So, will you heed the warning about not digging up the mounds, clinging to the demonic past?"

"Demonic? Look, Lee, the Adena hardly had the benefit of hearing vast pseudo-wisdom from the blessed lips of Bright Star Monson."

She'd done it again: let her temper get the best of her. For the second time, she'd managed to insult Bright Star, but the drivel Lee was spouting really upset her. He looked shocked.

She forced her feet up the hill before she could say something more direct about that horrible, screwed-up cult leader. Monson was the one who was demonic! He obviously went to great lengths to control people, scare people. She was certain he'd left those stars on the mounds and that was what poor Grace was trying to tell her. He no doubt wanted Kate out of the area at any cost.

21

"Okay, I get it," Grant said with a tight smile when they'd finished a fish-and-chips dinner uptown at the English pub that evening.

"Get what?" Kate asked.

"You're fidgeting like a kid having to wait to open presents Christmas morning. Let's head back, and I'll show you the vein of mica. We'd better take a spade and trimmer out with us, because, like I said, it's pretty hidden by undergrowth."

"I have tools in my car—but right. We'll use yours. The foliage is probably why I didn't spot the seam when I was looking for a water source out there. That was the day I saw Brad and Lacey together."

"Maybe she's going to be good for him. But he said she's only here for a few more days visiting her parents before she heads back to Cleveland. I think he may be the one who got her to disband her greeniacs, because it sure wasn't me. I got the idea they intended to protest at the mill at least a second time. Brad was also helpful today, telling people he was just filling in for Todd, so maybe everything will work out if he can sell his paper mill or get it back on its feet. And stay off the booze."

They went home—was she thinking of it as home now?—changed their clothes and headed out back with a spade and large pair of hedge clippers. Kate was excited to be walking out toward the mound with tools, even though they were soon headed past it.

After they'd returned from Keith and Velma's and Grant went back to the mill, she had spent the afternoon at Tess and Gabe's new place, making sure it was ready for their homecoming. Workers had completed the remodeling of their old house on the other side of town, and Tess's attached day-care center was almost finished. The sawdust on the floor and sawhorses still there reminded Kate of the sad remnants they'd found of Grant's bird's-eye maple tree up on Shadow Mountain. The precious, living heirloom that had held his childhood tree house and had watched over Mason Mound for decades had been slaughtered like some Adena had been in death chambers uncovered in this area. And she was still as far from getting into Mason Mound as—as she was from forgiving her father.

Once Tess and Gabe returned, if Grant still refused to let her excavate the mound, what excuse would she have for staying here? She couldn't impose on him longer. And she certainly wouldn't stay with newlyweds setting up a house and business. Should she work with Carson to convince the state legislature to force Grant to let them dig, and turn him against her forever? Carson had hinted at marriage more than once, but that once-cherished goal of them as more than research and excavation partners seemed all wrong now. She wanted to hold Carson off, as much as she wanted to urge Grant on.

As they approached the mica seam, she saw that

Grant was right. The side of a shallow ravine they walked into was completely overgrown with ivy and bishop's weed spilling over it from a treed ridge on top. But she could tell there was something dark beneath the drooping foliage. A frisson of excitement shot through her. She would feel this way if she was about to uncover the entrance to the mound, but at least she might find some clues that the Adena had used the mica here. She was going to find the right moment and ask Grant for permission, hoping he'd give her that, at least.

"So how did you know this was here, since it's obviously been overgrown for years?" she asked as he began to cut some of the foliage back, then pulled the tangle of vines away. In the dim light under the forest cover, the rock beneath glinted.

"Our gang of friends knew every foot of this forest when we were growing up. In the autumn, when the leaves were off the trees and we'd had a couple of frosts, we used to be able to see this from the tree house. and we checked it out."

"Did you make things out of this mica, like little arrowheads, or something like that? Adena usually used flint or chert for their working arrowheads and spear points, even ax heads. But mica is so shiny, they liked it for decorations and oversize ceremonial weapons— like those left in their tombs."

"I hear you, Professor. It's a short walk from here to the mound, so you'd expect to find mica artifacts in there."

"Exactly. Grant, since you still don't want me to excavate the mound, would you mind if I worked here? If enough of this plant growth is cleared away, I might be able to see where someone chipped at the mica, maybe even the shapes of what was taken out. Everything I'd need to see would be close to the surface here, no deep digging. It's a long shot, but…"

"You'd never prove it was the Adena, rather than the Shawnee or even pioneers, would you?"

"The Adena had distinctive shapes for their arrowheads and ax heads. I could make a good case for the Adena because, especially in their burial chambers, some of their tools and weapons are oversize, as if they had to be special for the afterlife."

When he didn't answer, she stopped talking. She didn't want to upset him about digging even here. But another idea suddenly hit her. Little Jason's dreadful drawing included a huge ax head. Did it mean the boy had seen an Adena ceremonial one? More likely he just drew it large because one he'd seen in a book looked scary or important. It had impressed him. Kids that age paid little attention to size or perspective. Grant had said he would talk to Jason, then hadn't mentioned it again. She'd have to question the boy on the sly.

"Well, if you think you can get something useful for your research out of this mica bed, sure," he said to her delight and surprise. "I'm all for your studies, Kate, as long as it lets the dead stay dead, as my grandfather said. But maybe you should only work on this with someone out here, considering we've had trespassers who cut the tree, and you thought you heard something outside last night. But I'd rather you don't get Carson Cantrell out here."

"How about Kaitlyn?"

"Can you trust her?"

"To help me work on this, at least. My instinct is to

trust her, but I'll need to know her better to be sure. Thanks, Grant."

"Oh, yeah. I haven't mentioned the fee."

"The fee?"

"Kind of like a finder's fee, not only of this mica, but because I've found you."

He put the clippers down and took the spade from her hands and dropped it to the ground. The mica seam glinted beside and above them in a sudden shaft of setting sun. Grant's hands came strong around her waist as he pulled her to him.

"Just a couple of these for a down payment," he said, his voice husky, as he kissed her lightly, then lingeringly and tugged her even closer.

Every nerve in her body came alive. "How many is a couple?"

"Oh, forgot to say—kisses are just for starters."

She was going to say something flip but, as ever when Grant touched her, everything except him flew out of her mind. She tilted her head so the kiss could deepen and looped her arms up around his neck to hold him tight. Her breasts flattened against his chest. If he had pulled her down on the gritty ground at the edge of the mica wall, she would not have protested.

They seemed to prop each other up as their kisses lengthened and deepened. She loved the feel of his hard back muscles, his shoulders, the crisp hair on the nape of his neck. His body seemed carved from the wood he loved. He pressed her against the mica wall, which was good, because she wasn't sure she could stand, even clinging to him, without that solid wall of rock behind her.

His hands left her bottom and marauded over her

hips and waist. He pulled her T-shirt hem up and lifted one hand under it to cup a breast through her bra. His kisses came harder, more demanding. He was devouring her, and she wanted more.

He turned them so that his back was against the mica and locked her to him again, hips to hips. She felt dizzy, no longer earthbound but soaring. The slight stubble on his chin scraped her cheek. She was certain the whole world was tumbling down around them in bright, sparkling shards of—

Grant broke the kiss and looked up. They heard a cascade of mica before it hit them, like a waterfall of tiny rocks coming down at them from above. Grant yelled and pulled her away from the wall as more mica gave way above them and then a big chunk bounced down, just missing them. He dragged them back as more rocks fell and exploded in smaller pieces where they had stood.

Despite their ragged breathing, they heard a grunt from above, then footsteps spitting mica that rained down again in a fine, black powder.

"Someone did that," Grant muttered. "Stay here—stay back."

He turned and ran out of the ravine with her right behind him. They clawed their way up to higher, flatter ground, then raced to the spot above where they'd been standing.

"No one here I can see," she gasped, out of breath.

"Gone by now. I told you to stay back, but I should know by now you do your own thing."

"Wish I could."

He turned and looked at her, squinting into the red,

setting sun. "We won't argue about that now. Let's check for footprints."

She glanced at the open glade fringed by a thick stand of trees, wondering if someone could still be there. If he or they had run, they hadn't gone far and could be watching. Wasn't that area ahead of them where Brad had buried his dog? She followed Grant over to the lip of the ravine. "Could it have been a natural occurrence? Mica stratifies and flakes easily."

"Not a coincidence," he insisted. "Awfully good timing, especially with all that's happened lately. I didn't see much previous rock litter down there, so rocks hadn't fallen recently."

Her heart was hammering so hard from his touch and her run up here and from her renewed fear that someone or something was still stalking them. They stood carefully on the mica ledge, peering down. "You know," she said, "the forest—ravines, too—are usually the sites of lurking evil in primitive myths and more recent fairy tales."

"Thank you, Professor Grimm. Would you quit talking like that? The dead Adena are not haunting you—or me—and we've got to find what living bastard is. Let's go back to the house before it gets dark. But what just happened means you can't excavate here or you might get hurt—or buried from above."

Buried from above. The words snagged in her brain. Like the Adena dead nearby.

"Grant, please. I didn't mean this should spook us— keep us away. I'll ask Kaitlyn to bring another student or two, and we'll set up a guard above us."

He didn't answer until they made their way back into the ravine. If she excavated only the mica seam here, would someone harass her? Considering what had happened to Paul and Todd, maybe this wasn't even about her. That would mean Grant was the target.

Grant was shaken but also angry. The rockslide had missed them only because they'd jumped away, warned by the fine mica dust and chips before the larger rocks crashed down. Those could have broken bones—or caved in their skulls. All he needed was another nightmare that he was back in the death chamber, stealing from skeletons with crushed skulls. And, unlike Kate, who he thought was hearing things outside windows or even making that up, they had both heard someone scurry away above them, and it sure as heck wasn't some Adena ghost or Beastmaster running amok in these woods.

But who would profit from his demise, or Kate's? The same idiot who had shot at them up on Shadow Mountain? Surely not Brad or Lacey, though Brad was his heir in his will—and knew it. Grant couldn't quite picture Carson Cantrell getting his hands dirty, though of course, like Kate, who had seemed fine with dirt and mica on her hands and under her fingernails this morning, Cantrell must excavate with the best of them. Or could Cantrell have seen him kissing Kate and her eager response? Who else hated his guts?

"I guess," he told her as they trekked back toward the house, "you can check out the mica seam if you can get a couple of guards as well as Kaitlyn for company. Not Professor Cantrell, okay?"

"No, I'll only use him to get permission for the others to come. He's got a busy teaching and speaking schedule anyway and can't get away much. I can't thank you enough, Grant, really."

"We were rudely interrupted back there," he said, taking her hand in his as they neared the mound. He'd agreed she could research the mica only to keep her working on something Adena that wasn't the mound itself. "Let's remember the finder's-fee payment continues daily if you're so eager to dig."

"It will keep me out of trouble during the day, right?"

"Except for getting in trouble with me at night, and—" He released her hand and ran toward the mound as they neared the house.

She saw what had upset him and chased after him. The hawthorn bushes guarding what she was certain was the opening to a horizontal entry shaft were not just sick and old, but very, very dead. He'd steered her away from the entrance on their way out to the mica seam, or they would have seen this earlier. It was almost dark, but he could see yellow leaves scattered under the brittle branches. Even the grass and moss at their base was brown and dead.

"I know those were old, but someone's poured some kind of herbicide on the ground. You didn't?" he muttered.

"No way! I wouldn't. I swear it wasn't me. When I get some help out here—just for the mica seam—I'll have them take a sample of the moss or grass to the lab, see if we can find exactly what killed these bushes."

He gripped her wrist as they stared at the entry area to the mound behind the skeletal hawthorns. She didn't flinch, but, unspeaking, slid her hand up to entwine her fingers with his. He tried to stay strong, but he feared whoever had killed Paul and hurt Todd was now after him.

22

Kate was thrilled at how swiftly, for once, her Adena research plans came together. Finally, something was getting done! One call to Carson and the next afternoon she had Kaitlyn Blake and two other graduate students, both eager young men, released from their archaeology seminar to assist at the mica seam. It lifted her spirits. It was a step in the right direction.

As she'd promised Grant, she had the two guys take turns atop the ridge, keeping an eye out as the others worked below. Bill Bosley and Sean Armstrong were eager to help. Bill took the first watch above, while Sean and Kaitlyn, under her guidance, cleared the rest of the ivy away. Standing on ladders, they started at the top of the seam with the long-handled soft brushes Kate had hoped to use in the mound. They cleared any clinging soil, cobwebs or dead leaves so they could discern patterns and shapes better.

"It was neat to see how the Adena are honored in this part of Ohio," Sean said as Kate supervised. "I mean, we passed the Adena Regional Medical Center on the way here, and then there's the Adena Mansion, but I haven't seen that yet."

"I have," Kaitlyn chimed in from the other ladder. "It was built for Ohio's Governor Worthington and is the site of early Adena remains, one of the first mounds excavated. The mansion was named Adena because that was the Hebrew word for *delightful place.* So that site gave the name to the ancient civilization, not the other way around. And you know what, Professor Lockwood?" the young woman asked, looking down the ladder at her. "Governor Worthington wouldn't let anyone excavate his mound, either. It took someone else to own the property before they could dig."

"I'd forgotten that," Kate said, thinking she wasn't going to share that tidbit with Grant.

"Read about that," Sean said. "When the Ohio Historical Society finally got permission to dig, they found a bunch of bodies in that mound as well as precious artifacts."

Kaitlyn, as if not to be outdone, continued the conversation. "What I think is way cool is the Adena Mansion was designed by Latrobe, the same man who designed the U.S. Capitol in Washington. If I hadn't fallen in love with archaeology, I think I would have been an architect."

"Maybe we should go to the Adena Mansion and you can give me a tour," Sean said.

Kate could see Sean really had eyes for Kaitlyn, which reminded her of her graduate-school days. More than one student on early digs had wanted to date her, but she'd been enamored of Carson. And, sadly, Kaitlyn seemed to want to dominate others with her knowledge. Had she been like that when she was so young and naive? And had she mellowed and learned better? She'd better if she hoped to fit in here in Cold Creek.

"How's it going up there, Bill?" Kate called to their watchman on the ledge above. "We'll change around every hour. Sean's turn next."

"Fine. Great view. Believe me, I'll yell if I see anybody. I really don't think that rock fall could have been accidental—not the bigger rocks, anyway."

Kate used a short-handled, soft brush to clear the lower face of the seam after the upper part was cleared. Then with a powerful headlight on her safety helmet— she'd made everyone wear one today—she scanned the face of the mica seam. Yes! She was certain this spot could have provided small pieces of mica to decorate garments or masks.

But she also discovered evidence that larger pieces had been removed. She thought she saw large shapes that could be ax heads and spear points, and historic tribes would not have used spears after bows and arrows were adapted in the area around 300 to 400 AD. Of course, the weather over the centuries could have made the pieces of chipped mica erode and widen. But artifacts in the mound would hold all the answers to her questions.

Eternally frustrated at not being able to excavate Mason Mound, she tried to rein in her excitement. She'd been taught not to jump to conclusions, and she should take that to heart in the bigger mysteries she needed to solve. Who was hurting—even killing—Grant's friends? Who had shot at them, thrown rocks at them? Bright Star and his lackeys, like Lee? Or worse, because it would devastate Grant—Brad, maybe with Lacey's help?

"I think there's something up here," Kaitlyn called down. "It was protected from the elements by the over-

hang of the ledge. That ax head you sketched for us earlier—I swear there's the shape of one here. You know, it's
a lot like the Toltecs and Aztecs used, too. Dr. Cantrell
has been lecturing about how many smashed skulls are
being unearthed near Mexico City and how that could
be a link to the Adena mortuary practices."

"A link in what way?" Kate demanded, appalled
Carson could be teaching a Toltec-Aztec-Adena link
theory, which would make all her Celtic-Adena work
seem pointless. "The Aztec civilization came after the
Adena rose and fell."

"But the Aztecs are descended from the Toltecs, so
they had a lot in common, and the Toltecs and their ancestors could be forebearers of the Adena. Dr. Cantrell
says the Toltecs started out as hunter-wanderers, so they
or their ancestors could have wandered clear up into this
area in prehistoric times."

Kate was stunned. Carson had never once suggested
that to her.

"Fascinating and creepy," Sean said. "Skulls from
human sacrifices, thirty-four of them found so far in
Mexico City, possibly dedicated to their sun god that
required human blood. Dr. Cantrell says that there have
to be stronger laws everywhere to prosecute and pun-
ish tomb robbers."

"Well, he's right about that," Kate admitted, trying
to compose herself and not wanting to berate these students for just passing on what they'd heard from Carson-
on-high. Perhaps he had been promoting the Toltec idea
just to make them think broadly. "Kaitlyn, let me take a
look at what you found."

Kate steadied the ladder, and Kaitlyn climbed down.
The young woman heaved a huge sigh. "The profes-

sor's right about most everything. But I think he's still undecided about whether this mysterious come-and-go advanced Adena civilization was really the Celts of Europe or a Toltec-type migration from the area of modern-day Mexico."

As excited as Kate was to get up the ladder, she almost missed the first rung. Had Kaitlyn read her thoughts and was trying to comfort her? Or had Carson told her not to get Kate too upset so that she'd quit her work here?

Sean jumped in. "It's just that he theorizes a long trek from there is more probable than a Celtic sea voyage from Europe and then a trek inland from the East Coast—until someone—maybe you, Dr. Lockwood—can prove different."

She clung to the ladder carefully as she went up. She was excited to see what Kaitlyn had pointed out, but devastated that Carson had not told her, despite all her work with the Celts, that he might be shifting his theory to the Toltec tribes. She had to talk to him face-to-face. And she had to get inside Mason Mound and find some link to the Celts.

Going up the ladder, she called down to the students. "I can't recall if the Toltec-Aztecs have oversize artifacts in their tombs."

"Yes, with weapon heads," Kaitlyn said.

Sean would not be outdone. "Yeah, but those are sacrificial, ceremonial or mortuary ones," he explained. "Cantrell said that just last week, at his lecture, Kaitlyn, remember?"

Kate kept climbing. Whom could she trust? Maybe not even these eager young students. What if Carson had sent them to urge her on, make her move faster, even do something rash? The article he'd sent about the thefts in tombs in Italy, now this. Was it all to force her hand, get her to go around Grant? She wanted to trust Grant, but could she? Sometimes she was sure Grant knew more about the mound than he was saying. And she admitted that going behind his back to talk to Jason about his big ax-head drawing meant Grant couldn't completely trust her.

Kaitlyn interrupted her thoughts. "See? Over there to your right a little more."

Kate directed her headlamp up, over. Suddenly, in stark relief, the silhouette of an ancient ax head stood out. She drew in a silent, hard breath. First a water source nearby, now this. The ancient Adena had been up here, had chipped an ax head out of this mica seam eons ago. And, perhaps, had killed their own sacrifices with it and left it to honor their gods or their dead in Mason Mound.

That evening, after her dig team had gone back to Columbus, Kate prepared supper and waited for Grant. He'd called to tell her he'd be late, and she'd filled him in on their finds in the mica seam. She'd also told him Kaitlyn had taken a sample of the poisoned grass and a limb of a hawthorn by the mound entry to have it tested. But he was still later than late, and she was worried. Had something happened at the mill? Had he and Brad argued again? Or something worse?

She took dinner out of the oven and put it in the microwave, where she could reheat it. Why didn't he call? She hated to act like a nervous wife and call his cell if he was in a meeting or with Brad. She'd hoped to take him out to see their work—and the silhouette of the ax head—after they ate but soon it would be dark.

She saw a truck on the road but it didn't turn in. She

walked clear out to the road. The truck looked like the one Grant was driving while his was being repaired. It had pulled off at a spot down the road, along the fringe of the woods. Was he going to check on the mica seam on his own, so he could discuss it with her at dinner? She'd told him she'd left one ladder out there. Was he going to judge what they'd done and then tell her she couldn't—or could—use a team to excavate Mason Mound?

She locked the house as she went out the back door. If Grant wasn't headed in a roundabout way for the mica, maybe he wanted to check the mound entrance without letting her know.

Looking for him, she walked into the forest, past the mound, heading for the mica seam. Maybe he'd heard something about intruders out here again and thought the tree thieves might have returned for more timber.

· He wasn't near the mica, either, so she turned around to head back toward the house. But there, through the trees, she saw a blur of his light blue shirt. Grant was heading for the stone cairn where Brad had buried his dog.

She stopped where she was and crouched behind a tree. He was kneeling over that little mound of stones as if he'd come to pray there. He took out a piece of paper. Leaving Brad a note, telling him he'd found the grave?

He scribbled something on the paper and put it on the ground, then proceeded to remove the stones from the pyramid, placing them on the ground one by one. Surely, he wasn't going to dig up a dead dog. Or did he think Brad had also hidden something else in that grave?

Hating herself for being the spy when she had wor-

ried someone was watching her from the forest, she
saw Grant produce a trowel from his back pocket. He
started to dig. Not far down he pulled up a small box,
not a dog's skeleton for sure. Maybe Brad had his pet
cremated and only buried its ashes.

He fiddled with the box then finally opened it. Though
she couldn't see his facial expression, she knew he was
upset. He bobbed his head once sharply, as if he'd cursed.

She watched him put the box back, push soil back on
it, then, consulting his paper, pile the stones, evidently
just the way they'd been before. He stuck his trowel in
his back pocket, clapped soil off his hands and jogged
back in the direction he'd come.

As soon as he was out of sight, Kate ran back toward
the house. Brad had something hidden there, maybe
on top of the dog's skeleton. So now, not only was she
going behind Grant's back to talk to Jason about his
ax-head drawing, but she was going to dig up that box
under the stones.

That evening, Grant was obviously in a bad mood.
He didn't talk much at dinner, excused himself and
went to his room, where he banged around and, Kate
thought, made phone calls. He raised his voice a couple
of times, but she couldn't tell what he was saying. She
had the feeling he might be talking to Brad.

He eventually reappeared. He looked relieved when
she told him that the grad students weren't coming back
until the weekend. He said nothing about digging up
Brad's box, and she certainly didn't tell him she'd followed him. If Grant could keep secrets—though she
knew this could just be a private matter between two
brothers—she could, too. Tomorrow morning, as soon

as Grant cleared that door, she was going to get answers. She wouldn't give up until the pieces of a puzzle came together. But where would she even find the pieces? Not by asking Grant, for sure, as he was hardly talking and finally disappeared to go to bed. No kiss, nothing, after all that enticing talk and touching Monday night. She hoped he didn't think she'd poisoned the hawthorns at the entrance to the mound, though she was grateful to whoever did.

"So where has Brad been staying?" she asked him at breakfast the next morning. "Is he still doing okay at the mill?"

"With Lacey. Her parents are still up at their cabin, and he's with her at their house in town. He says they don't know, that they think he's still living here. For sure, they'll find out, so I told him I wouldn't lie for him if it came to that."

So maybe that's what they were arguing about on the phone last night, she thought. *If he was talking to Brad.*

"Good move," she said. "Lies only create eventual disasters."

Grant leveled such a strange look at her that she trembled. Resentment? Anger? Worse, hatred? He got up from the table. "You're right about that," he said. Maybe she'd misread him. "As for Brad's work at the mill, the same. Helpful, supportive, yada yada. Gotta go, Kate. You have plans for the day? You promised you wouldn't go back out to the mica seam alone, and I'm holding you to that. Or out in the woods."

"'Beware of the woods' sounds like good advice for Little Red Riding Hood, but I hear you, master of the manor," she said, aware she was stalling for time to decide how to answer. If Grant could go behind her back... maybe lie to her, then...

"I plan to stop to get that Adena tree trunk from Nadine today. I'll call her first," she said.

"I can go with you this evening. It's too heavy for you—both of you."

"Then I'll just pay her for it, and you and I can stop for it later. I'm sure she could use some extra money right now. I've been wanting to visit her."

"Great. Sure."

She didn't tell him that she was also going to drop in at Todd and Amber's house to chat with Jason—after she dug up Brad's box under the stones in the woods.

23

Grant slammed his office door and swore when he spilled hot coffee on his wrist. He hated being in such a foul mood, but he was furious with Brad…with Kate… with himself. He was angry at Kate, but he also wanted to grab and kiss her, and that might be dangerous. He had to either keep her close or get her out of his life.

As soon as Gabe and Tess returned from France this weekend, would Kate leave town? He wanted her to stay away from the mound, but he wanted to keep her in his life, and that looked impossible. And then Brad—

His brother knocked on the door and stuck his head in the office, as if summoned by Grant's thoughts. "Keith said you wanted to see me. A production problem this early—or more dire warnings about me and Lacey?"

"I don't care about that, other than, like I said on the phone, you'd better tell her parents and not think you can hide out from them. Her dad's good with a shotgun and—"

"And her mother still likes you, not me. Look, we've got a load of oak coming in soon, and I should be on the cutting floor."

"Close the door and sit down."

"Wow, this is big. What?" he asked, perching on a chair across from Grant's big desk.

"You told Kate you had a dog—Max, I think it was—a collie, no less, that you buried in the woods. What are you, a fiction writer?"

Brad glared at him. One leg bounced, so Grant knew he was nervous. "Okay, when I was walking in the woods one day, I think she spied on me. I made up that story on the spot to get her off my back. I'm quite sure you like her on your back in more ways than—"

"Cut the cuteness. That pile of stones, even if off the beaten path, is not exactly subtle. Someone else could find it—I did."

Brad shot straight up out of his chair then leaned toward Grant, stiff-armed with his fists on the desk. "Only because Miss Adena Archaeology told you, I bet. Did you dig it up? Oh, yeah, I know it's *your* woods. Well, did you? We took vows we'd never so much as ask where each of us hid our stuff."

Throwing himself back in his chair, arms crossed, Brad looked as if he was ready to have a tantrum. His face was red; a vein throbbed on the side of his neck. Wanting to face him down, Grant came around the desk and sat on it so he almost hovered over him.

"Keep your voice down," Grant said. "Yeah, I dug it up, but so what since you—or someone else—had obviously moved it somewhere else. You didn't sell it, did you? Even so much as mention it to someone— like Lacey?"

"Are you nuts? You think I'd be back here if I sold it? I'd be bailing out my mill instead of working at yours if I got big bids for that! And I'd be nuts to try to sell it anonymously on eBay or anywhere word would get out!"

"How about somewhere it wouldn't get out? Someone who wants it for a private collection or museum? Since it's not out in the woods with your imaginary dog, just assure me it's someplace safe and you aren't asking anyone for advice about where to sell it on the black market. What if Paul did that, and look what happened?"

"Yes. Yes, it's someplace safe. Have you located Paul's? Do you know where Todd's is? If someone's found out about our stuff, it's not from me."

"As you said, we're not to tell each other where we keep them. I just want to be sure yours is safe, since it was missing from the box. And why didn't you take the box with it, since you went to so much trouble to have a silk-lined nest made for it just in the shape of the large arrowhead?"

"Which I've come to realize is actually a spear point."

Another smooth subject shift, Grant thought, and not a good sign. He'd also avoided the question of whether he'd told Lacey. Surely she hadn't seduced the artifact out of him to support her Green Tree passions. "Maybe not a spear point," Grant told him. "Kate says that artifacts destined for Adena tombs were often oversize, and Adena spear points are long with leaf-shaped points and a rounded stem, and yours wasn't, so it probably is—was—an arrowhead."

"My, my, but you and the professor have been having intimate talks. Look, if you're still so damned worried about keeping her and her archaeo-maniacs out of the mound, get rid of her. I mean, send her away, get her off your property and out of your life. I don't think you can have it both ways. Besides, maybe she lusts after the mound and not you!" He paused for a moment. "The fact you're not punching me or throwing me out tells me you've thought of that."

"I'm not an idiot, Brad."

"Okay, how about this approach if you don't want to burn bridges with her? Tell her you got in the mound alone when you were a kid and took that deer-head mask. Tell her if she helps you put it back—no questions asked, no one informed—that you'll let her excavate the place, but don't mention the rest of us who have things—or, in Paul's case, had. We don't need big fines, bad publicity or prison time."

Grant's insides knotted. That would make Kate a liar, but would she go for it? That was a solution he'd thought of. Only he'd considered asking Brad and Todd to let him put their relics back in the death chamber, too—and if only he could locate Paul's. Not that he believed taking the Adena artifacts caused a curse, but to lose Paul and then have Tarzan Todd fall was such an eerie coincidence.

Brad's voice sliced through his agonizing. "That is, if you want to keep Kate here." He got up and edged toward the door.

"The woman's been all over Europe," Grant said, standing and turning. "Her idea of a vacation is going to see her younger sister out West and excavating ancient Anasazi garbage dumps while she's there. It would be Lacey all over again, wanting to get out of Cold Creek, unhappy living here."

Brad put his hand on the doorknob then froze. "Maybe not. Kate's a whole lot smarter than Lacey, and the fact she's been all over might mean she knows what she wants, is willing to settle down." He gave a wry little smile. "Here's an idea. Marry her and she won't be able to testify against you—just kidding. Take care of yourself. I don't like the pattern of two of our old buddies going down. I'm watching my back and you'd better watch yours."

Strange, Grant thought, but his tone had sounded like a threat, a direct warning at the very least. Suddenly, he was desperate to move on, to change the subject.

"Oh, one more thing—not important compared to Kate," Grant said. "I was on the phone last night with the owner of a lumber mill outside Madison, Wisconsin, that received a huge amount of bird's-eye maple last week."

Brad's eyes widened as he turned back. He looked as upset as Grant felt, almost as if he'd been caught at something. "Our tree?"

"I think so. He's sending me a couple of wood samples, so keep an eye out for it. And one of the pieces has nails in it. I think that might be where our tree house crashed off when the tree hit the ground."

"Yeah, I'll watch for that, and we can check the nails. Let me know if he can trace the source. You do realize you just said that the stolen tree was not important compared to Kate, don't you?" he asked as he went out and closed the door.

For the first time since Brad had been home, Grant appreciated his advice and yet there had been a sense of menace to it. But Kate seemed to always operate on the up-and-up, so would she ever go along with entering the mound to put an item back for one man before— or instead of—taking them out for all mankind, as she liked to say? More likely she'd never forgive him for lying to her, misleading her this long. And, mound or not out her back door, would Kate ever be content living in Cold Creek, living with him?

After phoning Amber's mother to be sure she could drop by later, Kate got a small spade out of her car trunk, took a pen and paper and hightailed it straight for the place Brad had buried his dog. She marched past the mound—after taking a good stop-and-stare at it—and past the mica seam, since she'd told Grant she'd steer clear of both sites, at least until Saturday, when her dig team would come back. But he hadn't told her not to get near this pile of stones. And he didn't know she'd seen him dig here.

Looking all around, trying to buck herself up that no intruders would be in the forest this early, she did the same thing Grant had done last night. A quick sketch of the stones in case Brad, now Grant, too, knew how they were piled. An easy dig to that wooden box she'd seen Grant unearth.

The box was fine wood with a nice grain, but marred by soil and scratch marks. Fully expecting to find a dog collar or some memento of Brad's dog in it—but why would that have upset Grant when he saw it?—she fumbled with the corroded metal latch and opened it.

And gasped.

The box was empty. The inside was beautiful with gathered blue-gray silk, formed in a perfect shape for something that was no longer here. Something that had left mica dust and had lain here that was perfectly fitted to this form. A large—overly large—leaf-shaped arrowhead.

* * *

Still trembling with anger after reburying the box and replacing the stones, Kate rushed back to the house, washed her hands and went out to her car. She threw her tools in the trunk atop the others she'd brought along, hoping there would be some Adena dig she could work on in the area. The morning sun had heated the car's interior. She didn't mind, sitting there, feeling inwardly chilled on the warm June morning. She didn't start the motor, but her mind raced.

She would guess that Brad—maybe with Grant—had found the mica arrowhead in the same area where her team had found the shape of the ax head yesterday. He—or they—might have taken that arrowhead, and Brad had buried it above where he'd interred his pet dog. But had they found the ax head or other artifacts that came from the mica seam? Had Todd been involved, too, maybe had taken the ax head, then told his eldest son, Jason, about that or even showed it to him? These relics needed to be traced and studied, not buried or shown privately.

"You can't keep treasures—and the truth—buried." She repeated one of Carson's classroom mantras aloud.

She started the car and headed toward Todd and Amber's house.

Kate was in a hurry, but she accepted a cup of coffee from Amber's mother and was filled in on Todd's progress. "Slow, but after all the tests, they know what they need to do," she told Kate. "Ruptured spleen, but at least he can live without that. The doctor is operating on that today. Oh, by the way, we wanted to thank you again for getting that apartment where Amber could stay free at night with your friend in Columbus. We are so very grateful to you, and it's good to see Grant have a chance at real happiness again."

So much for her plan to talk to Todd about the ax head later today, Kate thought, but she was deeply touched by feeling appreciated here, at least by some people. As for Grant being happy—she wasn't so sure about that. But she realized she would love to make him happy. As much as he frustrated her, she would love to love him.

As soon as she could, Kate went out to the backyard, where the McCollum kids were playing while their grandfather kept an eye on them. She chatted with him briefly and was touched to see how the kids stopped their running around long enough to greet her. She finally managed to corral Jason alone over by the picnic table.

"So, I was thinking about that interesting drawing you did for your dad," she told Jason as they sat close together on the bench.

"Mom said he liked it okay."

"I'll bet he did. But I was wondering why you drew an ax head and blood, since when your dad fell, I didn't see an ax or blood."

"No, that was the other time. I wanted him to know I felt bad when I got hurt, too—like, I understand he's hurt bad."

"Oh, you fell, too? When you and Dad were chopping down a tree?"

He shook his head. "I didn't fall. In the attic I found the ax and it was really cool, but I was playing with it and cut myself bad."

"Oh, I see. I'm sorry about that. Did the ax have a handle on it?"

"No—just the top part, a kind of shiny black stone, and pretty sharp. I needed eleven stitches," he said, thrusting out his arm to her where she could see the pale red marks. "I didn't know it was hid in the attic. Mom was pretty upset, but Dad said he'd put it somewhere else. He found it when he was little, playing with Uncle Grant. Miss Kate, is my dad gonna be all right? I get mad at him sometimes, but I love him, and if he died I'd be really sad I didn't tell him that more."

Grant knows about the Adena arrowhead and ax head! And what else? Fighting to keep calm, she put her hand on the boy's shoulder and gave it a squeeze. "It may take a while, and he'll need your help, but I'm sure he'll get lots better."

She was right that Grant, Brad and Todd—maybe Paul—had found some Adena artifacts near the mica seam and hidden them. Yet her thoughts flew to her own father. *I get mad at him sometimes, but I love him, and if he died I'd be really sad I didn't tell him that more.*

As Jason went back to play with his brothers, she recalled how she, Tess and Char used to play in back of their house. She remembered her mother calling them in, saying that Dad would be late or wouldn't be home tonight. And, as angry as she was—she knew she had to stop hating her father.

24

Instead of heading home—that was, to Grant's—Kate drove straight to Columbus.

She tried to keep her mind on her driving, but she kept rehearsing tirades to Carson and Grant. Right now, everything annoyed her—the Columbus traffic, the fact she didn't have a faculty parking pass and had a long walk across campus, how big and old the Smith Laboratory anthropology building was and how their department had to share it with swarms of students taking physics, math, astronomy, public health and even film studies. Yet she really missed teaching here.

Most of all, she was upset about having to face Carson. She was no closer to permission for excavating Mason Mound, and he was still trying to force her to do so anyway. He was bombarding her with news about smashed skulls in Italy, setting up his grad assistants to push his new Toltec/Adena theory, which would ruin years of her work because his articles and speeches would have more clout than hers if she fought him on it. And she was ready to do just that. But she still didn't have the missing link of an artifact that the European Celts had in common with the Adena.

She knocked on the old oak door of Carson's office. "Enter!" he called out. She opened the door and went in; at least he was alone. How many hours had she spent in here, soaking in every word, entranced, challenged? The first time he'd kissed her, she'd been backed up against the wall, fondled and propositioned, and, like a fool, she'd thought it was wonderful.

He finally looked up from his laptop computer—then quickly shut it.

"Kate! What a surprise! You should have called, darling. Come in. Close—and lock—the door."

"This is business, Carson," she said, simply closing the door and pulling out the chair next to his cluttered desk and sitting to face him. He had the copy of the Beastmaster mask Kaitlyn had made hanging over the desk. It was mounted in a sort of glassed shadowbox, glaring down at them, the symbol, she thought, for all her failures.

"Let me guess," he said. "Grant was so impressed with your mica dig that he's agreed to let you excavate the mound, and you wanted to tell me in person so we can lay plans."

She dropped her big purse on the floor as a barrier at his feet where he'd wheeled his swivel desk chair closer to her.

"How about this?" she countered. "I'm totally unimpressed and appalled with your new Toltec theory, which you hadn't told me you were promoting in classes and who knows where else. And I'm here to tell you I'm still not ready to excavate Mason Mound."

"Ready or *able*? Kate, you've got to either get into that mound now or get out of Cold Creek! Once your sister and the sheriff return this weekend, I don't suppose you'll be sticking around. Back to Celtic digs in England?"

"Did I tell you they are back this weekend?"

"I think Kaitlyn mentioned it. That you wanted to continue the mica-seam work with her help even though they'd be home Saturday."

"She reminds me of myself."

He rocked back in his chair, planted his elbows on its arms and steepled his fingers before his face. His forehead had furrowed the minute she'd come in and refused to lock the door. She'd never bucked him like this—on anything. It was time to stand up to him.

"I knew she would," he said. "She's the best of you— bright, eager, willing..."

"I'll bet."

"That's unworthy of you. But I can understand how you'd be upset with yourself for having the opportunity to make the find of your career and have it fizzle out over female emotion, because you've fallen for Grant Mason."

She surprised herself that she had no desire to deny that. "I have made some finds, established some facts."

"Facts? Haven't I taught you anything? So-called facts—and artifacts—are elusive, subject to interpretation—to theorizing. Facts do not speak for themselves, and you'll need help on that. But I heard about the silhouette of the ax head Kaitlyn spotted. What else?"

She wanted to blurt out more about Jason's drawing and his admitting his father and Grant had found the relic itself. And that she'd seen the silken shape of what she was certain was an Adena mortuary arrowhead and had hope of tracking those items without even having to excavate the mound. But, to her own amazement, she didn't. "I'm theorizing that chips from the mica seam are the size to be used on funeral garments or shamans' masks," she said.

He sat up straighter. "Such as that?" he asked, pointing back at the mask watching them from over his desk. Carson's eyes narrowed at her as if he could probe her thoughts. "Kate, if you could ever find an identical or even similar mask to Celtic ones, like the Beastmaster, it would make your reputation. What are your last-ditch plans to get in that mound before you leave the area? Kaitlyn says what appears to be the shaft entry has nothing but some dead trees blocking it. Let's make an entry—make our move."

"Dead hawthorn trees that someone poisoned, and it wasn't me."

"So I hear. The lab test will find out what but not by whom. If it had been you, I'd give you one of those gold stars you found. Any more information on those?"

"Not really. I'm quite sure—that is, I theorize," she said, sarcastically, "Bright Star Monson left them there with hopes of either saving or damning the souls of whoever lies within those mounds. But you don't really believe some of the Toltecs journeyed all the way from Mexico and turned into the Adena, then later were progenitors of the Aztecs, do you?"

"It makes as much sense as the Celts—especially since you can't prove otherwise. When I was in Washington for that Smithsonian talk, I went to the American Museum of Natural History. Kate, there's a fantastic Toltec orange clay vessel that has a face on it that could be linked to the Adena pipe shaman. His earrings are identical, and the face is similar. We know both groups had human sacrifices with smashed skulls. Look, dar-

ling, I don't want us to fall out over this. How about I
come down to Cold Creek and together we make our
last-ditch case to Grant Mason to get in that mound?
The clock is ticking."

Her inner turmoil nearly swamped her. She loved
Grant, wanted to work with him, not against him. But
if he cared for her, why wouldn't he let her have what
she needed and desired, to dig in that mound? He'd been
so helpful letting her work on the mica wall, so was it
just the mound itself that was untouchable?

"Kate, like I said," Carson went on, pointing a finger
nearly in her face, "either get in that mound or out of
town—out of Cold Creek and out of Columbus. Back
to English digs, where you evidently belong."

She glared at him, speechless. He was right. Wasn't
this man always right? She hated that. But he was a
master manipulator, just like Bright Star Monson, who
held such sway over Lee and Grace. And even if she
couldn't quite trust Kaitlyn Blake, she wanted to rescue
her from Carson, so it wouldn't take the young woman
ten years and a lot of *sharing of resources,* as he used
to call it, to figure that out.

"You have one last chance," Carson said. "Either pull
this off now or give it up, and I'll take over. I'm having
a lawyer draft a deposition I can use to gain access to
the mound by extending the definition of *eminent domain.* Just think, with a dig team from here, you could
be in that death chamber in hours. Or else I will be,
without you."

She grabbed her purse, got up and headed for the
door. She pulled the old-fashioned key out of the lock
and tossed it onto his desk. "Just so Kaitlyn doesn't accidentally lock herself in." She walked out, and since

he was probably expecting her to slam the door, she closed it quietly.

As she went down four flights of stairs, she realized she had closed a door on Carson—his power over her, at least. If he stopped the dig team from coming back on Saturday, so be it. For the first time in years, she felt she was on her own in her career and private life. But she wasn't sure she had the strength to either defy or leave Grant.

Kate picked up food at a favorite Chinese restaurant in Columbus and drove back to Cold Creek. She figured she'd get home just before Grant if he was on time. It might be the last day she was there playing dutiful wife with food on the table, worrying if he was late. Once she challenged him on what Jason had said, he might ask her to leave. She wouldn't like going back to her childhood home, but she could handle it for a couple of days until Tess returned. Maybe she'd see if Nadine was still interested in buying the house when she stopped this evening to purchase the Adena tree-trunk sculpture. At least she'd have a modern piece of art to remember her time here in Cold Creek if Grant asked her to leave.

When she arrived she saw his car was already in the driveway. She grabbed the food and hurried into the house. "Grant?" She put the food and her purse down, then walked into the living room. What if he wasn't all right? What if, like Paul and Todd, something had happened to Grant?

She could see through the picture window that he was out by the mound. At least he was safe, looked all right, although she could tell he was furious. Another tree cut down while he was away?

She ran out the back door. When he saw her, he started shouting. "I didn't give you permission for this!"

"For what?" she cried as she approached the mound and looked where he was pointing.

The dead hawthorn trees were missing, exposing the mound area she was sure held the entry shaft. Despite some ground cover, she could clearly see a section was indented with the telltale signs of old digging, which had caved in the curve of the mound just slightly, probably from Hiram Mason's time.

"I didn't do that," she protested, hands on her hips. "And what if I did? They needed to be cut and hauled away. So you think I'm going to dig into the mound while you're gone, even though it's clear you don't want me in there? I've been gone all day, Grant. I wouldn't do that, because you didn't give me permission. Don't you get that much by now?"

"I— Okay. I jumped to conclusions. But then *who?*"

Her anger evaporated when she saw the forlorn look on his face. For a moment, she glimpsed the little boy in him, like Jason, devastated at losses he mourned.

"How long have you been gone?" he asked, his voice more quiet. "This wouldn't take long to cut it and have it hauled out. You didn't hear or see anything? It can't be the tree thieves trying to threaten or hurt me again."

"I was here awhile this morning then visited Todd and Amber's kids—Todd had surgery to remove his spleen today."

"Yeah, I know," he said, raking his fingers through his hair so some of it stood on end.

"And I drove to Columbus to see Carson."

"Isn't that cozy?"

"No, it wasn't. You know, you don't trust me, so I'll just move back to Tess's old house. This isn't going anywhere, we aren't going anywhere, and—"

"Hey, you two." Brad's voice interrupted from the backyard as he strode toward them. "Grant, I wanted to get here before you did, but Keith said you left early. Oh, I see they hauled the dead stuff away but haven't delivered the new saplings yet. I figured you'd want the same thing Grandpa put in—hawthorn. So, Professor Kate, I read up on hawthorn before I ordered it. Latin name, *crataegus monogyna.* Impressive, huh? I suppose you know its Celtic symbolism? Gotta admit I didn't, but the woman at the nursery I ordered from did."

For a moment, Kate almost felt she was back in Carson's paleobotany class years ago. "Yes, but I'm sure your grandfather didn't have Celtic symbolism in mind when he planted hawthorn trees," she told him, aware that Grant was hanging on everything they said.

"I just thought it was so ironic," Brad said, coming closer. "Grant, you're upset. I really meant to be here before you. Sorry for the surprise. I'm just grateful you let me take the foreman job—even temporarily—and wanted to help out around here. I know you've got a lot on your mind."

"True," Grant said, looking at Kate instead of Brad. "I do."

"So," Brad said, clapping his hands once. "I'll just get on my cell and find out why the new trees aren't here yet, if there was a problem. Be right back."

"Sorry I thought it was you," Grant said, taking her arm and gently turning her to face him. "Really. I'm just uptight."

"I understand."

"So what's he mean about the symbolism of the hawthorn?"

"As he said, it's Celtic, not Adena—that is, unless the Celts became the Adena. I'm wondering if your grandfather planted hawthorns there because that's what was there when he entered the mound years ago—and was planted there long before him."

"You mean the Adena might have originally planted them there and they reproduced over the centuries? So what's the deal about the hawthorn? That those long, sharp thorns have the message 'Keep out!'?"

"In Celtic beliefs, the hawthorn was associated with death, so in Europe, they're sometimes found near Celtic burial sites. But I—I hadn't even thought of that. They could be a link, just like the oversize weapon heads. Grant, like ax heads enlarged for burial sites in both Celtic and Adena culture, the planting of hawthorns could be a common element!"

"Because of the thorns, you mean the Celts linked hawthorns to death?"

"They do look forbidding and lethal. But we—Celtic scholars and archaeologists—believe it was probably because a cut hawthorn branch smells like decaying flesh. It's been proven the chemicals in each are related. You know, as if to remind worshippers or intruders what lies within the tomb or mound—what lies ahead for each of us."

"Yeah, I noticed years ago that the cut branches stink. But there, see. You have another link between the Celts and the Adena without even disturbing the mound."

"Before Brad gets back, I want to tell you that I figured out why Jason drew a picture of his dad being cut by the big ax head. Jason says he cut himself on that very thing hidden in their attic and had to have stitches. And that his dad told him that Uncle Grant was there when Todd found it years ago. Grant, that ax head is valuable, important and precious!"

Grant sank onto the big stump of his lost maple tree as Brad came bursting around the side of the mound again. "The nursery I used said we should wait to plant until later in the summer, so I said okay."

Grant muttered something she couldn't make out. Was he going to turn on Brad for this attempt at mending bridges? Was he going to turn on her for quizzing Jason about that drawing? Here, she'd been ready to walk out on him, on this mound, and now its access had been made easier by Brad.

Truthfully, all she wanted to do was stay here, talk things out with Grant. Yet he still stood in the way of what she wanted most in life—or was *he* what she wanted most?

25

After Brad left, Kate and Grant shared dinner and talked. He was trying hard to be careful what he said. For one thing, he felt bad he'd accused her of cutting down and hauling off the hawthorn trees. For another, now that the mound entrance was free of hindrances, he felt as if he was the only thing standing between Kate and the mound.

"Yes, that's true," he admitted after she brought up the ax head again. "Todd and I found that out behind the house. We were young—grade school—and, of course, thought it was cool—our secret."

"You probably didn't even know they were Adena at the time. When I've talked to groups of elementary kids about prehistoric lives, they can't even grasp the time frame."

He nodded, grateful she was trying to help him out. He was actually tempted for the first time to just come clean with her, tell her all of it, but Todd and Brad were involved, too. Sometimes he wished the two of them could sell their artifacts to ensure their shaky futures. When they took the things, they knew it was wrong, but not illegal. But they'd kept them for years, even after they did know the consequences. When Gabe got back in a few days, maybe he could handle this, finesse it, though Grant figured he'd say they had to hand everything over.

He took another long drink of wine that went well with the Chinese food Kate had brought. They'd already had a heated discussion when she wouldn't take his money for the food, but they were both making a big effort to keep the talk civil now. Man, why did things have to be so complicated between them? He'd love to scrape all the layers of his lies away, just hold her and make love to her.

"Was Gabe in on this?" she asked.

"He was away then, and we never told him."

"By *we,* you mean just you and Todd?"

"I don't want you interrogating him while he's hurt."

"Of course not. Does Brad know?"

"I'd like you to leave him out of this. He'd get upset, and I need to keep him on an even keel right now. This is between you and me."

"I'd like to think so, but you haven't answered my questions very directly." She stood and tossed her napkin hard at the table. He could tell her temper was going to show again. Her wineglass toppled over, but it was empty. "Then if it's between us," she said, "I have a confession to make. *I,* at least, want to tell the truth."

He waited for her to demand to know if he had hidden an Adena artifact, but she didn't. "I was waiting for you in the front yard yesterday evening when you drove by. I followed you, because I wanted to know if you were heading for the mica seam and why. I saw you dig up the empty box above Brad's dead dog."

He jumped up, leaned stiff-armed on the table. Brad had said she'd spied on him, and now—if she knew the

box was empty, she'd dug it up, too, seen the shape of
the big Adena arrowhead.

"Forget the dead dog. *You* keep beating a dead horse!"
he shouted. "Okay, Brad once had an Adena arrowhead
he found on our property. But from now on, any old artifacts we find here are off-limits to you, including anything in that mica seam or buried under a pile of stones!"

"You want me out of here, because you're hiding
something!"

"Yeah, I'm hiding that I want you and love you, and
that's just not going to work out, is it?"

She looked too shocked to respond, but what he'd
blurted out staggered him, too. Yeah, that was the
truth—how he felt about her, and the truth that it would
never, ever work.

"Grant, I want you to know—" she said as his cell
phone sounded. She stopped in the middle of her thought.
The familiar tune confused him for a moment as if it
came from another world. He turned to the walnut side-
board and reached for his phone, glancing at the number. "Keith," he told her. "He's home, but maybe those
wood samples came. Just—just a second. Keith, Grant
here. What's up? Did the bird's-eye maple pieces arrive
from Wisconsin after I left?"

"The timber thieves have been here! They took a couple of prime oaks! Three, way back behind the house.
You said, when they hit next, you had a lead to find
them and—"

"When? When was this?"

"Velma wasn't here today, so we're not sure. At least
five, six hours ago."

"Call 911 to get Jace there. I'll be over later, but I'm

going to check the place they cut up my tree on Shadow Mountain first."

"What's wrong?" Kate asked as he ended the call and jammed the phone in his shirt pocket.

"The tree thieves hit Keith's place for prime oak. I'm going up on Shadow Mountain to see if they try to hide there until they cut it up and get it out of state."

"But since we found their cut-up place, they wouldn't return, would they? Besides, we got shot at there."

He raced into the kitchen and grabbed his car keys. As upset as he was about the trees, he was relieved there was an excuse to stop her from grilling him. She followed him to the front-hall closet, where he fumbled behind hanging winter clothes and produced a rifle and box of bullets.

"We don't know it was them who shot at us," he argued. "They may not even know we were there. You ever hear of a citizen's arrest?"

"Grant, you can't! I'm going, too."

"No. Too dangerous."

"I'm coming, too!" she insisted and grabbed her purse from the hall table. He almost laughed at her. He had a gun and ammo; she had—what?—lipstick and a wallet?

But he was tired of arguing with her, fighting her. And he really didn't want to leave her here alone. She was right he needed a security alarm and motion light detector out back, especially if word ever got out there was literally treasure on these grounds. Did she believe any of what he'd told her?

"All right," he said as he headed for the front door with her behind him. "But there are certain conditions.

You will stay in the truck if I get out. You will get down on the floor if I say to. Understood?"

"Of course. See how well we could work together on other things? And just in case we end up spinning off that mountain road up there again, I wanted you to know I care for you, too."

That revved him up even more despite the fact she was getting too close to his secrets again. His defenses were going down. But he knew he could lose her if he refused to answer questions—and lose her if he told the truth.

Kate thought Grant drove too fast, obsessed with getting to the spot where the thieves had dissected his maple tree. It was dark by the time they reached Shadow Mountain, so she felt doubly nervous on the narrow, twisting road upward. The old Mason Mill truck rattled, and he said it needed new tires. Maybe she shouldn't have come along.

He was quiet, but she had to talk. Yet she knew, at least right now, not to start with accusations and arguments again. "I can't believe someone could haul huge horses, their hitch and one or more tall trees up this road. Have you thought of that? They'd be crazy to come back here. How did they get your tree up this road?"

"There's better access up the north face of the mountain, but it takes longer to go around. So we might be there in time. Keith said they cut them at least five or six hours ago."

"We won't be able to call for help unless Lacey's parents let you use the phone that someone cut the wires on just three days ago—if they've had it repaired by now. How did Keith sound?"

"Mad as hell. All this makes me feel he's my brother as much as Brad is. I'm going to park in the old driveway, where the former farmhouse once stood, to keep my distance. And you're staying in the truck."

"Maybe we'll see the horses in the field. Then we can drive back to bring Jace up here, because we'll know the thieves are there again. Please, promise me you'll be careful."

"You, too. Stay put. Stay down."

Using only his parking lights, he drove in the old farmhouse driveway. They bounced along, hidden from the field by a line of pine trees. When he turned off the engine, the blackness became a second, solid wall around them.

"This won't take long," he told her. "They're either here by now or they changed venues. Sit tight and keep the doors locked. I'll be right back—unless I find them. Then, I swear, I'll bring them back hog-tied."

Grant hiked into darkness through the trees with his rifle, a big flashlight and three coils of rope over his shoulder. If the thieves were there, he'd have to make them tie each other up.

Keeping his flashlight off, he stayed on the edge of the field, just outside the fence. He stumbled in a hole, went down on all fours, grateful he didn't sprain or break his ankle, but he couldn't turn on a light until he was sure no one was here. He got up and walked into the fringe of the woodlot near the shed where he and Kate had taken cover when they were under fire.

No sounds here but that of shifting leaves and a few

crickets. Not even lightning bugs, because they seldom came up this high. If the oaks were being hauled up here, surely the thieves would have arrived by now. He was deeply disappointed but relieved he wouldn't have to use the gun.

He waited awhile longer, listening, watching, thinking. He, Brad, Todd and Paul—were they thieves, too? The thought tormented him. He was willing to wait all night, but Kate would be worried. So he wouldn't stumble again, he turned on his flashlight and, keeping the beam low, swept the area with it. Jace had found cartridge shells up here, but from a common make of hunting rifle—not enough evidence to even question anyone.

The beam of light caught something bright red in the grass. Grant knew instantly what it was. He bent and picked up the wrapper. Clove gum, the kind Lacey always chewed. Her breath had always smelled of its tart, clean aroma. Sometimes he could tell when she was creeping up behind him from the scent. Had she been creeping through these woods from her parents' place, with Brad, and why? Of course, maybe they'd just walked over here to see the evidence of the sawed-up tree Brad had loved, too.

Grant jammed the wrapper in his pocket and hurried out of the fringe of dark forest, back toward the truck, keeping the light low again. He pushed his way through the screen of pines right beside the truck. He didn't see Kate in it!

He sprinted the last few yards.

Yes, thank God, for once Kate Lockwood has followed orders. She had scooted down in her seat.

In general, she had tried to toe his line, hadn't she?

More than anything, she wanted to get inside that mound, yet she'd heeded his wishes. *I wanted you to know I care for you, too,* she'd said.

He put his face close to the window glass so she could see it was him, but she was already fumbling with the inside lock. He opened the driver's-side door, slid the ropes and rifle back onto the floor behind the driver's seat, then climbed in.

"No sign of anyone," he told her as he closed and locked the door. "So maybe that *was* the thieves who shot at us before, and they've switched venues. I hope, at least, they still use the same mill in Wisconsin, but they might be too smart for that. I used to think it was probably some down-and-out local, unemployed good old boy, maybe a truck driver between runs who had the hauling capability, but now I'm not sure. It scares me to think it's someone I know—someone who has access to big saws and knows how to bring a big tree down right."

"Someone from the mill, you mean? Then they would have insider information to let them know when you and Keith aren't home."

He turned sharply to face her. "You mean Brad?"

"It was just a general question, but I'm learning not to trust people I want to trust, people I thought I could, namely Carson Cantrell."

"Good. I know what you mean. It's nothing definitive, but I found a gum wrapper from the kind of gum Lacey chews all the time."

"A strong clove smell? I noticed that from her."

"Yeah. But I'm trying not to jump to conclusions just because I found a discarded relic tied to someone."

"I hear you—again."

"Kate, you didn't mean that you can't trust *me*, did you?"

"I—I don't know. Will time tell?"

Unsure what would be a good comeback, he started the truck. The headlights came on, illuminating part of a big, broken, old painted sign leaning against the pines about fifteen feet straight ahead of them. Against a dark blue background, the white words glared at them in the lights. Treat Yourself To The Best.

Kate gasped. "That wasn't there before!"

"I sure didn't see it. You didn't see anyone, did you?"

"In the pitch-black? No, but some sick joker must have been so close when he put it there. Maybe someone is watching you or me. You're right. This is someone smart—and it's personal."

He turned the truck around fast, then hit the accelerator to send them bouncing down the old driveway. "I'm tempted to get my rifle and see if someone's hiding behind that sign. But I don't want another bullet in the tires up here—or in me."

He turned out onto the road so fast they fishtailed. Finally, just before they started down the mountain, he slowed. "The old barn up there used to have a Mail Pouch Tobacco sign," he told her. "I think that's part of it. But I can't remember if it was painted on or nailed on. So, not only is this a wild-goose chase, but we're the stupid geese."

"If not Lacey, still mad at you, maybe Bright Star is harassing us—especially me. He's bright, all right, but warped, diabolical. And what's the real message of *Treat Yourself To The Best?*"

Grant fought to keep calm, to drive the sharp turns carefully. It was black as pitch up here, and he was grateful they met no one heading up and that in the rearview mirror he saw no vehicle pursuing. As if to assure himself as well as her, he kept talking. "There are lots of Mail Pouch signs in this area. But—hey—I did like that message, even though we seem far off from treating ourselves to the best right now."

"Speaking of messages out of the blue—or the dark," she said, "you're not afraid, are you, for your own safety, after what happened to Paul and Todd?"

"You think it's a message like I'm next, so I might as well live it up now—treat myself to the best?"

"From the first you thought losing your tree was a personal warning or threat."

"It scares me that little brother Brad has everything to gain if I don't own the mill and the house. I think he's listening to Lacey too damn much. A man sleeps with a woman, his defenses go down."

Kate wondered if that was why Grant had not tried to take her to bed, even when she knew he wanted to. Because then he'd have to give in to her desires, too, and that included not only him, but the mound.

26

Kate waited in the house with Velma while Keith, Grant and Jace took flashlights outside to survey the site where the big oaks had been cut. They came back in and slumped at the kitchen table while Velma put huge dishes of homemade strawberry ice cream in front of each of them.

"No coffee this late," she said. "Trees cut or not—police work or not—people need their sleep, or they just crash and burn, and caffeine will get us all wired."

Grant glanced Kate's way. He felt as exhausted as she looked, completely drained physically and emotionally. But he dug into his ice cream.

"Gabe's gonna be shocked at what's happened since he's been gone," Jace said. "It's been a dead end—didn't mean to word it that way—on Paul Kettering's death. Todd's fall, an accident, far as I can tell."

Keith nodded and reached over to pat Jace on the back. "Maybe Paul's was, too, though I hear his wife doesn't want to accept it. Maybe he just lost it, went berserk for some reason. Then the tree trunk he was carving fell on him."

Kate groaned inwardly. She'd meant to stop by Nadine's tonight to buy that very sculpture, but she would first thing tomorrow. She pictured Paul's fine carving of the Adena shaman. Carson had claimed that the earrings and the face of that well-known Adena figure and the Toltec face he'd seen in Washington had strong similarities. She needed to check that online tonight, however tired she was.

Everyone thanked Velma for the ice cream. Jace promised he'd be back first thing in the morning to check for truck tracks and hoof prints. Grant huddled with Keith for a while, evidently consoling him about the trees.

At Grant's house, they got out of the truck in front of a pitch-black house. "I usually leave lights on," he said, "but we left in such a rush." He got his rifle out of the truck and put his other arm around her shoulders as they started to walk in together, but he pulled her to a stop. "What's that sound?"

She cocked her head. It was a warm, windy night with leaves rustling, but that hum was not the trees, not an animal sound. "I think it's far away."

"Or maybe just out in back. Weird. Let's go in, but I won't turn on a light."

They went into the dark house and locked the door behind them. Their eyes adjusted to the dark as they hurried into the living room to peer out the back. Inside, the sound was muted but still there, a hum, a buzz. Singing? Chanting? Gooseflesh popped out on Kate's arms, and her insides cartwheeled. Out by the mound?

The mound seemed aglow with wan lights. Moving lights! It flashed through Kate's mind that maybe Carson had a dig team out there, working at night. On important or dangerous digs, that had been done. But the lights were mostly atop the mound and seemed so otherworldly.

"What in the...?" Grant said. "And don't tell me it's Adena ghosts, though that mound's haunted me for years."

He grabbed his rifle again. With her right behind him, he strode for the back door.

Chills shot down Kate's spine. The sound was like a hollow drumbeat. And some sort of wind chimes? Singing, too. She almost, finally, believed in ghosts. That she'd find the shaman Beastmaster dancing atop the mound and the entry shaft open like a throat that had disgorged its dead. No matter what Grant said, whatever the odds or barriers, she had to get in that mound once and for all. Or else she would run screaming through this forest and through life like Grant's poor grandmother, who'd thought that spirits were after her. Was she—were both she and Grant—losing their minds?

They started to climb the side of the mound as they had a few days ago to see if gold stars lay atop it. And then she had a premonition of who and what this might be.

They peered over the top of the mound. Bright Star! Bright Star was dancing with three women—Grace was one—while at least twenty others knelt in a circle around them, all holding candles within paper shields and humming. Muted shadows dipped and danced, too. At first, the two of them just stared aghast as Bright Star's voice— musical, almost magical—chanted, amid drumbeats and gentle chimes. "Dead goats to deathly shadows, but my sheep won't go below, for in my light they glow..." On and on, chanting insane words within the rapt circle of people.

And, despite the loose-fitting gowns of the women, they all looked pregnant. Yes, even Grace looked pregnant, though not many months along.

Kate glanced at Grant's profile. Eyes wide, he looked stunned, but he was angry, too. She reached for his arm, but he scrambled up to more level ground and started shouting. "You're trespassing, Monson. Sorry to interrupt the séance or party, but those candles could light this foliage on fire. I'm going to ask you to leave my land now or else I'll have you arrested!"

The sounds halted. Bright Star looked as if he'd been shaken awake or slapped out of a trance. Could this man—all these people—be on drugs? Before Grace and the two other women who had been dancing around him could turn away, Kate glimpsed gold stars on their chests. Bright Star had lied. He always lied, so how deep was he into enslaving these people?

He came forward, walking unsteadily. For once, he was dressed all in black, more like his people. "Ah," he said, his voice still holding its singsong quality. "I see you have the woman with you, Mr. Mason. Everyone—" he turned to call behind him "—guard your flames. And you two," he said, turning back to Grant and Kate, "guard yourselves from evil. You never know when you will join the lost pagan dead. What a good lesson to see the goats like the Adena separated under the soil from the sheep like my flock."

"That's a good way to describe your people," Kate said. "Sheep. Maybe sheep to the slaughter if they stay with you."

"Always the wayward woman. But I will prepare a kingdom for mine own."

"On the old grounds of the lunatic asylum, you mean," Kate countered. "That sounds like your sort of Eden."

"Back to the bus, back home!" Bright Star called out. People rose and began to file quietly down off the mound, near where Kate and Grant had climbed up. He turned again to them, leveling a look of pure menace at each of them.

"I see you have a weapon of war, of destruction in your hands, Mr. Mason, owner of this place of pagan imprisonment. And you, woman, always the soul of a heathen. Death can come like a thief in the night, so beware you don't join the heathen dead—both of you."

When he stalked off, tears streamed down Kate's face, but she wasn't crying. She was hysterical with laughter and disbelief. "Back to the bus?" she spit out. "All that pseudo-religious mumbo jumbo to those poor robots—sheep—then back to the bus? And he sees himself as their Messiah. Jesus talked about separating the ungodly goats from his precious sheep. But then, back to the bus…"

Grant put the rifle down, gave her a little shake and pulled her into his arms. "You're losing it," he told her. "But I don't want to lose you. Kate, we're both punch-drunk from exhaustion—too much of everything."

She locked her arms around his back, pulling him tight to her. "But he's so unreal, so ridiculous, isn't he? I feel like *Alice in Wonderland* and I'm going to wake up soon."

"It's a nightmare, not a dream. And talk about curses—he's it. Come on. I'll watch the mound from inside the house, and tomorrow's another day. We both need some rest."

She hated letting him go. Despite the fact that, in a way, he was her worst enemy, he was also her love. They climbed carefully down from the mound, but Kate tugged him back just to take a look at the entry. She wanted to be sure Bright Star's cult members hadn't opened up the entry. No, it looked naked but still sealed. That was another reason she had to get inside to do a controlled, scientific dig. She could just see Monson's maniacs—and that included her cousin Lee and poor, pregnant Grace—coming back here to defile the remains of ancient people's lives. And hers and Grant's.

It was a pretty crazy idea, Kate thought late the next morning on her way to Nadine's house, but what if Bright Star was behind the tree thefts? He had members of his group who did manual labor of various kinds, including Lee. If he stored cut-up trees on his piece of property, he had guards watching for strangers day and night. They had some horses and other animals on their grounds. Perhaps he knew Grant would go out looking for Keith's trees and that would leave the mound available for their—whatever rite that was she and Grant had witnessed last night.

Talk about nightmares! Last night, falling exhausted in bed while Grant kept watch out the picture window, she had dreamed Grant was dancing with her, watched by the Adena, and then he'd put a Beastmaster mask on his head and led her down, down into the dark depths of the mound.

Kate hit her fist on the steering wheel as she missed

the turn to Nadine's road up the mountain and had to turn into a driveway, back out and retrace her path. She hadn't meant to, but she'd slept in this morning. Grant had been gone when she got up, so it was late morning already, and she didn't feel fully awake. So much was upsetting her. Everything about the mound and precious Adena artifacts, the fact Grant said he didn't have them and asked her not to talk to Brad about it. And especially what she'd checked online before she collapsed into exhausted sleep last night. The Toltec sculpted head Carson had cited as a possible link did bear some resemblance to the Adena shaman Paul had reproduced on the tree-trunk statue she hoped to buy from Nadine. Again, she'd promised Grant she wouldn't try to take it with her today but would wait for tonight so he could help her load it in her trunk. She couldn't wait to put its picture on her website, right next to the Beastmaster's mask she'd made, though there were only general similarities between those two. So far, she had as good a claim to the Celts as Carson with his Toltec theory.

She'd called Nadine to say she was coming and saw her looking out a front window, waiting for her. It seemed strange to go in the front door for once, instead of through the side entrance to Paul's shop.

"Things are still in a mess, but an organized one," Nadine told Kate as she ushered her in. Kate could see she'd lost weight. Her jeans were baggy, and she wore one of Paul's shirts. "My sister's been staying here, helping me pack things, donate things, mostly get ready to have my nephew list Paul's remaining works for sale on that eBay website. She's gone to the grocery store, but I'd love to have you meet her."

"If the two of you could use extra help, please let me

know. I'll be here for at least a few more days. So your illness has not been making you too tired?"

"I'm taking my meds, and I work in spurts. Cry in spurts. My sister's been a godsend, but I'm sure you understand that."

"I do, indeed. I miss Tess and Char when we're apart, which is most of the time. So you haven't thought about moving closer to your sister—to your doctor in Chillicothe?"

"Someday maybe, but I just can't leave this area right now, not after all these years and memories here."

"Then would you still be interested in buying my sister Tess's place? I'd be happy to show it to you, and she'll be back this weekend."

"Do you think she'd rent it? Then, of course, if she had a buyer, I'd move on."

"She might. I can sure ask her."

"Well, let's take a look at that carving you want. Grant called to say the two of you can drop by tonight so he can help you move it. He worries about you, I think," she said with a hint of a smile. "Here, coffee, while we sit down and chat in Paul's studio. Cream or sugar?"

"No, this is fine, thank you," she said, taking the mug. She smiled at the wording on the cup. *Paul Kettering Studio, wood carvings, au naturel.*

Kate was surprised Nadine had to unlock the studio door. Inside, every sculpture was draped in cloth.

"I know it sounds strange," Nadine said, taking a sip of her coffee, "but I don't like his carved beings looking at me. They are all mythic, strange. I'll proudly keep ones of plain old nature, but those fairy-tale types— Well, I'm relieved you want that Adena one."

Kate doubled the price Nadine suggested. "It means a lot to me," she explained as she took out her checkbook.

"Then you are getting something else with it," Nadine said. "I almost forgot about this. Found it when I was going through reams of Paul's sketches in his filing cabinet. He had the words *Adena artifacts* scribbled on it, so you might as well have it. Oh, and it was dated about twenty years ago, so he did it when he was in his teens. Now, where did I put that?"

Kate stared at the carving that was now hers. Maybe the sketch Nadine was searching for had preliminary sketches for the carving. That would be very special.

"Oh, here it is!" Nadine said. "Glad I found it because I'm wearing out again. Naps. I take a lot of naps. Here you are—yours!"

Kate took the sheet of parchment in her free hand and put her mug down with the other. She was shaking so hard she slopped coffee on the concrete floor. The pen-and-ink document dated twenty years ago was divided into four sections.

She gasped as she realized what she was looking at. On one quarter of the paper, Paul had sketched a leaf-shaped arrowhead that perfectly matched the shape and size of the one that must have been in the empty box Brad had buried. Beside that was an Adena ax head that would fit the form in the mica seam. Next was a drawing of an eagle pendant that would have been cherished by both the Adena and the Celts—by Carson's Toltecs, too, no doubt.

But the most intricate drawing—though it was no doubt much smaller than actual size—had fine details, shading and crosshatching of its mica-chip skin and sharp horns. Glaring at her from the paper was the eyeless mask of the Celtic Beastmaster.

27

"Kate? What is it? Are you okay?" Nadine's voice cut through Kate's shock as she stared at the sketches Paul had made years ago.

"I— Yes. Maybe more than okay." She felt she might collapse on the floor in hysteria—or else hit the ceiling in exultation.

"Nadine, this mask," she said, pointing at it. "I realize Paul drew this two decades ago, but do you know where he saw it? Or the other things here?"

"Oh, it's a mask? Wow, someone like a witch doctor wore that? You've seen that somewhere?"

"Not an original."

"Maybe it's something he saw in a book. With all the mythical things he carved, maybe he researched the Adena. See, it says *Adena* down by the date."

"But these other items here, this ax head and arrowhead, are Adena and were found in this area, on Grant's property to be exact. And this eagle pendant is similar to ones that are Celtic—the ancient European people I study. Where could Paul have seen that?"

"I have no idea. I didn't even know him well then, and he was always looking for new ideas here and there." Nadine sank into the single chair. Confusion and exhaustion shadowed her face. Kate regretted quizzing her like this, but if two of these artifacts existed, why not the other two? The pendant would be enough to support her theory, and the mask would prove it, no matter what Carson insisted about artifacts not being facts.

Nadine gave a huge sigh, as if she were deflating. "Since poor Paul isn't here and two of those things were found on Grant's property, maybe you'd better ask him."

"Oh, yes," Kate said. "Believe me, I intend to do just that."

In the old days, Kate would have called Carson for advice and support. But she drove directly to Grant's and retrieved her Beastmaster mask from the basement. Even though Grant had protested about it at first, he'd never moved it off the Ping-Pong table.

She unwrapped and displayed the mask on the large, wooden coffee table in the living room. She took a tiny easel that displayed a photo of Grant's parents, put the photo aside and leaned Paul's drawing on it right next to the mask. And then she began to pace and plan.

This had to be done right, said right. She made herself eat something so she wouldn't be at a disadvantage when she faced him down. Still, as exhausted as she'd felt this morning, energy and adrenaline surged through her.

She continued to pace in the living room, reciting aloud various approaches.

All the while, she kept glancing out at the mound through the big glass window.

It was just after five when Kate heard Grant's loaner truck, which made a lot more noise than his own. She

also heard the garage door go up and a truck door slam.
Next came the sound of a key in the lock, then the garage door to the kitchen opened. She stood her ground
by the coffee table, then moved in front of it so he
wouldn't see what was on it until he was fully into the
room. She didn't want him throwing a fit and retreat-
ing before they had it out once and for all.

"Kate, I was going to phone you, but we got really
busy with new deliveries today, and I was on the phone
to that Wisconsin mill and the highway patrol about
my tree. The name they had for the seller was bogus,
but they're going to get the police there if some oak—
Keith's oaks, I bet—comes in. They promised to make
an arrest, so there's a chance, anyway."

He tossed his keys on the end table and walked to
her. He didn't even take his cell phone out and put it
down somewhere as he always did, as if to officially
end his working day.

"What?" he said, stopping a few feet from her. "I
can tell something else happened. What?"

Before he could hug her, she stepped aside. He frowned
at her, then at the coffee table with her display.

He sucked in a sharp breath. "That's the mask you
made, right?"

"What other could it be?"

"The one you said Carson's latest protégée made.
Whatever one it is, I don't want it here!"

"Did you think at first it might be the one Paul drew?"
she said, lifting the sketch from the small easel and extending it to him.

His expression shifted from surprise to anger. "Nadine gave you this?"

"Yes. And I didn't even ask her for it. She knew very little about it, but I figured you'd know a lot."

He tossed the sketch on the coffee table and slumped on the soft couch. She couldn't stand still. She started waving her arms in wild gestures.

"Talk to me, Grant! I'm finally onto your scheme to keep me ignorant of the Adena relics from this property, from the mound."

"And?" he said, his voice a challenge.

"For starters, where is this eagle pendant in the drawing? And this detailed mask? I can believe an arrowhead—even a prehistoric one—and an ax head were uncovered outside the mound on your property, but you and your buddies hardly dug up this beautifully carved piece of an eagle necklace and a bone, horn and mica Beastmaster mask. I don't think either of them would be this intact just buried in the ground. They had to be somehow protected from the elements and centuries of people. Either of these relics are what I've been looking for, the pot of gold, El Dorado, proof that the Celts, or an offshoot of them, became the Adena! Did your grandfather get these out of the mound in '39, and you have them now, like family heirlooms, hidden away in secret because keeping them is illegal? You've lied to me, haven't you?"

"I don't have the arrowhead. Brad moved it and won't say where it is. But there was no dog buried out there, any more than there are likely to be Adena corpses—skeletons—in the mound."

"You're not answering my questions—again. So Brad lied to me, too? Did your grandfather say there are no human remains in the mound?"

"I didn't overhear if there are or not. I just know I

promised my dad and grandpa that no one would enter the mound."

She started to pace again. "Oh, right—let the dead stay dead. But the truth is, you can't keep treasures—and the truth—buried," she said before she remembered she was quoting Carson. "Your grandfather's keeping it a secret didn't help your poor grandmother, did it? Don't you think if your grandfather had let someone responsible dig there, it could have helped her? Then she wouldn't have imagined that Indians were coming out of there to chase her. Maybe she wouldn't have died the way she did."

"You should talk! Who supposedly saw the Beast-master lurking outside Tess's garage? Who heard it outside the window here?"

"Yes, that mound haunts me, too. And you said it has haunted you, so let's—"

"It's true Todd has the ax head, but he's put it someplace besides the attic where Jason cut himself on it."

"So you're saying you don't know where it is, either?"

"Look, the four of us made a boyhood pact, a blood oath on our friendship, that we would hide what we'd found—"

"What we'd found," she interrupted. "If you *found* that pendant and mask Paul drew, you were in the mound!"

"But we vowed never to tell anyone, never to sell them, no matter what. And sit down. You're driving me crazy."

She sank onto the edge of the coffee table so she was facing him but was out of his reach. Had she gotten too close to this man? Was she the one who was crazy to

think she loved him when he stood in the way of everything she wanted—or thought she did? The crazy thing
was she wanted to throw herself into his arms right now.

"But you're men, not boys," she argued, trying to keep
calm. "Times are different. Can't you, Brad and Todd
decide to hand the artifacts over, even let the mound be
carefully, respectfully excavated? Were there two or four
relics your grandfather brought out? When you found
them as a boy, maybe hidden in your attic, Todd got the
ax head, Brad the arrowhead, but you and Paul… Grant,
do you have the mask, since Nadine seems to know nothing about this?"

"You have it all figured out, Professor, so you tell me.
You might as well make things up as you go."

"I can't believe you're so stubborn."

"Isn't that the pot calling the kettle black?"

"All right, here's another theory, since you refuse
to deal in facts. I think you were probably the alpha
male of the buddy group. Older than Brad, and it was
on your property, with your peer group, so you got first
pick of the relics."

"Love the language. Alpha male, buddy group. Very
social worker-ish. Isn't that your sister Char's baili-
wick?"

"Stop always trying to change the subject. Worse,
you're starting to snipe at me like Carson, and I'm done
with him."

"I like the sound of that at least."

Ignoring that, she plunged on. "So, of the small eagle
pendant and the large, scary-looking mask, you took
the mask, right?"

He heaved a huge sigh. "Right," he said.

She finally took a deep breath. She realized it was a

good thing she was sitting down when he blurted out the truth for once, a chink in the barriers he'd built against her. They stared hard into each other's eyes.

"You want to see it, follow me," he said.

He got up and strode out of the room so fast, she was shocked again. She scooped up the mask she'd made for comparison, just in case he tried to pass off a fake on her.

She could hardly keep up. He headed for the basement door, turned the light on and thudded down the stairs. She hesitated one moment at the top. Why had he finally given in, even a little bit? She could trust him, couldn't she, if she went down there with him? He did care for her—that was a fact, wasn't it?

She hurried downstairs behind him. He had gone into the game room, where her own mask had been on the Ping-Pong table until today. Though he clicked on the overhead light there, he also produced a flashlight. He went back out to the furnace and was on his knees, feeling under it, until he produced a small, metal box from which he took a key. She hovered in the doorway then went over to put her mask back in its box on the Ping-Pong table before joining him again.

In the game room, he slid away a hutch with boy-hood sports trophies on its shelves. She expected to see a safe in the wall, but it was only more oak panel-ing. He pulled out five loose planks to reveal masonry brick beneath. He picked up a huge hook that looked like a weapon. She backed up another step though she wanted to watch his every move.

A terrible possibility hit her. Could Grant and Paul have argued over keeping their relics hidden? Paul needed money, but then, Brad, maybe Todd, did, too, so did they threaten to sell their artifacts, and Grant had to stop them? No, she was thinking crazy things. But was anything crazy if Grant Mason actually produced an authentic Beastmaster mask from his basement, when she'd been sleeping so near the object of her desires—other than him—these past ten nights?

She moved closer as he slid the big, old hook into a slight split in the masonry. A long crack there outlined three blocks that he slid out. From that space, he pulled a three-foot-square black metal box. It didn't look dusty or dented; he must have had it out recently. And with it, slid out one of her business cards.

"What's that doing there—my card?"

"Call me crazy—or in love. I thought if anything happened to me, someone would know to call you—to let you deal with this."

As furious as she was with him, that hit her hard. She blinked back tears and couldn't speak as he unlocked the box and lifted the large lid. She came close—too close that she blocked out the ceiling light. She took his flashlight off the floor and trained the light on the box as she knelt beside him, and he pulled out crushed tissue paper. Her hand was trembling; the beam of light bounced.

"Is this what you want from me?" he asked. "This and the mound? I was hoping it was something else, more fool me."

He slid the big box at her, and she lifted the last layer of paper. She gasped.

Staring up at her, it was so big and horrible and so beautiful! In her poor rendition of it, she had the size all wrong, but if it had been intended for the tomb and an afterlife, of course it would be large.

"Oh, Grant," she whispered and burst into tears.

Shaking hard, she tried to get hold of herself. He couldn't take it back now, could he, hide it again, throw her out, off the property? The answer to all her work, all her dreams! She could have kissed that fierce face, centuries old, despite its grotesque, glazed leather skin studded with delicate mica chips, some missing now, and its broken teeth of some beast killed long ago by arrowhead spears. And, amazingly, the human-skull base—it had been a large person, tall like the Adena—was intact, and the tips of the stag horns were still barely tinted, probably by blood. Blinking back tears, she studied the eyeholes where a real shaman had peered through—one descended from the Celts, not the Toltecs or any others!

To prove it was real, she touched it once, on the leather snout protruding from the flat-nosed human skull. It needed to be carefully preserved—at least as kids they hadn't played games with it.

"Grant, in this good shape, it's a find to match the Danish Beastmaster cauldron! It had to be preserved in the mound, not just buried."

"Yes," he said, as if this had cast a spell on him, too. She saw she was not the only one blinking back tears.

She jumped when his phone rang. He let it ring twice and squinted at the screen to see who was calling. "Keith," he said.

He took the call while she stared raptly at the mask. He'd finally admitted it was from the mound! But every time Keith called, something was wrong. Had the timber thieves struck again, or did that Wisconsin mill have a lead on a delivery of his oak trees? Nothing but this stupendous find—her missing link—mattered right now.

"He what? Damn! He's been doing so well. You think Lacey left him? Maybe she was better for him than I thought if he's off the deep end now. Yes, I'll be right there."

"What?" she asked, coming out of her trance. "Is Brad okay?"

"He must have had booze stashed at the mill somewhere, because he's drunk and lecturing Keith from the high catwalk above the saw line, saying he should have half say in the Mason Mill because Todd won't ever be back to work. Kate, I've got to go, talk him down. Let's put the mask back in safe storage for now, since you know where it is. We'll figure out how to handle all this when I get back."

"Can't I keep it out?"

"Will you just compromise here?" he demanded, putting the lid on the box and locking it. "What if Brad's suicidal? He could fall or jump. I need to go!" He pushed it back into its little tomb, and she shoved her business card in after it.

Picturing the horror of Todd's free fall from the tree, she helped him shove the three masonry blocks back in place. Brad mattered; living people mattered, yes, even more than buried treasure.

Grant pocketed the key.

They stood, bumping shoulders. "We'll work together on this," he told her. "I thought Brad was safe from himself—and I want you to stay safe."

He hugged her hard and ran upstairs, leaving her to put the oak panels if not the hutch back in place. She sat on the floor with her back to the blocks, as the guardian of the precious mask that lay within, just behind her. She wasn't angry with Grant for the crime he'd committed and the lies he'd told her. After all, he'd shown her the mask and he'd hugged her goodbye. Surely, everything would be all right now. They would work together on this.

She just sat there, waiting for Grant to call, still stunned by all that had happened and amazed she had no desire to phone Carson, despite the magnitude of this find. She loved being so close to the proof her years of work and research had been right. After sitting for maybe fifteen minutes or so, she heard footsteps upstairs. Oh, no! Had Keith called Grant with bad news? Or could it be that Brad had come down from the catwalk at the mill and come here, missing Grant? Who else but the cleaning woman had a key to this house?

She hurried up the steps. "Grant?" she called as she rushed into the living room.

Standing with a pistol pointed stiff-armed at her was Carson Cantrell.

28

At first, Kate's mind wouldn't register that Carson was actually here, in Grant's living room, so close to the mound. And with a gun pointed at her. *Too many shocks today, too much to handle...*

"Carson, did you come here to force Grant to let us dig? How did you get in?"

"Let's just say I'm here, darling, and your Grant's not."

He picked up the sketch of the four artifacts from the coffee table. "Paul Kettering was quite a good artist. It was a tragedy he died. He contacted me about selling his eagle pendant and hinted that he might have access to a deerlike antlered mask."

"Which you failed to mention to me, knowing it would make my case."

"And *your* name, instead of mine. He said he needed an expert opinion, then changed his mind, even though I'd offered him an outrageous amount of money. He threatened to expose me for wanting those items for my private collection if I wouldn't keep his secret. There was no going back."

"You—you killed Paul?"

"It was ruled an accident and rightly so, since we struggled. But then, wouldn't you know, I couldn't find where the man had hidden the pendant. I couldn't rely on you, either, two-timing me, choosing Grant over me after all I'd done for you. Do you think you would have moved up in the department or the academic world so fast without my mentoring and collaboration?"

"I— No, of course not. Please put that gun away, and we can still work things out."

"Too late, dear Kate. You have completely disappointed me, but I have hopes for Kaitlyn now. So let's get the mask out of the basement and get into the mound before darkness descends."

She gasped. How did he know where the mask was? This was too much, too fast to reason out.

"You asked how I got in here," he said. "Keith had a copy of the house key made quite a while ago from Grant's office at the mill."

Keith! If Keith was working for Carson, Grant was in terrible trouble.

Grant jumped out of his car and rushed into the mill. He scanned the catwalk above the now quiet, deserted cutting floor. There was no sign of anyone. At least Brad hadn't done this in front of the staff.

"Keith? You here? Brad?"

Keith's distant voice came from the big back sliding door where seasoned wood to be cut or treated was brought in by a forklift.

Grant ran around the big suspended cutting saws and conveyor belt toward the door. He scanned the area for Brad, praying he hadn't jumped or fallen to this concrete floor. He saw in his mind's eye the long-decayed, displayed corpses of the Adena, those honored in death, and the servants or slaves who had been sacrificed with them, laid out on low beds on the floor of the tomb with smashed skulls…a nightmare from the depths of time.

He stopped in front of the high, half-open door that led to the back lot with its pallets of tall stacked wood. Thank God Brad wasn't on the floor, but where was Keith?

He was about to yell for Keith again, when he heard a noise and turned. Keith swung a two-by-four so fast Grant felt a breeze. Instinctively, he tried to duck before his head exploded. He fell to the floor.

"And, of course," Carson lectured, "Keith's own set of keys was how he got in here to plant the bugs."

"*Bugs?* What bugs are in this house?" Kate demanded.

"Not those damned mosquitoes outside by the mound at dusk. Covert listening devices. Velma's been so helpful monitoring what was said here in this room and keeping me totally informed. She'd never texted before, but, in exchange for a few nice things, she's been a real trouper, too."

Besides betraying Grant for money, Keith and Velma must be out to hurt Grant because that would hurt Gabe. Another brother had quit the mill, but Keith must have stayed for revenge, and Carson had made it workable and worthwhile.

He went on. "I told Keith I'd pull the bugs out of here, so that tinhorn sheriff's deputy won't find them." She watched, stunned, as he pulled something from behind a framed photograph on the wall and something else from inside a leafy plant.

"Very handy, small and flat. Voice activated. These look just like a flash drive if anyone stumbles on them," he said, pocketing them. "You know, I had to cancel an important conference call to drive down here today when Velma texted that you had started rehearsing aloud what you were going to say to Grant about the four Adena relics. I figure one of them is the eagle pendant I'm owed, but I want the others, especially that Beastmaster mask."

"Keith's willing to kill, too, isn't he?" Kate asked, horrified. "Todd took Keith up climbing just before he fell. He must have made some cuts in Todd's harness that frayed during the next climb. But why? To put pressure on Grant to let us dig? And poor Todd was so sure of himself aloft, he missed that."

"Ah, pride goeth before a fall. Finally, you are showing a glimmer of intelligence in all this. As I said before, your rush of feelings for Grant blinded you. You should have done your homework. Didn't I always stress that?" He shook his head and shrugged. "I thought Grant would buckle under pressure, starting with losing that big maple tree that guarded the mound. Here on the edge of Appalachia, families like the Simons clan are thick as thieves—timber thieves."

"Keith is the timber thief? He's the one who shot at us on Shadow Mountain?"

"The one thing he did on his own, and it was stupid. He figured if you and Grant were gone, I could deal with Brad Mason. But we didn't need the law on our back, especially not your new brother-in-law, who would make it his life's work to find who killed you and Grant. At least Keith finessed his own trees being cut."

"He cut his own oaks so Grant wouldn't suspect him?

Was he up on the mountain the second time we went? He just mocked us with that old Treat Yourself To The Best sign."

"By that time he'd gotten it through his thick skull not to eliminate you two and tick off the sheriff. But you and Grant couldn't figure any of that out on your own, could you?"

"The amazing, the illustrious Carson Cantrell, always teaching me something new. Why start all this in motion by cutting down Grant's amazing tree?"

"Keith thought it was to shake him up. The truth was it was to open up the area near the mound for what should have been your excavation camp. Now it will be mine. I'm paying Keith well, but he and his brother, who used to work for Grant, were already making good money from that little arboreal sideline. I'll have to warn them not to use that Wisconsin lumber mill again."

Keep him talking—and boasting, Kate thought. She had to outthink him, keep him here, keep him calm.

"So you say Paul contacted you, but how did you find Keith?" she asked.

"I know you're stalling, but I have to admit I'm proud of how this all came together despite how devious and disloyal you've been to me. When I first learned about Mason Mound from archival information, which I now have—"

"I should have known someone stole that from the university archives!"

"Don't interrupt. Anyway, about that time, the *Chillicothe Gazette* and the *Columbus Dispatch* were full of articles about the kidnappings here, including your sister's. I was hoping there would be someone mentioned in the paper I could contact who could turn the screws on Sheriff McCord to force him to make Grant let me excavate Mason Mound. Keith turned up. He was mentioned as the *sole survivor* of the Simons family in distress, because of the sheriff's arrests. And here Keith worked for Grant Mason, mound owner, who was Sheriff McCord's best friend. So rather than Keith quitting the mill like his other brother did, I hired him to work for me to find a way to get to Grant."

"Grant felt Keith was almost like another brother," Kate said.

"That's why you should have stuck with someone with brains, darling. Namely me. Now you've made yourself my enemy."

It hit her hard that Grant had made a mistake with Keith, but she'd made one far worse trusting Carson all these years. He was a master manipulator and idea thief but also a murderer. She could see that Carson must be demented. He reveled in being the big man here, knowing the answers, smug and proud to lord it over her, just as he'd always done with his students in class.

"Carson, I know this sounds like an old movie line, but you can't get away with it. Gabe—someone—will find out, and you'll get your own small tomb of a prison cell for the rest of your life—if not the death penalty, especially if you set up Grant and hurt me."

"Bright girl that you are, you didn't suspect me, did you? Not Carson sitting in his distant, tenured, academic ivory tower, because I had Keith and Velma do all the dirty work around here."

"Including Keith wearing my Beastmaster mask to terrify me when I was trapped in Tess's garage?"

"I was tempted to try to do that myself, but he knew the territory. But as the ignoramuses of the world say, that's past history now, when history is always past. The Beastmaster *vision* was only one of my attempts to urge you to get in the mound, but you utterly failed. Let's get the mask out of the basement so we can head out there now."

"To the mound? It's still sealed," she insisted, not budging.

"My darling, I had the mound entry dug out this morning while you were out and about. Keith's brother is nearly finished reopening a narrow path through the entry shaft that was dug out decades ago."

"So you poisoned the old trees there to clear the way."

"Keith did," he said, waving the gun at her. She realized she'd been so shocked and angry she'd almost forgotten about what he must mean to do with that gun. That terrified her but it infuriated her, too.

"You'll say you found nothing inside, but you'll keep or sell whatever's there, won't you? Or keep things for your very private collection?"

"Kate, the basement. Get the mask now, or you won't be around long enough to enter the mound with me."

She had to keep him here, not allow him to rob the mound. Keith must have called Grant into a trap, a deadly one. But too much time had passed to warn him, and her cell phone was in her purse in the bedroom. She'd give up ever getting a glimpse into that mound if it meant she could keep Grant safe.

Grant swam up from the darkness. He was being dragged by his feet, the back of his head on concrete. Had he fallen from a tree? He was outside. There was a breeze. He felt too sick to even open his eyes. Was it time to get up and get to work? His head hurt. Bad.

Someone dropped his legs. Maybe Kate had called the medics. They would come in a chopper, and she would flag them down. She had a child in her arms. She loved kids, which surprised him. And they loved her.... He loved her, too, wanted children with her.

As he lay there, dazed, he heard a loud noise. He smelled sawdust. Someone was taking his tree! He had to stop them, but he didn't want Kate to get hurt. He'd make her stay in the car. He wanted her, even at the cost of the mask, the mound...

He opened one eye. Keith. Keith was hard at work, driving the forklift with a huge pile of wood, coming closer. Maybe they'd gotten his maple back, the tree house, too.

No, hadn't Keith hit him with a board? Or had he dreamed that?

Keith was driving the forklift toward him. It stopped. Keith was shouting. "This is for my family, but I swear, your sheriff friend's gonna join you in hell soon!" The metal arms rose higher and tilted to drop the whole pallet of wood on him.

Carson was waving the gun again, then pointing toward the basement with it. "I appreciate your finding this hard to believe as it all finally comes together. You had your chance, Kate, and you blew it. Could have had me, too, but it's too late. Lead the way down into the basement and get me the mask."

Her mind raced. If the listening devices were only in the living room, he didn't know where the mask was in the basement. "Grant took the key."

"At least show me where it's hidden so I can get someone in here to free it. Is it in a safe?"

"Why didn't you bug the basement, too? Maybe my bedroom and his?"

"Would that have been X-rated? Or would poor Velma have heard sweet nothings whispered? Actually, I thought about it. Now, move. Do it, Kate. You are expendable now if you don't do exactly as I say. I think you'd like a glimpse into the mound despite the fact I have only myself to thank for that."

She saw things clearly—too clearly now. He had planned for Grant, like Paul and Todd, to meet with an accident. He'd failed with Todd, but he'd still removed him from supporting Grant. And when Brad inherited the Mason property, Carson probably figured he could deal with him easily. And the pistol Carson pointed at her was not just to make her obey him. No, he'd told her too much and knew she wasn't going to be useful to him now. He meant to kill her, too.

Grant rolled away as the heavy boards crashed down near him. Dust rose. He half crawled, half clawed his way behind the nearest stacked pallet of wood. So dizzy. Hurt all over. Head pounding. Feeling so defeated but furious. Almost buried alive. His bones could have been broken—his head crushed like those in the death chamber with smashed skulls.

Grant figured it would take Keith some time to realize he wasn't under the pile of wood. He heard the forklift motor shut off. From one wood pallet away, Grant watched Keith get down, bend over the big mound of wood, then haul a few pieces off the top.

When Grant touched his head, his hand came away

covered with blood. He wiped it off on his shirt and edged away, around another huge pile of uncut planks. The dust was clearing, and Keith was madly pulling boards away, trying to find him, see if he was dead.

Grant felt so woozy but knew it would be suicide to stay and fight. He moved diagonally so Keith couldn't look down the alley of woodpiles and spot him. He had to call for help. But his phone wasn't in his pocket. No doubt it had fallen out or was smashed as he could have been.

Grant felt to see if his car keys were still in his jeans pocket. Yes. So all he had to do was get to his car, get out of here, get help.

He heard Keith swear and then the forklift started again. The man was skilled with that, and fast. Had Keith shoved rocks over the mica ledge at him and Kate? And what else? Could he be working for or with Brad? Brad had tried to get along with Keith lately, and they'd talked a lot.

Staggering in a zigzagging path down the tall stacks of tree trunks, planks and cut wood, desperate to get clear to his car, Grant tried to keep Keith from catching a glimpse of him.

29

Even if Carson killed her, Kate didn't want him to get his hands on that authentic Beastmaster mask. He was the real beast here.

On the way down the basement stairs with the gun pressed to her head, Kate wondered if she dared try to pass off her mask on the Ping-Pong table as the ancient one. Or if she did show him the real one, would he be so stunned at its magnificence, like she'd been, that she could catch him off guard? She could get his gun, shoot him if she had to, run upstairs, get help for Grant.

She decided not to risk passing off the mask she'd made as the authentic one. Carson was familiar with it, and the Ping-Pong table had lights above it, so he would see the mask clearly. She could try stalling, especially since Grant had the key to the box, though she supposed it could be opened by force.

She led Carson into the game room and easily removed the five wood panels, since Grant had not replaced the hutch. He'd left the big hook on the floor, too. Could she hit Carson with it or one of the wood panels? She took her time maneuvering the heavy masonry blocks onto the floor.

A terrible thought hit her. Here she was, showing

Carson what Grant had just entrusted to her care. If she and Grant managed to get out of this, would Grant ever believe that she hadn't meant to give his treasure away?

She was hoping Carson would get frustrated with her slowness, offer to help, lay the gun aside for even a moment, but he didn't.

"These blocks are heavy, and the box back here is, too," she told him.

"You're a strong girl. Take your time. I've got klieg lights out back if we enter the mound after dark. This Glock and I can be very patient. And Velma told me that Brad is living with Grant's ex, so I don't expect him to show up here. Today, we have plenty of time, just you and me."

She struggled to slide the box out, hurting her wrist and breaking her nails. She shoved her business card back inside the dark space. That Grant had wanted to be sure someone phoned her if he was gone and someone found the mask was not for Carson to know. She cherished the thought that Grant had at least done that for her, and before she made him tell the truth.

"Like I said, Grant has the key, so I can't open it," she told him.

"But you're very good with an excavating needle pick, aren't you?" He tossed one onto the floor beside her. "Use it to pick the lock. Ah, just think, the real thing at last. Proof of the Celt-Adena link. Does it help to know that you were right? I'd say the size of the box means it is quite spectacular."

"I don't know how to pick a lock," she said.

"Try it. Do it. Now."

She hated this man. She was going to stop him whatever it took.

* * *

As soon as Grant cleared the corner of the building, he broke into a full-out sprint for his car. It was only then he realized how dizzy he was. He reeled, went way off balance.

The buzz of the forklift motor stopped. He heard a shout behind him, followed by footsteps.

Grant lifted one hand to his head as if he could steady himself. With his free hand, he dug for the key in his pocket as he ran. If Keith caught up to him, he'd be no match for him in this condition. Now that he'd tried to kill him, there would be no holds barred.

His fingers seemed clumsy. When he glanced at his car again, it seemed to tilt, almost to stand on end.

He aimed the key for the lock, but it, too, seemed to be moving. He scratched the door paint, tried again.

Keith was close, too close. Desperation and rage poured through him. This man he'd trusted had tried to crush his skull like Paul's, like those long-dead Adena.

As Keith lunged for him, Grant grabbed at some hanging plants outside the mill. One came loose by its chain. Gripping that, he swung the plant at Keith and connected with his jaw. He went down on all fours, then scrambled up and lunged at Grant again.

Although Kate could not manage to pick the lock of the box, Carson didn't put down the gun to help her. "All right," he muttered. "Bring the box. No more Q and A, no more stalling. I'll take it like it is."

It was heavy, but she lifted it in both arms. Her skin was so slick with sweat she almost dropped it. She managed to keep the needle pick, though she wasn't sure what good it would do against a gun. But she held the pick tight under the huge box as she slowly made her way up the stairs. However pitifully small, she'd try to stab him with this pick when she got her chance. She had to keep fighting the most primitive fight-or-flight response. Stay calm, look for a way to outsmart one of the smartest people she'd ever known.

Outside, she was shocked to see only one man near the mound, a tall, muscular guy who greatly resembled Keith. And the mound—the entry was open. She could see a narrow passage into it!

"Take the box and guard it with your life," Carson told the man.

She managed to hide the pick before he pulled the box from her aching arms. She trembled from the strain, excitement and terror. If she went in there with Carson, she knew she wasn't coming out. How she had longed to get a glimpse of the interior, but now she wanted to run. Should she risk that, let him shoot her in the back? Maybe Gabe could trace the bullet and gun to Carson— if they ever found her body.

"You first," Carson said and gestured with his gun toward the dark, gaping entry. "Didn't you used to say you wanted us to explore things together?"

"You'll need a lot of light in there," the other man said, putting the box down and handing Kate a big light and Carson a smaller one. "You won't believe the stuff inside. Creepy, like some horror show. Man, can't wait to close that up again. I'll wait here."

Kate knew what her fate was then. He did intend to leave her inside, shot or not. Even if he interred her alive, she would run out of oxygen. Carson would be back soon to take artifacts from here, either pretend to be shocked to find her body—or get rid of it. He'd make his name with a careful excavation and claim her Celt/ Adena theory was his.

* * *

Grant hit Keith with the plant a second time, again in the face. The big man fell back onto his rear. Keith rolled over and lunged at him again.

Grant managed to sidestep the attack. Maybe his equilibrium was improving. A car horn blared. A door slammed. Someone driving by saw them. He heard Brad's voice. "Keith! Grant! What in— Stop it!"

"It's him!" Grant grunted. "Him!"

"Him what?" Brad shouted and pushed them apart. Keith swung a fist at Brad and connected with his jaw.

"He tried to kill me!" Grant shouted. Dizzy as he was, he pulled Keith away from Brad and kneed him in the groin. The man he'd trusted doubled over and threw up. Grant shoved him to his knees, facedown in his own vomit. "He climbed with Todd the day before he fell, probably sabotaged his harness! He called me and said you were drunk, on the catwalk inside. It was a setup so he could kill me!"

Brad scrambled up and helped Grant subdue the bigger man. Grant pulled the length of chain from the hanging plant and wrapped its links around Keith's wrists behind him.

"And you believed him about me being drunk again?" Brad muttered, as he spit out a tooth. "Thanks a lot."

"No, thanks for helping. When the Mason boys stick together, look out."

"Together again. You know, you look like hell," Brad said.

"Dizzy. Can't drive. Take me home. I've got to call Kate, tell her what happened."

"You need a doctor. Let's call Jace first to come arrest this bastard. He must have been killing off Gabe's friends to get back at him. So, the Simons boys stick together, too. I was probably on his hit list next—that right, Keith?" Brad demanded. He picked up his tooth and put it in his pocket. He was bleeding from the mouth.

"Let me borrow your phone," Grant said. "I'll get the sheriff, but I gotta call Kate first."

He dialed her number but she didn't pick up. He couldn't imagine she'd leave the house where she'd finally found the mask. She wouldn't take it out of its hiding place and go to that damned Carson—would she? He was hoping that he and not that horrible mask was the answer to all her prayers.

Praying hard, clutching the needle pick in her right hand, shining a bright beam of light ahead of her, Kate entered the dank dirt passageway into the mound. Behind her, Carson held his gun on her. He prodded her in the back with it more than once. It was much too narrow in here to turn on him and try to stab him with this little needle pick.

The thrilling moment of discovery she'd always longed for was ruined now. Whether it was the Adena who had passed through here centuries ago, Grant's grandfather decades ago, four scared boys or just Carson's lackey today, all she wanted was out. Even her passion to know what lay within was nothing next to her desperation to live.

And here, in this very passage linking life and death, what had sacrificial slaves or prisoners thought they would find within as they made this final journey? Praise? Honor? A glorious afterlife? She knew one thing. Once inside, she had to ignore whatever wonders or horrors she saw and concentrate on finding a way to escape.

She was sweating, but she shook with chills. Her stomach cramped. Dust bit into her nostrils, fierce fear into her heart. She could feel herself breathing harder in the scant, stale oxygen, hemmed in by the big log beams that lined this passageway. Suddenly, it opened into a low, broad space with a beamed ceiling.

She almost stumbled over a pickax Carson's man must have left inside. "Well," he said. "He didn't have my safety lecture in my Archaeology Fieldwork class."

If she wasn't ready to cry, she would have laughed. At one time, like an idiot, she would have thought that was clever. Now her moment of triumph in the tomb was going to be a deadly disaster.

As their light beams probed the interior, they gasped in unison at what they saw: two elaborately dressed, intact skeletons with dust-covered weapons and jewelry arrayed around them, guarded by prone corpses with smashed skulls.

Life—the idea of life with Grant—had never seemed sweeter. *Now or never,* she thought. "Oh, Carson, look there!" she cried. "Another Beastmaster mask!"

She flashed her beam of light directly into his eyes and ducked. The gun went off, echoing, seeming to shake the chamber, though the sound was probably muted outside.

She crawled away from him, waiting for pain, but she had not been hit. *Yet.* Carson cursed, used his light, then scrambled for his gun instead of her. It had landed on the wooden bench where the two main corpses lay. For a moment, their shifting light beams made it seem as if the dead bodies moved. It wouldn't do her any good to run out when Carson's lackey waited there. In that split second, she spotted something better than the needle pick she still held. She grabbed a big ax head near her.

As Carson spun toward her with the gun, she lunged and hit him with the ax head, cutting his neck. With a cry and a curse, he threw her back against a support beam, then raised the gun.

Just like the day she and Grant kissed at the mica seam, a small cascade of dust sifted down on them. Above, something rumbled. Carson, holding his bleeding neck with one hand, looked up for a moment and the cloud of dust turned to a dribble of dirt. She leaped away as he tried to cover his eyes. Dust and dirt in larger chunks cascaded at him. He covered his head and tried to duck.

He shot where she had been. He screamed, trying to clear his eyes as the two beams above them groaned and sagged, then gave way. The earth beneath Kate's feet seemed to shift. With a huge belch of dust and shudder of earth, the roof of the burial chamber caved in.

Kate threw herself under the corpses' bench and covered her head. When the rumbling sound finally stopped, she lifted her head and, coughing up dust, opened her eyes. The wan light that had marked the exit was gone, covered by a mound of dirt. She was trapped in utter, solid blackness with the dead.

30

After Jace arrested Keith Simons, Grant insisted that Brad drive him by the house on the way to the Adena Regional Medical Center.

"Her car's here," Grant said as they pulled up.

"So—a good sign."

"Then why didn't she answer her phone? If she went outside for something, I think she'd take it with her."

He'd filled Brad in on showing her the mask. Brad admitted he'd moved his arrowhead to his safe-deposit box in the bank. Together, both walking wounded, they got out of the car and walked toward the house.

"Kate!" Grant bellowed inside though it made his head hurt more. At least most of his dizziness had subsided. He didn't stop to wash the dried blood off his head or change his shirt. He'd been urging Brad to call the town dentist right away and take his tooth in to see if it could be reimplanted. But now nothing mattered but Kate.

He went down to the basement. The light was on. He saw the hiding place was open and the box gone. Had she betrayed him?

"Grant!" Brad shouted down the stairs. "You'll never

believe this. Keith's brother's out by the mound. Ned, the one who you said got ticked off and quit the mill."

As exhausted as he was, Grant ran up the stairs and straight outside. Dusk was edging toward darkness.

Ned saw him coming and shouted. "Hey, I was hired to dig out this mound. She's with that professor guy," he added, holding up both hands and backing away. Grant figured he was probably going to grab the shovel behind him for a weapon. The mask box lay just beyond, so had Kate turned traitor?

"He—I mean she," Ned stammered. "She hired me to dig out the entry. Hey, what happened to your head?"

"Get off my land. Go see if you can raise bail money for another of your lunatic brothers, because Keith's been arrested."

"For taking trees?"

That news staggered Grant. Keith and Ned were the tree thieves. But that was secondary to finding out who'd really ordered Ned to dig out the entry to the mound. He didn't want to enter it ever again, but he had to get Kate and Carson out here, so he hoped he didn't have to fight Ned, too. He watched the big man glance at the shovel, and then he ran into the trees.

Grant turned and gasped. It was true that the entry to the mound had been dug out, but it was blocked maybe six or eight feet in! Could Kate be trapped? He knew how desperately she'd wanted to see inside, yet he couldn't believe she'd do this. How could Kate or Carson have located Ned? He'd believed Kate when she'd said she was done with Carson, yet...

No, he believed her. He loved her.

He ran for the shovel and attacked the soil blocking the entry. Through the thickening gloom, Brad appeared. "i called Jace. He'll be here as soon as he locks up Keith."

"Call the volunteer fire department. We can use these lights. I think Kate's trapped inside, maybe with Cantrell!"

"Okay. Okay! I'll be right back to help you dig."

His head and heart pounding, Grant hacked at the huge plug of dirt—and then he hit a barrier of broken log beams.

Until the noise and shuddering of the mound stopped, Kate kept curled up with her hands over her head. She'd been certain her skull—like the two bodies here, like Paul's—was going to be smashed. But the low-built bench with the corpses above her had protected her from the worst. She was sure Carson had been crushed. She called out his name but there was no response.

She had a pocket of sooty air to breathe but for how long? She edged blindly into the pitch-black space. Where was that ax head? If she could find it, she could dig with it, but she felt nothing like that nearby. She reached up onto the bench to see if she could find another sharp mica weapon or instrument. Her hand snagged only bones. She pulled back. Her own gasping for air echoed strangely as if the corpses above her were breathing.

Although she could see nothing, she had to find a tool to dig her way out. As she crawled carefully through the darkness, waving one hand ahead of her, her thoughts cleared. She had so much to live for. She loved Grant and prayed he'd want her. And she had to forgive her father, to tell him so. She'd get to know her little half brothers, spend more time with Tess and Char, get married and have babies of her own. Her career was important, but here—trapped within the burial mound—the most important goal was life. She had to get out.

However hopeless she felt, she started digging with her hands. She breathed in stale air laden with dust. Grant's family motto of *Let the dead stay dead* haunted her. She wanted to breathe fresh air again, see the sunlight. She wanted to hold Grant. But she swallowed a scream when she heard another rumble and more dust and dirt settled itself just ahead of her.

Grant and Brad dug like madmen before nine volunteer firefighters rushed in with picks and shovels.

"I think some beams inside must have collapsed. We think two people are trapped," Grant told them. In the cooling evening breeze, he realized there were tears running down his face. As darkness descended, they brought in more klieg lights. The area around the mound turned bright as day.

He'd recognized all of the guys but one. Out of breath—praying that Kate had air—he stood back with Brad and watched them work.

The fire chief, Mike Thomas, who also owned the pharmacy uptown, came to talk to him. "You've been bleeding bad, Grant. Want me to clean that up or call the squad? Looks like you need stitches."

"We need the squad to help Kate when we get her out. What about maybe going in from on top of the mound?"

"I sent a man up to look. He saw a depression there, but no hole, so we might only cause more cave-ins with weight up there. It all depends on where the victims are trapped."

Where the victims are trapped. The words echoed through Grant's stunned mind. He tried to tell himself the fact they were in an ancient tomb didn't mean they were dead. Kate had to be alive. It would be too much if she died where she'd most wanted to discover things. They'd only begun to know each other. He couldn't bear it if she was buried with her Adena.

Kate continued to dig with her hands in the area where she thought Keith's brother had opened the narrow passageway. For so long she'd wanted in, not out of here. Her arms were weak, her back ached—her regrets hurt the most. The stale air was dwindling, because she was breathing hard, too hard. Hard work, she'd never been afraid of that, helping Mom when Dad left, studying long hours, working jobs to put herself through college for what her scholarship and grants didn't cover... reaching for goals. It was hard to breathe...exhausted... light-headed and faint...

But then someone was digging beside her. "Carson?" she muttered and slumped against the dirt wall. But no voice, no other sounds but her own rasping breath and someone else digging.

Someone was lifting her, laying her out on the wooden bench with the corpses. She was floating in air, surrounded by mica-covered faces and something bright in her eyes and over her face...like a mask...a Beastmaster mask...

Strange voices, not Grant...not Carson...not the one who helped her dig...

"Okay, got her. She was partway to us. Slide her out."

"She breathing?"

"Oxygen mask in position on her face. Turn it on. Now!"

"Kate! Kate, it's Grant. Take a deep breath. Breathe, sweetheart."

"Grant, was she crushed?"

"Not this woman. No way!" Grant said, but his voice caught and he sucked in a sob.

She opened her eyes and tried to blink away the dirt and soot. She was not on that bench with the Adena. Living, moving men had her on a kind of gurney. The lights were so bright they hurt her eyes. Was it the next day? How long had she been inside? She looked around, dazed, confused, seeing face after face of Cold Creek men who had somehow dug her out—and hadn't someone gotten in to help her dig? She kept sucking in big breaths of sweet air.

When Jace and Brad came up to stare at her, she pulled the oxygen mask off. "Jace, Carson Cantrell's inside. Buried under beams and soil. He had a gun. He opened the mound and forced me in."

Jace turned away, yelling to the others that there was another person inside.

"Grant," she said weakly. "Is the mask okay?"

He smiled through his tears and took her soil-caked hand. His head was bandaged. He had blood all over his shirt, and she was filthy, but crazy joy surged through her. She was alive and Grant was, too.

"The mask is safe," he said. "And I'm giving it to whatever woman agrees to live here and marry me— and dig this mound out the right way. Now, put that oxygen mask back on your face."

"Okay, but no more lies or masks. I'm going to marry

the man I love, even if he only owns an anthill and won't
let me near it."

He squeezed her hand and kissed her gently before
he put the mask back on her face.

Two days later at 9:00 p.m., Kate and Grant waited
for Tess and Gabe to arrive at the Columbus airport.
People who had deplaned streamed past them. They
watched a happy reunion between a soldier dressed
in desert fatigues and his family. Kate blinked back
tears at their joy and her own. She'd called her father
and talked to him for two hours. He'd said she and
Grant should visit in autumn. As soon as the mound
was cleared as a crime scene, she was going to lead a
team to excavate it. On Monday, she had to testify in
a hearing in Columbus about Carson's death. They'd
recovered his body—crushed under tons of wood and
soil in the mound—and some stolen and black-market
antiquities in his house. But right now, she felt nothing but relief.

When the story of Carson's crimes had hit the local
and national media, Char had called from out West,
worried about Kate, asking if she should come back
and take care of her. Char, the bleeding heart. Kate had
thanked her but had assured her she had someone to
take care of her now.

"Wow!" Char had exploded. "Maybe I'd better get
my bod back to good old scenic Cold Creek. Seems to
me like a hot spot for finding mates! No way i'm going
to marry a man out here. Wish I could stop them from
drinking and roughing up their wives and kids."

Kate and Grant held hands, watching for the newlyweds, since the arrival board said their plane had landed.

A cluster of people came at them, and then Tess and Gabe appeared, beaming.

"Hey, you two, thanks for being here," Gabe cried as Kate and Tess hugged and the men shook hands. "And you two were holding hands and you have that look— right, Tess?"

"I'll say they do," Tess said, grinning and rolling her eyes. "I'd recognize it anywhere now. But wait till we tell you guys about our trip. It was so fabulous and ro- mant— What? *What?* Did something besides you two getting closer happen while we were gone? Oh, Grant, you have stitches on the side of your head."

"Are you okay?" Gabe asked. "What happened? Is everything all right in good old Cold Creek?"

Kate and Grant had decided not to spring the news of Paul's death and Todd's accident on the newlyweds first thing. But where to start? All she could think of now was, no matter what terrible things had happened, she and Grant had a great, new beginning.

* * * * *

Author Note

Kate's story is book two in the Cold Creek trilogy. Tess, the youngest sister, was featured in the first book; Kate, the eldest, in this novel; and Charlene, the middle sister, will appear in the third book. (You have heard all the things about middle children acting out, haven't you?) The three women have very different personalities, yet they share the excitement of finding their lifelong mates—and the curse of danger until a happy ending.

I'm not certain, after writing more than fifty novels since 1982, why I didn't use the fascinating Adena people before this book, because signs of their lives are all around where I live in Columbus, Ohio, and points south to the Ohio River. Some five thousand mounds and earthworks attributed to them are in these dramatic sites, some quite small on private land, some long ago pillaged or excavated, some untouched.

Highbanks Park, a short distance north of Columbus where my husband and I sometimes go for picnics, has several Adena mounds. Like some others, they have been worn away and rebuilt. The Adena pipe—which became Ohio's official state artifact in May 2013—is in the Ohio Historical Museum in Columbus, and the Adena Mansion, a historic site, is just a short drive away near Chillicothe.

Thanks again to our friends Dr. Roy and Mary Ann

Manning for their tour of the Chillicothe area and for answering questions. I did, however, create the village of Cold Creek, based on places in southeastern Ohio on the edge of Appalachia. I did my undergraduate work in a college in that area with its dramatic foothills, mountain, quarries and creeks.

The Beastmaster Cauldron actually exists with its depiction of the antlered Beastmaster surrounded by animals over whom he holds sway. He is depicted on the so-called Gundestrup Cauldron, a photo of which can be found online. A lot of information about the Adena and their cult of death can be found at www.adena.com and numerous other sites. Where they came from and where they went after being such an advanced society for that time is the subject of much argument and conjecture, as in this story. Beastmaster masks, like the one from Mason Mound, have not been found in the New World, but it is surmised to be a Celtic shaman mask.

Most of us have beasts of some sort lurking in our lives or minds. I'm reminded of William Golding's line from his novel of inherent evil, *Lord of the Flies:* "Maybe there is a beast…maybe it's only us."

Needless to say, the characters in this novel are all products of my imagination. There is no one at Ohio State University on whom Dr. Carson Cantrell or Kate Lockwood or the graduate students are based.

I hope you will look for the next novel in the trilogy, which will pick up the stories of Tess and Gabe, and Kate and Grant, with a special focus on Charlene.

Please visit my website, www.karenharperauthor.com, for other information or just to say hi.

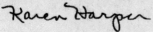